To Our Cousin
Claire Eleana Gillis
M.P. Webb
October 2009
Book One

Marooned in Africa

Marie Pierce Weber

authorHOUSE®

AuthorHouse™
1663 Liberty Drive
Bloomington, IN 47403
www.authorhouse.com
Phone: 1-800-839-8640

First published by AuthorHouse   8/27/2009

ISBN: 978-1-4389-7303-6 (sc)
ISBN: 978-1-4389-7304-3 (hc)

Printed in the United States of America
Bloomington, Indiana

This book is printed on acid-free paper.

To my husband, Jack, who made this work possible with his unfailing support, insightful critique and encouragement!

To John Thompson, bookseller, who set me on the right path.

To Carolyn Weber Lewis, Ph.D., who gave most generously of her time, expertise and opinions.

To my enthusiastic readers:

Evie Connelly
Len Coopersmith
Diann Gordon

For My Lifelong Friends

❖❖❖

"That is a good book which is opened with expectation and closed with delight and profit." – A. B. Alcott

Contents

Prologue

PAULA MAHREE THORNTON IS a young woman working on her Ph.D. in Biology. She has a congenial personality, which combines the best in female nature with the independence and self-reliance of a man. Nature has endowed her with comely looks, long legs and ash blonde hair. But these assets make no difference to her—as being a Palomino, with flowing white mane and tail, makes no difference to a horse.

It is her joie de vivre that makes her most attractive. Life to her is like stepping-stones: each stone is a choice—each choice is an adventure, sometimes mental, sometimes physical, but most often a combination of both.

She has led an athletic life: from gymnastics competition and horse-vaulting to distance riding; from hiking to cliff face climbing and rappelling; from tennis to yachting; yet she loved the study of plants and animals, which led her to seek an advanced degree in Biology. Her life has been a journey of discovery... with an affinity for challenges.

Fear to her is merely ignorance... and danger is crossing the street without looking both ways.

When she has a purpose, it becomes her focus, and she pours herself into the effort until she achieves her goal.

All of her life, she has had the encouragement and support of her parents, siblings, relatives, friends and teachers. But, support of any kind is gone now...

1

Marooned

THE YACHT BECAME ALMOST vertical as it climbed the huge waves, before the pause at the top and the sickening plunge into the trough behind the swell. With each climb, Paula was tossed aft into the galley, and with each plunge, she was flung forward between the bunks towards the bow.

I'm going to die if I don't get into a bunk and lower the storm net, she thought. But thinking safety... didn't make it happen. She felt herself slide, and then tumble towards the lab door in the bow. Now! She thought, grab on to something; she had only fleeting seconds to save herself. Opening her eyes, she felt dizzy and nauseous, but she needed to see the pipes that ran down the sides of the bunks. It was the only thing to grab hold of... to hold on to... until the next pitch towards the bow.

Her fingers found the pipe, but it was tight against the bulkhead and provided only a fingertip hold. Can I hold on? God, give me strength... please! Up, up went the yacht, the pull of gravity and inertia was immense and her fingers began to slip. Both hands! She thought. Hold on with both hands!

The pause at the top of the wave would be only momentary... before the sudden drop forward, which would tear her fingers loose. She concentrated for timing... as she had never concentrated before...until she felt her weight begin to shift, like a handstand pause on the uneven parallel bars, she brought her legs up and at the same time flexed her elbows, using the momentum of her weight moving under gravity, to twist herself into the bunk.

With a practiced movement, she pressed the button to

lower the storm net. Safe, exhausted and suffering from a concussion... she fell unconscious.

PAULA MAHREE THORNTON AWOKE to the gentle rocking motion of a moored boat. She sensed from the feel of the boat that it was a clear day, free of the stormy weather she vaguely remembered. The urge was strong to resist waking completely–to go back to sleep for a little while–to see what little dreams would come.

As the foggy cocoon of sleep parted, Paula startled... she was asea! In an instant, the nightmarish memories of heavy rains, screaming winds, and mountainous seas, came rushing back to mind. She remembered being tossed about the cabin, and her desperate struggle to get into a bunk and lower the storm net... to be held safely in place.

Fully awake now, she became aware of a bumping and scraping at the bow. Prodded into action by the aggravating thumps and rasping sounds, she released the storm net and rolled onto her side. With the movement came waves of nausea and the dizziness of concussion, which forced her to lay back on the bunk, groaning... seeking the relief of oblivion... only to be brought back by more jarring thumps and tortured scrapings at the bow.

Paula concentrated on keeping her head movements to a minimum as she reached, in slow motion, for the ledge of the opposite bunk; hoping the pounding in her ears and the cold clammy sweat would soon pass. The boat smashed and grated along the bow... again and again... before she was finally on her feet. With her eyes closed, she stood hanging on to the upper bunk rail, waiting for the awful spasms of nausea and the trembling weakness to go away.

When Paula opened her eyes, it was to see the cabin in a shambles. The deck was littered with supplies and sailing gear. She took a deep breath to steady herself, and smelled the foul odor of vomit and the sharp stench of urine. Moving aft, she braced each step against the jarring impacts on the forward hull... all the while desperate to find the strength to continue.

Damn... she raged inwardly. What the heck were they doing

to the boat? Somewhat strengthened by anger, Paula wobbled to the galley table, certain she would collapse there in a spasm of dizziness... but her distress did not worsen. Marveling too soon at her good fortune, she was knocked aside by a violent crashing at the bow.

In a blind rage at the vicious abuse of the boat, she staggered to the hatch and threw it open. The bright sunlight poured in, forcing her to close her eyes and turn away. She groped in the mess drawer for sunglasses, but found only welding goggles. While using both hands to put them on, she was pitched into the galley sink, by yet another brutal crunching at the bow.

Letting out a low growl of frustration—rage overriding her weakness—Paula ascended to the cockpit to chastise the idiots who were ruining the boat. Reeling from the exertion, but impelled by her anger, she reached the deck, turned forward, and screamed, "What the heck do you thi ..." before she realized... there was no one there. Worse than that, there was nothing there—nothing but the sea. She turned slowly, for a huge lump had come up in her throat. It was cutting off the breath needed by her racing pounding heart. Nothing! Just wilderness! No one! Just the sea... the rainforest... and me! Jolted once more by a teeth-jarring thump, she pulled herself along the rope rail towards the bow.

Between spasms of nausea and waves of dizziness, Paula peered over the side into the water. There she saw a line and cleat snagged like an anchor on the reef. With each surge of the outgoing tide, the boat was pitched unmercifully against the sandbar. She stumbled back to the galley and found a pair of small tin snips in the mess drawer.

She rested to let the dizziness subside and to gain strength, which came from another jarring crash at the bow. Stunned, incredibly weak and shaking as if with palsy, Paula pulled herself up the companionway and out along the rope handrail towards the bow. Using two hands, she managed to cut the stout line that held the yacht in destructive bondage to the unforgiving reef.

Freed, the yacht was lifted away from the reef on the next incoming swell. Paula made her way aft to the control panel and pulled the lever to drop the anchor before the boat could be carried back against the reef, with even greater force, by the running out of the tide. She felt immense relief, but an overwhelming weakness and slithered to the deck. On the next inward swell, she slipped down the hatchway into the galley where, with great determination, she secured the hatch before sinking into oblivion.

PAULA CAME TO AMID a mess of unstowed sailing gear. The light no longer seemed so bright. She hurt everywhere, even her toes and teeth hurt. Moving her head a bit, Paula could see the salmon streaks of the sunset through the clear, plastic cover on the ceiling vent. She was very thirsty. Her lips were dry and chapped and her tongue felt fat and fuzzy. She hated to move... she was so incredibly sore and stiff; there was no part of her body that didn't explode with pain as she arose from the deck. The boat was calm now. She reached the sink, and pulled a paper cup from the dispenser to fill with fresh water. Sipping the water, she opened the food locker for some Sea Toast crackers. She hoped they would settle her still queasy stomach.

Paula pushed the loose clutter off the booth seat, slumped down and rested her head on her forearms on the table. She felt so weak. Every inch of her body radiated pain. She wanted to think, but she couldn't get her mind around any of her thoughts. They were like wisps of smoke; the minute you moved toward them, they dispersed. She gave up, sat up, ate two crackers, sipped the water and took some aspirin. Numb with fatigue and pain, Paula made her way to the clean opposing bunk, shed her filthy clothes on the deck and crawled into the cozy cot. In a moment, she was asleep.

TAP... TAP-TAP... TAP... TAP-TAP-TAP; peeved by the tapping noise, Paula pulled herself out of the fog of deep sleep and turned over. No waves of nausea, no throbbing behind the eyes, not as much pain, but there was a particular gross discomfort. Dragging herself further awake, she realized she was soaked in sweat and the air in the cabin was absolutely fetid. Lifting her eyelids just enough to orient herself, she forced herself to reach up slowly—because movement was pain—to the porthole over the bunk to release the toggle and prop out the porthole window. The fresh and cooler air flowed in over her.

Sighing, she sought to escape back into the healing darkness of sleep, when she became aware of an insistent and ever-familiar bodily urge. Annoyed, she rubbed her eyes fully open to find the sun shining high over the forest on a beautiful day.

Tap... tap-tap... tap, came the sound again; it seemed quite close. Groaning, she pushed herself up and peered through the porthole. A gull was pecking at the mussel-filled seaweed caught on a guy wire, where it was attached to the deck. It made her wonder how long she had been sleeping. In what must have looked like slow motion mime, Paula got out of bed. She felt hollow, thin and brittle, and was exceedingly stiff. Putting her feet on the deck, she was able to rise without feeling faint or dizzy, and shuffled off to the head to satisfy Mother Nature.

She turned to the lavatory, to wash her face and hands, and glanced in the mirror above the sink. Her heart flip-flopped in her chest. Her startled intake of breath caused a sharp pain near her breastbone. Her pulse began to race... she felt the onset of shock as sweat broke out all over her body and she grew faint. Holding fast to the sink, willing herself not to succumb to the darkness... she glanced in the mirror again. Who was that hideous person she saw in the mirror? That can't be me! Her common sense took over, but her heart still fluttered making her breathing ragged. The face she saw was gaunt with deep black circles around sunken eyes. Bumpy blotches of purple-black, edged in the color of dried yellow mustard, covered her skin. Jagged cuts had closed with dried oozed blood on swollen skin. The lips were puffy and cracked. No Halloween mask had ever been so ugly.

Terror seized her already overloaded nervous system as the thought of some awful tropical disease ran through her mind. Breathing in ragged gasps, shaking as with ague, she peered closer, trying to control the fear that brought panic.

She saw mottled bits of blue mixed in with the black and that the yellow was splotchy. The vise gripping her lungs lessened a bit, and the hammering of her heart softened so she could stop gulping air. Inhaling deeply to slow her pulse, she looked down at her arms and legs, which were covered with the same unsightly purple-black and blue blotches edged in dirty yellow. The release from paralyzing shock made her feel faint. The disfigurement was only the various stages of healing bruises.

Relief flowed over her, allowing her sense of smell to be strongly offended by her deep breathing. Crossing to the shower, Paula drew on her physical endurance to bathe and wash her hair. After tending to her numerous cuts with peroxide and bandages, she put on clean sweats, and with the last of her tenuous strength, she put on water for tea and soup.

She had been battered over most of her body. While some places were much sorer than others, nothing had been fractured or broken. Now that she was aware of her unique predicament: marooned alone on a wilderness shore of West Africa... she knew she had indeed, been very lucky.

Paula forced her complaining body to the task of finding her sunglasses, so she could go topside to enjoy the beautiful day while she waited for the water to boil. Nothing had changed but the tide. The water glinted silver and gold, reflecting the streaming sunlight from the cloudless pale blue sky.

Amongst the sparse trees and clumps of greenery growing on the high sheer cliffs at the southern end of the cove, Paula recognized cormorants, storks and herons. Her eye followed the cliffs as they extended west, out into the open sea, where the ragged peaks turned to curve north. There, the rim dropped down in lumpy jagged pillars, decorated by sentinel-like pelicans, before the rim disappeared into the sea. Her eye continued across the wide opening to the sea, to a towering rock wall, which continued north until it met a mass of jumbled rocks. The rocky rim fell sharply until it became a ragged jetty, which continued its eastward march to the beach, where it disappeared into the rainforest wilderness. All along the sandy beach, on the east side of the cove, there was a thick forest of tall trees towering above dense jungle-like greenery.

There, great flocks of squawking gray parrots with bright red tails rose together in synchronized waves; they dipped and swirled and then rose again before settling gingerly in the treetops. The yacht was anchored in a huge cove almost completely surrounded by land. On the west side, through the opening to the sea, she saw a mass in the distance... maybe just rocks or possibly an island. She contemplated the almost circular shape of the cove, thinking it might be the remains of a sunken volcano... when the kettle whistled.

Paula wondered how long it had been since her last meal. She breathed in the rich smell of the chicken noodle soup, then sipped and munched on Sea Toast. Idly, she wondered what day it was, and where she might be... when she remembered the battery-operated date-clock in the lab. Forcing her stiff and resisting body out of the booth, towards the pile of dirty clothes on the deck by the bunk, she removed the key fob from her jeans belt loop and unlocked the bulkhead door to the lab. It was the 17th of January 1960—five days since she had gone aboard the yacht to stow her gear.

What in the world had happened? The only thing she remembered was being forced to her knees and pitched backwards... and then nothing. She ate a bit more of the hot soup, and ferreted from the smoke of her memory a few isolated events. She remembered repeated vomiting. She remembered repeated sliding from the galley to the forward bulkhead.

She remembered her desperation; her life depended on getting into a bunk... to lower the storm net to hold her fast. She mentally thanked her father, who had devised the storm nets for the safety of his children when they sailed the often-choppy waters of the Chesapeake Bay, and she was even more thankful that APCO had agreed to install them on the Expedition yacht.

Once safe, the hammering of the torrential rain and the crashing sound of huge waves breaking over the boat barely registered. The whistling wind, and the horrific pitching and yawing of the boat gripped her, in moments of consciousness, like the panic and terror of an inescapable nightmare.

Suddenly, her appetite was gone. Paula put the rest of the soup in a container, and put the container in the sink. She didn't even try to open the refrigerator; certain it would be a mess. The damp bedding had dried out with the portholes, the ceiling vents and the hatch all opened for cabin ventilation. The enclosed space smelled better, but it was still rank so she took her tea topside.

She sat watching the teeming bird life in the forest beyond the beach, where she saw many brightly colored songbirds, which were too far away to identify. Not so, the swirling flocks of gray parrots, the shoebill cranes and the fishing white pelicans. All together, the birdsong, raucous calls and squawks made a delightful distant concert; one that was making her sleepy as she sat in the warm sun with the soft, cooling breezes riffling her clean hair.

Leaning back, she brought her legs up to rest on the cushions she had taken from the seat locker, and let her mind wander back to her arrival at Lagos, where the tanker was to off-load the yacht and the six-man Expedition crew. The yacht, this beautifully designed boat under her, had been especially outfitted for the biological Expedition. It contained a complete lab in the spacious forward compartment, four bunks, two heads with lavatories, two commodious showers, also with lavatories, and a large comfortable galley amidships with a U shaped dining booth big enough to seat six comfortably. Aft, were two private cabins, one for herself and one for Professor Miles, and the storage lockers for sailing equipment and comestible supplies. The yacht was a marvel of beauty and efficiency with a modicum of luxury.

There had been unusual seas the evening before the yacht was to be launched–no one had an appetite for dinner; everyone had gone to bed feeling queasy. Heavy rain was forecast for the morning, so Paula decided to stow her personal things on the yacht before the bad weather arrived. The next day, they would cast off to sail for three months, collecting samples from flowering vines that grew behind the swampy beaches and along the river deltas.

Sandy, the radioman, had asked her to stow his tool box when she went aboard, saying he would install the batteries, which powered the VHF communications radio, the interior lights, the alarm, navigation and ventilation systems, in the morning. He was calling it a day, which made her chuckle at the time. Sandy was a former Navy Seal, the electrical and mechanical expert of the group, and he was feeling seasick.

TWO HOURS LATER WHEN she had finished stowing her gear, Sandy's tools and the lab supplies, Paula looked at the sailing gear piled in the corner and decided to let the men stow their own gear in the morning. She reached up to open the hatch from the companionway steps when the deck rose up suddenly; she was forced to her knees and tossed backwards, where she lost consciousness.

What could have happened? Why was she forced to her knees? The yacht wasn't damaged. She seemed fine except for the deep sea debris clinging to guy wires, cleats, rope rail and the furled sail and boom. Paula remembered her vomiting; remembered being tossed about the cabin in the heavy seas. She remembered her struggle to get into a bunk to lower the storm net; and the deafening sound of the wind and driving rain, but not much else. How had the yacht come off the tanker? Had the tanker sunk? What could have happened? She was too tired to think about it, she needed rest. Going below, she closed the hatch and ceiling vents before flopping down on the bunk. She fell asleep to the chatter of bickering gulls.

THAT EVENING PAULA FINISHED the soup. Then she tried to clean up some of the litter in the cabin, but soon headed back to bed, feeling dizzy and nauseous again; bending over was too much for her concussed head. During the next two days, Paula did the clean-up work in stages, resting frequently and napping when needed. As the cabin became ship-shape, her natural optimism chased away the subliminal feeling of despair that was creeping over her. Each day her aches diminished, and her appetite improved, which gave her more stamina for the clean-up chores.

She tried not to dwell on the puzzle that had put her in this predicament. She just wanted to get the yacht organized, get stronger, and sail the heck out of here—back to civilization and her friends.

THE NEXT DAY, PAULA put the smelly soiled clothing and bedding in a mesh sea bag, and hung the bag over the rail in the water for a few hours, allowing the flow of the high tide to act as a washing machine. Later, when she went to bring the bag up, she found it too heavy for her to lift.

Chagrined at her lack of foresight, she thought: what is this, a test? Daddy, are you at it again? Her father used to make up tests for his children when they were sailing. Paula had thoroughly enjoyed the mental and physical challenges... but it wasn't the same now. Her problem wasn't just a fun test thought up by her Dad; she was completely alone with no one to point out the folly of her choices... all she had now was her training.

She sat and thought for a bit; then she took the main halyard off the reefed mainsail, and ran it through the end of the spinnaker boom to the line holding the bag of wet clothes. The spinnaker boom acted like a clothes pole, which was braced against the mast and kept the wet bag out over the water. With the sail winch, which raised the mainsail halyard to the top of the mast, she was able to bring the sea bag up out of the water. Paula let it hang off the rail until it stopped dripping. She then sat the wet bag on the deck, removed the spinnaker boom and belayed the line around an aft cleat. She pinned the clothes to the line still attached to the main halyard and raised the line with the winch, until all her wash was fluttering in the breeze.

Paula's self-confidence soared as she watched her laundry blowing in the wind. Coping with the problem had given her flagging spirits a much-needed boost. Each day she slept less and did more. Each day she hurt less, and today she felt good enough to open the refrigerator.

It was gas operated, as were the stove and hot water heater. Nothing would have spoiled from lack of refrigeration, but ... surprise, surprise! None of the containers had broken or spilled their contents. All had been new and unopened. Everything had its own compartment. Plastic containers had been preferred over metal or wax, and the wisdom of the choice was evident. A little rearranging was all that was required. Even the eggs had survived in their foam-insulated plastic box. Once these were gone, it was powdered eggs, and the foam insulated box would be used to store perishable lab samples. Delighted with her find, she celebrated by having scrambled eggs, bacon and baked beans for a late lunch, early dinner, with canned pears and mint tea for dessert.

THREE DAYS HAD PASSED since Paula found herself marooned in the cove. She had raised the SOS pennant to the top of the main mast, and in the evening, before the moon was up, she fired a flare. People should be looking for her, she had been gone eight days.... maybe the rest of the crew was gone too. Maybe being aboard the yacht had saved her life while the others had perished. She did not know what to think, and speculation was distressing.

THE NEXT MORNING, OVER tea, Paula decided to treat her situation like another test from her father; the difference being, her decisions now could mean life or death. There would be no cautioning "ahem" to make her rethink her choices. She made the mandatory list: first, get well. Second, get shipshape. Third, get organized. Fourth, make a plan of action. She was already doing step one, and had a good start on step two. Today she would have the cabin ship-shape. Tomorrow, on the low tide, she would tackle the ocean debris topside. She still felt some occasional dizziness and had put out the swimmer's ladder in case she fell overboard. She wore the flare gun in a holster while working, so she could signal if she saw a passing ship or plane. Without batteries, the radio didn't work, nor did the ceiling fans, lights or the automatic sailing equipment. She had no idea how to set the radio up to work off the generator, or if that could even be done.

Step three: get organized. She had been doing things as they occurred to her.

Step four: make a plan of action. She needed to rig the yacht so she could sail her alone. On the next incoming tide, she would start the engine and motor closer to the shore and around the perimeter of the huge cove. See what was needed to handle this baby alone. She didn't have to worry about running aground, as the west coast shelf of Africa had a sharp declension beyond the low tide point... plus, she was now convinced that the cove was the remnants of a volcanic crater.

Along with the decision to be proactive, came a feeling of control. She took her cup of tea, a pad and pencil and headed for the cockpit. She listened to the lulling sound of shimmering waters lapping softly against the hull. The gulls wheeled and turned, looking for handouts, crying stridently for attention. A gentle breeze fluffed her hair and caressed her sun-warmed skin.

Paula closed her eyes and, unbidden, she saw herself going aboard the *Just Cause* that fateful evening. She remembered the snatches of conversation she'd heard as she passed the bridge on her way out. "...an unusual sea..." "...but nothing on the radar..." "...nothing unusual on the weather map..." "...forecast is for heavy rain" "...does remind me a bit of a seismic sea we had..."

Paula's eyes flew open and her mind raced. Seismic, that means earthquakes, maybe undersea volcanic eruptions and possibly tsunami waves! If an undersea volcanic eruption caused a tsunami, there would be no warning unless there was seismographic equipment monitoring the area of the eruption.

The unusual seas could have been the result of early tremors. If there had been an eruption, there might have been a tsunami. A tsunami wave could easily lift the yacht off the deck of the tanker and sweep her away. If the yacht was picked up on the crest of the wave, unmanned, she would automatically turn and slide down the back side into the trough behind the huge wave; then the yacht would climb the succeeding tidal waves and be sucked out to sea by the enormous ebb tide of a tsunami. That could explain why I was forced to my knees as I was leaving the galley; it could have been the sudden rise of the anchored tanker on a tsunami swell.

It would also explain the severe battering I received. The yacht had been climbing huge waves, and then falling into the troughs, and I had been pitched back and forth in the cabin like a rag doll. Paula closed her eyes again. It all made sense. Why every inch of my body, including my face, had been bruised; how the yacht had come off the deck of the tanker; why there were so many deep-sea plants plastered to the boat topside; why cleats had been torn out of their reinforced bases and two guy wires had snapped; why no one has come looking for me—or, if they have been looking, why they haven't found me.

Paula felt tremendous relief. The not knowing had been harder to bear than the awful but plausible explanation she had just surmised. Soon, she would be ready to lay a course back to Lagos. She was much stronger now, in mind as well as body. She felt confident she could handle the sixty-two foot yacht by herself, if she stayed in sight of land. She would just follow the coast north, for she knew she had to be south of Lagos, closer to the Equator, because of the jutting landmass, which is the bulge of Africa, off the Gulf of Guinea.

IT WAS ANOTHER DAY before she was ready, for her mental energy still exceeded her physical stamina. Paula was a seasoned sailor. Her family had spent most of their summer weekends sailing their thirty-three foot ocean-going sloop in the Chesapeake Bay and Atlantic Ocean. She knew better than to shove off unprepared. While she chaffed at the delay, it worked to her benefit as the high tide peaked at 9:20am on the day of her departure. This would give her good light, without a sun glare on the water, to find a way through the sandbar reef into the open sea. Then she would have the whole day to sail before the tide turned again, when she would anchor for the night.

Paula set the jib sail and let the breeze and tide take her to the cliffs. Under the light breeze, the yacht handled very well, but she realized she would have to leave the helm to lower the sail. Maybe the spanker would be best. That way, all the control would be aft, all pushing, no pulling. She came about as she approached the cliffs and dropped the anchor. She reefed the jib and set up the spanker. This fore-and-aft sail extended by a boom and a gaff, usually from the mizzenmast, would be ideal for solo sailing. She could easily handle the sheet from the helm. Yesterday, using the inertia starter to start the diesel engine, she had motored around the cove at high tide. Sailing along the length of the opening to the sea, Paula found no place to cross the sandbar. She came about, reefed the sail, started the engine and motored slowly past the opening to the sea, looking for a place to clear the keel. It was early afternoon when she again came alongside the jetty. On the last pass, the sea flowing over the reef was lower, and she saw the actual reef better, not just the surf breaking over it. It was a solid mass of sandbar and barnacles. The huge tides of the tsunami and the following gale winds had lifted the yacht over the reef into a vast tidal pool. She wasn't going to be able to sail her way out. Crestfallen, down but not out, she came about and decided to motor closer to the beach.

When the high tide had ebbed so that the reef was exposed, the immense tidal pool became like glass, so smooth that only the breeze brought the little whitecaps. The opening to the sea was less than forty-five degrees of the immense, almost circular cove. Paula felt certain the opening to the sea was the side that had broken down during the volcano's eruption.

I can't believe it! An aircraft carrier could get lost in here! The yacht and I are prisoners! I couldn't be safer, or more alone, if I were home in bed! Returning to her morning's anchorage for the best visibility from the open sea, she thought: if nothing else, I'll be bow first into the prevailing winds and the incoming tide.

◈◈◈

MORNING HAD TURNED TO late afternoon; Paula was hungry, tired and despondent by the time she'd dropped the anchor, reefed the spanker and stowed the gear. Going below, she made herself a cup of coffee, which she laced with hazelnut liqueur, while entering her frustrating day in the Log.

Exhausted by disappointment, Paula took another coffee treat with her to the cockpit. She used the binoculars to scan the shore, watching the birds vying for roosting places in the treetops for the night. She enjoyed their unpredictable antics. Seemingly all settled... the trees would erupt in a flurry of wings and strident noise. The sky would fill with riotous color and syncopated motion and then, minutes later, all would be settled again... maybe. The evening was getting cool. Paula decided to go to bed early after a last look at the magical African twilight, as it vanished into the black-gray and orange-gold sunset.

It rained hard that night. It had rained some almost every night, for the cockpit was often wet in the mornings, and some days there were brief, heavy showers too ... and this was supposed to be the dry season.

Exploration

A SHAFT OF EARLY morning sunlight fell full upon her face. Paula awoke, and stretched to find the soreness from her bruises almost gone. This brightened her spirits, chasing away the gloom that had set in yesterday after the futile attempt to leave the cove. She needed a plan; she could just sit here and wait—for who knows what—or go ashore and explore. She heard her father's voice saying, "Choose the best of your options; follow a logical plan and prepare, prepare, prepare!"

Yes, I'll go ashore and explore to the north, for there could be something just beyond; there could be a river flowing to the sea, with a settlement not far upstream where I could contact the *Norsk Star*.

OVER TEA, AFTER HER oatmeal breakfast, Paula took her hiking checklist from her backpack and made an exploration list. Her plans provided hope as she began to assemble her kit. She did not plan to be out overnight, but prepared to improvise if necessary. Two complete changes of clothes, extra socks and underwear, plus her poplin camouflage shirt and camouflage hat, cliff-climbing sneakers and her rubber-palmed gloves, half-chaps and rain poncho. Plus the sundries: yellow soap, facecloth, small towel, squat candle, extra wood matches, spare shoe laces, bandanas, spare nylon cord and duct tape. The first aid kit went in a special pocket on the outside of the backpack and she put a specimen collection kit in the straps above it. The camera, film, diary, her wallet and extra ammunition went in the secret waterproof pocket between the frame and the pack.

When all was packed, she attached her pigskin half-chaps across the top of her backpack, in case she should need them to venture into the underbrush. She filled the expandable outer pouch below the first aid kit with high protein granola and fruit bars, enough for a week, and a packet of tea bags. This was her insurance. From her hiking experience, she knew to expect the unexpected, so she prepared not for one day, but for a week.

She chose to wear her brown khaki walking shorts, lightweight tan knee socks with her canvas and mesh crepe-soled hiking shoes, and a long sleeve white shirt with chest pockets. She wore her 5in1 (whistle, compass, matches, fork and spoon) on a soft red nylon cord around her neck under her shirt collar and tucked into her shirt pocket, with a collapsing plastic straw in the pencil slot. She had a plastic bag with electrolytes, potassium, aspirin and chewable vitamin C (from APCO) in the right shirt pocket. She had small refillable containers of bug spray, sun block and her lip balm in the pockets of her shorts.

THE EMERGENCY BELT HER father had designed for hiking and mountain climbing was designed to sit low on the hips so it would not interfere with carrying a backpack. It could also accommodate a holster for her .22 Magnum pistol, which Paula wore on the right side. On the left she looped a sheath for the hunting knife in place of the special kit for pitons, hammer and links, which were now at the bottom of her backpack with a hundred feet of line. The machete she wore in a sheath slung over her shoulder and across her chest for easy access. She didn't plan on going into the jungle-like growth along the edge of the rainforest, but, if she needed the machete, she would have it.

The backpack was made of waterproof nylon reinforced at corners and seams. It had insulated sleeves on each side of the first aid kit for water bottles: one bottle was metal with a cup lid, which could be used to heat water, and one bottle was plastic with a retractable drinking spout. Last on the list were a few miscellaneous items: sunglasses with elastic safety band, a small packet of tissues, which she put in her other shorts pocket with a bandana, the individual packets of little wet towels to sanitize hands supplied by APCO for the Expedition and her special penknife, a gift from her twin brother on her graduation. It was her usual hiking gear except for the .22 Magnum and the machete. She had hiked for years with this same equipment, and more if she was camping out overnight.

Standing on the drop-down loading platform off the stern, she pulled the cord to inflate the dinghy, tossed in the oars, her pack and stepped aboard. She fastened the oars in the oarlocks and shoved off. The tide was coming in, which made it was an easy row to the beach. Jumping out, Paula pulled the dinghy up into the cover of the brush. As she cut some greenery to cover the dinghy, she questioned her caution, reasoning: I'm alone here; it's a long swim back to the yacht with this backpack... better safe than sorry. Paula looked at the wide swath made by the dinghy, and walking backwards to the surf, erased it and her footprints in the sand with a leafy branch.

HER CANVAS AND MESH hiking shoes were good in water. They released the water and dried quickly. She walked in the surf to the rock rubble that looked like a jetty, being wary of the barnacles, which were as sharp as razors.

Atop of the rocky land spit, Paula could see for miles to the north. There was nothing but the narrow sand beach, the ocean and the dense forest. The scene was primeval. Now she knew how Robinson Crusoe felt. A few miles down, beyond a curve, there appeared to be another land spit like the one on which she was standing. That would be her goal for the day. It could be further than she thought. With such a sameness to the vista, it was hard to judge distances. The flesh on her arms prickled with goose bumps... while she loved hiking and exploring, being alone in an exotic country with a vastly different and possibly hostile culture was quite daunting. She needed to be back on the yacht long before the dusk.

Paula decided she would turn back at three p.m., which

would allow for an afternoon rest and snack, and give her more time on the return in case she was tiring. She was keenly aware that this would be more physical exercise than she had had in weeks, even without the concussion. She was in good physical condition and accustomed to strenuous physical exercise, but there had been no place to walk or jog on the tanker. The deck was so windy that the Captain had ruled it off-limits. They had been limited to calisthenics, jumping rope and the mini-trampoline. But walking was what she liked to do best, especially hiking for long distances.

Walking at the edge of the surf was relaxing and cooling. It seemed no time at all before the sun was high overhead, and it was time for a snack. Rounding a curve she saw, not far ahead, a fallen tree, which lay across the beach into the surf. It looked like a good place to rest. She had already reached and passed the land spit she had seen from the jetty. When she had topped the second land spit, it was to see more of the same: beach, sea, thick forest and an irregular shore line, which could conceal the very stream she was trying to find, so she continued on. She would make the downed tree her turn-around point.

PAULA SAT IN THE shade of the huge root ball and leaned against the bole of the fallen tree. She ate a granola bar, drank some water and took her electrolytes. She rested, with her eyes closed, and tried to distinguish the different birds she heard. There must be hundreds, all vocalizing out at the same time. She loved the lulling musical sound of the impromptu avian orchestra.

Startled awake, she heard the sound of the waves, the cries of the gulls, the daytime sounds of the forest and voices. Paula instinctively hunched down closer to the tree trunk. She glanced around and realized the voices were coming from the same direction she had traveled. Dragging her backpack behind her to cover her tracks (earlier, she had walked atop the log from the surf), she scrambled into the deep hole left by the uprooted tree when it fell towards the sea. From her foxhole-hiding place, she could see six natives walking on the firm sand at the edge of the surf. The two in front had feathery plumes and ivory bones in their high, elaborate hairdos and colored cicatrix on their faces. They wore intricately decorated kitambas over their loincloths, which were draped like togas under the right arm and over the left shoulder. Gold loops surrounded their ears, which had been pierced top and bottom with the holes enlarged by ivory disks. Both wore spiral coils on each bicep, tooled leather wristbands and woven leather strap sandals.

These are clearly important young men. What were they doing here? Where did they come from? The other four, who were following at a discreet distance, wore their plain kitambas more like capes over their loincloths. Their only decoration was the tattooed patterns on their faces and chests. They wore no ornaments. Their hair was short and their ears were unadorned. These four carried bundles on their heads. All had weapons: bows and arrows, lethal metal-tipped spears, clubs called walinkas and long sheaths for the machetes.

The first two young men were deep in discussion. Paula took out her pistol, terrified at what might happen if they saw her. They did not look like cannibals, but they looked fierce and unfriendly.

As the natives neared the fallen tree, Paula understood a few words of their discussion. The taller one, with many gold-colored bands on his upper arms, had seen one of her footprints and was convinced it was the footprint of a Sea Goddess.

His companion did not think it was a footprint at all. "It was just a mark from a fallen coconut that had been washed away by the surf."

The taller one disagreed. "It had the shape of a foot without toes. The Baharike does not have toes, only feet. I have seen these marks in the sand before... evenly spaced... coconuts do not fall evenly spaced."

Up close, these men looked even more savage and dangerous, making her heart skip a beat.

They passed by, walking into the surf to round the tree, without so much as a glance towards the end of the tree where

Paula was crouched, hiding. Her chest tightened, her heart thumped, and she strained for air when they came so close. With great relief, she watched the natives continue down the beach engrossed in their discussion. When she could no longer hear their voices, she fled to the dense foliage at the edge of the forest, dragging her backpack to obscure her footprints in the sand.

At the base of a mahogany tree, she dropped down to compose herself. There was a ringing in her ears, and she was shaking all over. Her breathing was ragged as she gulped air to slow her racing pulse. She had never been so frightened. With a shaky hand she holstered her pistol, and leaned her head back against the bole of the tree. Looking up, she saw a large grayish-black monkey with a white oval on his nose, sitting on a low branch, watching her. Suddenly, he squealed and ran away, traveling through the trees like it was a walk in the park.

Unbidden, a picture of herself scampering through trees flickered through her mind. She had strengthened her upper body and toughened her hands for gymnastics by swinging and hanging and pulling herself up on the limbs of the maple trees in the side yard at home. The trees here were shaped like the maple but much bigger, much taller, with the lower limbs being at least twenty-five feet off the ground.

Feeling a bit calmer, Paula crept through the foliage and looked down the beach. The natives were now just distant spots and still traveling away from her. Now, she had to get back to the yacht as fast as possible, but she dared not go back in the open surf. She would be too exposed and too easy to see. Traveling through the dense foliage was the only option. She put on her protective half-chaps and reapplied bug repellent and donned the stretchy rubberized cotton gloves to protect her hands. Fastening the backpack straps to her waist to drag the pack behind her, she parted the foliage and headed deeper into the thick vegetation.

In a few minutes she realized dragging the backpack wasn't going to work. She had already snagged it a half dozen times, soon it would tear; besides, it left a clearer trail than footprints.

She would have to go back and travel on the beach close to the edge of the undergrowth. They would only see her footprints if they came up to the forest. If she saw the natives returning, she could always duck into the foliage.

Paula backtracked to the fallen tree, obliterating the marks of her passage. She looked for any leaves she had damaged and snipped them at the base—much less obvious—tossing the snippets into the deep brush. The sand was firm close to the greenery, and she left only vague tracks. She came to an uprooted palm tree, which was leaning against a mahogany tree. It looked like a ramp made to gain access to the lofty branches of these huge trees. She thought of the white-nosed monkey and smiling to herself, thought, why not!

Paula changed to her pebble-tread cliff-climbing shoes and redonned her half chaps; put on her camouflage shirt and hat, and tied a line on her gear. She made her way up the palm tree by using the long straps from her backpack as a loop around the trunk to pull herself forward and up. When she reached the big limb, she sat and rested, for the climb had been harder than it looked.

Once her backpack was hauled up and put on, Paula felt pleased with herself and much less vulnerable. She mapped, by eye, a route to the next tree. In a few minutes, she found the knack: up a branch or two, down a branch, hang, swing down, balance beam to the center and then map out another route to the next tree. Unused muscles were coming into play, but soon she was having more fun than she had had in years. Without her special tread sneakers and the rubber-pebble-palmed gloves, she wouldn't be able to do this.

She saw no more monkeys, but found going too high in the trees set off the birds, the cormorants, darters and parrots nesting high above in the mahogany forest and mangrove swamps. At one point she saw the natives, but only as wee specks, far away. As she rested, she wondered if she had done the right thing in avoiding them. Maybe they were not hostile. Maybe it had just been their sudden appearance, which had scared her. She had read about the various tribes of the west coast of Africa while aboard the tanker. In general, natives with painted faces were warriors and most were hostile. Tattooed natives were usually important members of the tribe, with those bearing cicatrix were leaders. Cannibals favored facial distortions of the nose, lips and ears as well as the filing of the front teeth into points.

THE TIDE HAD TURNED when Paula came to the land spit forming the cove. Here, she felt she could travel safely in the surf to the dinghy. Even if the natives turned back, they wouldn't be able to see her; but she must make sure not to leave another footprint in the receding tide. She hung her shoes and socks around her neck and walked in the deeper water; though she was tiring, the adrenalin of fear fueled her muscles.

Paula speculated: what if I had approached them, and they were hostile? I would have been at a disadvantage even with my pistol. No one knows where I am—or if I'm even alive. Better to be alone and alive than a captive in some unimaginable situation. She dragged the dinghy to the surf; the smooth band of sand looked so obvious to her—like a sign that read: *This way to fresh meat!* Digging in her pack, she took out her hundred-foot line. She tied the line to the dinghy, then jumped out and pulled it up past the water line. Back at the forest, she took a leafy branch, and walking backwards, began to remove the *sign* of her passage. She reached the dinghy and pushed it into the water, holding the line to keep it from being swept away, as she erased the rest of the marks to the sea.

It was ebb tide, which helped the row back to the yacht where she let the air out of the dinghy and secured it in the locker. She raised the loading platform, and dogged it tight. Then she pulled in the swimmer's ladder and secured it in place. She wished the security systems were functional. Oh, how I miss those batteries!

The foghorn! It was operated by compressed air! Running the engine yesterday would have pressurized the air storage tank. If I attach a line to the foghorn chain and tie it to the rope-rail that runs around the boat, and someone leans or pulls on the rope-rail, it will sound the foghorn! Ten minutes later her alarm system was in place. Too bad I don't dare test it, she thought, feeling pleased with herself.

Going below and securing the hatch, Paula felt safe. The windows were all portholes. There were three ceiling vents, each fifteen inches square in the cabin housing. One in the galley, one in the aisle above the bunks and one in the lab, all with exhaust fans, which, alas, also ran on the missing batteries.

Paula showered and put on clean sweats, for the evenings were cool. She ate a few granola bars and finished the pears with a cup of mint tea—all the while watching the jetty until the last of the twilight faded. When it was dark—no moon or stars... and no flare tonight—she got in the bunk and snuggled under the blankets. It felt so good to lie down. The aspirin was taking effect, and feeling safe, she slept.

THE CLAMOR OF THE gulls awakened her the next morning. The tide was coming in bringing with it the anchovy schools, a favorite food of the gulls. Immediately, Paula looked out the porthole; she could see no one. Rising, she checked all sides... nothing. She looked through the eyehole in the hatch—clear. She unlocked the lab and stood on the swivel stool to look through the movie camera viewfinder... nothing; no one was hiding on the boat or in view on the shore. She felt sure she was alone. If the natives swam out to the boat, surely they would have had to touch the rope-rail to come aboard... if they were able to attain the deck at all. Relocking the lab, Paula moved to the galley and breakfast. She felt famished, and had oatmeal, grapefruit sections and biscotti; over coffee, she entered her beach excursion in the log.

WHILE SHE HAD BEEN traveling through the trees, she had come across vines with unusual flowers with fuzzy pods like poppies. She had quickly picked several and put them in her specimen case. When she finished the entries in the log, Paula took the specimen case out of the refrigerator and into the lab. There she spent the rest of the morning identifying and photographing the specimens and partitioning them for later analysis. The work was going well when she stopped for another cup of coffee. She glanced out the bunk portholes as she moved into the galley, and felt reassured; the beach was empty. She munched on a protein bar with dried fruit and nuts and drank a large cup of water before returning to the lab.

The heat in the forward compartment was enervating without the fan in the ceiling vent, so Paula left her work to nap. She needed to get into the routine of napping during the heat of the day. Being so close to the Equator, there were about fourteen hours of daylight each day, not including the late and early twilights, which were special times of beauty, peace and tranquility with lusciously cool breezes.

Twilight was also the time of day when the birds returned from the day's wanderings to roost in the tall trees with a great deal of squawking and flurry and sudden raucous eruptions, before finally settling down. In the mornings, they gossiped softly as the sun rose... before the pandemonium of leaving on the day's business. The subtle nighttime sounds of the rainforest were replaced with bellicose daytime chatter; while the noisy and always-hungry gulls flew off to the nearest sushi bar.

Breathing deeply of the distinctive smell of Africa, Paula slept.

3

Specimens

ALTHOUGH THE FLOWER SPECIMENS she had collected were new to her, they turned out to be an already described species. The fuzzy pods, however, seemed to be an unknown genus. As soon as some of the seeds were dry and could be powdered, she would try several different solvents to extract organic constituents.

She hoped to identify some new alkaloid with sedative properties in conjunction with the research by the Expedition, as well as being part of her Ph.D. studies with Dr. Miles. Every culture in the western hemisphere and Europe seems to have discovered, or used, at least one plant for its psychotropic (mind-altering) effects... as a sedative, hallucinogen or intoxicant. But relatively few were known from the continent of Africa—except, of course, the ubiquitous cannabis, which was found in Africa. So, the pods she had gathered were an interesting find.

In her element, Paula did not notice the day fade away until she was unable to see by natural light. Stowing her work, she prepared her dinner. She scanned the beach with the binoculars from the porthole; but she could not see into the jungle-like growth that edged the length of the beach. A thousand fiends could be hiding in that dense foliage.

Before she lit the gimbaled oil lantern, Paula closed the plastic shades on the portholes and ceiling vents to keep the light from being seen on the beach. She entered her day in the Log before going to bed; where she felt snug and safe and where her jittery feelings subsided. The awful fear of fleeing for her safety was a first for Paula, and it had jangled her nerves.

She lay on the bunk with open, unseeing eyes, thinking: I have to get control of myself. I'm not being reasonable; the natives have no reason to pursue me. More than likely, they don't even know I'm here. It was just such a shock to wake up to their voices; to see such savage faces so close to me that had pushed my panic button.

Paula felt foolish. She had reacted with fear... unreasonable fear, for the first time in her life: she had stood her ground in a black bear charge, scaring the bear off with blasts from her whistle; she had climbed a tree to escape a cougar that had doggedly followed her up the tree, until her brother arrived and fired his pistol; she had come across a nest of rattlesnakes while climbing a cliff face, and had managed to block a strike with her hat; she had lost stirrups and reins on a run-away horse galloping through the woods—and had managed to ditch with only minor bruises; she had gone aground while sailing on a windy day—when she jumped out to lighten the load, a gust of wind whipped the boat away, keel-hauling her through the choppy sea, until her friends could drop the sail and haul her aboard.

She was no stranger to danger, but this was the first time she had ever felt threatened by people. It gave a whole new meaning to the word... danger.

Feeling calmer, she began to attribute her irrational reaction to the *Robinson Crusoe Syndrome*. She was alone... marooned in a hostile place... and the natives were cannibals... even though she knew cannibals in Africa were rare and found only in remote areas of the interior... the part known as the Dark Continent.

THE ARBOREAL TRAVEL BACK to the yacht had made the muscles in her shoulders and back sore; but traveling through the trees had made her feel in control, which had dominated the fear. Paula had not spent much of her life truly alone away from home; there had always been back-up of some kind. Now, she had only herself. Now, she would live or die by her decisions.

Paula thoughts rambled to her interesting findings in the lab, and then to the troubled Expedition. Had the Professor and the crew survived the storm... tsunami... whatever? Was anyone looking for me, or the yacht? It's been twelve days. Maybe I need to plan a way out, on land, but which way should I go? All the maps were with Dr. Miles gear, which he had not yet brought on board. Then again, since I have plenty of supplies, maybe I should just stay put. If I go off wandering, and help comes, they might never find me.

Or worse, think I perished in the storm. No, the yacht is too ship-shape for me not to have survived. They'd notice that. And so thinking, she fell asleep.

AT EARLY LIGHT, PAULA awoke and pampered herself with *little dreams*. The garbled chatter of the shore birds vied with the strident cries of the gulls as they dove on the anchovy schools. After drifting for a bit, she arose to feel all her sore muscles as she moved about opening portholes for cross ventilation, for African nights can be cool, requiring blankets and closed portholes. At each porthole she looked out searchingly. Nothing that she could see had changed.

Feeling better after the mental pep talk of last evening, Paula made oatmeal, opened a can of grapefruit sections and took some aspirin. She ate in the cockpit with her attention focused on the beach and the stone jetty, thinking: if the natives come this way, they will have to cross the jetty, to avoid the mangrove swamp that lies beyond the greenery lining the beach.

Coming back through the trees, she had crossed a forest trail that might have been the route the natives had traveled to the beach. It was about a mile up on the other side of the jetty. On her morning walk in the surf, she had paid little attention to the thick vegetation lining the beach, but on her return, she had been cautious, watching for other natives. If the group she had seen returned and went up that trail, they wouldn't see the yacht at all. From the trees, only the mast and the distress pennant had been visible. She fervently hoped that she had not somehow left them a reason to go looking for her.

PAULA SPENT THE DAY in the lab. The seeds from the pods were encouraging. She was glad she had brought her own microscope for Dr. Miles kept his with his gear. She needed more of the seeds from the pods to continue her analysis. Tomorrow, she would go and gather another supply of the pods.

Since she had been fleeing through the trees for her safety, she had not taken the time to dig out her camera to photograph the flowers, pods and vines; thereby documenting their habitat and growth forms... an oversight she had to correct. At lunch, she checked the tide. As near as she could tell, it would be high tide late tomorrow morning. She could leave early and be back for the ebb tide.

THE FOLLOWING MORNING, PAULA wore her dark green, knee-length tights with green knee socks and half chaps. She did not plan on walking in the surf, so she wore her cliff-face scaling sneakers with the pebble tread, for better traction in the trees... because she intended only arboreal travel. Get the pods and get back! Don't take any chances! She told herself. She wore her camouflage shirt and tucked her hair under the camouflage French Legion style cap. She added rations for another week to her pack... sort of like insurance... if you have it... you won't need it! She left the machete, extra film and her wallet on the yacht. She started to remove the cliff climbing gear, but changed her mind. It was the one thing, if ever needed, for which there was no substitute.

During her usual breakfast, Paula thought about her last hike before leaving for Africa. It was just the six of them: her parents, her twin brother Eric, her older sister Sallee Anne and her brother Scott, who was the eldest. They had spent a three-day weekend on Hawk Mountain. Hiking up the rarely used rugged trail on the back of the mountain, which was only a rocky space in the deep woods. She had carried almost the same gear plus a sleeping bag and tent as well as a few cooking implements.

The day after the hike up the mountain, they had rappelled off the promontory cliff face to a jutting shelf where they ate lunch. Then, they made cliff face ascents back to the top and camp, where Mom and Sallee Anne had dinner ready. Paula loved the campfire evenings and the delightful, often funny, stories told while catching up on their everyday lives. Eric always had tons of funny animal stories from Veterinary School. Scott had made Captain in the Air Force and had all sorts of anecdotes about flying. Sallee Anne was deeply involved with her painting and with practicing the piano for the occasional concert, but she still found time to design clothing for a few select collections; she loved mimicking the couturiers with a French accent, which kept us in stitches. We all wondered when she found time to sleep.

Mom told stories about the horses or the family; she never mentioned her Income Tax Preparation business. Often her stories reminded us of being kids again. Dad enjoyed his tenure as a Professor at the University of Delaware in the Engineering Department; yet he still found time to putter in his shop. He had two new patents pending. The evenings always passed too quickly, but winter was the best time to go to Hawk Mountain to avoid the crowds that flocked to the summit by car, spring and fall, to watch the hawk migrations, which were awesome.

The next day, with somewhat lighter loads, they had hiked back down the boulder-strewn mountain trail. Who would have ever thought that her next hike would be alone—on a deserted beach in West Africa?

So MUCH HAD HAPPENED since then, it was hard to believe it was only a month ago that they had all been sitting around the Christmas tree opening presents, and just three weeks ago when they had returned from Hawk Mountain.

Her muscle stiffness had progressed to twinges as she gathered her gear and her courage to get going: collect the pods, take the corroborating pictures, and get back, fast! She dropped the rear platform, inflated the dinghy from an air canister, and then tossed her gear and oars aboard. Lastly, she reattached her foghorn alarm before stepping into the dinghy to row ashore. She cut fresh greenery to cover the dinghy and taking a leafy branch returned to the surf and backed her way to the forest to obscure her tracks.

SHE TOOK ADVANTAGE OF a thick vine hanging nearby, and climbed hand over hand, using her chap-covered legs around the rough vine. She sat and rested on a stout limb to catch her breath... feeling pleased with herself: her upper body strength had not failed her when she needed it most. The best gymnasts were preteens, but Paula had kept her lithe, spare frame and had competed in gymnastics all through her college years. While in graduate school, she had coached at a private gymnastics school and had often used her skills to demonstrate to the youngsters the various steps for each move.

Once rested, she made her way through the trees. It was slow going, for she had to find new paths as the trees looked different going in this direction. She moved higher in the trees, for better cover where more branches met each other in the middle terrace, nearer the canopy, but not so high as to greatly disturb the nesting birds.

Once past the swamp, Paula found the going easier. It was still early morning and cool, for this was the west coast, with Mount Cameroon looming in the distance; the sun had not yet arrived to turn the forest into a sauna. The birds and tree animals were all awake, calling and chattering to one another. With the cacophony of sound, it was not necessary to try to move silently. Still, it took over an hour to reach the trail that led into the forest.

Climbing higher in the trees, to cross the trail, she froze. Two of the native bearers were walking up the trail from the beach. Paula remained still—barely able to breathe in her leafy aerie until they were well past—they almost saw her, for she thought them to be long gone. Why were they still here? Shaken by the unexpected encounter, for these men still terrified her, she moved with caution on her way to find the vines; get more samples of the fuzzy pods and get back to the yacht—fast!

With her mission accomplished, Paula rested once she was back past the forest trail. She considered traveling on the ground, since the natives had gone into the forest almost three hours ago. She sat, reapplying her bug repellent and taking a drink of water, when she heard excited voices. Startled, she climbed higher in the tree, until she was concealed by the dense foliage; she pulled out her pistol and waited.

In a few moments, the owners of the excited voices came into view. It was the tall warrior with all the gold circlets on his arms and his shorter companion. Only two of the bearers were with them. They were coming from the direction of the yacht. These four men must have continued past the path when she was looking for a place to cross over it. Had they gone far enough south to see the yacht?

She could not make out their conversation, but they were clearly excited as they hastened towards the forest trail. The tall warrior stopped, held up his spear, turned and spoke to one of the bearers, who put down his load and took off towards the forest trail at a run. The other bearer also put his load down, before he moved off into the undergrowth with the shorter warrior. Paula worried: were they looking for her? The tall leader sat down by the bundles and waited.

Her heart plummeted. Could they be looking for my trail? Have I left some *sign*? Because of her heavy application of the eucalyptus-citronella bug spray, she had caused little concern to the denizens of the trees, for they did not smell her as human. But the birds, which mostly had no sense of smell, would occasionally lift off from their roosts if she climbed too high.

She wondered: did they find the dinghy, or had the startled birds alerted him to my presence? What had made him go past the trail to the jetty? It was he who was convinced that the footprint in the sand had been that of a Baharike. What was a *Sea Goddess* anyway? I'll have to sit tight and wait; he's too close for me to move undetected. Right now I'm completely hidden... as long as I don't make any noise... unless he can hear the hammering of my heart or my labored breathing.

Each minute waiting motionless was like forever. The tall native just sat staring out to sea. He made no attempt to look around. Maybe it wasn't me that had caused him to stop here. Maybe this was where he first saw the footprint of the

Sea Goddess. She was starting to gain a little hope in her high hide-away.

In an hour or so, the shorter companion came back to the beach. He sat beside the taller man. Their conversation was low and fast, none of which she could hear. The sun was high when three of the four bearers returned, and moved the bundles into the shade a short distance away from the leaders.

Paula thought: no one has looked up into the trees; either they know I am here and don't want me to know that they know, or they have something else in mind. Before long the fourth bearer returned. Much gesticulation and excited conversation followed. She caught only snatches: "... to the village..."– "...with Masula..."–"... not the long trail..." The fragments of conversation gave her no clues or ideas.

After a noon meal and a short rest, the natives gathered up their goods and, in the manner of players on a golf course, strolled down the beach to the forest trail. Relieved, Paula waited another half hour. She ate a trail bar, drank some more of her water, and took her electrolyte tablets. Climbing down the tree to traverse the lower branches, she took care not to disturb the birds. It was harder to travel here. There were larger spaces between the limbs, and she often had to go up, cross over, and then go back down again. It was tedious and tiring but she was fueled with the desperate desire to get back to the yacht and safety. Here, without protection, numbers mattered. On the yacht, she could always maneuver evasively around the huge cove... if necessary.

Paula had passed the stone jetty when she heard the distinctive whump-whump-whump of a helicopter in the distance. Grabbing a stout vine, she slid to the ground. With joyful excitement, she pushed her way through the foliage and ran out onto the beach.

She ran along the beach looking up for the helicopter, ready to fire her flare gun. It was still high tide and the beach was narrow. She stopped for a moment, listening, when a net settled over her head, shoulders and arms and was instantly pulled tight.

Paula whirled around, stunned. There stood the six natives.

The two leaders were smiling. Thank God, no filed teeth. Disgusted with herself for being so careless, and annoyed that the helicopter hadn't come yesterday; she sensed struggling would be futile and degrading. If ever she needed her wits about her, now was the time. It was odd, but now that she was captured, the terror subsided and defiance took its place. The natives had been searching for a *Sea Goddess* and a *Sea Goddess* they would get. She must not seem to be afraid... she knew that from her encounters with wild animals that could sense fear. So she stood defiant and let her anger show in her eyes. She would never let them know of her gut-wrenching dismay.

The sound of the helicopter was getting louder. The natives pulled her into the undergrowth, took the flare gun from her hand and tied her bandanna over her mouth. All heads turned as the helicopter came into view. It flew in circles over the *Just Cause*. The pilot hailed the yacht with a bullhorn, calling for Paula by name. When it seemed that the helicopter might be coming over to land on the beach, the natives melted into the lush undergrowth, taking Paula with them. From a short distance, they watched as the helicopter hovered close to the boat, and two men jumped into the water to swim to the yacht.

Paula could see that the natives were agog, watching this curious, whirling bird. With the gag over her mouth and her arms clamped to her sides, she could not tell them by word or *sign*—that the helicopter had come for her. They thought her to be a Baharike, a *Sea Goddess,* and it was possible they did not connect her with the yacht at all. She was a prize, and in a fatalistic way, she knew they were going to take her with them, but why? No... thinking that way brought desperation and irrational fear. If she was going to survive, she must look strong, act strong and above all, be strong. Men, in her experience, admired and coveted strong women, and these were men... men who could be astonished!

She would bide her time. She needed to know the foibles of these men before she could escape. She needed to use their weaknesses against them. They knew nothing of her, and she would keep her talents to herself. She would play on their superstitions about the Baharike, and their obvious respect and admiration for her as a creature of the sea.

Yacht Found

Once Sandy and Greg were in the water, the helicopter headed for the beach. Greg reached the yacht several strokes ahead of Sandy, and heaved himself onto the loading platform and grabbed the rope rail. Instantly the foghorn sounded, so startling Sandy that he fell back into the water.

"Did you do that?" he sputtered. "You scared the heck out of me."

Greg reached down to give Sandy a hand up, saying, "Took a few seconds off my life too! All I did was grab the rope rail, like this." The Klaxon foghorn sounded again.

Sandy raised an eyebrow in question; he looked at Greg and said, "Looks like our gal has set herself an alarm. I wonder why–for protection or as a signal? Obviously, she's not here."

It didn't take them long to make an inspection of the yacht. It was evident Paula had survived the tsunami and the following stormy seas, for the yacht was clean and tidy, showing only minor effects of the rough passage: a missing cleat, a missing eyebolt and a couple of broken guy wires. They found the hatch locked, but the key was stowed in the hidden key holder. The lab door was unlocked, and inside it looked like Paula had work in progress.

"Seems to me our fearless Paula might be out collecting samples." Sandy called out to Greg, who replied, "Yup, dinghy's gone. One of us should stay here until Paula gets back. Want to toss for it?"

"Nah," Greg said, "I'll stay. I can get started on the repairs.

We can't hoist the mains'l until those guy wires are secured. Would you bring my ditty bag with you tomorrow?"

"Sure, no problem; anything else before I swim back to the chopper to get the news aloft?"

"Nope—just don't forget the batteries." They both chuckled at the irony before Sandy dove into the water and swam, with long strokes aided by the incoming tide, to the beached chopper.

When Sandy and Ace, the helicopter pilot, were airborne, Sandy radioed Captain Nils, Master of the *Norsk Star* with the good news that they had found the *Just Cause* unharmed. Sandy could hear the hooting and shouting as Captain Nils passed the word to the crew on the bridge. It had been fourteen days since the yacht went missing on the 12th of January.

The APCO choppers had arrived on the 17th to search for the missing yacht, bringing medical aid for the victims of the tsunami. The initial search was based on a message that had been received on January 15th from a fishing trawler, about the sighting of an unmanned yacht in the Bight of Biafra. Using the co-ordinates given, the helicopters made two search flights a day, for four days out to sea.

On the 22nd of January, the *Norsk Star* arrived at Port Harcourt for repairs to her storm damaged bulkheads, which in effect, moved the search area to the southeast and along the western-most coast of Nigeria and the northwest coast of Cameroon.

The noise of the helicopter precluded casual conversation, giving Sandy time to think about all that had happened since the 11th of January, when they had anchored off the Slave Coast of West Africa.

During the day of preparations for disembarkation—of the yacht from the tanker—the crew and passengers had suffered motion sickness from the disturbed seas. Unknown and far distant undersea eruptions had caused vast unusual seas, as the gigantic swell gained strength and headed towards land in the Bight of Benin.

The *Norsk Star*, being empty when the tsunami roared into the bay, had risen up on the swell and then heeled over on her anchors while the tremendous force of the wave passed, which physically catapulted the unmoored yacht into the trough behind the wave. After the wave passed, the empty tanker had bobbed back upright, like a cork. The injuries on board the tanker were minor because the daylong triple motions of the seas had forced the passengers to their bunks. The off-duty crewmen were in their hammocks. Only the officers of the watch were on the bridge; and they had the moments during the massive ebb tide, before the enormous wave struck, to warn the crew and passengers to brace themselves for a tidal wave.

For days, the crew of the *Norsk Star* provided communications, medical help, supplies, clean water (desalinated from the ballast tanks) and rescue coordination for the devastated town of Lagos. APCO (Asher Pharmaceutical Company), the funding corporation for the Expedition, sent two helicopters to search for the yacht; but had first filled them with needed medical supplies and personnel.

The last eight days had been a constant search for Paula and the yacht. Without the yacht and its lab, there would be no Expedition. Everyone was now pleased to be able to get underway with the project. It had been decided that if the yacht was found before the end of the month, in good order, they would go south to the Ogooué River where there had been no tsunami damage. There, they would still be in the rainforest, the likely habitat of the types of plants they sought.

As TWILIGHT APPROACHED, GREG was surprised, and then very concerned, when Paula did not return. He was feeling the isolation and frustration Paula must have felt at not having radio communications. He could tell no one that Paula had not returned. Greg was getting a tiny taste of the dire circumstances Paula had experienced, being completely alone, for the past fourteen days. He put himself in her shoes and wondered what he would have done? Would he have had the courage and strength of mind to continue to function as Paula had done? He put his useless conjecture aside as the worry became insistent. Where was she? Has something happened?

The foghorn alarm suggested she might have been afraid... or maybe it was just a signal... right! A signal for what?

Greg's imagination began to run wild. To control his conjecture, he started on the fiberglass repairs, which had to be done in stages. He would need power, which he did not have, to run the drill in order to attach the eyebolt, before he could swedge the guy wires to it. He felt a redesign of the power supply was needed. Too many vital operations relied on the batteries, with no other back-up power sources. He decided to use his time to plan the changes.

Greg went for paper and pencil. When he opened the locker, he saw the logbook with a protruding page marker. Curious, he opened the log and read Paula's entries from the 17th to the 25th, which stunned and amazed him. He was overcome with worry and feared foul play, since she had not returned from going ashore today–damn–the very day they had found the yacht.

The following day, late in the morning, Greg heard the helicopter return. Watching from the yacht, he saw them unload and inflate a large dinghy. Into the dinghy went the crates of batteries, boxes of fresh foods, their duffle bags, several long tubes and a box with a ribbon on it. Tossing in the oars, Sandy pushed the dinghy into the surf. The tide was coming in and it would be a tough row out to the yacht; so Greg raised the anchor, started the engine, and motored towards the beach.

Sandy tossed Greg a line to make fast, and asked, "What's in the box with the ribbon, a cake?"

"Yup," Sandy replied, "A surprise for Paula. Where is she anyway?"

Greg hesitated and Sandy looked him in the eye and asked, "She didn't come back?"

"Nope, and wait until you read the log book." Greg felt a lump rise up in his throat and had to stop talking for a moment. "I found it last night when I was looking for some paper to sketch out a few electrical changes."

Sandy stood stunned at the news. Gaining some control, he said, "Let's get these batteries installed so we can radio Ace in the chopper. With the surrounding cliffs, we may not have a signal strong enough to reach the tanker without a booster on the antenna. Ace can relay the problem to the Professor when he gets airborne, and radio back to us."

An hour later, after Sandy had read Paula's entries in the log, and installed the batteries, he hailed the chopper.

"*Just Cause* to ZLA 9. Come in. Over."

"ZLA 9 here. I found a dinghy with the APCO logo hidden in the underbrush. I piled some coconuts on the beach in front of it. I also found deep footprints, like someone running on the beach, over towards the jetty. The deep footprints stopped and then turned and walked into the forest. It was hard to tell exactly, what or who had made the footprints, because the rotors had blown a lot of sand around when I was looking for a spot wide enough to clear the blades and not have the runners in the surf. Do you have contact with the tanker? Over"

"Not yet. Paula did not return yesterday. Greg found the logbook and it seems there was a band of six natives, possibly hostile, who might have been stalking her. She had some fuzzy pods in the lab and might have gone ashore to gather more. Let the Professor know as soon as you're airborne. We need to make some fast decisions here. Over"

"Copy that, I need to be off anyway, the left runner is almost awash. Over."

"That's a ten four, Ace; thanks for the ride. Over and Out."

Sandy and Greg watched the copter rise and swing out over the cove as they motored back towards the sea opening by the reef, which was also a better site for radio reception.

Captain Nils had sent charts of the area. He had marked the place he thought the yacht to be, and confirmed that it was the largest of three sunken volcanoes, the one with a rim just below the surface along the opening to the sea. Captain Nils felt the only way to get the yacht out was to raise the movable centerboard and use flotation devices to clear the rim. This task would require diving equipment to place the flotation devices, a ship's cradle to hold them in place, and another boat to haul her across the reef once she was floated high enough above the water.

The needed work was a convenient distraction. Sandy had installed the antenna booster and then manned the radio, contacting the tanker while Greg finished his repairs, and started on the needed electrical changes. Based on the helicopter pilot's report, Dr. Miles had informed the Nigerian government that the yacht had been found, but Paula had gone missing. They, in turn, promised to contact the proper authorities in Cameroon, for the cove was in Cameroon territory.

Sandy and Greg worked through the heat of the afternoon making the changes to the electrical system. Once the ceiling vent fans were operational, the cabin space became pleasant and comfortable. They decided to power all the electrical systems directly from the generator when the engine was running, which included charging the batteries. This would, in essence, make the batteries back-up power, not the primary source when the diesel engine was running.

When they had finished making the electrical changes, Sandy looked at Greg and said, "You want to motor back to shore and take a look at those footprints?"

"Yeah, let's do that!"

Ace was right. They couldn't make much of the prints. Some were deeper, and then they became confused with many impressions at the edge of the undergrowth. It looked like there was a trail, really just a bunch of indentations, no clear footprints going inland; but the razor edged plants, thorn bushes, and trailing vines made it impossible for them to follow the scuffed sand very far.

"We aren't properly dressed or equipped to do this," Sandy yelped as his shorts and leg caught on a wait-a-bit bush.

Greg helped him extract himself and replied, "You're right, it's getting late, and we haven't told anyone what we're doing. What if we get lost or ambushed too. Then what! Let's go back and tell the Professor what we've found. Let him decide what we should do, okay?"

"Yup, sounds good to me."

The Professor, when confronted with the possibility of abduction, contacted APCO. APCO then contacted the officials of Nigeria, who were hosting APCO's research efforts. They, in turn, contacted the Cameroon Republic, as the yacht was in their territory. The Cameroon officials immediately agreed to send a search and rescue team from Yaoundé, which was less than two hundred miles away. The team should arrive tomorrow morning.

The next morning, Sandy and Greg rowed the recovered dinghy to the beach to wait for the searchers. As promised, the rescue team arrived mid-morning; a native tracker and two United Nations soldiers who examined the footprints, now barely depressions in the sand, as it had rained during the night.

Greg gave them a picture of Paula and told them about her wilderness skills. The soldiers told them, in English, "There are certainly no cannibals or even hostile tribes within hundreds of miles. More than likely, Miss Thornton went into the forest for relief from the sun and has just gotten lost."

Greg and Sandy knew differently. Paula was too experienced to wander off into unknown thickets. They showed the logbook to the soldier in charge, but he dismissed the stalking implication as hysterical, female imagination.

But the native tracker said to the soldiers in French, "The trail into the forest supports the theory of abduction."

Immediately the soldiers followed the tracker into the dense undergrowth, saying, "They would keep in touch with the yacht by radio."

When they had gone, Greg told Sandy what the tracker had said to the UN soldiers in French, adding, "Let's keep this to ourselves until tomorrow, when the rest of the team arrives to float the yacht out of here. Maybe the tracker was wrong, and they'll find her wandering, lost."

"I hope so." Sandy muttered. His feelings of guilt, for not installing the batteries on that fateful day, were almost unbearable. After a bite of lunch, they worked on the changes to the electrical systems, which kept them both busy for the rest of the day and into the evening, when they had a transmission from the UN soldiers.

"Search and Rescue to the *Just Cause*. Come in. Over."

"*Just Cause* here. Over."

"The tracks are heading into the mountains. The group is traveling single file and it is difficult to establish whether or not Miss Thornton is with them. They have more than a day's head start on us and if it rains again tonight, tracking will be very hard, if not impossible. Over."

"Thanks for the update. Over and Out." Sandy turned to Greg, "Damn, I thought this was the dry season!"

"It seems there is no such thing in a rainforest, just less rain at times. We'd better contact the Professor and let him know the status of the search—not wait until tomorrow—in case there is something else he can do."

Professor George Miles was distracted by the news. He had not contacted Paula's family, hoping she would turn up smiling, with a full sample case. He couldn't put it off any longer. Getting patched into a landline, George placed the unpleasant call to Lisa and Charles Thornton in Oxford, Pennsylvania.

Late in the day on the 29th of January, the *Just Cause* was floated out of the cove into the Atlantic Ocean. On the 30th, she headed south to the Ogooué River. A net filled with supplies, a VHF radio, and a letter from Professor Miles had been left, covered with a small tarp and strung high over the beach, near the place where Paula had left the dinghy. They had booby-trapped the line with young saplings so that the weight of a monkey would release the sapling and fling the monkey high into the trees. There were only two saplings usable for this purpose; they hoped it would be enough.

There was literally nothing else they could do. It had been five days now since they had found the yacht. The UN soldiers and guide had been forced to return as they had lost the trail. APCO promised to keep the pressure on the government of Cameroon, which was in a state of flux, merging the French Cameroon Republic, which was a United Nations trust territory, with the British-administered southern territories of The Cameroons. The joined territories were to be known, simply, as Cameroon.

5

The Rainforest

THE NATIVES KEPT PAULA confined in the net but removed the gag after a short time. Then, motioning to her for silence, she was prodded forward with the tip of a sharp spear. What was happening to her was so far beyond the realm of probability, and filled her with such distress that it was an emotional, as well as a physical struggle to continue on with the dignity and disdain she had assumed upon capture.

The native bearer in front of her was deferential, and held back the thorny bushes, vines and branches as she passed, but even so, it was a severe physical strain to walk and duck with her arms pinned to her sides. She was close to faltering when her captors stopped and removed the net.

Paula soon found that it was not out of consideration for her difficulties, but because she slowed them too much—trussed up like a mummy—since one indignity was exchanged for another. They tied a rope around her waist with two leashes: one to the native leading, and one to the native following. But the relief at being able to move her arms for balance and forward motion was immediate.

The natives did not break trail in the dense, prickly undergrowth. They seemed to be able to pass through any mass of tangled vegetation with ease, using their spears as adroitly as a person uses their arms. This was a bit of woodsmanship she had yet to learn, and so suffered many scrapes, pricks and scratches from thorny plants. The native in front of her was no longer moving as much vegetation as he had, when she was bound in the net.

Once they reached the animal track, the pace picked up

a bit, but not much due to the rate of climb. Paula had lost all sense of time and distance while her attention was fully occupied trying to escape the evil thorny vegetation. She now began to note the rise in elevation, and the direction of travel. Paula knew from experience how to gauge the distance traveled on foot per hour; she knew they had been in the *rough* for three hours before reaching the open trail; maybe they had traveled five miles, no more.

Time passed, no one spoke.

When the natives had removed the gag, she had asked them, in English and in French, what they intended to do with her? The leader had just prodded her with the tip of his spear, gesturing for her to be quiet. The natives did not speak at all on the trail; they used only hand signals among themselves, none of which she understood. I must be careful... should they speak... not to show understanding, she thought. Right now, that's my only advantage. She tried to plan for eventualities: she felt they were taking her to their village for a reason. She might be a trophy—if they thought her to be a Bahariki. If so, they will take good care of me until they reach their destination. My best chance for escape, then, lay in being docile and submissive to lessen their watchfulness. I must show them courage, stamina and stoicism to gain their respect, if I am a Bahariki, but why not also be an ordinary woman—with a woman's foibles?

For now, attached to a native in front and behind, there was no escape.

With time to think, Paula became morose. If only I had waited another day before venturing out again. I allowed my ego to push me into a reckless situation, by wanting to be the first one to find an unnamed plant. Now, I will be lucky to survive. How had they known to circle around to get in front of me? Their woodscraft is superb. That they could travel easily in the dense, seemingly impenetrable underbrush was more than proof of it.

The question that worried her most, as she trudged up the winding mountain path, was if the natives knew she had been traveling in the trees. She must make it seem that she was afraid of heights to lessen their suspicions, if any. It amazed her that people almost never looked up for a quarry; several times she had avoided hunting groups in the mountains by climbing trees. If only the natives would talk amongst themselves—give her some clues. She knew the two leaders talked, but only when too far away to be overheard.

As the day progressed, Paula knew she was being watched surreptitiously. She had followed their command and did not speak, but she had also assumed her gymnastic presence. It was an attitude of inflexible concentration, a mien of detachment. It was a cloak against doubt and distraction, one with which she had a long-time familiarity.

At rest stops, she was given water first. No one touched her. Water, and later food, was placed beside her so that she had to sidle over to it, for they always tied her between two trees. Were they afraid of her? Did a Sea Goddess have powers? She wished she understood the appellation. Whatever their reasons, Paula was grateful for the deference.

The long African twilight was almost gone when they arrived at a wide clearing beside the trail, which was surrounded by a high, thorn boma. Two stakes were pounded into the ground and Paula was tied between them. She was given a skin to put on the ground, and a robe to use as a blanket against the night chill. Later she was given a cold meal of meat and fruit served with hot broth.

She was exhausted from tension and worry. In only moments after her meal, she was asleep. The natives then examined the contents of her backpack, and found nothing they needed to remove. They had already taken her .22 Magnum pistol, the flare gun and her hunting knife.

Morning was heralded by the multitudinous sounds of early birdsong, and bits of whispered conversation. She lay still, trying to hear what was being said, but only made out a word here and there, which gave her no useful information. She heard the term *Bahariki* used several times. It was clear they thought her to be a Sea Goddess, whatever that implied; she must be sure to take advantage of this mystical appellation to keep them in awe of her.

Moments later, her bindings were tugged; she opened her eyes to a gourd of hot coffee, with a hint of vanilla, and a steamed cabbage leaf rolled up like a crepe with a paste of berries, nuts, and grains inside. Even though she had been abducted, she wasn't being mistreated, and the food was good.

When she finished her meal, the two men who had walked with her yesterday took the ropes looped around her waist, and led her into the forest where they tied the ropes, one on each side, to young trees. A few leaves were placed at her feet and she was left alone. Paula was horrified. What were they doing? Why have they tied me here in the underbrush? Are they going to leave me here like this? Am I to be some sort of sacrifice? Terror arose. She struggled with her bonds until she heard stealthy noises in the bushes behind her. Whirling in fright, she saw one of the natives crouch down, in an unmistakable stance, not far from her. Paula had to stifle a wild urge to laugh–her terror had been such that she was not far from hysteria. Nothing would be gained and much would be lost by showing such weakness. This was just the universal morning ritual; nothing would be gained from constipation either.

THE MARCH RESUMED A short time later. In places where the track was steep, the native in front provided help and support through his leash. It would have been impossible for her to climb these trails if they had not freed her arms. Most of the trail was a gradual climb but the switchbacks were often quite steep and badly eroded. The rainforest continued thick and impenetrable on either side of the track.

Two of the bearers led the way hacking away infringing growth, followed by the bedecked young men–who did no work except to carry their weapons– and then came their little ménage-a-trois.

They continued climbing all morning, stopping only for water. At noontime they again had a meal of dried meat and fruit. The two-hour stop in the heat of the day was a blessing. Still, no one spoke a word. Their silence amid the incessant cacophony of forest sounds gave the march a dream-like quality.

As the daylight faded into the long African twilight they reached a wide ridge. Beyond the flat expanse of the sloping lichen-strewn shoulder was a panoramic view that stretched for miles on the western side of the ridge. The taller trees growing up from the mountainsides were dripping with the pinks, purples, reds and whites of the flowering creepers, which were contrasted by the myriad shades of green in leaf and vine. Some of the trees were covered with hats of flowers that were so dense the supporting greenery could not be seen. In the rays of the setting sun, the flowering treetops looked like they wore halos of shimmering gold or iridescent white. In other circumstances, the incredible sea of color and the awesome beauty of the vistas would have been, in themselves, worth the trip. It was a marvelous change from the dense shadows and closed-in feeling of the hillsides.

Her warders quickened the pace along the mostly open and downhill track. A few stops were made for gathering, at which times her leashes were given to the aloof leaders, who ignored her as if she didn't exist. She returned their courtesy by sitting cross-legged in a yoga-like position, chanting: aaahooom, aaahooom. She knew her mantra worried them and their discomfort gave her a modicum of pleasure.

They followed the ridge for a few miles before arriving at a mud hut, surrounded by a thorn boma. This was obviously an oft-used route, and she wondered why. It was not obvious if they had acquired something from the ocean: but who knew what was in the wrapped bundles the bearers carried on their heads with such impressive agility, as only two of the bundles were opened at the campsites.

Paula thought about the distances they traveled each day. She thought maybe ten miles yesterday and maybe fifteen today. Combined, it was probably only a day's travel from the beach for the natives, without a prisoner. The wide spot beside the trail with the high thorn boma was probably their usual lunch and rest stop, if they didn't spend the morning slogging through the swamps.

Dinner was served and Paula amused her captors by using the spoon in her *5in1* to eat the stew served in a hollowed out gourd. She always wore the *5in1*, even at home, in classes or in the lab. It was her trademark. She had casually determined the direction they were traveling by the occasional shafts of sunlight that penetrated the canopy, but had confirmed her opinion on the twisting trails with the compass, which was set in one end of the *5in1*. On the other end was a whistle; the middle was a waterproof barrel that held wooden matches; with the spoon and fork hinged on either side, making use of the match barrel as a handle. Paula used the spoon to eat while the natives ate skillfully with their fingers.

After dinner, Paula went right to sleep. When the moon was high in the night sky, a tree hyrax, a very noisy and horrid-sounding fellow, rudely awakened her. His mating call sounds much like a person being hacked to death with an axe, as it escalates in pitch and volume to a fearful end. This was the first time she had been awake when the natives were asleep. She knew escape would be impossible even if she were not staked in the hut, for she could hear the natives snoring as they sheltered from the rain under the long eaves of the hut. Now would be a good time to put on clean underwear and socks and her hiking shoes. Feeling around in her backpack, which she used for a pillow, she came across the switchblade penknife her twin brother, Eric, had given her for a present. She had forgotten about it. She put it in her pocket. It would give her confidence to have it close. Finding the small, fat casserole candle, she lit it, and using her water bottle with the packaged towelettes, had a quick wash before donning clean underwear and knee socks.

What a difference being clean made, it felt wonderful. Not wanting the natives to know she had changed, she put on the same outer clothing along with her half-chaps, which covered enough of her hiking shoes to make them look much the same as her sneakers.

Closing her eyes, Paula listened to the soft patter of the nighttime rain on the thatched roof, and wondered, if she had not been with them, would all the natives have slept inside?

Probably not, probably only the aloof leaders would have used the hut. She fell asleep smiling at the thought of their unaccustomed discomfort.

MORNING CAME ALL TOO soon. This day was no different than the one before it, except that the vistas were absolutely intoxicating in the morning sunlight. Paula could see for miles in every direction, valley upon valley of rainforest covered in a profusion of bright colors; and far and away, the dark, cold blue of the ocean fading into the lighter, warm blue of the horizon.

The ridge of the shoulder narrowed and became rocky, claiming her full attention before it dropped into a crease filled with an impenetrable growth of dock (wild celery), which grows to eight feet and is crowned with feathery white blooms. It is a favorite food of mountain gorillas. She wondered if they were high enough for mountain gorillas. The dock did not look like it had been harvested recently.

The theme song from the movie, "The Bridge on the River Kwai", kept running through her mind as they slogged through the dense, dark creases. Some were steep and narrow; some were shallow and wide; some were a series of hillocks, with each one dropping lower before they again regained the wider mountain shoulder. With each emergence from the vales, the view of the mountains snaked away in front of them as far as the eye could see, shaded by the giant podocarpus with their yellow trunks, and the lower acacias with their dull, gold blooms. The hillsides were covered with clumps of tall tree ferns, stands of thick bamboo and euphorbias of the richest green. Behind them was the towering peak whose flanks they had skirted the day before, haloed by a misty cloud. Paula felt they must be around 6,000 feet high, possibly more.

All day, they kept to the ridge, which went up and down like a lazy roller coaster. The trail went down more than it went up: through open rocky scree–populated by aloes with fat long leaves, wood ferns that sheltered near large rocks, and thickets of blackberry bushes hiding between the boulders– before the track again dipped down into wooded creases of bamboo, hypericum, and sedum. The breeze from the updrafts and the occasional dappled shade made the heat of the sunny ridge tolerable, but Paula would have been lost without her homemade French Legion hat.

THE NATIVES DIDN'T SEEM to mind when she rummaged in her backpack at rest stops or used the bug spray and sun block, or took aspirin or electrolytes. It made her wonder if they had examined the contents of her backpack that first night, when she fell asleep immediately after dinner: the thought startled her. Why am I falling asleep so quickly after dinner each night? Are they drugging my food? If they are... whatever they are giving me has no side effects. I feel good when I wake up, not dull or groggy... and... my anxiety is diminished! I'm not happy about my situation, but I'm not frantic either.

AT DUSK, THEY CAME to another mud hut. This one was barely visible from the trail for it was built behind boulders in a wide, flat space that overlooked the steep, forested valleys to the west. Here Paula stopped... stunned... enthralled by the beauty of the scenery before her. Trees were artfully dotted with masses of white flowering mistletoe; and tucked into the Master's canvas, here and there, oranthus, with its dark green, seemingly black foliage, and draping clusters of bright red tubular flowers. Below, in an icing of golden green moss on horizontal limbs, were spikes and clusters of magnificent orchids, some creamy white, some lavender, or some a deep burgundy-red. The entire vista of magnificent flowers was made luminous by the orange-gold backdrop of the setting sun.

Nothing had prepared Paula for such a spectacular sight. She sat mesmerized by the grandeur and fabulous beauty that so few would ever see. Paula watched until the sparkling and shimmering magic faded and was gone. Never again would a sunset compare to this one. Each flower that was touched by the refracted rays of the setting sun had shimmered and sparkled as if it were encased in crystal. Paula's mind was blank; she was filled with peace and remembered: some good comes of everything.

THERE WAS ANOTHER CACHE of food hanging from the roof of the hut and plenty of dry firewood inside. Paula was glad to stop for the day; the rough ropes around her waist, above the emergency belt, had chaffed her skin. Once staked out in the privacy of the little hut, she applied ointment from the first aid kit to relieve the soreness and hasten the healing; she also put more aspirin and electrolytes in the small plastic bag she kept in her shirt pocket, for she recognized her fatigue as an electrolyte imbalance from so much sweating.

After dinner tonight, she was going to make some plans, but after she had eaten, she closed her eyes to think, and was soon asleep.

LATE THE NEXT MORNING, they started to descend the far side of the mountain. Just past mid-day, they came to a small spring-fed pond nestled at the base of the hillside. A thick stand of bamboo surrounded one end of the pond. Large stones were interspersed along the far side with tall graceful ferns and clumps of the decorative leaves of the herb, sansevieria. From the spring bubbling out of the hillside to where they stood were shrubs with bright green foliage resembling laurel mixed with the darker green agauria. Here her handlers removed her lead-ropes and gestured for her to take off her clothes and bathe. She was given a stick about four inches long and an inch thick and told to smell it. It smelled of honeysuckle and cedar, neither of which was native to Africa.

The men retired to the wide, flat clearing shaded by tall trees. There, around a fireplace made of stones, she could hear their mumbled talk and laughter, the first since her capture. Paula reveled in her bath, washing her hair and then her clothes, which she placed on rocks, in the sun to dry. She used her small towel to dry herself and dressed in clean clothes from her backpack. It never occurred to her to wonder why she had been given this treat. She went to the leaf pallet the men had prepared for her. Sitting in the dappled shade of the fragrant podocarpus tree, she felt totally renewed at being clean and was pleased to eat a meal without being staked.

In the three and a half days that she had been their prisoner, Paula had not been molested, and her intense fear of these men had diminished; but still, she remained wary. Her captors were still careful not to talk in her presence, so she had no idea of where they were going, or even how far they had yet to travel. But, in truth, the unknown disturbed her thoughts little, for she was consumed with watching out for critters in the dense foliage, or the placement of her feet while walking; or... she was sleeping.

Paula was now completely sure they were drugging her food. It was unusual for her to fall asleep the way she had been on this march. Even at the lunchtime stops, she fell asleep as soon as she finished eating. But, she awakened easily, feeling well rested. With this thought she was roused by a clapping of hands, and turned to see her warder gesturing to her to pack her clean clothes. Paula was amazed to find her washed clothes dry and soft, even her heavy socks were dry.

Minutes later they were back on the trail again, but with one big difference; she was no longer on leashes. Walking downhill on the gentle, forested slopes, feeling the soft updraft breeze, was pure delight. She had not realized how much she had detested the leashes.

The spectacular views and vistas of the ridge changed to a world of camouflage greenery, and the "Bridge on the River Kwai" jungle-travel music ran constantly through her mind. She knew there was still a great deal of danger, for she was a captive subject to the whims of her captors; but, for the moment, she was enjoying herself.

The slopes gave way to a wide, grassy plateau where the spring water pooled before meandering off in a rivulet. It was late in the dusk, for this had been the longest day of travel so far, but she felt as if she could go on forever. She was not at all tired. The electrolytes had made a big difference in her stamina. Against the hillside, there was a cave-like recess under the mountain face where she was staked for the night. A fire was built in front of the recess and while she waited for her meal, she rested against her backpack and pretended to fall asleep.

After awhile one of the natives said to the other, "The Bahariki walked like a queen today after her bath."

"Yes, she was different after the water. Maybe she draws power from water."

There was silence. Soon she heard a scuffling and peeked through her eyelashes to find her food set out before her. She decided not to eat it. If she could lay awake and plan, she would be better prepared for whatever might come. She was now sure that these men could tell the slightest difference in her manner. She had to maintain her status as a Bahariki; she had to do things to let them know she was different, special.

Since she was now positive they were drugging her, Paula kept up the pretense of sleep to have time to make her plans. Whatever it was they were giving her was marvelous. She didn't have bad dreams, awoke refreshed and was not mentally lethargic, nor was her appetite changed. Was it also the reason why she felt so little anxiety? Later, when they were asleep, she ate only the food, leaving the broth, drinking only the fresh spring water she had in her travel bottle. She needed to know which they were drugging, food or drink. Predictably, she was soon asleep.

The natives did post sentries, but it was done covertly, so they could watch the Bahariki without her knowing she was observed. They saw everything, even when she had been alone in the hut. It was then that it was decided that she needed water for her body. They had seen her fatigue and had worried that she would die on them before they got her back to their village.

Her rejuvenation after her pond bath had proved them right. From now on, they would follow the trails that led past springs, waterfalls and ponds. There was more danger from the big cats near watering places, but mostly the cats would keep their distance. They knew that it was groups of men like these that were their greatest enemies.

The next day they traveled on the wide plateau above the escarpment. There were springs and small ponds aplenty.

There were also a great many gazelles and antelope. The sun was fierce, but the cooling breeze was constant. Paula loved the smell of Africa. It smelled like no other place she had ever been before. She was sure it was unique to the continent. It was an earthy smell, a fertile smell and a musky smell all rolled into one. In the rainforest, the smell was diluted by the dense greenery and flowers. She wondered if the earthy smell could be connected to the fact that there were more diverse animals per square mile in sub-Saharan Africa than any other place on earth. The high plateau ended late in the day and they wended their way down to the grasslands below.

The tall leader gave a lilting birdcall, and the others started up a singsong chant. Tapping their spears and walinkas together, they made a loud, rhythmic noise to accompany the beat of the vocalization. At the same time, the pace was increased to a quick jog. For five miles they moved in this fashion across the savanna towards the cliffs.

In the midst of the twilight, they came to a sheer cliff with a dead ebony tree at its base. A thick live vine was entwined all around the dead tree, up and through the dead branches. The agile leaders climbed to an adjacent cliff ledge. Two bearers followed but one remained on the lowest branch to help the Bahariki. The remaining bearers gave her a boost up to the branches and helping hands reached down to grab her. Paula feigned a fear of climbing, clinging to the vine with her eyes closed. The last two bearers, using force, tugged her loose and pushed her up to the bearers, for the other one had come back down to lend a hand; they grabbed hold of her arms and dragged her up to the ledge. Behind, the last two bearers scrambled swiftly into the tree and onto the ledge.

In the last of the light, Paula saw some movement at the base of the tree... lions? Peering over the edge, she saw three female lions. One lioness roared angrily and leapt up the tree trunk, but she could not hold her great weight long enough to reach the lower limbs. She dropped back to the ground with vicious snarling and hissing.

Oh, my! That was the reason for the hurry. What if I had

not been able to run for five miles? The speculation caused her great angst; this was Africa—not a walk in the park!

Dinner was a brief, cold affair: meat, fruit and nuts, but later she had delicious hot broth. Paula withdrew into a recess in the cliff face. She was almost asleep when she realized they had not staked her out, and smiled to herself when she realized why.

After a hot breakfast of oatmeal, bananas and coffee, she gave another good show of being terrified of heights by clinging desperately to the vines while being lowered to the plains. Once down, they again resumed the ground-eating jog and the rhythmic chant with the steady beat of spear on walinka. Running this way, moving to the beat, made it seem as easy as walking. After five miles or so, they came to a path that climbed over and down a steep hill, before entering the partially treed plain before the forest beyond. It felt wonderful to be in the forest again and out of the hot sun. The cooling shadows of the woods suited her. She loved the trees. She knew there were big cats in the forest too, but she felt quite safe with her escorts. Soon they came to a wide, well-worn path. Here, the pace was increased.

They did not make the usual stop for the noon meal and rest, only a short stop for a snack and water. This was quite curious, as their stops had been like clockwork in the time of day and duration. They did stop at a small spring, where she washed her face and filled her bottles. It was about mid-afternoon when they began to climb again. Topping the rise, a grassy valley lay before them at the bottom of the forested hillside, with a stream running through the valley and a palisade-enclosed village beside it. The tall leader took out a horn and blew on it three long blasts before they descended into the valley. In an hour, on reaching the gates, the entire village was assembled to greet them.

The Ndezi Village

THE FIRST PERSON SHE noticed was a tall, well-muscled man who had the look of being all business. He was attired in a long, red kitamba with an elaborate beaded edge, and around his forehead was a matching beaded band with large fangs woven into it. His face was tattooed and his ear lobes were deformed and fitted with ivory discs. He wore a massive necklace of gems, carved beads and ivory that lay completely across his shoulders. It was stunning. Behind him to his right was another impressive man, one of the best looking men she had ever seen. His tattoos looked like an eye mask worn by Zorro, but they did not cover his identity. He had unusual brown-green eyes that she felt saw right through her, into her mind and heart. His finely sculpted eyebrows not only conveyed meaning, but also changed his expression when they moved. The look in his eyes mesmerized her.

Her captors each took an arm and led her up to the pavilion where these impressive men stood, and the taller captor said, "Father, this is the *Sea Goddess* of whom you have spoken. I am pleased that it is I, Mbundo, your eldest son, who has brought her to Bolbonga, the great chief of the Ndezi."

"You are a good son, Mbundo. You make me proud. What do you say now Suruna? Our sons have made us proud this day."

The eyebrows moved–the eyes sparkled and the voice of wisdom spoke: "Our sons have made us proud every day of their lives. We have been most fortunate, as fathers, to have such dutiful sons."

"We must have a feast tonight. Let us honor Mbundo and Masula for their triumph. Bolbonga wishes it so."

A great roar went up from the crowd. Paula was led away by the women to a large, roofed platform on stilts, with woven lattice around it from the floor of the platform to the ceiling, much like a birdcage. There was a bamboo screen on the side nearest the palisade, which she later found contained the usiku chungu (night pot). In the center was a stone and clay oven with a pallet next to it. Scattered about were several small stools and a stack of hides and worn blankets.

The women returned with basins of hot water and soap sticks. They also brought cloths for towels. When they attempted to wash her, Paula said in her best Swahili, "siyo gusa!" (Don't touch). They left hurriedly, running to tell Bolbonga of this problem. They had brought with them a platter of fruits and nuts; while she surveyed the village from her bower, she made up for the missed lunch

Paula then washed in the warm water–the bug repellent kept the bugs from biting, but it attracted dirt–and put on clean underwear with her form fitting knee length shorts, which she wore when scaling cliff faces, and a white long-sleeved shirt. She wore tennis socks and her climbing shoes and brushed her hair until it gleamed. She washed her brush and sweaty clothes in the soapy water, rinsing them in a bucket of cool water. She spread her clothes on the clay oven to dry. Then, she lay down to take a nap. The women had not returned.

THE FEAST WAS IMPRESSIVE. A long, low table had been set up in front of the Chief's pavilion. It was covered with bowls of food. After a speech from Bolbonga about the worthiness of their sons, he bade the assembly feast in their honor. The four men: Chief Bolbonga with his son, Mbundo and the Medicine Chief Suruna, with his son, Masula, sat on pelts at a low table inside the pavilion. Here, the leaders could look out over the low trestles set up for the feast. Paula was at a similar low table, off to the side of the pavilion. She sat with five other women, who all ignored her, as they ignored one another.

After the men had served themselves from the wide

wooden bowl, the servers brought the food to the woman's table. Not one of the women reached for the food. Paula, who was quite hungry, feared these women would turn on her if she reached for the food; so she was quiet and still all evening. Bolbonga and Suruna chose to ignore the women completely, and engaged in banter with their sons.

When the feast was cleared away, there was ritual dancing around a large fire accompanied by drums and flute-like pipes, which added to the merriment. The village women kept the men's cups filled from earthen jugs. The only women not serving were those sitting with her in the pavilion. They sat like frozen statues, not eating, not drinking, and not talking. It was ominous and unnatural. Maybe later, she would find out why.

When Paula yawned, her attendants came and escorted her back to her aerie, followed by a guard who took up duty at the bottom of the steps. This time the attendants did not try to undress her, but saw to the fire, piled pelts on the pallet and left. Paula was exhausted by the tension and the implied hostility of the women at her table; her nerves were frayed from their sinister attitude. After she folded her now dry clothes and put them in her backpack; she wanted only to sleep, and curled up to the fire in the little oven in the center of the floor. But, she could not rid herself of the ominous feeling; these women hated her, but why?

BOLBONGA, CHIEF OF THE Ndezi, was at once smitten when he saw Paula. This was a rare sensation for him, one that set his loins tingling. He studied the proud approach of the Bahariki who walked like a queen, her footsteps firm and sure, and who stood like a queen, tall and straight with her head up high. She had the regal beauty of a goddess with her bright, silvery-gold hair, lightly tanned skin and flashing emerald-blue eyes, which gazed at him unafraid. Her attitude was poised, almost disdainful, and this also pleased him. With this Sea Goddess for a wife, the drums would make him the most famous chief in Africa. Already his Ndezi warriors were the largest and most powerful warrior tribe within a moon's walking distance.

Bolbonga became chief of the Ndezi at age eighteen, when the dreaded Tutus ambushed his father's hunting party. The feared cannibals took the unfortunate survivors captive. Two bearers, who had been scouting ahead for a campsite, later found the awful carnage with the remains of their Chief. They hastened back to the village to tell the tragic tale. Bolbonga took charge of organizing the rescue of the captives—for the sortie had to be swift—or the men would be lost. The Tutus lived in an impregnable mountain valley, more a cleft than a valley, and once back through the hole that led to the small valley, they would be safe and the captives would never be seen again.

BOLBONGA WAS A PROUD young man. He was tall, strong and smart. He made the decision not to go to the site of the ambush, but rather to lead a direct foray to the tunnel-like gap that led to the Tutu village. They would have to cross a wide river infested with crocodiles, snakes and irritable hippos to gain the time needed to make the rescue effort a success. He whispered instructions to two fast runners who gathered materials and went ahead to install a stout line from a tall tree across the river to a tree on the other side. When the warriors arrived, they climbed the tall tree and placed their hands on a piece of bamboo and slid down the stout line to the other side.

Because of his cleverness, the hostages were saved and Bolbonga became the unanimous choice to succeed his father. He was a wise leader, but suffered from an aggrandizing ego.

Now, at thirty-eight, Bolbonga was still a prime specimen of manhood, who craved the thrill of sexual conquest. His other wives had been ordinary and docile, no challenge at all: and his present queen was a virago of the worst kind, sly, subtle, mean and extremely annoying.

DURING THE FEAST THE chief questioned his son closely about the Bahariki. Mbundo told him she was brave, intelligent, strong, sensible, proud yet flexible. Her only fear had been of heights and climbing. With a laugh he related the trouble they had experienced in getting her up to the cliff ledge, and then the even worse difficulties of getting her down again. Mbundo felt it was just a womanly trait, this fear of heights, for she had been stoic even when very tired. Nor did she ever complain or falter, even when they had to run for miles through lion country. He told his father of her curious need for body water and bathing and how it seemed to strengthen her.

Bolbonga was pleased to hear all these things, for tribal customs allowed the wife who ruled the household, and who was called the *first* wife, to challenge any new wife to combat, in order to keep her place, authority and title. He was certain Kira would challenge the Bahariki.

While it was not unusual for a warrior to have more than one wife, it was rarely objected to by the *first* wife if her husband and the new wife would allow her to keep her position as head of household, and not be made a servant to the newcomer. If a husband or his new love would not allow the *first* wife to keep her position of authority, then the *first* wife could challenge the newcomer to combat to keep her status. Wives were an important basis for judging wealth, and therefore status, in the tribe. Land within the palisade was finite and a significant source of wealth... along with wives, children, goats and chickens. Wives, besides supplying gratification for the husbands and babies, represented a work force, for the making and preparing of items for trade. The goats and chickens were essential food sources, and always a source of wealth for barter.

Kira had been the chief's *first* wife for eighteen years. She was a shrew and termagant and Bolbonga no longer sought her bed. He wanted a beautiful wife, someone special to gratify his ego. He had no need of sons as he had three: Mbundo, by his first wife who had died in childbirth, and two lazy sons by Kira. But Kira was tough and mean and he knew she would never step aside, for she reveled in her status as the chief's *first* wife. Bolbonga was certain that Kira would challenge the Bahariki, for she would want to retain her despotic dominance over her household.

◈◈◈

COMBAT RULES HAD THE right ankles of the antagonists tied together with about twelve inches of thong between them. Their left arms, above the elbow, were bound to their sides. At a signal, each would try to knock her opponent to the ground without falling herself. If they both fall, the *first* wife keeps her status as household ruler, but must accept the newcomer as an equal, not a servant.

If only one remains standing, she has the right to keep her vanquished opponent as a servant; or if the husband chooses, he can give the victor a knife, affording the winner the right to slay her opponent. Killing is rare, as most women prefer to have a servant to perform the unpleasant duties of the hearth, and another pair of hands to tend the vegetable gardens, care for the animals, clean and repair the hut as well as produce more handcrafts for trade.

Kira's status was enviable. Not only did she already have two vanquished wives as servants, but she also had their three young daughters as a work force. This gave her wealth for barter among the native women and purchasing power with the trader.

Bolbonga was pleased to hear that the Bahariki was strong and unafraid. He was ever so weary of Kira, who had the ability to make his life miserable without subjecting herself to discipline. Kira used this cunning skill like a whip on his other two wives, who both wished Bolbonga had given Kira the knife. Once under Kira's domination, they had become like zombies in his bed, and neither had given him sons.

Bolbonga hoped this magnificent Sea Goddess would vanquish Kira, and he would again know peace and tranquility in his home, because he would offer her the knife.

The next morning Bolbonga was disturbed while at his breakfast by shouts and loud excited jabber. Looking out from his dais seat in the open pavilion, where he ate his meals and held court, he saw that the white trader had arrived in the village. Good, he thought, he is finally here. The old man is late this year. But he is in time to tell the Bahariki she is to be my wife. He can explain the rituals and customs to her, and I will buy the Bahariki many wedding gifts from him.

The trader, Max Mason, came once a year to trade with the Ndezi. Here, in this mountain-rimmed basin, the thick-set, white-bearded South Afrikaner traded for elegant and intricate ebony carvings often embedded with valuable gem stones; bizarre ritual face masks carved from the fragrant, yellow-variegated podocarpus, often inlaid with red mahogany or black ebony; intricately woven baskets of grasses with petrified flowers or pods and carved beads; beautifully carved bowls, platters and utensils made from burnished teak wood; as well as many other exquisite handcrafts. Max would not trade for ivory or pelts; only for gold, gems and handcrafts.

Thirty bearers accompany him for the transporting of trade goods over the mountainous forest trails. Max has trucks that supply the permanent base camps, which are set up at various points along a seven hundred mile route. Among the goods desired by the natives are: skeins of fine wool, which will be woven into kitambas for the men; colorful bolts of cloth for pambisha, the sari-like dresses worn by the women; sewing needles, thread and scissors; metal flensers for cleaning hides; matches, salt and sugar; glass beads and thin copper wire; combs and mirrors; hunting knives, machetes and razor-edged metal arrow and spear tips; as well as awls, shaped metal chisels and other hand tools used by the natives.

The Ndezi are always glad to see Max on his annual visit to their village. It is a time of fun and festivity for all, as the natives love to trade and barter. He is well respected and the price he pays for their goods is always fair. For special pieces, he has been known to be quite generous. On this visit Max has a new partner with him, Jon Caulfield, who is a tall young man in his early twenty's with wavy, honey-colored hair, dark topaz-blue eyes and beguiling dimples when he smiles. Jon is fluent in African languages and dialects, English, French and German; a complement to Max's Bantu, Afrikaans, Dutch, English and French.

Max lured Jon into accompanying him on his next trading jaunt with tales of adventure from his past treks. He knew Jon joined him with an ulterior motive, but Max hoped he would get hooked on the freedom and excitement of a trader's life. His years of traveling the mountainous rainforest regions with only the company of his native bearers, had been a bit lonely, and Jon's company on this trip was a delightful change. Max found his ideas and conversation interesting, and his knowledge to be diverse. But best of all, Jon knew when to sit quietly and listen to the endless variations in nature's orchestra with the wild crescendos, the tympanic interjections and the trilling permutations... all performed by the unseen denizens of the deep rainforest.

BOLBONGA SUMMONED MAX IMMEDIATELY. "Your time of arrival is good. Mbundo, my son, has brought a Bahariki from the lake by the sea. She does not speak our language. I wish to marry her in two days. Kira has challenged her to combat. You must tell her these things before you trade. The combat will be at dusk tonight. You will not frighten her for she is strong."

Max motioned to Jon to accompany him to the prison pavilion, where the guard removed the traders' weapons before they went up the wide ladder steps. Max and Jon climbed to the large platform high above the ground, which was covered by a thatched roof with a wide overhang. In the center of the roof was a smoke hole for the clay oven, which sat on a stone base in the middle of the floor. The sides of the platform were constructed of horizontal bamboo poles lashed to the uprights from floor to ceiling.

Paula had been allowed to keep her backpack in her prison aerie. Only her weapons: her pistol, flare gun and hunting knife, had been confiscated. The switchblade knife, the butane lighter and the candle had been overlooked or considered harmless. Somehow, her survival belt had also been overlooked; maybe they thought it was a decorative part of her clothing.

Max and Jon were both startled to find a white woman as the object of Bolbonga's attentions. They were even more amazed that the so called Bahariki was well groomed with a regal bearing and seemed unfazed by her predicament. They immediately understood why the chief would want her for his bride. She was lovely: tall with silvery gold hair, sparkling emerald blue eyes and a smile that drew you in close and made you feel glad.

Both Max and Jon were accustomed to the native practice of capturing women for servants and wives, but they stood aghast at the prospect of the chief taking a white woman for his wife. Usually, white captives were traded back, as they brought high prices... but taking whites also brought severe repercussions.

"HELLO, MY NAME IS Max Mason. This is my partner, Jon Caulfield. We are traders. Do you speak English?"

"Yes, I do. I'm an American. Thank goodness you've come! I don't know why these natives have abducted me. Do you know what they want of me? Or why they have they brought me here?"

Side stepping her direct questions, he said in a polite, conversational tone, "Will you tell us how you, an American, came to be here in Africa?"

As Paula's story unfolded, Max and Jon were stunned by her ordeal on the storm-tossed boat, and amazed by her courage when stranded alone in the cove. They understood her rueful dismay that rescue had arrived just as she was captured. Both were impressed by her fortitude and determination; and her incredible ability to keep up with the natives on the arduous trek back to the village, (which Max mentally estimated to be more than a hundred and fifty miles) and now she appeared to be none-the-worse for the impossible strain of it all.

After hearing Paula's story, Max and Jon were doubly distraught. There had been headline stories in the newspapers and urgent messages over the bush radio about her. A large reward had been posted for Paula Thornton when she had been swept away aboard the yacht, the *Just Cause* during the tsunami. At least six nations were looking for this woman.

Max said to Paula, "I need to speak with Bolbonga. Jon will stay and answer your questions as best he can. This is his first trip as a trader, so he does not yet know all the customs of the tribes".

Max had to handle Bolbonga carefully; he was all ego.

"Chief, the woman your men have captured came to Africa as a guest of the government. She came from across the great sea—from the mighty nation of the United States of America. She was separated from her group by a huge wave, a tsunami, which caused a great disaster in Nigeria. A very large reward has been offered for her safe return."

Bolbonga narrowed his eyelids and set his lips in a grimace, becoming querulous at the thought of losing the Baharike. "This is the Republic of Cameroon. The Nigerian government does not interfere here. You would be wise not to discuss this matter further unless your safety means nothing to you."

Max knew the threat was deadly. He could not pressure Bolbonga for three hundred warriors to thirty bearers was no contest. Dismayed and frustrated, Max trudged back to the prison pavilion to tell Paula and Jon of Bolbonga's inflexible position.

"MY DEAR, THE CHIEF is smitten with you and refuses to discuss your release. He wants you for his bride. At the moment, Jon and I can do nothing to thwart him, as he has already taken our weapons and has my bearers under guard. At dusk this evening, you will be challenged to a test of skills by Kira, the chief's *first* wife, and then in two days, after ritual preparations, he plans to marry you."

Jon, outraged, blurted out, "Why don't we refuse to barter and leave? Once gone, we can send a runner ahead to the radio."

"The chief is crafty," Max replied. "I think he will suspect us of a ruse if we don't trade at all. But I had another idea: we will make our prices so high, that the natives will get disgusted and refuse to trade, or only trade for a few things. Then, once the trading is finished, we can leave as usual."

With a plan, Max and Jon went out for the first time, not to trade. And Paula had a glimmer of hope.

With the trading soon over, Max and Jon were ready to leave by mid-afternoon, but were surprised by the wily Bolbonga. He sent an armed escort with them on the long walk back to their jungle camp, saying it was for their protection, as they would not arrive at their camp before dark. The escort not only carried all the weapons, but it precluded sending a runner on ahead. Max did not see how it was possible for them to evade these delaying tactics and his thoughts turned to Paula's grave plight.

MAX KNEW THE COMBAT would take place in the long twilight of the evening. If Miss Thornton survived, she would wed Bolbonga in two days time, after the women had made her ready for him. The horrid preparations: a clitorectomy, tattooing of the face, enlarged ear piercings and shaving of the head and pubic area, were really mutilations designed to mark the bride as the personal property of another man. Maybe, just maybe, Bolbonga would not want to mar her special beauty and would spare her from the ritual preparations. Max had been too distraught to tell Paula the gruesome details.

THE TRADING PARTY AND their escort of fifty warriors arrived at the thorn boma camp as the dusk waned. The warrior escort returned their weapons and melted into the night. Jon and Max listened to the chanting, and the rhythmic beating noises, made to frighten off predators, as the escort jogged their way back to their village. Noise, and lots of it, was a very effective deterrent to animal attack.

As soon as the din faded, Max went to the radio. He never took the radio into the villages, for it required a treetop antenna to transmit in the mountains; so Bolbonga was not aware that Max had this capability. In most of his jungle camps, Max had long ago put antennas high in the lofty trees, in order to be able to communicate with the permanent bay stations where the supplies were kept.

"Base camp four. Come in. Base camp four, urgent you reply. Over."

The radio crackled and Max wondered about the batteries. The heat and moisture of the rainforest used them up quickly.

"This is base camp four. Over."

"Sampson, this is Max. We found Paula Thornton today in

the Ndezi village. She's the American woman who was washed away on the yacht when the tsunami struck Lagos. The chief has refused to trade for her, and plans to marry her in two days. Contact Enugu Station and Captain Reverman and tell him it is imperative that they send armed military choppers to base camp four by first light tomorrow for a rescue mission. Once the choppers cross the mountains, we will fire flares to lead them to the Ndezi village. We will man the radio until we have confirmation. Do you read me? Over."

"Base camp four; we copy. Over and Out."

JON TOOK HIS COFFEE and pipe to the base of an African tulip tree, where he could listen to Max's transmission. He remembered the only other time in his life he had felt so depressed and useless. Shortly before he was eight, his ten-year-old brother Thomas, had vanished when the charter plane bringing him home from a National Scholastic Achievements competition was reported missing with his teacher and the pilot of the private plane. Months of searching produced no clues.

Then, after unusually heavy rains in the mountains and massive river flooding, part of the wreckage was found in the Benue River in Nigeria. Everyone was stunned. This was more than three hundred miles north of the filed flight plan. Searchers later found the hull of the plane and inside, the seat-belted, bony remains of both the pilot and Thomas' teacher, but no trace of Thomas.

Jon didn't tell his father that one of the reasons he wanted to go trading with Max was because his trading route took him up the Benue River, making a huge five hundred mile circle in and around the region surrounding the river where the plane was found. Thomas could be living in any one of these remote native villages with amnesia or something. The close contact with the entire population of a village while trading was a distinct advantage over other search measures.

Jon would give anything to find his brother alive. Thomas had been his best friend. He had always watched out for him, and every afternoon, after tea, Thomas shared with him the new things he learned that day with his native tutor, Kaizii.

Thomas was always kind, never bossy or superior. On his eighth birthday, Jon began his nature lessons with Kaizii, but the joy was gone without Thomas to share the excitement. In a few months, when Kaizii's grandson, Loboda, became eight, Jon's father allowed Loboda to join the lessons. From then on, his grief began to lessen, as he reveled in his newfound childish superiority over Loboda, which soon became camaraderie.

The two years, before he was packed off to public school in England, seemed in retrospect, to be but a blink of an eye. Yet... he remembered times of loneliness that were simply unbearable. His twelve years of formal schooling were a panacea for a lonely boy. He was constantly surrounded by other boys at school, and long weekends and holidays were spent with his aunt and uncle and four rowdy cousins at Woleston Hall, the family estate in Berkshire. His summer holiday was spent in Africa with his parents and sisters on the tea farm. They were the icing on his cake.

LAST JULY, WHILE ON a graduation holiday to the Albert National Park in the Congo, Jon had met Max. Together they had traveled to the remote interior to visit the Pygmies, whose legends fascinated Jon. In conversation, Max had regaled Jon with stories of other primitive and remote tribes, and his adventures deep in the rainforest. Before they returned to Lake Victoria in Uganda, their friendship was sealed, and Jon had accepted Max's invitation to join him in January, for his next three-month trading tour. And here he was, sunk again in regret and frustration, feeling completely helpless.

MAX, LIKE JON, SOUGHT a bit of solitude with his pipe to think about strategy. He had been trading with the natives in the remote regions of Africa for almost twenty years. This was the first time he had been unable to negotiate for the release of a white captive. While he had been able to amass a fortune from the trade goods he brought back, his original mission, in the guise of a trader, had been to rescue a boy stolen from a safari camp. After the successful return of the boy, Max realized he had enjoyed the rescue adventure more than he enjoyed being a soldier of fortune. That experience started him in his present line of work, which he still enjoyed, more for the adventure and exploration than for the profit.

The authorities now relied upon his judgment when rescuing captives—since he had become well acquainted with the different tribes and their whims. While he had heard about the missing lady scientist, it never occurred to Max that she might be in the area he covered on his trading route. The possibility was not even a probability, for she had been lost at sea. So, Max was unprepared, both mentally, and physically with goods, for serious barter.

He knew Bolbonga would have been quite impressed with a shiny brass French horn and the noise he could make with it, or a power bow with metal tipped arrows, or even a sheepskin-lined coat for the cold nights. So many simple treasures could have been offered to make the trade irresistible to him. But, alas, even if Miss Thornton survived the combat this evening, unless help arrived first thing tomorrow morning, it could all be too late.

Suddenly the radio sputtered to life. "Base camp four to Max. Come in. Over"

Max grabbed the microphone and replied, "Max here. Over."

"Captain Reverman has agreed to the arrangements you requested. Two helicopters with twenty armed soldiers will be here at base camp four before first light. Over."

"Good. Jon and I will leave camp with twenty armed men at four a.m. We will fire flares from the forest to guide the helicopters to the village. Samo will be here in camp manning the radio. Over."

"That's a ten-four Max, good luck! Over and Out."

The Combat

PAULA WATCHED AS THE party of traders left the Ndezi village under escort. Did they usually escort the traders, or was there another reason? With a sinking feeling, Paula realized she might be on her own—with no help coming from the traders. It was like watching a rescue ship sail away just as your feet felt the cold waters swirl into your sinking vessel. She had to think and plan. There wasn't much time until dusk and the contest. She needed to warm-up. Starting slowly, with humming and gyrating added to the stretching, she began her warm-up exercises, for gymnastics. As expected, she drew attention when she started to romp around her prison bower. Paula tried to disguise the exercises with wailing, thrashing her arms about, and throwing herself to the floor, pounding and kicking. The watchers smiled at her anguish and went away laughing among themselves at such a weak and frightened woman. Kira would make short work of her.

Between the clay oven, and the bamboo screen for the privy, Paula practiced the difficult Valdez Lift, which used the back and stomach muscles to arch the body and then a leg and arm to spring to her feet from a supine position. The dive-roll, the Valdez lift, the lay-out, the aerial, the back spring and hand spring had all been a part of her floor exercises in competition, but she couldn't practice them here. She needed the element of surprise in her favor.

As Paula lay on the floor, mostly concealed from watching eyes by height and angle, she did sit-ups, push-ups, one arm and two, leg-lifts and stretching exercises. When she turned on her back to rest, she noticed that there was a large limb about five feet above the smoke hole in the roof. By sliding around on the floor, she could see that all the foliage on the limb had died from the heat rising from the clay oven. But towards the trunk, the foliage was healthy and dense.

She estimated that it was more than eight feet from the top of the oven to the smoke hole in the peaked thatched roof, and she wasn't sure if the roof would support her weight. Unbidden, a picture of her father climbing to safety flashed across her mind. His rappelling line had cut through the soft rock face of a jutting boulder to become trapped between the huge stone, with all his weight hanging beneath the rock. Firmly wedged and unable to free his line, he had used the folding grapnel and the thin flexible wire line in the survival belt to snag a sturdy tree branch. He had then climbed hand to hand up and over the top of the rock.

That's how I'm getting out of here! Tonight! Paula thought. She had never had a reason to use her survival belt, but with the image of her father clearly in her mind and his demonstrations of how to put it together, she would lose nothing by trying. She had been so engrossed in the details of her memories that she had not noticed the approach of dusk. In equatorial Africa, the days are the same length year round, and dusk is just a softening and paling of the light, like a three-hour dimmer switch turning slowly off.

IT WAS THE SOUND of many voices, all commingled to a steady hum, which attracted her attention. Rising, she went to the lattice surrounding the platform. Following a tall graceful and good-looking woman were the crones of the village. She thought the woman might be Kira, the chief's wife, one of the women who had been so icy at dinner last night. The woman, Kira, wore only a thong. She was bare breasted and wore no jewelry or ornaments. Behind the crones came the rest of the village. There were no children to be seen, or even chickens or goats. Scanning the village, she saw the small children on the far side, in a corral with the baby goats... kids playing with kids. 'What horrible things were going to take place that the children and domestic animals need be protected?'

She heard noises on the ladder steps and a matron (not one of the wizened old crones) came up to the platform. The woman talked gently while she removed Paula's blouse, bra, shoes, socks, and her tights. She seemed satisfied when she saw her hip-rider panties and made no effort to remove them. The woman gently pushed Paula onto a stool and started to braid her hair tightly, adding smelly grease to each braid as she worked. When she had finished with her hair, she rubbed the same grease all over her body with a practiced professional touch.

The woman led Paula to the bars of her prison. Looking down she was surprised. Below her in the clearing there were now two more young women, both clad in brief loin cloths, and greased like Kira, who went to them and tied their right ankles together, leaving about twelve inches of thong between them. Then she bound their upper left arms to their sides. The tied women looked at each other intently, and made no move until the drums started. Then they burst into action.

One woman shot her hand out with her pointed fingers and long nails to gouge the eyes of her opponent. In swaying to avoid the attack, her opponent was tipped slightly off balance. In the blink of an eye, the attacker yanked hard on the thong with her tied leg to further unbalance her opponent. The opponent had followed through the off-balance sway by leaning forward, which kept her from being toppled backwards when her ankle was jerked. As they moved, Paula saw that one woman had a white stripe down her back and the other a yellow stripe. This helped her to follow the skirmish, for the moves became faster, as the women twisted this way and that. Each woman constantly jabbed at the other, while making constant tugs on the ankle thong, which kept them both struggling for balance.

Paula was held spellbound by the ritual combat. Some of the blows clearly hurt, while others were made only to off-balance the opponent before a sharp tug on the ankle thong. Both women were now sweating and the drums were beating at a furious rate. Neither one was able to hold off the arm of the other as they had both become too slippery. It seemed the fight would go on forever or until one or the other dropped from exhaustion, when the woman with the yellow stripe lunged forward with her head lowered and struck her opponent squarely in the gut. Too late, the woman with the white stripe tried to turn aside. There was so much sweat and grease that her right arm was ineffective as it slipped over her opponent's head and back. As the woman with the white stripe folded forward from the stomach blow, yellow stripe whirled and gave a mighty tug on the thong and brought the side of her hand down on the back of white stripe's neck.

White fell and did not attempt to rise. Jeers and shouts arose from the audience; the crowd parted as a most imposing black man came forward. He was tall, well muscled with shoulders like John Henry. He pulled out his knife, bent down and quick as a wink, cut the thong. Just as quickly, he turned and slit the top of the right ear on the fallen woman.

Paula drew in her breath and waited for more mutilation. But none came. She would never know that the fallen woman was the *first* wife of the powerful man, Jomba, and mother of his son. The challenger was also to bear a child by Jomba, and wanted his protection for her child, which was her right according to tribal law. Mruna, the *first* wife, hated the woman, Sutto, who had brazenly seduced her husband with her wanton ways. She would fight to banish the slut. When Jomba cut the top of her ear, it was her penalty for losing to Sutto. He loved Mruna very much and hated that she would now have to allow Sutto in her home, not as an equal because Jomba would not take Sutto as a wife, but not as a servant either. More like a permanent participating guest. Jomba was embarrassed and ashamed that he had succumbed to Sutto's wiles when Mruna was recovering from childbirth. Jomba helped Mruna to her feet and took her home; Sutto followed.

Gently the matron prodded Paula towards the ladder. When she appeared below, there were many hisses and rude noises. Clearly, I am the underdog, Paula thought, as she was guided to the center of the clearing. Another matron came forward with the thongs and tied her ankle to Kira's. Then the woman tied her left arm to her side before she bound Kira's left arm. She heard Kira murmur. "Asante Mzazi." (Thank you, Mother.)

They stood thus for a few moments. Paula noted she was taller than Kira and probably had a few pounds on her too, but the look of rage in Kira's eyes gave her a distinct advantage. Rage made strength. She would have to surprise Kira at the outset or this woman would see her dead. Her hate was palpable. Two women came forward with pots of white and yellow paint and were sent away by Kira's mother. There was no need for color markings to tell the opponents apart this time.

The drums sounded the start and in an instant Paula pushed off and tucked her upper body into an aerial—knowing it couldn't be completed—but hoping both would fall, leaving her fate up to the Chief who so desired her for his bride. The stunning move so surprised Kira that she stepped back, putting all her weight on her left foot, which allowed her tied right foot to be jerked out and lifted off the ground by the swinging upward force of Paula's aerial. Kira's astonished fall backwards raised her right leg even further, far enough for Paula to save herself by landing on her hands and flexing her elbows to push for a spring-back onto her free left foot. It all happened so fast that the crowd was stunned to see Kira landing on her back while the Bahariki rose backwards to stand on her feet.

Amidst a collective sigh from the watchers, Bolbonga walked up to Kira's side with a wicked-looking knife; he leaned down and slit the thong. He then turned and presented the knife to Paula, hilt first. The crowd gasped. It was a signal to Paula that she was expected to kill Kira.

Looking Bolbonga in the eye, she read his anticipation; she also saw the threat lurking there. Paula lowered her head and bowed to give herself some time to think; she was not going to kill anyone for sport, or to please these ghouls. The actions of the 'imposing' man came to mind. She raised her head and took the knife. Pivoting on her toes, she knelt down and raised the knife above the unflinching Kira; what bravery, what courage! Without another thought, in a swift motion,

Paula slit the top of Kira's ear. She stood, bowed again to the Chief, and walked through the parting crowd to the ladder of her prison bower.

The assembly was stunned at Paula's insult, and her utter disregard of Bolbonga's order to kill Kira. Her great show of mercy was interpreted as defiance, not ignorance. Bolbonga himself wondered, but his years of wise rule produced a quick decision. She had seen Jomba so punish Mruna. She was not aware of the customs. Bolbonga realized the Bahariki could not know that only the husband had the right to inflict ear disfigurement on the loser. He decided she was not defying him, she did what she thought was expected of her. With this thought, Bolbonga addressed the crowd saying, "We must cheer the Baharike for her stunning skill in defeating Kira. We must admire her for her mercy and kindness. She does not know our ways, and has misunderstood her role. I forgive her for not doing her part in the ritual."

Bolbonga turned and swung his arm out to Paula, who had turned to listen to his words. At first, there was only a smattering of cries, but when the crowd perceived that Bolbonga was truly pleased and not embarrassed, the whole village broke into cheers. After Bolbonga returned to his gazebo, where he spent most of each day, to await his dinner, the crowd dispersed and returned to their normal duties. But there was much jabbering and excited talk, as well as speculations about the unexpected and thrilling moments of the evening. They attributed to Paula strange and mystical physical powers; adding too, her ability to enchant, for Bolbonga's mother, Misha, who had prepared her for the contest, spoke with admiration of her calmness and courage.

Bolbonga, although conflicted by the unexpected outcome, was also pleased; the Baharike would be a queen among queens, and soon everyone would be talking about him and his splendid woman. But, best of all, Kira had been deposed. Soon, she would no longer be the chief's *first* wife, but a servant subject to punishment, for any misbehavior, no matter how slight.

◇◇◇

EXHAUSTED BY THE TENSION and stress of the day, and the physical contest of the evening, Paula ate some of the fruit left for her and finished the tea she had brewed earlier. Kimbata, the guard, brought up a large pot of hot water. The woman who had prepared her followed with soap sticks, sponges, cloths and pots of unguents. When the woman approached, Paula shook her head from side to side and pointed to the ladder. Since Paula would soon be her son's new wife, Misha bowed her head in acceptance and retired. The hot water had been left on a shelf behind the bamboo screen, where the privy pot sat.

Paula hung a blanket over the lattice at the back of the enclosure, and began her ablutions; as she bathed, she regretted dismissing the woman so quickly, for who was to wash this grease off her back?

Just then, the woman spoke: "Misha nahuku." (Misha is here.) Without a word, Paula put out her hand with the sponge; Misha took it and washed her back for her. She then sat Paula on a stool, where she undid the braids and called for more hot water. When the braids were undone Misha left her to wash her hair alone.

Kimbata brought more hot water. When Paula was finished bathing and dressed, Kimbata brought her dinner. She ate everything but the pudding in which she mixed a sleeping capsule, and left it for the guard. She had seen him eating her lunch dessert and knew he had a sweet tooth. Sated, she lay down next to the opening of the clay oven and was soon asleep.

WHEN THE HOUR WAS quite late, before the full moon rose, Paula put on her half-chaps and rubberized specimen gloves. She wished she had her .22 Magnum and the flare pistol, more for a feeling of control, than for help with her escape. She still had the wide curved hunting knife that Bolbonga had given her to use to kill Kira. In the confusion of the unexpected, everyone had forgotten she still had it. Paula now slipped it into the side of her half-chaps where she could get to it easily.

❖❖❖

IN THE DIM LIGHT from the clay oven, Paula went through the steps of assembly for the grapnel. Lastly, she took one of the little gas tubes from its secret cover on her belt and screwed it on to the eight inch long shaft of the closed grapnel. Taking aim she flicked the canister switch with her thumb.

The closed grapnel flew towards the limb, shot past its mark and would have gone to the top of the tree, taking the line with it, if it had not hit another branch, which knocked the grapnel open... for Paula had neglected to anchor the end to her backpack. The grapnel fell and the thin woven wire became snarled in the leafy branches.

Paula lay down and feigned sleep. No one came. She lay for half an hour and then tugged on the grapnel. It fell some more, but then it stopped. Paula put all her weight on it and tugged hard, it held. She lay down again for a bit; she was sure the drugged guard was now asleep. The whole village was dead quiet two hours after dark, and it was now midnight. There were sentries and guards posted at the gates, but they were on the other side of the village.

PAULA ATTACHED THE WRIST and foot loops to the wire, and fastened her backpack to the bottom of the line. Standing on the clay oven, she put her hands and feet in the loops and pushed her right hand far up the wire before bringing up her left hand: then her right foot followed by her left foot to keep the line taut. She had climbed hand over hand many times, but always with a leg around the rope or in the L-shaped power position. This thin, flexible wire was hard to control. She had never used the foot and wrist loops before and found herself wishing for a guide on the emergency belt to control the sway of the wire. The climb was laborious. It seemed to take forever. She kept twisting around and her backpack, which was attached to the end of the wire, kept banging into the clay oven, which now held only embers.

The roof hole was smaller than it looked and she abraded her skin on the jagged pole ends as she wormed her way through. It was almost impossible to keep the line straight, even with her weight in one of the footholds. After she had passed through the smoke hole to her waist, she realized she would have to go hand over hand until her legs were through the smoke hole. Her muscles were quivering from the great exertion. For relief, she rested her elbows on the roof. She no sooner put her weight on the roof, than she heard a loud crack and a roof support snapped; energized by fear–fear that someone had heard the noise and, looking in the direction of the sound, would see her body half raised out of the smoke hole–she rose hand-to-hand, terror fueling her tired muscles.

Moments later she reached the branch, and scurried into the cover of the dense leaves. She put a gloved hand over her mouth to muffle her noisy breathing and waited. The full moon was rising, but there were some scudding clouds in the sky so the moonlight was intermittent. When the moon was behind a large cloud, Paula scurried back to the wire and hauled up her backpack. Safe again in the cover of the leaves, she removed the loops and slides from the wire and reattached them to her belt.

After the clouds passed the moon, she could see the grapnel about fifteen feet overhead. The wire had snagged on one branch, and the grapnel had wound itself around a limb below it. It was a long way up, and it would take precious time to untangle.

She was desperate to get away from here, but she had to have the grapnel. Besides, if they found it, they would know that she had no special powers, only special stuff. She needed, more than anything, to keep them worried about her unknown powers. Paula pushed the button on her watch to light up the dial. It was well after one in the morning. She only had a little more than five hours to put some distance between herself and this village.

Forest Flight

PAULA SAT CONCEALED BY the leaves, listening to make sure no one was stirring. She climbed to the limb where her grappling hook was snagged. The limb was wider than a balance beam, but it swayed low under her weight. She sat astride and groped for, and found the grapnel, unwound it and closed the hooks. She tugged on the wire, but it was tangled in the greenery on a thinner limb that might not support her weight.

Paula wrapped her end of the wire around a dead branch caught in the leaves, and yanked with all her might; hoping the wire would break free of the leafy branches above. A loud splitting sound followed, as the whole branch broke off and came hurtling down. In a flash she tossed the closed grapnel to the limb beside her. It swung around and banged open, stopping the leafy branch in its fall towards the roof of the prison. Frightened, her heart beating so fast she could hardly breathe, she lay prone on the limb... and watched the dangling branch swing back and forth. If anyone looked towards the noise and saw the branch swaying in mid-air, there would be pandemonium.

A thin cloud moved across the moon. Taking advantage of the deeper shadows, Paula made her way down to the limb above the dangling branch. She stretched out on her stomach and pulled the swinging branch up, and by feel, extricated the thin wire from the leaves. She looped the wire back through the V crotch at the base of the broken-off branch and lowered it silently to the roof of the birdcage jail.

Shaking from fear and an overdose of adrenalin, she scurried to the safety of the dense leafy growth; where she took long moments to calm herself taking deep breaths to slow her pulse. The cloud cover passed, and the full moon lit her way to retrieve the grapnel.

She felt a desperate need to get going, so she put the thin wire and grapnel in the top of her backpack; put her arms through the shoulder straps and fastened the waist buckle above the survival belt. At last, she was ready to flee. It was just after two am.

IN THE LIGHT OF the full moon, Paula could see over the palisade walls to the lethal, sharpened spikes set in the ground, for twenty feet or more around the perimeter. There was no dropping down from here as all the lower limbs of the trees on the other side had been removed to prevent the cannibalistic Tutus from sneaking into the village over the spikes.

An inane thought made her smile and relieved some of her tension. Now she really understood the expression *out on a limb*. The moon again passed behind a wispy cloud, but only for a few moments. Looking up to watch the cloud pass, Paula noticed that the upper branches of the tree were thickly knit together with branches of the trees on the other side of the bulwark. Way up there, she might find a way to cross into the forest so she could get away from here.

Up she went, like a sloth, slowly and carefully, climbing to the upper branches. She chose sturdy limbs, and found it easier to move through the foliage than she had expected. Paula climbed up high to the abutting branches, and saw she would have to go hand over hand until the limb on this side, sagged enough to allow her feet to touch the limb on the other side.

While heights had never bothered her, she was over sixty feet in the air and a slip here would be fatal. She moved out on the limb, stepping around small branches. When she was as far out as she could go on her feet, she dropped to straddle the limb, and then swung down under it with her legs still folded over it. Breathing deeply to relax and oxygenate her muscles, she released her legs from the limb. Hand over hand she moved until the limb started to bend under her weight. Grateful for the rubber-pebbled palms of her gloves, she inched her way out to the limb of the opposite tree.

She heard the splitting noise before she felt the drop, and grabbed for a vine hanging beside her. She caught the vine and grasped it just as the branch broke away. The vine held for a moment, and then she felt herself falling, even as she heard a great crashing and tearing noise when the vine pulled free from its lofty mooring. With a jarring thud, she came to a dangling halt. Glancing up, she saw that the broken branch and vine were caught between other limbs... at least for the moment.

Wrapping her chap-covered legs around the vine she still clutched, Paula slid down until her feet touched a limb below. Shaking uncontrollably, she scampered towards the bole of the tree; but she was still almost toppled by the immense force of the broken limbs crashing their way through to the ground.

Too shaken to move, Paula clung to the sturdy trunk while trying to calm her nerves, for she was shaking like a leaf. She checked for damage. Each part of her body responded without pain, but even better, she heard no movement or commotion from below. The great height gave her a feeling of security, almost like being invisible. Even so, she rested until the jitters stopped, before she continued on her way. She tested vines to hold onto while she moved from one tree to another. With the moon now high in the night sky, she was able to see her way through the forest.

Traveling in the trees though, was very slow-going compared to traveling on the ground. Paula worried that she might not reach the safety of her destination by first light, when her absence would be discovered, and a search party would be sent out to look for her.

Paula already knew where she could hide and be safe from the shrewd skills of her trackers, for she had seen a huge laprodis plant not far from the trail near a water and rest stop.

The full moon would last for three nights, giving her time to reach the mountain trails back to the sea. In the trees she had only to fear the leopard, the baboons and some snakes and spiders. At night, it would only be the leopard, but probably not this close to the village, for his natural prey was scarce here, and there were probably too many people for the reclusive, but dangerous baboons. Snakes would be curled up somewhere warm and hopefully her clothing and repellents would protect her from poisonous spiders and lethal bugs.

PAULA SOON FOUND A rhythm to her travel and used the energy of necessity and the fear of being hunted to keep her from tiring in her strenuous work. It seemed not long before she heard a few early calls from the birds high in the trees. It was time to move down in the trees, closer to the trail she had been shadowing. She saw the clearing where the trail diverged. It seemed familiar to her. Could this have been the place where they had stopped, before going on to the village? She had been led off the trail, into the undergrowth for her personal needs; there she had seen the huge laprodis plant, called the devil plant by the natives.

This laprodis was a very large specimen, at least seven feet high and thrice that across. It grew like a hosta with broad overlapping leaves that draped to the ground. If touched on the topside of the leaf, it produced a spreading rash that not only itched incessantly, but, if scratched, turned into boils that oozed pus with a terrible stench. The boils themselves were painful. When they broke open, they burned like hot needles. The pain was excruciating, and often, death resulted from massive infection. No other plant in the jungle was as taboo as the devil plant.

But Paula knew this plant. More often than not, in the bigger specimens, there was a dead center, as the new growth always came off the tubers growing outward. By using a stick and her rainproof parka, she could make her way to the center of the devil plant and be safe from all creatures. Not only was the devil plant toxic to the touch, it had a pungent odor like eucalyptus, which kept all bugs and rodents away. Only snakes, with no sense of smell, could slither about it freely, but they rarely did, as there was no prey, and the dried leaves, while no longer toxic, had hairs on the lower side that dried hard into tiny needles, like straight pins. But with all its faults, the devil plant had an invaluable feature. After the leaves had grown and opened, there was formed at the base of each leaf a tapered cylinder, shaped like a calla lily, which caught and held the rain and the dew. This was pure drinking water–with a straw. It held no microbes that could kill from within.

Traveling east, away from the trail, Paula soon saw the laprodis plant that she had remembered, but felt it was too close to the main trail. Traveling on, but leaving time to return if necessary, Paula found another devil plant, one that was even larger. It was growing in a small clearing, as other plants also avoided the devil plant, and this specimen was in glorious bloom. The towering bright red spikes were covered with clusters of draping dark red nodules, which looked faintly like a head wearing a feathered head-dress; the flower petals draped in gay profusion, shading from a burgundy red to a lipstick red on the curled edges at the ends.

Paula dropped to the ground, and used a dead branch to disguise her footprints to the devil plant. She had seen the natives tracking animals on her trek to the village, and had heard them once remark on what else had been on the trail, while she herself saw nothing.

HER ONLY CHANCE TO elude the Ndezi was that, by traveling high in the trees, she had left no trail for them to follow. Now, they must see no *sign* of her movements on the ground. Taking off her backpack, she fetched out her rain parka. Strapping her backpack on again, she pulled the rain parka over all, bringing up the hood and pulling the drawstring, so that only a slit remained for her to see through. With the dead branch, she lifted and poked the leaf litter she had trampled as she backed up to the draping leaves of the laprodis plant. Here, she turned and propped up the big leaves touching the ground, so she could crawl under. When safely underneath, she used the dead branch to brush away the traces of her entry, laying the branch inside for her exit later.

Safe from the toxic top sides of the leaves, she wiggled through a small gap in the sturdy leaf stems to the almost five foot circular dead area at the center of the plant. Some of the topmost leaves had turned inward over the center to form a roof five feet above her head. But it was the smaller under-leaves that held their treasure–shielded as they were from the sun and the birds–the little flutes of clear, sweet water. Paula took the hard plastic, collapsing straw from the pencil slot in her shirt, and loosening her rain hood, carefully drank four of the little flutes. She ate a granola and fruit bar and a banana she had brought with her from her jail, drank a bit more water and was ready for sleep. She stomped the area to break up the brittle, prickly dead leaves, which released their aroma, and masked her scent. Paula lay down in her rain parka, and listened to the joyful sounds of the awakening forest–and slept from fatigue.

Ndezi Search

TAMUBU LOOKED TO THE sky as the birds circled wildly above the trees. Someone was coming this way. In fact, a lot of someone or something was coming this way. The birds were calling frantically and flying scattered with no order, just panic escapes into the air. Tamubu climbed to the upper reaches of an old oak tree covered with creepers and parasitic air plants, and searched the forest for movement not connected with the breeze.

As he crouched, hidden, he saw a most amazing sight. Across the clearing, in the lower branches of the trees, came a white woman dressed for Safari carrying a sack on her back. She moved with assurance and ease through the trees towards him. He immediately thought of her as a Mitiriki, a *tree goddess*. He watched her descend to a lower branch of the tree, where she stopped and looked up straight at him and smiled, before reaching out for a dead branch.

TAMUBU WAS ENCHANTED. HER beauty stirred him, like a dream coming to life. Her silvery-gold hair framed skin the color of creamy lilies, evoking long buried memories, which caused an ache in his chest.

After the Mitiriki dropped the dead leafless branch to the ground, she moved nimbly to the lowest limb, where she sat, grasped the limb, and swung her body around to be suspended underneath the limb by her hands and heels, before she lowered her legs to a hanging position and dropped lightly to the ground, landing beside the leafless dead branch.

Tamubu was held spellbound. She moved like a goddess

of the trees with simian grace and agility. Tamubu's prowess at climbing trees was one of his better physical talents, but her movements made him feel awkward by comparison. The Mitiriki picked up the dead branch and, walking backwards, obscured the traces of her tracks in the heavy dew.

WATCHING HER, TAMUBU BECAME alarmed. She was backing straight into a kamikiza (devil plant). He was poised to shout a warning when she stopped, opened her sack and took out a mottled green cloak, which she donned after replacing the sack on her back. Tamubu watched fascinated, as the Mitiriki then turned to the kamikiza and carefully lifted the leaves, propping them up with the dead branch, so she could crawl in under the leaves. In a moment, the broad draping leaves of the kamikiza fell back in place. As he watched, confused and incredulous, the dead branch peeked out and did a dance where she had knelt. It danced all about the edges of the bush. Tamubu smiled. The Mitiriki was cleverly covering her tracks. It looked as though guinea fowl had been feeding there when she was finished.

HIS ATTENTION WAS DRAWN again to the sky. The birds that had settled down were again in flight and the forest was alive with their squawking and fearful cries. Taking a last look at the kamikiza, Tamubu climbed higher in the creeper-covered tree. He was now sure that a large party of hunters or warriors was coming this way. In his climb, he passed a huge python bulging with the meal it had recently eaten. He continued to climb. The python was sated and would be loath to move before his meal was digested. It would have been best for Tamubu to leave the area, but his boundless curiosity would not allow him to leave the Mitiriki.

Finding a suitable perch amongst the dense tufts of the parasitic oranthus, he pulled his mantle up over his head. It was brown and black, forest green and dark sapphire-blue in the manner of the panther, and when he was totally covered he was, for all purposes, invisible in the deep green foliage with its clusters of bright red flowers.

THROUGH A SMALL SLIT he watched and waited. Before long, the natives appeared. They scanned the ground thoroughly, and looked into the trees, pulling on vines, dislodging small critters and shooting arrows into the dense, green growth. It was a thorough search. One man was heading towards the kamikiza with his bow and arrows when a fellow searcher called out to him. He had found a place near where Paula had dropped from the tree, but he could not make sense of what he saw. The man who had been shooting arrows into the trees came, scanned the area, and said, "A python has made a kill here. See all this scratching; a python probably killed a guinea fowl or quail." Their observation took them away from the tree in which Tamubu was hiding. It also took them away from the limb where the Mitiriki had dropped to the ground. Even with her clever efforts, a skilled tracker might be alerted. But to read *sign*, you had to see it.

Tamubu felt the Mitiriki was probably safe under the leaves of the kamikiza. Even from his lofty hiding spot, he could not see into the plant, because of the many leaves that had turned inward, seeking the sun. He did not know there was a hollow center in the plant and that she would not have been seen even if the searchers had dared to lift the leaves. Nor did he imagine that she was already asleep.

WHEN THE SUN CLEARED away the morning mist, Tamubu decided it was time to reconnoiter. He fastened his gathering sack, herb pouch and weapons among the branches hidden by the dense foliage of the parasitic plants. Then he pulled his mantle up around his head. He had a pinch of leaves from his pouch in his hand. Slowly he rubbed the leaves to a fine powder in the palm of his hand. Chanting softly he raised his palm to his nose and sniffed the powder. He did this three times until the powder was gone. His cloak drifted down to settle softly in a heap over his belongings.

Moving as the breeze, Tamubu watched the searchers who were deployed throughout the forest. Hearing voices, he moved towards the sound and found many men gathered beside the trail. He positioned himself in the dense forest undergrowth, and listened to the talk.

A man, adorned in a vast necklace, was questioning the men. "What have you seen?" he asked.

The replies came: "We saw nothing."

"There has been no *sign* at all."

"We shot arrows into the trees and bushes. She was not anywhere."

"It is like she vanished into thin air."

Bolbonga shouted, "If she had wanted to vanish, why not before the fight? Why would she take such a chance if it wasn't necessary?"

His son Mbundo spoke, "Father, if you will spare me a moment, I wish to speak with you."

Bolbonga loved this son of his. He admired him too. He was a son to be proud of in any situation. So he said to the men, "Continue searching, we will meet here again when the sun is high." To Mbundo he said, "What is it you want to tell me that you do not want the others to hear?"

"Father, last night was the first night of the full moon. We have not had a full moon since the Baharike was captured. It is possible she has great powers during the fullness of the moon, for she is a sea creature. If this is so, then for some days she could be invincible. Maybe her victory over Kira was because of the rising moon. If this is true, we might capture her again only to have her disappear once more at the next full moon. We did not harm her. We treated her with respect. Maybe she spared us retribution before she left, for these reasons."

Bolbonga looked at his earnest son. His reasoning was good. The Ndezi hunters were the best in Africa. If there had been *sign*, they would have found it. No one can move through the forest without leaving a trail—except spirits and gods, flying bugs and birds.

At the noon gathering, the reports were the same: nothing was seen but the jungle animals and a small troop of Tutus, their cannibalistic archenemies. It was thought the Tutus were not a hunting party, only travelers on an errand. Bolbonga questioned each man as he arrived at the rendezvous. Each one had followed any spoor and all had been explainable, as being made by the denizens of the forest.

TAMUBU WAS NOW SURE that they were searching for the Mitiriki. He was almost ready to leave when he heard Bolbonga tell the assembled men, "The Baharike has proved herself to be what her name implies, a *sea goddess* or maybe, a *sea witch*. After the full moon she must again be captured with the net and brought back to the village to be burned alive." A rash of startled, indrawn breaths met this announcement. They knew the death proscribed for female sorcery, but, in living memory, there had never been any witches burned alive.

BOLBONGA LEFT THE GROUP after his meal and sought out a secluded, mossy place for his afternoon rest. When alone, he pondered all the known facts. Suruna, the Medicine Chief and his second in command, had reported to him that he had examined the platform jail, and the only *sign* was a small bit of broken roof thatch lying on the oven. It was as if she had flown out of the smoke hole. But, if she could fly, why had she not flown sooner? Did she need the power of the full moon as Mbundo suggested? The sentry must have had a spell cast over him. He was asleep and could not be awakened. Suruna had also suggested to Bolbonga that the Baharki might only be captured when the moon was waning, because her powers rose and fell with the moon and tides.

This could explain her ability to best Kira so quickly, to escape last night, to live on top of the water and to leave no trail. All these things would be possible for a sea witch. Bolbonga began to wonder if the Bahariki might have other powers as well; powers that could steal his manhood, or put him in a deep sleep like the sentry. With each imagined problem, Bolbonga became more vengeful towards the object of his passion. Especially when he realized he wasn't going to be rid of Kira and her subtle taunts, which will worsen with this debacle, making his life almost intolerable. The Bahariki was the cause of his embarrassment and shame. The more he thought about the Bahariki and the problems she had caused and the problems she could cause, the more he wanted to possess her and humiliate her. But what if she stole his manhood when he possessed her? If she was truly a sorceress, what manner of spells could she cast over him? It was too dangerous dealing with a Bahariki who might also be an evil witch. When found, she would have to die in the manner of her kind, by fire.

Feeling a surge of power and energy from his decision, he drew from the waist of his loincloth the shiny .22 Magnum pistol his son had taken from the Bahariki. Looking at it, he thought, maybe this weapon is cursed, and my carrying it makes my loins throb for her. I will have nothing to do with it, or her, from this moment forward. With this resolve, he tossed the pistol into the forest undergrowth.

RISING, BOLBONGA RETURNED TO the resting searchers. "The Baharike has probably eluded us, for we have covered a vast amount of ground without so much as finding a footprint. The full moon may be her strong time. We could be leaving the village at risk if we continue to have so many men out searching. There could be other Tutus in the area as well. That small party could have been a scouting party or a decoy to distract us. We will return now, and later choose search parties who will go on hunting—even returning to the great water with the house moving upon it. We will have our vengeance!"

TAMUBU HAD WATCHED BOLBONGA take the revolver from his waistband. He saw him look around at the others who were mostly napping. Then, without warning, he tossed the shiny trinket into the woods. Tamubu searched and found the place where it had landed, and covered it with a dead leaf. He would come back for it later when the hunters were gone. For now, he was pleased that the natives had decided to abandon the search.

BOLBONGA LED THE SEARCHERS back to the village at a trot. An hour later he was stunned to see two giant metal birds, with wings on the top of them, sitting in the vegetable patch. He was even more surprised after he entered the village to see that all his people had been captured. Soldiers with long guns were guarding the old men who had stayed behind. The women and children were sitting in the square. Before Bolbonga could react or issue orders, other soldiers came out of the forest to close in behind them. A military leader stepped forward and spoke through a bullhorn, "You are surrounded. Drop your weapons at once. Put your hands on your head, and walk quietly to the center square. Sit down on the ground, in rows, back to back. Failure to comply will mean death."

One warrior turned and threw his knife. It found its mark but bounced off the bandolier carried across the chest of the soldier. The assaulted soldier raised his rifle, aimed and shot the warrior through the eye. Fear, superstition and panic reigned.

Bolbonga raised his voice, "Do as the soldiers tell you. I am certain it is some sort of mistake. No one is to give any trouble, none!"

The soldiers herded the warriors into the square, sitting them close together, with hands on their heads. Several young boys were detailed to gather the weapons and place them under the prison platform. The dead man was left to gather flies, as a reminder of the penalty for resistance.

Suruna was sitting in the pavilion with his hands and feet tied. Bolbonga was brought to join him, and he too was bound hand and foot.

Captain Reverman stated his position, "The Ndezi chiefs have been charged with kidnapping an American woman. This is an offense punishable by a prison sentence for all who were involved. Suruna, the medicine chief, has told me that Miss Thornton escaped during the night. I don't believe that! What have you done with her?"

Bolbonga eyed the imposing military officer and decided not to try his patience, "We have done nothing with her. She was gone when we awakened this morning. We have been out searching for her, but did not find her. You can question any man in the search party, and he will tell you the same thing. We did not find as much as a footprint!"

Captain Reverman was well aware of the pride of these little kings. It would be impossible for them to invent a tale that told of their incompetence, and the failure of warriors and hunters to track a woman. Bolbonga would never tell a story that made him or his tribe look foolish, for these stories would travel faster than the wind and shame his boundless pride: a pride that was more precious than life itself.

Captain Reverman had heard the whole story of the capture of Miss Thornton from Suruna, while he was waiting for Bolbonga's return. He fully expected the chief to have her with him and was suspicious when he did not. These men can track a mouse—I've seen them do it. How could they not track a woman, and one that would leave a trail like paint on the ground?

There was a deep mystery here, one that called for information. He needed to talk to Max Mason. The traders had not wanted to be connected with the arrival of the soldiers. So, until Captain Reverman was in charge of the village, they had kept a low profile in the woods before returning to their forest camp to man the radio.

LEAVING ORDERS WITH HIS lieutenant, Captain Reverman took one soldier with him to the helicopter while he contacted Max Mason.

"Captain Reverman to Max Mason. Come in. Over."

The radio crackled, then loud and clear he heard, "Max Mason here. Over."

"We have a mystery here, Max. The chief and medicine man say Miss Thornton escaped during the night. When we arrived at the village, most of the warriors were out searching for her, and when questioned on their return—said they found nothing—as the chief put it—not even a footprint. Do you have any opinions about their preposterous position? Over."

Max was stunned! "Give me a minute, will you? This is quite a shock! Over."

"Take your time, Max. I need your best input here. Over and Out."

Max looked at Jon who had heard the exchange. "What do you think about that? Escaped and the trackers couldn't find the trail! Unbelievable!"

"Yes, totally unbelievable!" Jon frowned, then smiled, and then he leapt into the air and yahooed as he tossed his hat to the sky. "Great! Just bloody marvelous! Super!"

Max was surprised at this show of high spirits. Jon hardly knew Miss Thornton, but he too was mightily pleased. But how had she done it? Where had she gone? How had she left no trail? Neither one could come up with any feasible possibilities for her escape. No matter how she went, she had to leave a trail—or at least the occasional footprint. Only the birds left no trail and they were sure Miss Thornton couldn't fly.

"Max Mason to Captain Reverman. Come in. Over."

"I'm here, Max. Over."

"We have not a bloody clue! Do you think Bolbonga is lying to you? Over."

"It is highly unlikely. He has admitted that none of his men were able to track a woman. He has made himself a complete laughing stock if word ever gets out. Over."

"Yes, I see what you mean. He'd rather die than seem foolish. I would like to contact the leader of the Expedition and see if Dr. Miles can shed any light on this perplexing situation, with your permission of course. Over."

"Yes, do that and get back to me, ASAP. I have twenty men holding hundreds and once I have to start letting them move about, we could be in trouble. Over."

"That's a ten-four. Over and Out."

Max called his base camp four and had them patch him through to Enugu Station, where he was patched through to the *Norsk Star*. It seemed that the yacht had left the cove four days ago and had sailed south to the Ogooué River. In what seemed like forever, but was, in reality, only minutes, Max heard. "This is the *Just Cause*. Come in. Over."

"This is Max Mason, calling for Professor Miles, about Paula Thornton. Over."

There were the usual crackling noises when a sonorous voice said, "This is Professor Miles. Do you have news of Paula? Over."

"Professor, the *Norsk Star* is patching me through to

you from the deep rainforest in the Republic of Cameroon. My name is Max Mason. I am a trader. My partner and I came across Paula Thornton yesterday. She was well and unharmed, but she was a captive of the Ndezi Chief. Last night we managed to get permission for the Nigerian military Search and Rescue forces to rescue her today. The problem is: she somehow escaped during the night, leaving no trail. I repeat, she escaped and the best trackers in Africa found not even a footprint. Can you shed any light on how this might have been possible? Over."

"Only one idea comes to mind. Paula is a world-class gymnast and was to be our tree climber on the expedition. If she could get to the trees, she would be gone. She is incredible and a fearless climber. Over."

"Are you saying she can travel through the trees without going to ground? Over."

"What I'm saying is: she has that ability, yes. If she needed to protect herself from harm, she would not hesitate to do so. She is a rock face climber, a mountain climber, a long distance hiker, and the most self-reliant woman I have ever known. Will the Nigerians be able to continue their search and rescue mission in Cameroon? Over."

"Now that Miss Thornton has gone missing, it is doubtful. We just wanted to make sure the Ndezi Chief wasn't lying to us about Miss Thornton escaping without a trace last night. It was just so unbelievable! We'll keep in touch. Over and Out."

"What do you think, Jon? Think she could escape through the trees?"

"I loved reading Edgar Rice Burroughs' Tarzan series. We have the entire collection at home, but that is fantasy. Do you think it is possible?"

"I think it is the only answer that makes any sense," Max said. "What a gutsy girl! What a perfectly marvelous escape! But, now, where did she go? Is she trying to get back to where the yacht was stranded? It must be all of a hundred and fifty miles, possibly more, and she's alone. But, what else is there to think?"

"Max Mason to Captain Reverman; come in. Over."

"Max, that was quick, thanks. I hope you have something for me. Over."

"I contacted Professor George Miles, the Expedition leader. He said Miss Thornton is a monkey in the trees. Now the only question is: how did she get to the trees? But the professor also said she was a rock face climber; you know, one of those people who scale seemingly impossibly sheer cliffs! Over."

"Max, I owe you for this. Reverman Over and Out."

IN THE TREES! WHO would have ever thought of it? But it makes sense—how she's gone leaving no trail at all—smart, talented lady! But, if she left no trail, how do we send out a search party for her? We have no idea in which direction she went. Stymied, Captain Reverman decided to deal with the here and now, to round up those guilty of her abduction and fly them to Yaoundé. Even though the government was in a state of flux, the local authorities were functioning as usual.

BOLBONGA AND SURUNA, MBUNDO and Masula and the four bearers were loaded into the copter for the flight to Yaoundé. Bolbonga left his son by Kira, Ngunna, in charge with Jomba, his chief lieutenant, as advisor. Ngunna was only 16, lazy and indolent, but Kira would whip him into shape. She would be in her glory with her eldest son as acting chief. The sixteen soldiers left behind would guard the weapons, which were piled under the prison platform. Captain Reverman would retrieve the soldiers left on watch later today, on his return flight from Yaoundé. The copter should be back to the village in five or six hours.

It would be interesting to see what rescue plans the United Nations Search and Rescue Forces, or the new government of Cameroon would suggest. Paula Thornton was now their problem. Captain Reverman and his Nigerian forces had been standing ready, mobilized for a recon sortie, and therefore had been available for immediate help; so the officials of Cameroon had accepted their offer, while in the throes of internal government reorganization

"S&R 321, Captain Reverman to Max Mason. Come in please. Over."

The reply came instantly.

"Max here, 321. Over."

"We are returning to the Ndezi Village from Yaoundé. Unfortunately, there was no decision made about future rescue plans for Miss Thornton during the time we were there. The various agencies involved want mandates from their new superiors before committing themselves to a plan of action.

"The Chief of Police, however, did make a decision about who would be kept for trial. He let the four bearers go, as they were soldiers following instructions. He allowed Suruna to leave, as he was not a party to the kidnapping in any way. He booked Mbundo and Masula on the kidnapping charge and Bolbonga as aiding and abetting the crime... a good call in my opinion."

"Max, will you get in touch with Professor Miles again, and let him know to contact the United Nations Search and Rescue Forces at Yaoundé for further information about the efforts to find Miss Thornton. Over."

"Will do, right away. Captain, Jon and I want to thank you for taking the trouble and initiative to go to Miss Thornton's aid. We are at your service if you ever need us. Over."

"That's a ten-four, Max. Captain Reverman and S&R 321. Over and Out."

Dusk, the beautiful copper and gold twilight of Africa, had begun when the chopper arrived back at the Ndezi village. It disgorged the five happy natives. Suruna would now be acting Chief until Bolbonga returned. The short reign of Ngunna and Kira was over.

10

Tamubu

TAMUBU WATCHED THE SEARCH party leave at a smart trot to go back
to the village. He returned to his possessions and wrapped
himself in his cloak, settling in to wait for the Mitiriki to come
out of the kamikiza. He had seen much this day. There were
many things to think about, especially the recently stirred
memories of his early youth and the only other white woman
in his life. The memories of this long-ago white woman had
dimmed during his instruction years with Manutu to become
only scattered bits and pieces.

Now though, while he was still under the influence of the
psychotropic leaves, those dispersed memories seemed nearer
and clearer to him. He closed his eyes and examined closely
what he remembered: the shining silvery-gold hair, which
she wore pulled back and fastened behind her head; the even
white teeth of her full smile; the merry sky blue eyes, which
always noticed him while she rode the dancing horse; for he
loved to watch her ride. The lady nodded at him each time she
passed by, and he clapped his hands in glee.

This favorite memory faded to hearing a boy's voice crying
out for him. He couldn't remember the face, just the voice
calling, "Tommy, where are you? Let's go." He loved that
voice. It had always made him happy to hear it. But that was
all there was, just the sound of a cheerful, eager voice calling
to him, and the memory of a smaller, warm hand in his.

The next recollection made him wistful. It was of a man
reading to him as he lay in bed, before he fell asleep. The
man had a weathered face with a thin mustache and bushy
eyebrows that moved constantly to make him laugh as he read

the stories. He yearned for this man and his bristly kisses and fierce bear hugs. He longed for the clean, earthy smell of him, his warmth and his strength, but most of all, for the feeling of absolute security he felt when he was near.

His reveries ended. Were they just parts of his old dreams? Could you smell a dream? Why were the fragments always the same, no more, no less?

HIS PRESENT LIFE AND recall began with a time of fevered dreams and ague. Often he was in pain, but the fierce gods came and blew smoke up his nose, and the pain went away. Always there was the lyrical, soft voice of a woman telling him stories as she wove her cloth. During what he called, the dark time, Nanoka, with her soothing voice, was always with him.

She wore several gold bracelets, which made a rhythmic jingling as she worked. The sound was a comfort to him. He remembered the good days, when he was feeling better, when Nanoka would allow him to go outside to sit in the sun. On these days, she gave him lessons in the language of the Zuri Watu and its customs. She pointed out the birds, the trees, and the women washing or cooking. She would call the children over and have each one say their name and age and the names of their families. In this way he came to speak Bantu as fluently as he had spoken Swahili and English

On the bad days, the fierce gods came and blew smoke up his nose, while chanting to calm him. Those days he stayed on his pallet with Nanoka nearby. This went on for a long time until a white man came to the village. Nanoka and Sashono allowed this white man to examine him. He gave Manutu, one of the fierce gods, a special medicine which tasted awful, and from that day on, the fevers and pain diminished until they were no more. Only later did he learn that the white man had been a missionary doctor who had questioned his topaz blue eyes.

It was explained that his father was a Trader. His head had been shaved like all the other boys and his skin had been rubbed with koala nuts to darken it, so the missionary doctor had accepted his presence as one of the tribe. Even now, his skin was still the color of weak coffee. Sometimes Tamubu wished he had remembered sooner that Nanoka and Sashono had only adopted him. His illness had been so traumatic that his memories of his youth, before he came to the village, were only those wisps he thought to be recurring dreams. Once he began to think in Bantu, his youthful education and language skills were never called to use.

When Nanoka was near her end, she told Tamubu the story of his arrival in the village saying, "After I am gone, if you so choose, go and look for your birth family. Tell them you filled my life with love and meaning. No one ever had a better son." She asked him to understand how, during his illness, she had come to love him, feeling he was the answer to her prayers saying, "You were not conceived under my heart, but in it. When you did not question us about your family or going home, we accepted you as a gift from the Gods, and named you Tamubu, which means *sweet gift*."

Tamubu remembered his long childhood illness. It lasted through three or four rainy seasons, with two more rainy seasons passing after taking the missionary doctor's medicine, before he was well. Then his life became so interesting that even his few dream-like memories rarely intruded. And so, perched high in an oak tree, Tamubu's mind wandered back to the incredible life her devoted love had given him.

When he was feeling much better, he had asked Nanoka, "When will I be able to play with the other boys?" That evening Tamubu heard much whispering between Nanoka and Sashono, the man who ate from her pot. He heard their muted voices long into the night. He was disappointed when, the next day, he was not given permission to join the games. Instead, he was taken to the hut of the fierce god, Manutu, who was the Medicine Chief. Manutu had often ministered to him when he was sick.

It was dark inside the hut because there were no windows. It was a large hut of several rooms. The fire that burned was small, almost embers, and lit the central chamber but dimly. He and Manutu sat for a long time looking into the embers; watching the tiny fires flare as sticks were added to the coals.

Soon, Tamubu could distinguish many objects hanging on the walls. There were all sorts of weapons, and a row of grotesque ceremonial masks and decorations. On a shelf there were many gourds, some with feathers from different birds; bunches of leaves hung in the air along with strings of dried bones. This was all he could see without moving his head, and he was too intimidated to move anything but his eyes.

They sat for a very long time. Tamubu began to tire. He heard a grunt and looked up to see a gourd being offered to him. He took it and drank. It was the honey-lemon water that he liked so much. When he had finished, the man reached out for the gourd. He sat it in front of them. Looking Tamubu in the eye, with a glinting stare, he said, "I am Manutu, Medicine Chief. I am high priest to the spirits and gods and blood brother to Sashono, your father, who is the strongest and wisest man in this Nation. You are here because Sashono wishes me to show you your destiny, which is not to play with children."

Manutu leaned forward and again handed Tamubu the gourd for him to drink. Tamubu smiled to himself for Manutu had forgotten it was empty. Not wanting to embarrass this most important man, he lifted the cup to his lips, and was surprised to find it full of the sweet lemon water. When he was finished, he handed the empty cup back to Manutu, who pushed has hand back saying, "Drink it all." Tamubu had drunk it all, as he liked it very much. Still, wanting to please this man, he again lifted the cup to his lips and again he found it full. Tamubu was stunned. How could this be? Was he dreaming?

Manutu took the cup back and sat it between them and asked, "How many times did you drink and empty the cup?"

"Three," Tamubu replied.

"What did you drink?"

"I drank lemon water."

At this reply, Manutu arose, gesturing to Tamubu to also rise and follow him. They went into a smaller chamber, where the walls seemed to be made up of writhing snakes. Manutu raised his arms up high and stretched out his empty hands. Swirling his arms and hands in the air, he opened and closed his hands as if grabbing and then giving; he chanted as if praying, but in unknown words. Manutu spoke to those Tamubu could not see. Tamubu could only watch in awe as Manutu's hands began to glow with the aura of candlelight. Beyond his hands the blackness of the roof became fluid and fluttery, moving down closer and closer until Tamubu saw a kitu-kina, a cloak like Manutu wore, swirling above his head. As it hovered, Manutu chanted short lilting phrases, and then the cloak settled softly upon Tamubu's shoulders.

Manutu said, "This cloak must always be with you, as clothing, as a ground cloth or cover, or even as a dry place for your feet when you bathe. It will never get wet or soiled. It will never rip or be pierced, and it will grow with you as you grow. No one can take it from you. Only you will be able to remove it from your corporal self, when you have learned the ways of the spirits.

"You have been chosen for great things, which I will teach you. No one can harm you as long as you wear the cloak. Tomorrow, and each sunny day thereafter, you will accompany me into the forest to a clearing, which is guarded by the spirits. There I will teach you. You must bring nothing with you but this cloak and these charms, which I am placing about your neck. Never remove the charms for they are now a part of your spirit. Say nothing to anyone of what you have seen here or what has happened here today. The gods have chosen you as few are ever chosen. Do not betray their trust and speak of this great gift. You have much to learn. The secrets of the ages will be yours if you keep your own counsel."

So SAYING, MANUTU LED Tamubu from the hut. Sashono and Nanoka were waiting for them under the shade of a leafy aligna tree. The day was drifting into dusk, a time when the whole village usually gathered outside their huts, cooking and eating the evening meal. But this evening was different. There was no bustle, just a quiet anticipation.

When the crowd saw Tamubu emerge draped in a cloak of indescribable colors, they all cried out with a great cheer. Manutu raised his hands and quiet reigned. "This is Tamubu, son of Sashono and Nanoka and spiritual son of Manutu. The Spirits have chosen him. He is Dogo Mungu."

At this everyone fell down in homage and bowed their heads to the earth.

LITTLE GOD. WHAT DID it mean? He was so astonished at hearing himself so described that he cried out, "Do not fear me, I am your friend always." Tamubu could not believe that he had spoken thus, unbidden, and turned to look at Manutu and Sashono. They had removed their ritual masks and held them under their arms with their heads bowed to him. Nanoka was kneeling, with hands clasped and tears on her cheeks, beside them.

He did not remember ever seeing Manutu without a mask on, and he was surprised to see that Sashono, who was the Chief of the Zuri Watu and a very handsome man, looked exactly like Manutu, his brother. They were identical twins. Both had gray eyes with shiny green flecks, short white kinky hair and eyebrows, high cheekbones, long straight noses and narrow well-shaped lips. Tamubu just stared at them. They both smiled back at him revealing their love and pride. Manutu replaced his mask. Tamubu had often seen double when he was sick, now he knew why.

Manutu and Sashono clapped their hands and the people came to their feet and took up the clapping, then chanting and ritual dancing. A feast followed, and then the games, contests and revels that lasted well into the night.

TAMUBU OFTEN RELIVED THIS day in his thoughts. It was the end of his confinement... the end of his illness and solitude and the beginning of his life. He was allowed to go anywhere, when he was not with Manutu or Sashono. If he left the palisade, an escort of four warriors went with him. They were not close enough to intrude, just close enough to protect him. He did not carry weapons, as he had not yet learned proficiency with them, except for the walinka, which all boys received when they became eight, and the slingshot he had made for himself.

He loved his lessons. Manutu was endlessly patient and

kind. Tamubu also had lessons in wisdom and leadership with Sashono. There were specially chosen boys with whom he practiced wrestling and the use of the walinka. But it was with Manutu that he grew in mind and spirit. With him, Tamubu forgot the pain and suffering of his past and lived in a present of wonder and excitement

ONE DAY WHEN TAMUBU was out exploring, he came across a nest on the ground. There were some broken eggshells in it and one unbroken egg. Looking around, he saw no bird that seemed to be in distress at losing her nest. He waited awhile, but no bird came to possess the nest and the lone egg. He had found the branch from which the nest had fallen, but it was not possible for him to climb so high on such thin branches. So he placed the nest securely in a forked branch nearby, securing it with a twig through the grasses and hairs. He moved off into the tall grass and waited. No birds came at all. It was getting on towards sunset. He had to return soon; it was the rule. Climbing the tree, he retrieved the little nest with the tiny egg in it. While he was walking home, he saw the little eggshell crack in the nest in his hands. A little bird was hatching.

Running as fast as he could, he went straight to the hut of Manutu. So excited was he, that he entered before announcing himself. He could hear voices in the little room where he had received his cloak.

He stopped, not to listen, but to make sure he did not disturb Manutu, and heard Sashono say, "We both know Tamubu is chosen, but we must agree, between ourselves, that when he is a grown man, he will be allowed to decide his future for himself. Your sons, Benima and Kenga, are still young. They can be trained if they show promise. Nanoka and I have only Tamubu, and we have the most to lose. We have darkened his skin, and shaved his head, but his facial features are clearly those of a white man. It would be very bad for him if he discovered his heritage from outsiders. He must learn the truth from us."

TAMUBU WENT TO THE far side of the hut and sat in the darkness, away from the small fire. He wanted to hear no more, not now. He wanted so much to keep learning from Manutu, whom he had come to love. That Sashono, himself, considered him his own son had never occurred to him. As Chief, all the boys were his sons and all called him, Great Father.'

Tamubu knew that Sashono cared for Nanoka and tried to please her in every way. But not until Tamubu started his leadership lessons did Sashono ever speak to him or show affection. Deep inside he knew Nanoka was not his birth mother, but her love for him was so comforting and reassuring, that it was only natural for him to respond to it. Nanoka had been there for him through all his misery, day and night. She had been selfless and patient while caring for him. He did not care about any secrets. He wanted his life and learning to go on as it had these past months. He had never before been so happily engrossed, and he could hardly wait for each new day.

SASHONO PASSED THROUGH THE hut without seeing Tamubu in the shadows. When Manutu came into the room, he knew Tamubu was there.

"Come forward and let me see what you have brought with you." And so, without censure for his unannounced presence, he showed Manutu the nest with the cracked egg, which now had a small hole in it. Manutu recognized the egg as that of a small songbird with showy, golden feathers, and said. "The female must have been snared, for they are considered prizes and bring high prices from the Traders. You must learn how to care for this tiny bird when it is hatched. It will consider you its mother. It is a bug and grub eater. You will have to build a cage to keep it safe, find soft, down feathers to keep it warm, and prepare food and water for it. In this way you will learn the responsibilities of a parent. It will be one of your hardest lessons, for failure as a parent can mean death."

TAMUBU SAW THE BOTTOM leaves of the kamikiza move. He watched as Paula raised the leaves, propping them up with the dead branch. She crawled out from under the plant and removed the prop. Sitting away from the bush, she carefully wiped the parka with damp moss before putting it back in her sack. Walking backwards, she brushed the ground all around her. She passed close to a fallen tree leaning up against the lofty limbs of a huge mahogany tree, and continued on brushing towards a thicket, where she turned and brushed her way back to the leaning tree. Tamubu smiled, "This indeed, was a large flock of guinea fowl." Using the leaning tree as a ramp and ladder, Paula climbed to the lofty branches of the ancient mahogany tree and was gone.

11

The Simba-jike

PAULA WAS SURPRISED SHE had slept so well, considering the extreme stress of fleeing for her safety and the dire fear of being hunted; but rigorous exercise had always been good for her, both physically and mentally. She refreshed herself from the hidden flutes of water, and ate one of the granola bars–hoping she had enough for the journey back to the yacht. Finding fresh fruit was going to be a necessity. If she had known she was going to have to trek through the wilds of Africa, she would have paid a bit more attention to the study of indigenous edible plants! Now, she could only hope to find blackberries, bananas or pineapples; the fruits the natives had harvested on the trek to the village.

Even though her captors had not talked in her presence, she had learned much from them. The natives always wanted to be in a secure place, with a good fire, before the big cats came out to hunt, at the end of the gloaming. They did not fear the big cats when they were hunting them, but they did fear the big cats when they were the ones being hunted.

The best times to travel were early morning until noon, and after two in the afternoon until dusk. Breaking up the physical activity with food and rest at noon, doubled her endurance in the tropical heat and sun. It was now almost three and Paula knew the search parties would have passed this area long ago. But she wondered: are the Ndezi out there just waiting for me to appear? Have they left sentries hidden along the trail? Would it be safer if I waited until dark? But traveling in the trees at night was so slow and arduous. As it is, I don't think I'm even an hour's walk from the village.

Nope, I'll have to stay high in the trees, and hope I see them before they see me.

SHE BRUSHED OUT HER footprints to a leaning tree, which gave her access to the lofty mahogany trees. Paula had left a broken branch trail, so she could find the main trail again. Her compass was of little help in retracing her path in the trees. She needed to follow the trail the Ndezi used to come out of the forest in the right place. Getting just a few hundred feet off the trail, could take her far away from the right path back to the yacht.

As she moved along the arboreal trail, the ease of moving through the trees in the dappled, westerly sunlight gave her unexpected satisfaction. Her shoulder and back muscles were tight and her hands were sore, where her calluses had grown soft with disuse; but the discomfort brought back poignant memories of perfecting new routines on the uneven parallel bars. Her spirits began to soar as she applied her timing and rhythm to her movements in the trees with lessening effort as each hour passed.

Paula kept to the west side of the trail she was shadowing. It kept the shafts of the lowering sun with its deceptive light and shadows from shining in her eyes. With the good backlight, she moved up from the lower branches, which were the stoutest and the easiest to travel, having few small leafy shoots, but they did not connect as often, one tree to another. The myriad vines and flowering creepers craved the sun, and grew with a singular mind straight to the tops of the trees, into the sunlight.

In the middle terrace, there were more limbs branching in each direction and more choices, but also more foliage. Vines hung everywhere. Most of them were firmly attached and able to support her weight, but the odd one that wasn't could let her down, forty feet or more above the ground. She used the vines more as railings and handholds for security, as she balance-beamed along the limbs.

TO CROSS A LARGE open space, Paula used the grapnel, with a

line knotted along its length. Several times during the first few throws, she lost valuable time retrieving the grapnel from unsuitable moorings. But the security she felt by keeping to the trees made the extra effort worthwhile. And too, she had the feeling that competency with the grapnel might one day, come in more than handy.

Paula moved through the vines and creepers of the forest almost noiselessly, and stirred the birds not at all. Occasionally, she startled a monkey who screeched and scampered away. There were few monkeys in close proximity to a native village as they were competitors for the same wild foodstuffs, and themselves a source of meat for the stewpot.

She saw few snakes, but knew they were there, as were the spiders, mites and scorpions, all potentially dangerous. Her suede leather chaps provided good lower leg protection, and she had slathered her exposed skin with bug repellent.

Paula was so preoccupied trying to find paths through the trees, and still not lose sight of the trail she was shadowing, that she had no idea she was being followed on the ground.

Tamubu had kept his distance at first, but when Paula took to traveling high above the path, he had no choice but to follow closer, so as not to lose sight of her. He was amazed at the way this Mitiriki flowed through the trees: walking out on a limb, grabbing a vine or branch and swinging to the next tree; or swinging across large spaces on a white rope; or falling to a straddling position and swinging under the limb and dropping to the limb below... and, she did these things as easily as he moved on the ground.

They passed the area where Bolbonga had flung the pistol away... like a poisonous toad. Tamubu found it and tucked it in his quiver. He knew about white men and their guns, and suspected that the empty sheath hanging from the Mitiriki's belt might be home for the shiny piece of metal.

TAMUBU ASKED HIMSELF WHY he was following the Mitiriki; he could give himself no reasonable explanation; except for his boundless curiosity. He was even traveling in the wrong direction, yet he was so spellbound by his fascination, that he gave it no thought at all. Trailing this lone unpredictable woman was the most interesting thing he had ever done... he was totally captivated by her.

As THE LONG TWILIGHT faded, Paula moved directly off to the east, looking for another Devil Plant and some berries or pineapple plants. The undergrowth had thickened, which indicated that she was further from the village than the natives usually came for forage. Just when she thought she might have to sleep in the trees until the moon was up, she saw the small clearing of a laprodis plant and there too, taking advantage of the sun provided by the clearing, was a small stand of banana plants. She broke off two bunches, one near ripe and one still green. She attached the fruit to her backpack, donned her parka, and propped up the laprodis leaves to safely enter the sanctuary in the center of the devil plant.

She feasted on the fruit and drank copiously of the sweet water in the leafy flutes. As the dark of the night fell, Paula lay listening to the night-sounds orchestra. Only the shrill horrifying and escalating scream of the tree hyrax, a marmot-like tree dweller, disturbed the night.

Tamubu also helped himself to the bananas. They blended easily with his trail mix of grains and nuts for the leaf roll-ups he made for trail snacks. Before he settled himself for the night, Tamubu filled his gourd at a nearby spring. He was concerned, because he had not seen the Mtiriki drink that day. He did not know the secret of the devil plant.

THE CLOUDS COMPLETELY OBSCURED the full moon. The rain came, making a stygian darkness of the night—full of muted dripping sounds, which did not disturb Paula's sleep at all; for with only light meals, and extreme physical exertion, sleep became her fuel. The leaves of this devil plant so thickly overlapped the dead center that very little of the rain dripped in where she lay covered by her rain poncho. Most of the water followed the downward drape of the top leaves to lower leaves, or to the little flutes at their bases, which then overflowed down the stems to the ground. This rain pattern explained why the laprodis plant always grew outward: because most of the rainwater dripped to the ground on the outside perimeter of the plant.

Tamubu, wrapped in his cloak, was warm and dry–high in a tree nearby.

PAULA AWOKE AT FIRST light to the joyful trilling of thousands of awakening birds, and saw the heavy dew. She knew she would leave a glaring trail, evident even in the trees, until it dried up a bit. While munching on bananas and a trail bar, she thought about the unimaginable circumstances that had brought her to, of all things, sleeping under a toxic plant in equatorial Africa... while fleeing from vengeful natives. She longed for a cup of hot tea, as she drank deeply from the little water reservoirs at the bases of the center leaves. She used her straw as a siphon to fill her water bottles. Then, sitting cross-legged, with her pack as a table, she began to record the events of the past few days in her diary.

THE MORNING DEW EVAPORATES quickly when the sun rises in Africa. Paula reorganized her pack to make room for the bananas, and soon after, was back in the trees. The hot sun made a sauna of the wet jungle-like treetops where she traveled all morning–enduring the discomfort for the safety it provided. The ground was still wet enough to provide easy tracking, so when she came across a nice three-limbed tree crotch, she stopped, ate a granola bar and two bananas, and tied herself to the limb for an afternoon nap. In the early evening, the forest started to thin, and Paula knew the savanna was only a few miles away. At dusk, she went to the largest tree she saw and there made a bed for the night. It would be too easy to lose the trail looking for a laprodis plant.

The next day, about mid-morning, Paula had to leave the trees, for the forest had thinned to a sparse wood. She had seen no evidence of the Ndezi, and wondered if they had given up trying to track her when they found no *sign* of her passage. She hoped she had aroused their superstitious natures, for it was the only trump card she had to play. As she walked the wide wooded path, it felt different to her; making her wonder if she had somehow followed the wrong trail from the trees. When she reached the savannah, beyond which lay the thorny, boulder-strewn hills, Paula knew she had indeed followed the wrong trail.

TAMUBU HAD CLOSED THE distance even more that morning. He was skilled at tracking, and he knew she was oblivious to his presence. Also, he now knew that she drank from containers attached to the sack she carried on her back, but she passed many edible fruits and nuts and harvested nothing. He decided to weave a grass bag to carry food for her. She either did not know it was good food or did not want to be bothered carrying it through the trees.

IN TWO DAYS AND twenty hours of arboreal escape, Paula was only about five hours from the village on foot. Her pursuers should have overtaken her long ago, and could already be in front of her. But since she had somehow followed a different trail, did she have to be wary of them coming this way? Paula was glad to be traveling on the ground, for her hands were sore. Her calluses had blistered and broken open. She had put salve on them each night, but a few days without rough branches and sweaty gloves would aid the healing process.

The closer she came to the scrubby, boulder-strewn foothills, the harder the ground became; for the tree cover was thin here, allowing more sunlight through to dry out the soil. Paula moved at an easy lope, crossing the savanna before reaching the undulating hills in mid-afternoon. She was skirting the base of the hills looking for a path, when she came upon a small spring fed pool nestled behind large rubber plants. She took a moment to fill her bottles from the spring before she shed her clothes and bathed. What a luxury. It had been seven days since her swim in the mountain lake... which seemed like ages ago.

TAMUBU MARVELED AT THE fearlessness of this Mitirike. The whole area around the little pool was covered in lion spoor. While it was early for the lions to be out hunting, it was never too early for a drink. Tamubu skirted the big boulders to get above her, and watched with mixed emotions, as she bathed in the water, then washed her hair and her clothes. She laid her laundry on the sunny leaves of the rubber plants to dry, while she sat on a large flat rock, and fluffed her hair while it dried. She dressed in dry clothes from her sack; then wandered about gathering small twigs, dried branches and some dried moss. These things, she attached to her pack, with her almost-dry clothes, and climbed over the rough boulders towards a sheer rock face. Tamubu lost sight of her, but soon smelled the smoke, and moved higher in the boulders to a place where he could see the little fire on a high ledge with a cave-like niche, which was about twenty feet off the ground. How did she get up there? This woman was a constant surprise.

Today, Paula was going to have a cup of tea; she took the insulated cover off her stainless steel water bottle and put it between rocks beside the small fire. This way, the water was heated, but the metal bottle did not become soot-covered. She ate a banana and a granola bar with the tea. It was absolutely delicious. Why did ordinary foods taste so much better when eaten in the open? Propping her pack for a backrest, she lay back and, feeling contented, dozed off.

A low croaking call, like the sound of a secretary bird, awoke her. She listened, but did not hear it again. She dismantled her little camp, packed her now dry clothes, and descended to the pool to again fill her water bottles from the spring. She checked the direction with her compass. She had come out of the forest in a different place, but she could not tell if she was north or south of the trail she sought. Paula went south hoping to find a trail going east that led through the nasty wait-a-bit covering the stony slopes.

Tamubu watched incredulous, as Paula set out. It was here, in this thorn-covered scrub, that the simba-jike liked to hunt in the early evening; when the mongoose was out looking for sunning snakes, and the genet was hunting rabbit and rats. This was the time of year for cubs. The simba-jike would hunt for her cubs before setting out later with other female lions to hunt larger game.

He had scouted the area while Paula napped, and had found a trail over the mountain. He had also found dense spoor from the simba-jike. Her den was close. When he returned to the spring fed pool, he also saw simba's fresh prints in the damp earth. He climbed a tree and saw Paula was still asleep. He gave the low croaking call of the secretary bird to wake her as it was getting late. In a few hours all the female lions would be out hunting. That ledge, while high, was not insurmountable for a hungry lion.

Watching Paula, he saw that she was going to skirt the lower reaches of the hillside to avoid the thorny brush, which would give the simba-jike perfect cover for stalking her; so Tamubu moved above the simba-jike on the hillside. Now, he was nearer her cubs. He had watched the big cat slink into the thorny scrub after her drink, following Paula's scent; so he was not surprised to see the lion watching the Mtiriki as she walked along, oblivious to her danger. Crouching down, the simba-jike moved silently through the thorny underbrush to a point where Paula would soon pass if she continued on in the same direction.

Tamubu's arrows and slingshot were useless in the brush, so he hastened to the rocks where he had seen the simba-jike reclining while Paula was napping. Sure enough, there they were– three small cubs asleep. Stealing along silently, he reached over the log fronting the den and grabbed a cub. It hissed and struggled mightily, trying to scratch him as it squealed piteously.

The lioness was immediately alert. When pinched, the little fellow cried out in pain and terror. The female lion instantly turned and raced toward her den. The moment the cub cried out, Tamubu dropped him back with his littermates, and raced for a strong, young tree with lower branches too weak to support simba's massive weight... if she decided to climb up after him. No sooner had he attained the safety of the upper branches than simba broke into view. She smelled the air, and when it was man she smelled, she became cautious. The cubs were quiet now, hiding deep in the lair. Simba decided to check the cubs, which gave Tamubu an opportunity to drop from the tree.

He moved quickly on an angle to intercept the Mitiriki. He was sure she would see the trail and follow it, hoping to cross the mountain. These rocky caves were prime lairs for female lions that sought each other's company, especially when hunting. This was no place for the Mtiriki to be alone, uninformed and unarmed at dusk.

Tamubu reached the trail before Paula passed by. Scouting down the trail, he saw her below. He also saw two young female lions stalking her in the thorn bushes. He could hit one with his walinka, but would the other lion run or attack. As he reached in his quiver for a second walinka, his hand touched the cold steel of the pistol. He jerked the pistol from the leather carrier and in doing so, snagged the safety off. He pointed the gun towards the lions and pulled the trigger. The awful noise from the pistol and the whistling sounds of the ricochet from rock to rock, made the lions turn and run away. Paula instinctively threw herself into the bushes lining the trail—right where the two lions had been.

Tamubu laughed as he strode up to her and said in Bantu, "Do you always throw yourself into the lions' mouth? How have you been able to survive doing that?"

Paula was so unnerved that it took a moment before she realized what he had said. Then, before she gathered her wits to reply, she saw he was holding her pistol. Thinking she was caught again, she raged, No! Not again! Think of something! Scrambling gingerly from the thorny bushes, Paula gathered herself to rise. She was going to pretend to faint so he would have to carry her, just as Tamubu smiled, and put out his hand to help her up. Surprised, she saw he was not a native. His hands were the same color on both sides. Looking at him as she rose, she saw eyes, the color of a blue topaz, and dimples on either side of a beautiful smile. Closer now, she could see wisps of honey colored hair that matched the brows below the dulband on his head. His mouth was nicely shaped, and his nose was long and narrow. This man was not black, just tanned. He was dressed like a native, but differently from the Ndezi. He had no facial tattooing, skin piercing or enlarged ear lobes. He was talking to her in a Bantu dialect. She only caught a word here and there, but his manner and urgency were unmistakable.

TAMUBU HAD SEEN HER fear when he strode up to her. He had also seen the surprise when she realized he was not a native, especially not Ndezi.

"Come, we must go quickly before simba returns. This is her hunting time and we are close to the dens. There is a big tree just a way up the hill where you can be safe." Without asking her permission, Tamubu grabbed her hand and towed her up the trail. She saw the ancient oak tree surrounded by big boulders. Tamubu had pushed her off the trail towards the boulders when an angry roar froze them in their steps. There crouched the female lion whose cub Tamubu had pinched. She had them, and was calling for help. "Go quickly," Tamubu said to Paula. "I will distract her until you are safe. Go! Go now! But don't let her see you."

12

Tête-à-tête

PAULA WAS OUT OF simba's line of sight, as she scrambled atop the boulder. It was much too open and, judging from the gnawed bones, a feeding place of carnivores. She still had the grapnel and line hooked by her holster. She immediately tossed it to the oak tree twenty feet away. In moments, she swung to safety next to the bole of the tree.

Looking down, Paula saw two smaller lionesses join the large female lion. They ranged themselves in an arc: crouching, motionless, eyes focused, waiting for Tamubu to move. Keeping his eye contact with the large lioness, Tamubu, gave a loud shrill battle yell and rushed the simba-jike, brandishing his spear. Paula was stunned. But the surprise of his aggressive action gave him the few moments he needed to use his spear to pole-vault to the top of a boulder beside the lofty oak tree.

From there, he was able to leap for the lowest limb of the mature tree. Hearing the simba-jike's outraged roar, he hastily pulled himself up to a standing position on the limb, and was scrambling for a higher limb when he felt simba's massive weight hit the branch he had just vacated. Simba reached up with a mighty claw to snag her prey just as a strong hand grabbed his forearm, above the wrist, and yanked him out of her reach. Tamubu was astonished to look up and see the Mtiriki making her way to the uppermost branches.

Glancing back, Tamubu saw simba atop the rock getting ready for another mighty leap into the branches. With great speed, but less agility, he also climbed to the upper reaches and safety. The infuriated cat tried to follow him. Simba's great length and reach with her claws had snagged at his cloak, advancing her mind from the stalking and chase function to the kill mode. Even so, her claws could no longer support her massive weight, nor could the lighter branches, which snapped under her great bulk as she tried to advance. Paula watched the awesome fury of the great feline who protested mightily against the loss of a good meal. It was with great relief that Paula watched the lioness retreat from the tree.

GETTING SETTLED IN THE crotch opposite to Paula, Tamubu looked at her and smiled. He knew she had been watching his ascent. He had seen the fright in her eyes as simba's razor-sharp claws swiped at his cloak, just as her mighty pull took him out of her reach. Many times his cloak had saved him from harm, for not even simba's lethal claws could penetrate the fabric.

Tamubu had not yet recovered from his surprise at seeing the Mitiriki in this tree. He thought she had escaped to the rocks. From the high vantage point, he looked over to the boulder, where he could see a carrion leg dangling over the side. It seemed that choosing the tree had been a wise decision. She smiled at him and he, with a feeling of thrill, smiled back.

Tamubu started to speak, but Paula raised her hand, shook her head and told him in halting Bantu, "Speak slowly. I am just learning to speak Bantu. Do you speak English or French?"

Tamubu smiled and said, "Yes, I speak English, but have not for long time."

Paula was so grateful for his help, his courage and bravery that she just sat smiling at him, wondering if she should ask him how he came to be here? If he's not a native, what is he? After a moment, she broke the smiling silence saying in English, "Thank you for saving me from the lions."

Tamubu wondered what she would say if she knew that it was not the first time he had waylaid simba for her today. She was probably referring to the gun noise, which had chased away the young females before simba arrived.

He replied, "You save me too, asante."

"My name is Paula. What is your name?"

Tamubu thought this over. He had an English name, Thomas, as well as his tribal name, but he was not yet ready to declare himself English and subject himself to scrutiny.

With gravity he said, "I am Tamubu–from the Great Nations of the Zuri Watu."

Paula smiled and chuckled. He spoke English with a British accent.

Curious as to the cause of her mirth, he said, "Is funny?"

Seeing that she had been thoughtless, she hastened to say, "I was just surprised. You speak English with a British accent. I didn't expect that!

Tamubu had never heard English spoken by an American. He understood her words, but her accent and word use was odd. It took him a long moment to understand her meaning, before he said, "Your English is different. Who are your people?"

"I'm an American. Do you know the United States of America?"

As Paula spoke, Tamubu became excited. He whooped and laughed, as diverse fragments of memories flooded his mind.

"Are you a Yank? I know about Yanks! Americans were our heroes."

Simba again assaulted the tree when she heard Tamubu cry out. She would not stay much longer for she knew she had missed this dinner. But, being outsmarted made her very angry. She knew they would have to come down sometime; but, for now, her cubs needed food. She would come back later.

Paula was puzzled. Why would Americans be the heroes of Africans? Possibly he was not really an African. Maybe he had just been exposed to the sun for so long his skin was brown. "You say you're from a tribe, yet you speak with a British accent. Are you British?"

Reeling from a flood of new memories, Tamubu said, "Yes, from Kenya. The Zuri Watu scouts found me lost and sick. They took me home with them. "Soon, the simba-jike goes to hunt for cubs. We go to better place. Simba is angry. She come back later."

While Tamubu spoke, he had been rummaging in his bag and finally produced a leaf, into which he put several selections from the pouches. "Are you hungry? I have traveling food: nuts, grains and dried fruit."

Paula was pleased to accept the stuffed leaf. It was chewy and tasted of almonds and berries. She drank a bit of her water, and said, "That was delicious, thank you. I suddenly feel very tired. I must rest a bit." As she spoke, Paula tied herself to the limb before closing her eyes. She had no idea why she felt so tired, but the instant she closed her eyes, she was asleep.

TAMUBU SAT THINKING. THE floodgates had been opened. His mind was inundated with pictures, faces, stories and memories. He was like a person freed from amnesia. But he hadn't had amnesia. He'd had trauma, shock and a long siege of malaria. Over the years, other things had triggered memories, but isolated ones. Now, he needed time to think about the flood of new memories crowding his mind. He needed to think about them and put them in order.

He reached over to Paula and put the gun in her holster. It fit perfectly. He was glad that he had retrieved it for her.

The simba-jike had finally gone. He could hear her chuffing for the whereabouts of her female hunting companions. They could be her daughters, or other young females who had not yet mated. The food supply dictated the mating process in any given year. In a lean year, the males would eat the cubs if there were no other prey. Only with a full belly was the king of beasts a benevolent father.

Tamubu dropped down to a lower branch thickly covered with vines and the bushy parasitic oranthus. He secured his possessions in the greenery, and brought his cloak around his head to sniff the crushed leaves in his palm. He had only a short time to find a secure place for them to sleep... where they could have a fire and make a meal. The simba-jike could come back at any time, and she would come back, after she found food for her cubs.

Tamubu followed the trail into the stony hills. The trail led to a dead end at the bottom of a high cliff. The top of the cliff was the edge of a huge, sloping, grassy plateau that eventually connected with the arm and shoulder of the mountain.

On his return, above the foothills, he found what they needed. A high ledge, cut into the cliff face beneath a rock outcropping. It was inaccessible except from the branches of a tall, spindly tree growing out of the jumbled rocks below it. There were plenty of dead thorn bushes for a fire. This, in itself, was an indication that man did not usually come this way.

The ledge was shaped so that it was sheltered from rain and sheer on all sides. There were rifts in the overhead stone for a chimney effect so they would not have a problem with smoke. Tamubu was quite pleased with his find, and went back to get Paula. She should be waking soon. He had sprinkled a bit of a sleeping herb in her food. It would also relieve her tension from the encounter with the lions.

Paula untied herself in the fading light of the last phase of the full moon, looking up to see a sky dressed in wispy clouds with zillions of stars shining through like sequins on a ball gown. She sighed: the beauty of Africa was beguiling, for it hid its perils well. Tamubu had moved further down in the tree and simba was gone. She had not napped long, but she felt well rested.

Tamubu spoke softly, "We go now, before simba come back. We find good place for rest; up mountain—no food for simba."

"Isn't traveling at night risky?" Paula asked.

"Less risk now, simba hunts for cubs."

Paula put her rope away and climbed down the tree. She hurried up the narrow, winding track behind him, wondering why she trusted this stranger so completely. Maybe it was because he had put her gun back in her holster. How had he come by it? How did he know it belonged to her? She put her doubts aside. At least we are going in the right direction, away from the Ndezi.

PAULA WAS GLAD FOR the luminous sky; it helped her to see her footing on the rocky path, for Tamubu had a fast walk. She was delighted by the new sleeping place. It seemed no time at all before Tamubu had gathered a bundle of soft feathery fronds for their beds and kindling for a fire. By the time she had the pallets arranged in the narrowing angle under the rock overhang; Tamubu had a small fire going at the edge of the overhang. They had worked in silence. Paula sat on her pallet and said, "I'm going to make a cup of Earl Grey tea, would you like to join me?"

Like he fell in a pond... the thoughts came rushing back to him and covered his mind and filled his soul and made his heart beat faster. Thoughts he had not had since he was lost, returned to him. He remembered the plane, he remembered his brother... he remembered Kazaii.

Tamubu was delighted. He had not had real tea for a long time. "Yes, I have no tea for many years."

Taking the cover off her stainless steel bottle, she added a tea bag and set the bottle at the edge of the fire and asked, "How long is many years?"

"Since ten years old. The Zuri Watu drink coffee, cocoa, broth and lemon water."

"Why do you remember your age so exactly?"

"That my age when engine of plane gets fire. Pilot land in river. Pilot and teacher die as plane hit tree in water. I lived... got out of plane, through broken window to tree trunk. River full of crocodiles. I watch crocodiles drag arms out to river.

"How did you ever survive in the jungle, all by yourself, at age ten?"

"From skills taught by native tutor, Kiazii. He make games to play: games where I lost, have to find home; game where lion hunts me, I escape; or game I was lost, had to find food, get help.

"I was alone for days. Then hunting party pass under tree where I sleep. I follow them all day, make sure they not cannibals. When they make night camp, I sleep in tree. Morning, men look at me in tree. I go home with them.

"I get sick. Men carry me. Sick for many rainy seasons.

"I no speak Bantu, only Swahili. They talk to me with

hands. I sick, only want water." Sipping the hot tea, Tamubu thought: I don't sound right when I speak English. It took some minutes before he realized he was speaking English in native dialect, where many words included other small words, which were each spoken in English. He said to Paula, "I not used to English speaking. You tell me right way to say, I forget."

"If you like, I can do that. How long were you sick?"

"I was sick long time. Medicine Chief, Manutu and Nanoka, wife of Great Chief, Sashono, take care for me. They save my life. For long time, Nanoka tell me tribe legends and stories. She good storyteller. She spoke Swahili. She teach me Bantu with her stories. I had no distress or sadness... no longing for others. I was safe and secure. I was the center of their lives and important to them."

"Didn't you eventually miss your family or your home?"

"After the crash, I was occupied with survival, the journey and then the illness came and I did not think at all. I was sick with chills and fever through many rainy seasons. By the time I was well, I was important member of the village. My other life was like dream when you awake... only bits and pieces."

Paula poured her tea into the thermos top, and Tamubu produced a gourd from his sack. As he talked, he had been stirring what looked like a stew in a coconut shell.

"You must have been happy in your new life."

"Yes, I was happy with my life once I was well. But now, I am traveling back to my birth family."

"Why did you wait so long? Surely, you could have gone back sooner."

"No, it was only a few moons ago, when Nanoka was sick and near death that she talk of the missionary doctor, and of missing boy. Until then I had no wish to leave. It was only her deathbed story that made me remember other times."

"Why did Nanoka see the missionary doctor?"

"I had malaria and missionary doctor had quinine."

"Were you planning on crossing the continent on foot?"

"Yes, I like to go to new places. See new things. It will be a good walk."

I<small>T HAD STARTED TO</small> rain when Tamubu served the stew he had been preparing. It was the best stew Paula had ever eaten and she told him so. "Your stew was delicious, thank you for sharing."

Tamubu smiled his dazzling smile and said, "Your tea was delicious, thank you for sharing."

Paula smiled back at his subtle humor. "I don't know about you, but I am really tired. I am going to turn in."

Tamubu was puzzled, "Turn in to what?"

Paula felt like the Cheshire cat with all the grinning she was doing. "Turn in is an expression that means—go to bed. Good night."

"Good night to you."

This man was so different from anyone she had ever met before. He was self-assured, soft spoken, unassuming, forthright and somehow amusing. He was as comfortable in the wilderness as she was in the laboratory. She sensed his knowledge was as vast as her own, but as different from hers as night from the day. In only hours, she felt like he was a benevolent colleague. She felt him to be her peer in every way and respected him and his abilities as she did few others. But, most of all, she felt happy being with him. She didn't even know him, but she was sure of him … and, his smile was charming. His skin was darkly tanned, which made his kind blue eyes stand out against his honey brown hair and bushy eyebrows. He was tall, strongly built with broad shoulders and lean muscles. He had strong hands with long fingers and even white teeth and dimples. He moved with grace and ease as he put more sticks on the little fire.

Paula closed her eyes as Tamubu turned back to her saying, "We will wait for the rain to end. It will wash away our scent. If simba makes no kill, she will come hunt us."

Brought sharply out of her lethargic reverie, Paula asked, "Is she likely to do that?" Their confrontation with the lions had thoroughly robbed her of her courage… coming so close to being a lion's dinner had made her feel quite vulnerable.

"We safe here. Good to den-up for rain, unless need to travel. You need rest after escaping the Ndezi."

"How do you know about the Ndezi?" Surprised, her need to sleep vanished.

"I heard the searchers talk. They were close to the kamikiza. You sleep good, if you not hear them. They make much noise."

"You saw me hide in the Laprodis plant?"

"Yes. No one goes near those plants. They cause painful boils."

"So... you have been following me?"

"Yes. I thought you might need my help."

Surprised, confused, grateful, she whispered, "And I did, didn't I? Thank you." Humbled, Paula closed her eyes. Did he watch me bathe? She wondered as she drifted towards sleep. The knowledge did not change her good opinion of him, actually, it reinforced it, but it made her feel inane. It was too much to think about now. Tomorrow she would be able to cope better.

TAMUBU LAID THE END of a small, but long, log in the fire. When the end started to burn, he went to his pallet and rolling himself in his cloak, lay down. Still sorting through the unfolding, and jumbled memories Paula had awakened in him, he now had to deal with his disquieting thoughts of this amazing woman.

THE FIRST WARBLES OF the songbirds woke him long before dawn. He left Paula sleeping to hunt. He surprised a covey of quail and bagged two. They were roasting slowly on a spit when Paula, stirred by the smell, awoke.

"My goodness, you have been busy this morning."

"Yes, it is good to hunt early. You sleep well, it is late."

"The sound of rain has always lulled me to sleep. It is so quiet here compared to the deep forest. I must admit that the tree hyrax often ruined a night's sleep for me."

Tamubu chuckled, "It is safe to go down if you like. There is water here to wash. The rain has been filling the gourds.

This bowl is cassava, like oatmeal. It is for you. The quail are for dinner. They are a rainy day treat."

On her return, she found Tamubu gone. He was giving her space and privacy. She had just finished making tea, when she heard a shrill whistle and turned to see Tamubu step from the tree to the ledge with several large roots.

"These are for dinner. They are elephant's ear roots and taste like potatoes."

"Thank you for the porridge. It was good. Do you like to cook?"

"Yes. Men must be good cooks to live off the land when they go exploring. The women make the same stew each day in their big cooking pots. When you are out traveling, there are other choices, not just the gardens. Manutu and I would talk for hours while we roasted game birds. You tell me about you... about what adventures happen to now. Why American woman is alone in African wilderness?"

"You're right; it has been an incredible adventure. A storm marooned the boat in a land-locked cove—I could not sail away. I went ashore, and the Ndezi captured me and took me to their village. Four days ago, I escaped into the trees through the smoke hole in the roof of my prison. I traveled in the trees, so I would not leave a trail for them to follow. I do not have much woodcraft in the forest, but I knew the secrets of the Laprodis plant from my studies. I knew it would offer me a safe place to hide and rest."

"I was in the clearing and I see you come in the trees. I watch you go to the kamikiza, lift leaves to go inside. No one touches kamikiza. I stay to see what you do next. What studies told you such things?"

"I am a biologist, a person who studies plants. That is the reason I came to Africa. We are looking for several species of plants that have the power to relieve anxiety and pain, without becoming addictive. Do you understand what I mean?"

Tamubu smiled inwardly. He not only knew these plants, but he had already given her some after her escape from the lions. "You have said *we* several times. Is there someone with you?"

"Yes and no. There were six of us who came to Africa. But I was alone when the storm swept the yacht away. A rescue helicopter had just found the yacht when the Ndezi captured me. I am going back to the cove where the yacht is moored. It is about six days travel... on the ground."

Tamubu smiled at her subtle humor and thought: this woman will not make it back to her yacht alone—she is mzuzu (a tenderfoot).

Paula was thinking: what if he had not followed me? I would have been a lion's dinner. She had been badly shaken by the close encounter. Now, she doubted her ability to travel so far alone in safety. Trekking in Africa was **not** a hike in the woods.

Tamubu spoke first. "I go to gather." Without so much as a goodbye, he was gone.

13

Forest Travel

PAULA AROSE TO STRETCH and move about. A bed of fronds was better than a bed on bare stone, but it was still hard. She had spread her poncho over the pallet vegetation, and was using the thin metallic blanket from the first aid kit, as a cover. She was finding life in the wilds of Africa very harsh. Ordinary things: like fresh water, a safe place to sleep and enough food weren't ordinary anymore; and the daylight she required to write in her diary, was devoted to survival.

Two hours later when Tamubu returned, she was still scribbling away. So adept were his wilderness skills, that she did not hear him approach the ledge. For a while, he sat and watched her, caught unawares by a lost memory, for he too had once written in books. He had not done so, since the plane crash. The Zuri Watu have no written language, not even pictographs, all is memory.

It was at this moment, that he made the conscious decision to guide Paula back to the yacht. He would be speaking English again, which had already prompted forgotten memories, and he needed to remember how to speak English properly. Maybe in exchange, she would agree to further his education, from that of a ten-year-old boy to that of a grown Englishman.

Tamubu gave a bird whistle.

When Paula turned to see the bird, he greeted her with a smile. She felt an immediate gladness, and returned his smile with unexpected pleasure.

Tamubu had another bird, some plantain, berries, nuts and large chard-like leaves. He had plucked and eviscerated the bird in the forest, for entrails drew all sorts of undesirables, such as vultures and hyenas, as well as annoying insects.

So Paula was not sure what manner of bird it was that he added to the spit when she said, "I never thought it would make me so happy to see food cooking. You are a very good hunter/gatherer. I must confess to a lack of knowledge about the edible plants of Africa. The Expedition focused on finding plants with a medicinal purpose. The possibility of having to forage for food never even occurred to us."

"I noticed that. You passed many good things to eat and took nothing. The helpful plants you seek, do they take away worries and fears?"

"Yes, do you know them?"

"It is possible. There are many plants that help people in many ways. We will eat the quails when the tubers are cooked. The guinea fowl will be for another day."

Paula sensed that he was reluctant to talk about the helpful plants. But, right now, she had more pressing matters on her mind.

"I know you are on an important journey back to Kenya to find your family," Paula tilted her head and smiled, "But if you could spare a few days to help me get back to the yacht, I would be most grateful. My associates have resources that could help you to contact your family. The Corporation sponsoring the Expedition could arrange for you to fly back to Kenya; if you decided not to take a four or five month walking trip overland."

Tamubu fussed with the spit to give himself time to think. This is what he wanted. But he also wanted to travel to Kenya on foot. A plane would put him there too fast. He had already remembered his father's opinion of the natives, and he did not want to disappoint him... or embarrass himself. He needed time to adjust from thinking and living like a native, to being British again. Traveling with Paula could be the help he needed, before he met his family again.

Tamubu replied. "It would be good for us to travel to your yacht together. You do not have the skills needed to travel so far in safety. We can trade: I will guide you, provide food and keep you safe. For me, it will be an opportunity to speak English with an adult. It has been thirteen years since I thought in English. I have much to learn, and much to remember. Will you teach me?" Tamubu looked at her kind face and shining eyes, and wondered aloud, "Would you agree to this kind of a trade?"

Paula was overwhelmed with relief. He was right. She had thought of herself as invulnerable, because of the safety she had experienced while traveling with the Ndezi warriors. There may have been many dangers that they avoided, because the Ndezi could read the *sign* of the forest—dangers she didn't even know existed. She had already missed one trail. It was possible she could miss others. She was indeed, unprepared for wilderness travel in Africa, as once away from the main trails, everything looked the same to her. Even worse, on her own, she had almost been dinner for lions.

"I would be glad to serve as your tutor. In the last eighteen hours, your speech patterns and vocabulary have improved quite a bit. Are you thinking in English now?"

Tamubu was astonished by the question, and took a moment before answering. "Yes," he said, I am, but I did not notice it."

"That would explain the improvement in your speech patterns. You should keep on thinking in English as much as possible. You must have been a very bright boy. Your usage and syntax have improved significantly; maybe you haven't forgotten as much as you thought. If you continue to think in English, there won't be much for me to teach you, except maybe vocabulary.

"Speech patterns? Usage? Syntax? Significantly? Vocabulary? What do these words mean?"

Paula smiled, "Speech patterns are the way you speak your thoughts. Usage is the choice of words you use to express yourself. Syntax is the arrangement of your words as you speak or write. Vocabulary means all the words that you can use properly. Significant is with special meaning or important."

Tamubu was pleased by her compliments, and by her ability as a tutor. The use of the word tutor had again reminded him of the class distinctions that existed between his family, the house servants, the stable boys and the workers in the field. Even the nanny, who lived in their house, was not invited to sit in the parlor. He put his misgivings aside, telling himself he was their son, their first born, and living with natives did not change his heritage. But he did not want to shame them, himself or the Zuri Watu whom he loved deeply. He would use these days of traveling with Paula to improve himself before he returned to Kenya.

In the meantime, he had agreed to guide Paula to a yacht in a cove by the ocean; and he had no idea where the cove was located, or how far away it might be, so he asked, "Do you remember the way you traveled to the Ndezi village?"

"I remember it all. From the beach, we traveled through the thick undergrowth of the equatorial forest, until we reached a game trail. We followed this trail through the foothills, as we climbed to the mountain ridge. Our direction was due north until we left the ridge; then we went northwest from a vast plateau to the stony foothills; thru the forest we just left, to the Ndezi village. We traveled for seven days. Five days were ten-hour days, two days eight hour days. We probably averaged two point five miles per hour which would make it about one hundred and sixty five miles, more or less, from the cove to the Ndezi village."

Tamubu was amazed. He had not expected such detail from one who was so foolish about Africa. His task might not be as difficult as he had imagined.

"You remember the trail well."

"Maybe, but remembering wasn't good enough to bring me out of the forest on the same trail."

"You were high in the trees. The fork in the trail could not be seen. You followed the wider trail made by elephants. It is not a problem. There is more than one way to get where you want to go. We will find another trail. It will be a better trail because the Ndezi will not think of you knowing it. They can't track us if they don't see our trail." He smiled at her, and the charm of his dimpled smile, along with the sincerity in his voice, melted away her worries.

THE ROASTED LUNCH WAS ready. Tamubu had stuffed the birds with his dried seed, nut and berry mix, blended with some of the cassava from breakfast. The elephant ear tubers were soft and fluffy and tasted more like pancakes than potatoes. The big green leaves that looked like chard, had cooked down to look and taste like sweet spinach. It was a feast, the best meal she had eaten since the family celebration on New Year's Day... before she had boarded the tanker for Africa.

Looking at the sumptuous meal, Paula shook her head and said, "And to think I was going hungry with all this good food around me!"

"You passed many good things to eat. You did not eat them or take them with you. It worried me. I made this grass gathering bag for you."

Paula looked at the small net-like bag and a lump came up in her throat. She took several moments to examine the bag and to control her emotions before looking up, with a smile, saying, "This is a marvelous thing ... and you made it yourself. I am very pleased, thank you."

Tamubu realized he had been on edge when she just sat and looked at the grass bag. He wished he had not given it to her. It was a poor thing, not worthy of her. But when she looked at him, he saw the deep emotion he had evoked and his misgivings evaporated. She was truly pleased

"I know what we can do. We can have our first lesson. We'll see what you remember." Opening her diary to a clean page at the back of the book, she said, "I want you to write numbers to twenty and then the letters of the alphabet while I clean up from our meal."

She gave him the diary and pencil and turned to washing her *5in1* and the small wooden spoon Tamubu had used for cooking. The waxy leaves, which had been their plates, were gently wiped off with dried grass that she disposed of in the fire, and set aside. Tamubu told her he would use the leaves to wrap leftover pieces of cooked meat with the mint, for a later meal... saying ... 'the bruised mint masks the smell of meat on the trail.' Paula turned the spit where the guinea fowl was roasting over the fire, and glanced over at Tamubu. He had the look of a ten-year-old boy taking a test.

As she watched, he looked up, a triumphant smile on his face, and handed her the diary. She was astonished to see the flawless numbers and letters, upper case and lower case, gliding along the page in flowing script.

She took the pencil and wrote, "Repeat exactly what I write. Copy each sentence below. Print the alphabet, both upper and lower cases." She handed him back the diary. This was going to be fun. He was smart, and apparently talented.

In the time it took Paula to rearrange the pallet of fronds under her poncho ground cover, Tamubu had finished his assignment. Paula took the diary and her mouth dropped opened in amazement. He had written exactly what she had written... and had done it so well... it looked like she had written the lines twice herself.

"This is incredible!" she gasped, "Do you know what you have done here?"

"Yes, I did what you asked. Is it wrong?" Paula noted his impish smile.

"How long have you been able to copy exactly what you see?"

"I think since I was given my first crayon. It is the reason I won the Children's Talent Award in Kenya and went to Ghana to compete in the Arts and Science Contest. When I asked for help, I meant to say and do things properly. You use many words that I only guess at their meaning. I also need to understand the written as well as the spoken word on an adult level, not as a ten year old boy."

"Fair enough, now that you have had your little joke on me... and I have to admit, it was a really good one, we will proceed differently."

"You see, that is what I mean, what is proceed?"

"It means: to go on, or carry on, or continue." Paula felt really good about tutoring Tamubu. Now she could contribute to their alliance in a meaningful way.

"What was your project for the contest in Accra?"

Tamubu thought for a moment. The memories had

come flooding back after his unconscious mention of the contest. Until he said it, he had forgotten about the contest completely.

"I took a pencil drawing of horses running in a pasture in the foreground; with workers on a tea farm in the middle ground; and the Great Rift Valley in the background. It was a fantasy picture, done from a view above the subjects, but it was not entered. Before the judging, I did a pencil drawing of the fair from a gallery above the main floor. My teacher said I should enter it, as it could only have been done that morning. I took his advice, entered it and won first prize. That's why my teacher and I flew home on a chartered plane. We had to stay an extra day for photographs and interviews. My Father and Mother flew home as scheduled."

The sudden recall of his Father and Mother at the Talent Fair with him, made him want to be alone to examine these new memories.

"I will go and find a trail for tomorrow. We do not want to go back into the dens of the simba-jike. How are you at mountain climbing?"

Paula chuckled, "I would say I am better at mountain climbing than I am at traveling through trees!"

His astonishment was almost comical, so Paula added: "My family enjoyed scaling sheer rock faces when we were out camping."

Tamubu was fascinated, "Why did you do that?"

"Just for the fun of it... and the challenge; in the heat of the summer, we sailed in the Chesapeake Bay or Atlantic Ocean. We rode horses on trail ride competitions in the spring and fall. In the winter we climbed mountains and sheer cliffs... when there were no bugs, bees, bears or snakes. Our family usually did something together every weekend, and often took along relatives or friends to share the fun."

"I want to hear more about your family later." Tamubu said, and then he was gone.

Paula sat for a few moments and thought about the past twenty hours. "Thank you God for sending Tamubu to help me... so that I might help him." She said aloud.

Once Tamubu had begun to think in English, his speech patterns and syntax had greatly improved. He had been well-spoken as a boy. He just needed a bit of time to remember his past and to use his English.

The rain had stopped but the damp air was cool. Paula put on her camouflage shirt and spread the metallic blanket over her legs for a nap. The enervating tension of fleeing from the Ndezi, and traveling alone, had evaporated when Tamubu agreed to guide her back to the yacht; but as her worries melted away, they left her feeling exhausted, and she slept.

MID-AFTERNOON IS A GOOD time to *roam*. The curious urchins within the monkey family would be busy finding places to nap, not out grubbing for food where they might find his cached possessions. He made a huge circle, going back to the path Paula had missed, to the savanna and over the rocky foothills. The savanna had only rocks, tall grass, spindly trees and bushes and not much water, as Paula had said. From there he climbed to the grassy plateau and headed west, back towards the camp where Paula waited. The plateau was filled with antelope, bushbuck, topi, kob, hartebeest and probably others, so there would be lions, and possibly cheetahs. Not enough trees for leopards, but there was good water from mountain springs. With so much natural game, the lions would avoid man, a dangerous prey that often hunted them.

The sun would be fierce, bearable only because of the constant updraft breeze. The plateau ended at the sheer cliffs he had seen last night. Arriving back at their camp on the ledge, he found Paula sleeping soundly with the fire almost out. He gathered dried grass and twigs to rekindle the flame. He needed a hot cup of broth after *roaming* in the rainy and cool afternoon.

Once the fire was going well, Tamubu made cassava oatmeal with bananas and nuts, for a light dinner after the main-meal lunch.

Paula stirred and watched him for a while before sitting up to fill her metal bottle, to heat water for tea. "Did you find a trail we can use?"

"Yes. It will be rough, for it is not yet a trail, but only for one day."

"I have broken trail many times. I am used to it."

"Good. Tell me more about your family. Do you have sisters and brothers?"

"Yes, an older sister, an older brother and a twin brother."

"Twin brother? I thought twins were always the same—either male or female?"

"Mostly they are. But there are also fraternal twins; a boy and a girl, conceived at the same time, but from separately fertilized ova. We don't look alike either."

Tamubu was listening, but he was suddenly in the midst of remembering another set of twins, little girls, pink and sweet, about five years old. Unbidden, a series of pictures had come into his mind and he knew, instinctively, they were his sisters. When the reverie passed, he felt very sad, for he realized he had missed watching them grow up. He again heard the voice calling him, as it did in his dreams. He now knew it was his little brother Jon calling him, and he had missed his growing up too.

Paula sensed that his attention was elsewhere and took up her diary to plan another lesson. The afternoon soon turned to evening, occupied as they were with teaching and learning. Tamubu's formal education may have stopped when he was ten, but his innate education was vast and Paula was intrigued by it.

THE NEXT MORNING WAS damp and misty, but the hot African sun soon cleared the day. Tamubu mixed the plantain with ground-up nuts, coconut and boiled mashed taro and rolled the mix in pieces of chard for breakfast. Paula's metal bottle was filled with hot water, waiting for a tea bag. When she stirred, he said, "Good morning, did you sleep well?"

Paula knuckled her eyes open and stretched. "Yes, I did. I have not slept so well in weeks and I'm sure I have you to thank for it. I am so pleased that you have agreed to travel with me. It has banished my anxieties." Paula smiled to herself, then at Tamubu, "banished: sent away; anxieties: worries and fears."

Tamubu smiled back with an impish grin. "I see we start our lessons early today." In their short time together, they had found an affinity in their perception of humor by implication, and enjoyed bantering with one another.

Paula left for the morning ritual, and when she returned Tamubu was gone. He was proving to be very considerate. He had left warm water for her toilette, and something that smelled like muffins baking. I think I am getting the better part of this trade. "Thank you, God, for bringing Tamubu into my life." She said. "Please help me to help him too."

Paula had her things packed and was sipping her tea when Tamubu returned. They shared the roll-ups, which tasted like they smelled, like fruit and nut muffins. Paula was quick to compliment him. "I don't know what you do for a living (job), but you would make a great chef (chief cook)."

Their eyes met and the silliness of her sentence made them both laugh. "Am I clarifying (making clear, explaining) too much?"

At this, they both got the giggles, and the giggles progressed to amused laughter.

"No, it is good. Funny, but exactly what I need. On this rough trail I found for us, we will be far from the lions, but out in the full sun later today and tomorrow. Will that be a problem for you?"

"Not at all, I'm ready to go."

Tamubu doused the fire but left the pallets. They would make good fire materials for someone else, although it was unlikely that the Ndezi would come this way or discover their camp on the ledge. The rain had completely wiped out their tracks.

Tamubu took the lead. From years of traveling with Manutu, he had a ground-eating stride. Paula was, at first, a little pressed to keep up, but she soon found the rhythm of his stride, and stayed close to take advantage of his use of his spear to move the thorn bushes aside. Later, she acquired a nice walking stick for herself, but still she stayed close; she liked it that way. Tamubu stopped often for sips of water and brief rests. He was watching her closely for fatigue, but soon saw she was strong and faring well.

At mid-day, they finished the roll-ups and ate some of the other quail, while sitting atop a boulder in the dappled shade of a wild fig tree. They discussed the trail. Actually it was only a track, and sometimes not even that. He mentioned the likelihood of encountering poisonous snakes and spiders. Knowing the habitats of these venomous critters was the ounce of prevention needed. Other than the stops, they hiked in companionable silence.

It was odd, but she hadn't thought about critters at all when she was traveling with the Ndezi. Looking back, she realized she had been in the depths of despair and didn't even realize it. She, herself, had totally believed the façade she had acted out for her captors

A cooling updraft breeze riffled her hair. Paula wedged her pack between a large stone and the trunk of an olive tree, and used her jacket as a seat cushion preparing for a nap with a view. In equatorial Africa, mid-day naps are a way of life; for Paula, they were a necessity.

The thorn bushes of the morning had given way to jumbled rocks and boulders by lunchtime. In mid-afternoon the trail became a rocky ridge of loose scree, with the flanking valleys covered in a forest of ebony, podocarpus, African tulip and aligna trees as well as the oak-like bubing tree. Many of the ebony and bubing trees were covered with the dense green tufts of the parasitic black green oranthus, with its showy clusters of draping lipstick red tubular flowers. Intermingled and framing the oranthus were shyer flowering vines with pink or white blooms. Under the trees was a thick cover of agauria, laurel-like shrubs with bright apple green leaves, tall tree ferns and aloes with lofty spikes of creamy white flowers. In the distance, Paula saw a wall of steep cliffs.

She was getting used to Tamubu wandering off to gather foodstuffs when the way of the trail was obvious.

She was lost in the intense beauty of the scenery when she heard the shrill cry of an eagle. Looking up she saw the magnificent bird soaring over the valley. This would be a good area for nesting with its lofty podocarpus trees. Scanning the sides of the ridge, she saw a towering tree that had broken off near the top–probably struck by lightning. Attached to the uppermost branches was a huge nest. Paula watched in fascination as the eagle circled nearer to the nest. The bird had a dead animal of some kind in its talons. Two little heads appeared, as the parent landed on the rim of the nest, and began to tear the meal into bite size pieces for the gaping little beaks. With each morsel fed, the eagle turned to look at her. Paula decided to wait quietly, until the bird had gone off to hunt again.

She looked around for Tamubu, but did not see him. She called softly to him but he did not reply. No matter, she had a front row seat for one of nature's marvelous spectacles. The bird was not as large as the American Bald Eagle, and mostly brown with a tall, curved crest. In flight, Paula had seen mainly white under-wings with a white tail tipped in black. It seemed only a short while before the eagle hopped to a high exposed branch where it perched, with a long stare in her direction. Paula moved not a muscle, realizing the eagle was worried by her presence so near to its nest. Actually, she was not near it at all, unless she could fly like an eagle.

Suddenly the bird swooped into the air crying out with a series of high-pitched whistles and circled the ridge, swooping lower. Now would be a good time to move away, letting the bird think that its aggressive circling was scaring her off.

She put on her pack and her homemade French Legion cap when she heard a soft voice saying, "Do not stand up straight. Bend over as you move through the grass. The eagle will think he has frightened you away."

"Where are you?"

"I am here, do not worry about me. I will join you as soon as the crested eagle feels safe again."

For the next mile, the eagle made threatening circles with harsh, piercing whistles and low swoops, which forced her to fall flat on the ground, until she reached a long narrow swale filled with the herb sansevieria. At the edge of a tiny pool below a mossy rock spring, Tamubu sat resting.

"How did you get here before me?"

"I did not have to move all bent over as you did. The eagle didn't see me."

Once the eagle had gone off to hunt, they continued on the widening ridge until it joined the grassy plateau, where an oak-like bubing tree gave them some shade for lunch and a nap.

"Those cliffs, beyond the savanna, are our goal for today. It will take us to dusk to reach them. It will be necessary to rest and drink often, while we are in the open and exposed to the sun."

At a late afternoon stop Paula noticed that Tamubu had many scrapes and scratches from the saw-tooth grasses on his feet, ankles and lower legs, for his sandals gave little protection.

"You must sit here a moment and let me tend your cuts. I have an ointment that will heal them quickly and keep them from becoming infected." Her first-aid kit had its own pouch on the outside of her backpack, and in a moment she was swabbing the sores with peroxide before applying the salve.

"Now what you need is protection." Taking out a pair of her thick hiking knee socks, she insisted he put them on. His sandals fit snugly over the socks, but Paula was not convinced they were secure, and produced two long, nylon strings with which she stabilized the sandals, Roman fashion, lacing his legs up to his knees. Tamubu was quite surprised by her authoritative manner, and permitted her to tend his cuts and bind his calves, as he would have allowed Nanoka or Manutu. It seemed the natural thing to do.

"Asante," he said. "Already the cuts feel better. This grass is rough edged and cuts flesh easily. Your leg coverings give you good protection."

"They are called half-chaps. We can make a pair for you if we find some soft leather."

Tamubu walked on thinking, this woman is a never-ending surprise. She makes me feel glad. Further on, they came across a stand of wild oats where Tamubu showed Paula how to harvest the grain.

It was after six when they approached the base of the cliffs. Tamubu led Paula so they arrived at the best camping spot by accident. It was an open ledge that could only be reached only by climbing, rock face style. It was about thirty feet above the plateau. After she changed to her soft shoes, Paula climbed up to the ledge as Tamubu watched, totally amazed. She was like a fly! Were all white women so incredible? He then remembered the white woman of his dreams who made the horse dance—maybe so.

Using the grass bag he had woven for Paula, he filled it with small sticks and dried grass for a fire. He made a fagot of branches to be broken down as needed for the fire, and cut a fagot of pampas grass for bedding. In the tall matted clumps he found freshly laid francolin eggs and, nearby, a few sprigs of allspice and some wild shallots. These he tucked into his food sack.

"Be careful with the food sack," he called, "I found some eggs for breakfast." Paula hoisted all his gear, sacks, weapons and fagot bundles to the ledge by line and grapnel.

Paula instructed Tamubu to remove his stiff-soled sandals and climb in his stocking feet. She gave him the waterproof canvas covers used for storing her shoes in the backpack, to wear as booties, which fastened at his ankles with nylon strings. Tamubu then tied a line around his chest for the climb while Paula belayed the other end around a conical rock for safety. While the cliff was sheer, it diminished inward on the rise and up close there were enough handholds and toeholds to make the climb much easier than it looked. To Tamubu, it looked utterly impossible and to that end, he fortified himself with a pinch of his *roaming* herbs, for an out-of-body feeling.

The camping ledge was about ten feet wide and maybe twelve feet long in the widest area with narrow tapering edges on both sides. It was backed up by another forty feet of sheer cliff face, and was completely open to the sky. It was a wondrous safe haven from critters below, or above.

Without a word, they set about their tasks. Paula swept the loose debris from the area with a dead branch, destined eventually for the fire, before she arranged their pampas grass pallets. Tamubu gathered some small stones for a hearth before he started the fire. This way he could control the draft and rate of burn. Getting more firewood in the dark of night was out of the question. In no time at all they were settled in with the metal bottle heating water for the mandatory cup of tea.

Tamubu said to Paula, "You were telling me about your family last evening. I hope you will continue tonight. I have only brief memories of my family until I was ten. But I remember more about them while listening to you. The things you say often bring back forgotten memories."

In a natural way, like a man whittling on a stick, Tamubu organized, assembled and prepared the evening meal. Paula was absorbed watching him work, and after a few moments he primed the pump saying, "I have twin sisters. They were five when I last saw them. They looked so much alike, I couldn't tell them apart except by their personalities. Are you and your brother similar at all?

"We have similar characteristics: our eyes, hair color, smiles, and body builds are the same, as they would be for any brother or sister, but he is taller."

"Does he like to do the same things you like to do?"

"Eric and I both love animals. But Eric was completely fascinated by sick animals. He was always mending the wing of a bird, or the ear of a cat, or a scratch on a horse or the paw of a dog."

"Maybe your brother is not alone in liking to tend cuts on paws."

Paula glanced at his face as he worked. He had an impish smile with a twinkle in his eyes and a boyish tilt to his head.

She giggled at the irony. "Yes, you could be right. I was often his helper when he was tending to his wounded patients.

When we were in college, Eric went to work as an assistant (helper) to the local Veterinarian (a doctor for animals) during the summers and holidays. I stayed at home, rode horses and dried flowers for my sister and her friends.

"Eric and I had both taken gymnastics (using the body to leap, tumble and turn) as children and later we learned horse vaulting (leaping on and off moving horses) together. We worked as a team and had quite a good act going as part of a drill team, (horses and riders all doing the same thing at the same time) until Dr. Peters offered him a job as veterinary assistant.

"I stopped horse vaulting; it wasn't the same without Eric. I started pressing wildflowers (drying plants and placing them between pages of books) and herbs for a compendium (a summary), which I submitted it to the Natural Science Exposition and Fair in my junior (third) year of college. It took a third place and I was offered a grant (money to pay for school) to graduate (advanced) school, for biology (study of plants and animals) by Asher Pharmaceutical Company, known as APCO. So, Eric is studying to become a Vet (short name for an animal doctor) and I am working on my doctorate (advanced degree) for Biology."

"It would be easier for me, if you waited until I asked you about a word, before you explained it. The explanations mix-up what you are saying, and you say many interesting things.

"You mentioned an older sister. What does she do?"

"Sallee Anne is an artist. She is also a concert piano player, but gave it up because of the long tours. She plays locally but her passion now is painting, especially horses. Our whole family loves horses. My mother breeds and trains them for Dressage."

Tamubu leapt up. He just stood there looking at her with his mouth open. Hundreds of pictures passed in milliseconds before his eyes. Moments passed before he whirled and threw his hands in the air.

Startled by this display, Paula sat still and waited. After a bit, Tamubu sat back down and said, "I have had a dream for the past thirteen years of a woman riding a horse. She could make the horse trot without moving forward; turn leaping circles with his front legs while his back legs stayed in the same place; trot sideways or trot in slow motion. I think this woman is my mother."

Relieved that his actions were from surprise at the sudden return of old memories, Paula said, "Yes, those are Dressage or high school movements for horses. They require a well-trained and talented horse and rider combination. Do you have other memories of this woman, your mother?"

"Some. I see her tending to little girls with no faces. I see her in riding breeches giving lessons, possibly to me, or maybe my brother. I see her at the dining room table, directing the servants, and in the drawing room talking to faceless guests. I am remembering more of the man, my father. We did things together and he read to me at bedtime. I spent most of my time with a native companion, Kaizii, who taught me how to survive in the bush. Sometimes my younger brother went with us. If he didn't go along, I would always tell him what happened when I got home. We were quite close. I missed that with the Zuri Watu. I was kept apart from the other boys by my teacher, Manutu, who was the Medicine Chief of the tribe."

PAULA NOTICED THE HUGE improvement in his speech, especially when he spoke of the past. She realized the ten-year-old boy had been articulate for his age. She must keep him talking of his memories. It would be the best way to connect him to the present, for he would hear himself as he talked.

"WHAT THINGS DID YOU do with your father?"

"I would ride out with him for inspections on the tea farm. There were many decisions that had to be made daily: pruning, spraying, cultivating the soil, fertilization, planting new bushes, removing dead or diseased bushes and deciding when to harvest the tea leaves. Father kept up a constant explanation of the reasons for his decisions. I felt very important and rode out with him several times a week when I was not in school.

Sometimes we went to Nairobi for supplies. It was a long ride, the roads were terrible, mostly holes. The best part of the trip was visiting with friends to play croquet and badminton. I was also learning to play bridge, a card game. I liked it very much."

Paula said, "When you speak of your memories or your

past, your English is quite good. In a few more days, you won't need my help anymore."

"Asante." With a little smile, he tilted his head to the side, and continued, "If I won't need you... does that mean you won't need me?"

Paula raised an eyebrow at his wry smile, and replied, "In retrospect, I theorize that I have digressed by lauding your sophomoric phraseology."

Tamubu sat stunned, but only for a moment... before he broke into hearty laughter... the contagion of which, Paula could not escape.

When he could speak without laughing, he said, "A deal is a deal... I cook and protect until you are back at your yacht... no matter how verbose I get."

Now, it was Paula's turn to be surprised... and it was long moments before they could speak without giggling.

"Why did you remember the word, verbose?" she asked.

"It was our parent's way of saying they didn't care for someone... 'Mr. J. is so verbose about his garden.' or 'The Smiths are too verbose about their children.' Jon and I used that word for everything; verbose rooster; verbose dog; and sometimes... verbose parents!"

They laughed again until their sides ached; it was a good feeling.

TAMUBU'S FORMER LIFE WAS coming back to him in whole chunks. Some word of hers or a certain mention of her family... and suddenly a large piece would fall into place. He'd had no friends for the last fourteen years, Manutu had often said, "It is not your destiny to have friends here, just family. One day you will understand my meaning." Was this his destiny? Was Paula his meaning? He did not know the future, but in the present, he had never felt happier inside.

TAMUBU HAD NO FEELINGS of inferiority, but his memories of the class distinctions at home made him concerned about his acceptance. Paula's praise and encouragement were a balm for his apprehensions. Her actions and manner with him also gave him confidence. She treated him as an equal in all ways.

"Now, you must tell me about your parents." he said.

"My father is a college professor. He teaches engineering. He likes to invent things too. He made this emergency belt I am wearing."

"What do you do with it?"

Paula looked around. She only had fifty feet of wire, so she attached thirty feet of the nylon line too–that should be enough. Stepping back, she started to swing the grapnel in a circle, letting the circle get larger with each turn before she let it fly. It missed the top by a good fifteen feet, but the grapnel opened as it bounced and the claws snagged on a narrow shelf. Tugging to make sure it would support her weight; Paula put her hands through the wrist loops and, stretching up high, put her foot against the face of the cliff. Hand up to hand she rose, pushing away from the cliff each time she raised a hand. After about twenty-five feet, she rappelled back to the ledge. Paula rippled the wire and popped the grappling hook free of the rocky shelf.

Tamubu was amazed and spoke with excitement. "I saw the rope and the metal fingers tied to your pack. I was hoping to see what you did with it. Now I know how you crossed those large spaces between trees. I could see you swing, but I could not see what you used to swing on. Is that how you made it over to the tree when simba was readying for an attack?"

"Yes."

"I am glad you were there in the tree, it was a close escape. Did your father invent other things?"

"He designed a net blanket for the bunks on our sailboat so his children wouldn't fall out in rough weather. I asked the yacht designer to include them on the yacht we brought to Africa; they saved my life. My father's inventions have saved my life twice since I came to Africa. I used the emergency belt grapnel and line to escape from the Ndezi prison."

"You would have been pleased to hear the words of the Ndezi trackers when they could find no trace of your escape.

They were sure they were dealing with a witch, and were glad to go back to the village."

"Their superstition was my only advantage. On the plains, we had to escape hunting lions by climbing a tree to a high ledge. I pretended to be terrified of heights. They almost had to carry me up the tree. I was even worse when we left the next day, clinging to the tree and refusing to let go. It might have been because of my pretended fear, that they did not consider the trees as an avenue for my escape."

Tamubu, impressed by her cleverness said, "In the nations of the Zuri Watu, you would be a goddess of nature, a Haliiki. People would come to you for advice, and wash your feet and kiss your hands. It would be considered an honor to cook your food, clean your home, wash your clothes and care for your possessions. If you disapproved of someone, the whole nation would avoid that person. Your words would be repeated by each man and woman, for you have been touched by the gods and made one of them."

Surprised by the solemnity and essence of his words, Paula replied. "What I have done is learned. Yes, it took years of training and practice, but you could do it too, unless you are afraid of heights."

Tamubu thought: Her training is like the training I received from Manutu, special, different, and it sets you apart from all else. "I am not afraid of heights. Are you afraid of spirits?" Tamubu was smiling with a paternal fondness for a special child. "I will have to be careful with you. You are very clever."

"Yes, I might become a spirit and disappear in a puff of smoke!" She teased.

Tamubu tilted his head to one side and looked deeply into her eyes. Their gazes locked. His eyes seemed to penetrate to her soul. For a long time she could not look away; she could only speak with her thoughts; she seemed to float; she felt empty and free; time was suspended. Without moving his lips Tamubu said, "Put on your jacket, it is getting cool. This fire is small—it does not warm us."

Obediently, Paula reached down for her jacket and put it

on, still unable to break eye contact. She was beginning to feel sleepy. Her eyelids were very heavy, but she couldn't close them and break the union of their spirits.

"Now close your eyes; sleep and forget. When you awaken, you will be warm."

Paula slept instantly, her chin dropped to her chest. Tamubu arose and gently lowered her to the pallet, covering her legs with the thin metallic blanket.

He was astonished, thinking: she is a spirit savant, like me. Manutu bade me drink from the cup three times without refilling it. It had always been empty, yet my thirst had been quenched, my mouth moistened. Paula was able to take her jacket and put it on, without rising, even though she had been sitting on it. She had been able to hear him tell her to do so even though he had not spoken aloud.

He had wondered earlier why she asked no questions, and why he did not have to give her directions. She just did everything as though she heard his thoughts. Sometimes, she answered his questions before he asked them. He felt as though they were one spirit moving in two bodies. In pleasing himself, he pleased her and vice-versa. He had no choice but to follow her. He had no choice but to offer to guide her. She was his destiny... and this pleased him.

14

Nighttime Visitor

IN THE MORNING, TAMUBU looked at Paula with an impish grin, saying, "A person should not ask a question that he does not want answered; but... how do we proceed from here?"

Paula smiled at his use of a recently explained word, and replied with humor, "There's no doubt about it... we go up!"

"I thought you might say that." Tamubu sighed.

"Last evening, when I demonstrated the grapnel, I saw that this cliff face is uneven and will provide good hand and toe holds for climbing. I will show you." Leaving her gear to be hoisted later, Paula hooked a few pitons on her belt with her special hammer. The folding grapnel had been restored to her survival belt and the nylon line hung on her hip.

Off to the side where the ledge narrowed, the face was most jagged. Paula climbed steadily. Up she went like a fly on a wall. Tamubu had never seen anything like it. He was filled with wonder. She clung to the rock like a lizard.

Reaching the summit, she called, "I can see the mountain ridge from here. It is across a sloping savanna of tall grass, low brush and shrubby trees. I can see a waterfall high up the mountainside, gushing into a valley filled with dense vegetation."

Paula lowered the line to bring the gear up; Tamubu called up, "Just one more bundle–my things. Leave them there and go on. I have found another way to reach the top, but it is longer. I will catch up to you soon."

Paula chuckled to herself. She had seen the chimney crevasse and knew it offered a second approach to the summit. At least there, he would be able to rest often; climbing cliff faces used different muscles, and it **was** a long climb for a novice.

She gathered her pack, left the things he usually carried beside a wild olive tree, and started up the grassy slope. It was a steeper climb than it looked. When the slope leveled out a bit, she decided to rest and wait for Tamubu atop a smooth boulder; wondering what had placed the boulder here by itself in the open savanna... too far south for a glacier, must have been from a volcanic eruption; the thought of a boulder this size being spewed from a volcano miles away gave her an insight to the awesome power of a volcanic eruption.

Time passed; she began to worry that something had happened to him, and the further she went, the further she might have to go back... if he did not show up soon. Paula found herself wishing that she had waited for him before going on—then laughed at herself. What is he? Your security blanket! Don't be silly, she chided herself... but still, being alone without him felt like a catastrophe. Yes, she thought ruefully, he is my security blanket... wherever could he be? A bird twittered behind her. Paula turned to see it and there he stood wearing his impish smile.

"How did you get in front of me?"

"I must have passed you when I circled around a thicket of thorn bushes, before I saw the smoke from your fire. Am I in time for tea?"

Irked by the distress he had caused her and his casual attitude, she retorted, "Yes, in time for tea, but late with lunch!"

Tamubu was surprised. His value had been reduced to lunch. From some- where deep inside him came a tickled laugh. He could not remember ever being treated with such disrespect. The tickle erupted and he laughed joyously.

Unable to withstand the joy of his humor, Paula laughed with him, and then said, "Let's stay together. If I had gone back looking for you, which I almost did, we might not have found each other again."

Tamubu noticed the stress lines around her eyes and mouth. She has been through a bad time, and I was thoughtless. How could she know that I always knew where she was and what was happening to her?

Contrite, he said, "You might not have been able to find me, but I would have found you. I agreed to take you back to your boat... until I do, your safety is my responsibility; so, when I am gone, do not worry about me."

After lunch, and a nap in the shade of Paula's staked poncho, they hiked steadily all afternoon. In the early evening they reached the trail that climbed towards the waterfall. It was the end of the gloaming when they arrived, but Paula recognized the place immediately. "This is the pond where I bathed and washed my clothes on the way to the Ndezi village. Could I bathe again, now?"

"Yes. I will start the fire. Stay near that stand of bamboo. Snakes may still be lurking around the rocks for warmth." The twilight dark gave Paula a feeling of privacy so she took her time with her toilette, before returning to the fire. They ate the rest of the guinea fowl, cold sweet potatoes mixed with wild berries and coconut, and the chard-like leaves cooked with wild onions, mushrooms and spices. It was a feast for which she was truly grateful, so she said, "I will clean up from the meal while you bathe. Then we can have a lesson."

"We must take some time at the noon rest for lessons. It is too dark now."

"I have another idea for lessons in the evenings." She smiled at him.

Tamubu left for his bath. He was accustomed to basin washing and scraping his face with soap and his knife every day, but loved bathing and did so, when the opportunity presented itself. Manutu had firm rules: hands were washed before cooking or eating and after eating or rituals. The whole body was washed as needed; but most of the Zuri Watu were not so particular. Bathing, by immersing the whole body, was unusual; basin bathing was the norm. When he returned, refreshed, he asked, "Now what is this idea you have for evening lessons?"

"I would like you to tell me the story of the Zuri Watu, and of your life with them. You speak of Manutu as your teacher.

What did he teach? And Nanoka told you stories; what stories did she tell you?"

Tamubu said, "I must give this some thought. The story of the Zuri Watu goes back for a long time. It is a long story."

"Well then, just tell me about your life after you got well... or about Manutu."

"Manutu was my life after I got well. Nanoka still cooked and made a bed for me, but I spent all my daylight hours and many evenings with Manutu."

"What did you do that required so much time?"

"Manutu was my teacher. He taught me the ways of the birds, insects and animals. He taught me all about the plants, grasses and trees. He taught me to see, to hear, to smell, to know and to understand all the living and growing things around me. He also taught me to heal, to comfort, and help our people. He taught me to cook and how to live off the land. He taught me the plants that help the body when it is sick or hurt. He taught me the stars, the moons, the rivers and the fish in them. He taught me the ways of other tribes and the talk of the drums. It took him twelve years to teach me these things."

Paula was impressed. His education was far more thorough than many an education received at the finest schools. "Who taught Manutu all these things?"

"Manutu is the Medicine Chief of the Great Nations of the Zuri Watu. Only the *chosen* can be taught the ways of the medicine chief. I was *chosen* when I was twelve. Manutu was *chosen* when he was ten by Agurra, who was then medicine chief."

"Are you the medicine chief of the Zuri Watu now?"

"No, Manutu is alive and well. He will be medicine chief until he dies or until he finds the work too difficult. He is often out all day and all night with the sick. He has helpers, but they are not taught the ways of healing."

"Will you follow Manutu when the time comes?"

"That is one of the reasons for my journey. I must make a decision whether or not to accept the honor. Manutu has been training his sons, Kenga and Benima, but he says, 'They are not *chosen* by the gods'."

"Were you *chosen* by the gods?"

"Yes; but I cannot speak of this to anyone but Manutu. Even Sashono, the Chief of the Great Nations of the Zuri Watu, would not ask me to speak of these things."

"I was going to ask you what you meant earlier when you said to me, 'You have been touched by the gods and made one of them'. Is it the same as being *chosen*?"

"Yes and no. Touched, means you are special, way above ordinary, gifted. *Chosen* means you have a destiny to fulfill. I cannot speak for your future, but I do know you are special."

"What will happen if you choose not to follow Manutu?"

"That is a serious question, one that cannot yet be answered. Manutu has found a girl who has been *chosen* by the gods; but it is a difficult life for a woman, a lonely life–for she would have to remain a maiden always. He is training her as a helper now. Manutu is always looking for children who have been *chosen* by the gods, for children learn best. Once, for a long time, he trained a boy from another tribe. Manutu said he was the most gifted pupil, after me; but, the boy was called home before his training was finished. The boy's mother could not bear the separation, and had become ill from her grief. Some children who are *chosen* do not thrive on the long years of training, or being set apart from the villagers. Those that come from other tribes, often find the separation from family and friends a severe hardship, and the isolation unbearable."

"Does it always take twelve years?"

"No, most of the time, it takes a lifetime."

"I don't understand."

"Nor do I... but the learning never stops."

INTO THE ALMOST QUIET night air, there came a great thrashing and splashing noise from the pond. Tamubu leapt up and raced towards the noise. In a few minutes he returned holding out a large snapping turtle. "This fellow will make many good meals for us, some delicious soup, and provide a good cooking pot."

"How did you catch it?"

"I set a snare. When I bathed I saw the pointed V pieces missing on the leaves by the water, and used a wing-end from the guinea fowl as bait. I tied it to a stem of bamboo, and in front of the bait, I made a loop the turtle would have to stick his head through to grab the bait. When he grabbed the bait and moved back, he pulled the loop tight around his neck. Sometimes, if the turtles don't struggle, they get loose."

"Now I understand what you meant, when you said, 'to see, to know, to prepare'."

Tamubu was delighted by her observation. Only on the days that he had managed to surprise Manutu with his ability and the application of his lessons was he so secretly pleased. He did not question his feeling of pleasure, but accepted it, as he had with Manutu.

Paula, on the other hand, was taken aback and completely intrigued by their mutual awareness and rapport. It had only been a little over three days and she felt closer and more connected to this man that she did to her own family.

Tamubu set about breaking the turtle out of his shell. It was a process that Paula had never seen before and found repugnant. She walked away and began to gather the greenery for their pallet beds; using Bolbonga's razor sharp knife to strip the leaf fronds from the bamboo stems to cushion the large thick leaves she cut from the rubber plants. She banged the leaves against a tree trunk to rid them of bugs, before carrying the bedding to the narrow crevice behind the fire.

Tonight, they would sleep on the ground. By the time she was satisfied with her work, Tamubu had strips of turtle meat draped on a spit over the fire to cure. He used green coconut husks filled with wet oak leaves to make a smoky fire. The downdraft of cool air from the mountains carried the smoke away from the makeshift beds.

"We should keep watch tonight. I'll take the first watch. You get some sleep." Paula was tired, but felt like talking; so Tamubu made broth, for Paula was low on teabags. When the broth was gone, she felt sleepy and crawled into the narrow crevice, where she covered herself with the metallic blanket.

It had been a long and challenging day—emotionally tiring; her sleep was deep.

A LOUD AND CLOSE feral rasping cough shocked Paula out of her deep slumber. She knew that sound! She was seized by terror. Her heart hammered so hard, her breath caught in her throat. She looked, but saw only the smoky fire. Tamubu was gone. She reached, in slow motion, for her pistol. She felt a desperate urge to get to her feet, but was too petrified to move. Drawing on her desperate need, she softened her gaze to see beyond the smoky fire. There she saw a huge sleek and shiny black form move with stealth against the grayish black of the night; then two large, glittering, yellow orbs suspended in the dense black. Abject terror held her immovable; panic filled her mind, while shock froze her motionless.

A harsh terrorizing snarl and threatening hiss shattered the night. The beast was so very close, much, much, much too close. Under the cover of the metallic blanket, Paula withdrew her pistol. Her hand quivered so, that she couldn't look down the barrel. It was impossible to keep the black on black focused through the smoke, while looking for the wobbly sight. It seemed the long black shape was moving back and forth as would a caged animal. A lifetime later, the throaty growl moved off toward the pond. Stricken feeble in her bed, Paula waited: she had begun to hope the black leopard was gone, when the huge black form came back to the smoky fire, growling fiercely. After what seemed like forever, the flickering yellow eyes turned away and the deeper blackness became just a deep gray. Hopefully, the beast had gone back into the forest. A bit later, in the distance, she heard the agitated screams of a leopard. Was it another leopard? Or was it the one who had come to the fire?

She lay for a long time, unmoving, except for the jitters. Eventually her heart stopped hammering, her vision cleared, and she was able to draw a deep breath again, yet she still trembled. An hour must have passed before she saw Tamubu approach. He sat at the fire as if he was pulling a chair up to a dining room table.

"Is he gone?" she whispered.

"Yes, chuima is gone. She was a marvelous beast, wasn't she?"

"I wouldn't know! I was laying here saying my last prayers, while you were safe, high in that tree!"

Tamubu couldn't help smiling, even though he knew it would annoy her. "You were quite safe too; maybe safer than me."

"I'm quite sure you will explain that illogical (not sane) reasoning to me."

"Chuima could not see you with the firelight reflecting off your blanket. She could not smell you because of the dense smoke of the fire. Only if you had moved, would you have given yourself away. You had your pistol. You were not defenseless. I knew you would do the right thing and stay still. I had taken the meat and foodstuffs and climbed high into the tree. Chuima could have followed me. She is quite at home in the trees. It is what I expected her to do. I think she must have already fed this night. She seemed mostly annoyed at the presence of the fire at her watering spot. I left the food net hanging high in the tree, but I will put the turtle meat back on the spit to cure. You can keep your watch from your bed unless you think you might fall back to sleep again."

"Not hardly! I may never sleep again!" Tamubu chuckled, but in his heart he was aware of her bravery. Chuima had not been a tall man's length away from her. Seasoned hunters could not have been more fearless.

Paula could not believe he was actually going to go to sleep. He had wrapped himself in his cloak and was now prone on the pallet she had prepared earlier. "Are you really going to sleep?"

"Yes, it will be light in a few hours. I am tired. If you like, you can sit up and put the shiny blanket around yourself. I put some wood for the fire by your pallet."

It took several long minutes before she got over her indignation. After all, she reasoned with herself, he had to sleep too. As he pointed out, she was armed. Why was she making a big deal of sitting here? Even with all the talking to herself, she could not dispel her fear of unexpected and deadly night visitors.

MORNING SUN COMES LATE to a camp on the western side of the mountains. With the chattering of the birds, Tamubu arose. In the twilight of the morning, he could see Paula was gone. Surprised, but not worried, he set about making their breakfast. He retrieved the food sack from the tree, and set off to the spring for fresh water.

He observed the spoor of the denizens who had come in the night for a drink: chuima had been huge, possibly pregnant and near her term. She had left deep marks in the soft ground by the water. He saw the tiny heart-shaped prints of the dik-dik, the smallest of the antelopes, no larger than a rabbit; there were duiker prints too, a larger antelope, the size of a medium dog and signs of the smaller carnivores: civet, genet and mongoose. Among the forest dwellers that had come for a drink, were the tree pangolin, and the potto, a small primate with three digits opposing the thumb, a little fellow the size of a housecat. It had been a busy night at the pond, but chuima had been the only large carnivore last night.

PAULA WAS PERCHED IN a young African tulip tree, on the other side of the pond. She had been there since Tamubu went to sleep. She could see him from her perch, but her jangled nerves wouldn't allow her to sit, exposed, next to the fire. Seeing a lioness fifty or sixty feet down the trail was much different from seeing a leopard less than eight feet away with no means of escape. Just thinking about the incident made her heart pound.

Paula watched Tamubu go about his morning chores. She started to forgive him for being so casual about her encounter last night; but each time she forgave him, she also blamed him. It was the most terrifying thing that had ever happened to her.

But the indignation and confusion faded away when he looked up from the fire, and smiled at her saying: "You were so brave last night that I have made a special breakfast for you: oatmeal, fresh fruit and coffee."

"Coffee, where did you get coffee?"

"I found some bushes at the edge of the cliffs. It was one of the reasons it took me so long to catch up to you yesterday. I roasted them last night, after I roasted the oats we had gathered on the savanna. Do you like oatmeal?"

Contrition for her mean thoughts enveloped her. "Yes, oatmeal is my favorite breakfast." Never again would she disparage his decisions about wildlife on the trail. He had already put his life in danger for her. She must trust him to make the right decisions, as she had trusted no other near stranger before.

SHE LEFT THE TREE and joined him for breakfast, where he regaled her with stories of the various nighttime visitors to the water. He described each animal, its footprint, diet, and habitat. He also shared his theory that chuima had been pregnant and near her time.

Hearing this, tears welled up in Paula's eyes and she began to cry.

Tamubu was chagrined: what had he said? "Did I say something to upset you?"

"What if, in my terror, I had shot her? I would have been devastated by remorse; since, as you pointed out so succinctly, I was not in any real danger. The only reason I didn't shoot was because I couldn't get a clear shot with the smoke from the fire... and my wobbling hand."

Now it was Tamubu's turn to feel regret. He had lived in Africa for as long as he remembered. She had only been here a few weeks. He knew the ways of the big carnivores and she did not. He had been callous last night. And he, too, would have been filled with sorrow if she had shot the black leopard, for they were a rare species. "I expected too much from you; I ask you to forgive me for my heartless attitude."

"I know now, that you made your decision based on your past experience; but I have no experience, and I was scared witless."

They finished morning chores in silence and were ready to leave when Tamubu said, "Since you are familiar with this part of the trail, why don't you lead the way?"

"I would like that, thanks." Paula remembered well, the narrow eroded trail they had traveled down the side of the mountain. In some places the trail disappeared from water run-off and the wide, deep gashes had to be leapt. A few required the use of the grapnel, as the gaps were too wide, going sharply uphill, to leap in safety. By noon, they had attained the path leading to the ridge. It was a wide path, because the stony surface had little soil to support plant life, but here and there, a depression boasted an acacia or olive tree or the bright green agauria.

"The mud hut is just ahead near those saplings." Paula said. "It is a good place to stop for lunch. The view out over the valley is magnificent."

Paula was astonished as Tamubu produced onions, parsnips, carrots and beans, a foot long, from his food sack to make a snapper stew. "Where did you find all those vegetables?"

"If you know where to look, the savanna is a big garden."

This afternoon, she needed to rest while Tamubu made the stew in his versatile turtle shell. Closing her eyes, Paula felt humbled and dependent, for the first time in her life. This man was a miracle and her savior: turtle stew, fresh oatmeal, coffee, roasted francolin with sweet potatoes, and I was going hungry! Her short and stressful night caught up to her and she was soon asleep.

Tamubu had seen the signs of strain on Paula today. She was quiet and withdrawn with gray smudges under her eyes. To save her teabags, he had been making broth from powdered dried meat. He had given her a cup while she snacked on a francolin leg, a tangerine and some raw peanuts. He had added an herb to relax her and relieve the tension. She would feel much better after her nap.

Tamubu had a strange feeling, as he watched Paula sleep. He desired to be with this woman, to protect her, and always be in her company. When he awakened this morning to find her gone, he had been sharply disappointed. He blamed himself for allowing her to sleep on the ground. They had arrived too late for him to see that chuima came regularly to the water. Even so, he was remiss as the habitat was ideal for chuima. Why had he not taken his usual precautions? Had he been too interested in Paula, and overly caught-up in their conversation? He enjoyed talking to her as much as he liked talking to Manutu, who had told him often, "... it only takes one unguarded or careless moment to die." Chuima had been a warning.

The heat of the day caused an updraft on the mountain slope, and provided a cooling breeze beside the hut. They were several thousand feet closer to the sun on the ridge, which made the traveling hot and exhausting. Tamubu thought: here we have the safety of a hut for sleeping; here we will stay until the morning. So it was that her snack became lunch, for Paula slept until the twilight deepened.

15

The Jagas – Shawna

THE MUD HUT USED by the Ndezi on their travels had been constructed in an open space between two large boulders at the edge of the cliff. The boulders formed an L above the ravine, and the hut was concealed in this protected space. A thorn boma atop the boulders protected the roof and another boma closed the entry space from boulder to ravine. The rock-lined fire-pit, which was the congregating area, was built in the large open space fronting the hut over by the cliff. The opening to the hut itself was at an oblique angle to the fire-pit to prevent smoke from entering it. In all, it was a cozy nest, a safe and defensible resting place.

WHEN THE TURTLE STEW bubbled, Tamubu put his shell-pot to one side, covered it with a leaf to let it simmer, and left the campsite. In a hidden niche between large rocks and trees, he followed the rites for *spirit travel*, leaving his possessions safely hidden to *roam*. He followed the elusive animal trails through the woods, until he came upon a spring of fresh water. Later he found banana plants, date palms, cassava and ripe blackberries. Once Tamubu was satisfied that there were no marauders in the area, he returned and gathered the food he had found, taking a goatskin water bag to carry the water.

Paula was still asleep when Tamubu returned to the hut. His seat at the fire-pit was in profile to her, so he did not notice when she awakened. She watched drowsily as Tamubu prepared the foods he had gathered. The meals he made on the trail were remarkable–delicious and varied.

As she watched him surreptitiously, she began to see him

not as her savior, but as a man, a very attractive man, entirely different from any man she had ever known. There was an air of mystery and intrigue about him. This was the first time Paula had seen him without his cloak, which he now had folded under him, so he was naked except for his loincloth. She could see his strong broad shoulders, his deep chest and firm, muscular arms. She already knew he had beautiful long fingers on sculpted hands. His back was smoothly muscled tapering all the way to his waist. He was a big man, tall but lean, with defined thigh muscles like the legs of a runner. She had seen his shapely calves, when she tended to his cuts and scrapes. All in all, he was a handsome man and Paula wondered why she hadn't appreciated his sensuous masculine appeal sooner.

She felt very fortunate that she had met this remarkable man—with his unassuming competence and subtle good humor.

"I CAN'T IMAGINE WHAT I'd be eating... or if I'd be eating at all, without you." Paula spoke softly. "How can I ever repay my debt to you? You have been a paragon among men to me."

"I see it is lesson time; what is paragon?"

"It is a model of perfection or excellence."

Tamubu was keenly aware of her need for his knowledge and skills to stay alive; but he was surprised to hear her say so, in such flattering terms. He had been pleased to see her self-confidence return after the encounter with the lions, and enjoyed her vigor after the day of rest on the ledge. Facing the black leopard had set her back. Only now did he realize how much of an ordeal it must have been for her. She needed rest. The long days of extreme exertion in the heat and the confrontations with the big cats had depleted her reserves. "You only say that because it is true."

Paula was dumbfounded by his egotistical reply. After a surprised pause, she broke out in a startled, yet amused laugh.

"You are right; I only say it because it is true."

Paula returned his smile.

Tamubu said, "Lunch... well early dinner is ready. Are you hungry?"

"I am always hungry when you're the cook."

The turtle stew was ambrosia, like snapper soup with vegetables. The banana oat muffins were light and fluffy. The papaya and blackberry fruit cup with slivered coconut was incredible. Just-picked fruit had a sweetness and texture all its own.

Over broth, Paula remarked, "You prepare better meals over a wilderness campfire, than I ever made in a modern kitchen."

Tamubu smiled at her earnestness. "Asante. It is pleasant to cook for someone who enjoys your food." Tamubu felt the high level of mental communication arising between them again and said, "Do you believe in fate; that events happen because it is your destiny?" Paula cocked her head to one side. "I don't know; I never thought about it. Do you mean that we are not in control of our actions; that we are but pieces of a game moved about by a higher power?"

Tamubu smiled, "No; more like the choices we make, mostly without forethought, will lead us down different trails. If we choose one trail, we will encounter lions, and possibly death. If we choose the other trail, we may encounter an injured person needing help, who would have died had we not come along."

"When you put it like that, yes, I believe in fate. But I never thought of it as 'choosing my destiny'."

"You choose, because of your destiny. If you had chosen the less traveled path, when you were escaping the Ndezi, you would have come out on the savannah, where you knew the trail–a long way from the lion's dens. By choosing the wider, more frequented animal trail, you came out in the heart of lion territory, which eventually made it necessary for me to show myself to you.

"On my part, if I had not been attracted by the erratic behavior of the birds; if I had not climbed that oak tree for a better look; if I had just gone on my way; I would never have seen you enter the clearing and hide in the kamikiza. It was such an unusual thing for someone to do that my curiosity was aroused. I chose to stay, to see what else would happen. And in so doing, I followed my destiny in a way that I could never have expected. The behavior of the birds guided me to my destiny. Once there I had to choose: either I followed you or I went my way. Do you remember why you chose the more traveled trail?"

His perspective about destiny fascinated Paula. She had always just dashed along in life doing things because she wanted to do them, never once thinking that she was making choices of one destiny over another.

"I followed the wide trail, because I could see it from the trees. I did not know it was the wrong trail."

"Because your destiny was not to travel back to your boat alone; had you seen and chosen the narrow trail, you would have found the path south to the mountains. There I would have left you, and gone on my way across the plains towards the east. Now it is these choices... you chose the wrong path... I chose to follow you... that I call fate, which leads a person to his destiny.

"Our fates combined to have us here together. You needed me and I needed you, although I did not know it. You have wondered what you would be eating, or if you would be eating at all...

"Well, since we met, I have seen how embarrassed I would have been, if I had gone back to my people in a man's body with the attitude and social skills of a ten-year-old schoolboy. While my native learning is vast, it would not have helped me cope with the world of an Englishman. I would have felt ignorant and inferior with my limited understanding and my wrong English.

"Talking to you, for some reason, has not made me feel self conscious– only determined to learn. You have brought back many long buried memories–memories I need to know again to understand my family; feelings I need to remember to help me cope with the changes; attitudes I need to experience and understand, so I will not feel offended. I could not do these things without your help.

"The interaction between man and woman in the English world is vastly different from the tribal world. You say you can never repay me. I think it is I, who can never repay you. I will give you food and safety for a week or more. Your tutoring will give me the confidence to claim my heritage, for I am the first-born son. It will bring me acceptance for a life time."

Paula was deeply touched by his words and felt privileged to know this ethical man. Contemplating his words, she gazed out over the top of the forest at the last of the magical African twilight. A soft feeling of relaxation was borne on the breeze. The varied calls and whistles of the birds, and the dimly heard voices of the forest denizens, made a pleasing and melodic noise. Combined with the chiaroscuro in the color resplendent valley, it made Africa a wondrous place. A place set apart from the rest of the world, in beauty and in danger, with each one enhancing the other.

"Did you put something in my food to take away my nervous feelings? I was on edge all day. My nerves were jangled and I felt tense. But, I feel good now, relaxed and at ease... did you?"

"Yes, I did. You once asked me if I knew plants that gave relief from anxieties, and I did not answer. I did not know you well enough then to discuss my knowledge with you; so much has changed in the past four days."

"Was it part of your training with Manutu?"

"Yes. To be a medicine man, you must know these things."

"Would you share your knowledge with me?"

"It takes a long time to learn. I have no English names for the plants."

"If we come across a plant, would you point it out to me?"

"Yes, I could do that; but we may not see anything. Plants change in different places."

Paula knew that quite well from collecting wildflowers and herbs for her compendium, but she had a sudden inspiration. "Since you're an artist, could you draw the plants from memory?"

Tamubu's eyes widened and his face took on a look of utter

astonishment. "Yes... I could do that; I never thought about drawing. I would like that! The Zuri Watu do not write; there are no writing tools."

Seeing her surprise, he said, "With the people of the Zuri Watu all is memory, nothing is written. Everyone has a good memory. Messages must be remembered and repeated word for word. Stories are told and must be retold word for word. To change a message or a story is to be shamed. It is better to say nothing than to say it incorrectly. But with the plants, to remember incorrectly can mean death. It is a serious responsibility. A book to use as a guide would be an excellent tool."

Paula was elated. Tamubu was absorbing vocabulary and substance by leaps and bounds. His memory, and his ability to remember and use new words, was a constant surprise to her.

"Here, use my diary. You can draw the plant on one side, and write the description on the other." In the early evening twilight, Tamubu drew quickly. "This is the plant most used. It is the plant I gave you; the leaves are dried and crushed to a powder. It is called kimmea."

"Write where it is found, the time to harvest and the form needed for use. Write what it does, and the indications for its use and the symptoms it relieves." An hour later, Paula was looking at a drawing good enough to print, and a written description that looked like calligraphy... with no mistakes.

"This is simply marvelous. You are truly talented with your art. Could you do one or two each day? We don't have to worry about the English names for the plants just now. Whatever they are called in Bantu or Swahili will be fine."

"Yes, I will enjoy doing this; I like to draw. The Zuri Watu culture was so different that I never even thought to draw in all the years I was with them."

Paula was ecstatic. Tamubu's drawings and plant descriptions were better than any findings that might be obtained by the Expedition with the random testing of plants.

The world of the Medicine Man was the world of a secret

society. They gained their power through knowledge others did not possess. No medicine man would share these secrets except with a protégé, usually a son. Her good fortune from encountering Tamubu seemed endless.

"Is it a breach of confidence to share the information about plants with me?"

"Yes and no. Yes, because only medicine men are supposed to discuss the healing and helping plants. No, because you are not competing for their power. Telling you about the plants will never affect the tribal medicine man. Not every medicine man knows about every plant. The knowledge of Manutu is much greater because he is Kuzimu Akili."

"What is Kuzimu Akili?"

"It is a person that is able to communicate with spirits or become a spirit himself. It is a person who can communicate with others by thought, and can influence others by thought."

"How would being a Kuzimu Akili give him greater knowledge about medicinal plants?"

"In all the world there is nothing new. What is here has always been here. It is only the uses of these things, the combination of these things that is new. There are many ancient, but lost secrets about things that were once done, which are unknown today. It is the ability to communicate with the spirits who know the lost secrets that makes Manutu so wise."

As TAMUBU SPOKE, PAULA entered a plane of thought she had never experienced before. It was as though she herself was a spirit, for she felt weightless. She could see emanations surrounding Tamubu, hovering; were they protecting him? Was he a Kuzimu Akili too?

Smiling at her with his impish grin, he answered her question without speaking. 'Yes, I am Kuzimu Akili, as apparently, so are you.'

Paula liked this dream; it was so unexpected and surreal. 'Why do you say I am a Kuzimu Akili too?'

'Because you are communicating with your thoughts, not your voice.'

'Is that why I can see the spirits hovering around you?'

'Describe the spirits you see around me.'

'I see heads that are mostly eyes and mouths with wispy emanations for bodies.'

'How many do you see?'

'It changes. When I first saw them, there were five, then three, now they are gone.'

Tamubu was truly astonished. Manutu had said to him long ago, that the spirits of love protected him. Manutu had also seen the wispy emanations, sometimes five, sometimes three. Tamubu had never seen them himself, but when he *roamed* as a spirit, he often felt as if he had company.

'You will sleep now', he told her, 'when you awaken, you will feel safe and untroubled. The spirits of love will watch over you too.'

TAMUBU WAS EXCITED. HERE was great, unexpected ability. Manutu had seen the spirits hovering over Tamubu when he was a boy, sick and in pain. Manutu had not seen them in a long time; he supposed that, once Tamubu was well, they no longer needed to watch over him. Yet, Paula had seen them tonight.

He was not in pain or sick. Yet they were there. Was her subliminal power greater than Manutu's? Each time he had given her the kimmea she had become mutable. Her esoteric mystique flamed. These latent intuitions were strong, so strong that he was drawn into the flow with her, without the use of psychotropic powders.

Yet he was the one who controlled the flow, like a medium in a séance. He wished he could take her back to Manutu now. Her psychic abilities would astound Manutu, as they had astonished him.

Gazing at the star-studded sky, Tamubu's thoughts moved into the nether regions of the infinite possibilities of their powers combined. His imagination wandered the limitless deserts of possibilities... until he slept.

OATMEAL WITH BLACKBERRIES, a banana, and vanilla-flavored coffee was breakfast. Tamubu wrapped the turtle stew in wild celery leaves. He had congealed it with oat powder to the consistency of chicken salad. It would be a good lunch. The next stretch of the trail was very narrow and steep on both sides, making escape from chance encounters impossible. They needed to keep moving through this stretch of rocky scree, hemmed in with man-high walls of an almost impenetrable growth of dock, a wild celery with tall, white feathery blossoms. It was an arduous trail that took concentration and care. Even so, they made good time all morning.

Paula, still in the lead, clambered out of a steep narrow ravine bisecting the ridge, and stood upright to see a huge anthropoid about fifty feet down the trail. He just stood there watching her. They were both so surprised to see one another that neither moved, until Tamubu emerged behind Paula.

Then the huge ape became furious and screamed his defiance. His eyes turned red, his fangs dripped froth and he bellowed terrifying shrieks of challenge. Seizing a chunk of dead wood he rushed forward, stopped, swung wildly at the vegetation, and then, with a bellowing roar, rushed for the kill. The other members of the pack came to see what the clamor was all about, arriving just as he made his rush to attack.

Paula had immediately drawn her pistol when the bull ape issued his threats, for there was no place to go. She had to stand and fight. The startled and enraged ape shrieked his challenge as he charged, swinging out with the club, destroying the vegetation on either side of the trail. Paula took aim and fired at the rocks at his feet, sending shards of rocky splinters toward his hairy legs.

Stunned by the colossal noise and the sudden, awful pain in his legs, the ape turned and fled. Seeing the pack fleeing before him, the horrible ape turned back, raised his club and slammed it against a rock, where it broke into kindling. The valleys filled and reverberated with the terrifying noise of the frustrated bull ape, an awful noise that filled Paula with terror.

The menacing ape stood defiant, barring the trail. Paula advanced slowly; when he charged again, she fired repeatedly at his feet, sending more shards of stone flying into his already bloody legs. It was too much noise and too much inexplicable pain. The gruesome ape turned, and screeching his rage followed his already fleeing pack into the dense undergrowth of the valley.

Tamubu had been behind her with spear poised the whole time and he said softly to her, "You were wonderful! That was the best way to handle his charge, to make him turn and flee. If you had killed him, the other bulls might have taken up the fight with a thirst for revenge."

"Black bears make a lot of awesome noise in their rush to attack. Most of them could be scared off by several loud blasts on my whistle. Unusual loud noises usually cause wild critters to run away. It is a built-in survival trait. But with that huge fellow, I certainly wasn't going to rely on my whistle!"

"I think we must wait to have lunch, and make great haste to get past this narrow part of the trail."

"I agree. What incredible noises and terrifying shrieks he made!"

"You are a very brave woman. The bravest I have ever known."

As Paula reloaded, she said, "You give me too much credit. It was a case of do or die... and I wasn't ready to die!"

For the next few hours, the trail angled mostly uphill. The narrow ridge and the deep wide gaps gave way to a wider, grassy terrain, strewn with large boulders and loose stones, which supported blackberry bushes and scraggly fig trees. The sun had passed its zenith into the west, and the slight tree cover was appreciated.

Tamubu had seen no *sign* of the apes after they had vanished down the hillsides.

They stopped for the mid-day meal in a crevice made by two huge boulders. While the usual rest was needed; it was a poor place to linger and a bad place to nap. They could rest later, where the mountain trail opened up, and the big boulders changed to rocky scree.

In silence and without warning, the huge bull ape leapt from behind a tall crag. He was mad with rage and pain and clutched another dead tree limb. In an instant he charged with incredible noise and insane shrieks. He was so close that Paula instinctively took a step back, and her foot slipped into a narrow crevice, causing her to fall. The ape, sensing the moment of victory, bellowed wild screams and raced to smash her to bits.

Paula had her pistol out and carefully aimed at the dead limb in the ape's upraised hand. The force of the bullet hitting the limb splintered the wood into flying slivers, like tiny arrows. The deafening noise and then the inexplicable pain in his hand, arm and chest, caused the ape to clutch at his hand and flee in absolute panic.

Paula looked up to see Tamubu again standing over her, with ready spear.

He said, "Are you hurt?"

"My foot is caught between these rocks."

Leaning down, Tamubu found her foot firmly wedged. She would have to take her foot out of the shoe before he could free it. Once her foot was out, Tamubu freed her boot, while Paula hopped to a rock to sit to put her boot on again. Standing up to walk, spikes of pain radiated from her ankle.

Tamubu seeing her falter said, "Have you been injured?"

"Yes, I think I may have twisted my ankle." Paula sat again and Tamubu stooped, removed the boot and gently examined her ankle. There were no broken bones, but there was an area of increased heat, with a slight swelling. He took some powder from his pouch, added a few drops of water to make a paste, and applied it to her ankle. Paula suggested he apply a bandage wrap from her first aid kit too. She then changed to her climbing sneakers. Tamubu mixed some green powder with water and gave it to Paula to drink.

"Now, can you put weight on it at all?" Paula arose, and holding onto his forearm stepped forward, but the ankle was too painful to support her weight.

Tamubu said, "You will ride upon my hips. I will put my dulband around your back and under your arms, and brace it against my forehead. You will use your leg muscles to hold yourself on my hips, and use your arms to support your legs to keep yourself balanced."

Paula did as she was told. She was so embarrassed by her injury that she fell mute. The African version of a piggy-back-ride was an improvement since she did not have to use her arms to hold on. Tamubu had to ask her to relax her inner thigh muscles a bit, for she held his hips so tightly, he couldn't stride out. Paula was impressed that his walk seemed unchanged while carrying her.

They soon developed a rhythm in their movements, which caused an unexpected sensual desire to build in Paula at the nearness of his strong, warm body. Surprised that she could be aroused by her dependency on his physical strength, she forced her attention back to keeping a lookout for the vengeful ape.

Tamubu was having trouble understanding his feelings of joy. He knew he should be sorry for her injury, but instead, he was happy to have her so close to him. Her breasts moved softly against his back and even through the layers of fabric, he could feel the soft brush of her pointed nipples. She was riding his hips like a horse, letting her buttocks rise and fall with his steps. It took all the mental energy he could muster to keep his thoughts focused on the trail.

Immersed in their erotic reveries, it seemed no time at all before they reached the broad, forested trail, which ended the narrow ridge of the mountain arm.

"This is not yet a good place to rest; there are still too many places for the ape to hide for an ambush. Nor will a thorn boma deter that ape should he want to attack again."

"Are you tiring? You have carried me a long way."

"No, I'm fine. You are quite easy to carry. I hardly know you're there."

"We stopped somewhere near here for a rest when I was with the Ndezi. I looked down the side of the mountain and saw a cave and ledge about fifty feet down. See... ahead, there is a good tree where you can boost me up to wait while you look for the place I saw. I know it is nearby. I remember this veronia. It reminded me of a dogwood tree in bloom."

Tamubu smiled to himself. A little loss of self-reliance was turning her into a chief giving orders. He said, "You are right. It will be easier to find a place to camp by myself. You can sit on that big branch and wait for me."

Once around the bend, Tamubu hid his things to *roam*. He found the jutting ledge Paula had seen, but getting to it was impossible. The thorny forest undergrowth was much too thick. He wanted to find a place on the eastern slope, for the morning slope was cooler, but nothing was suitable or attainable. He was about to travel into the forest looking for an animal track to lead him to water, when he saw a dark spot where there should have been light. Going closer, he found a large boulder sitting on a ledge, and behind it, exactly what he was looking for: a small shallow cave made by the over-hanging bluff. Below the ledge were the tops of the trees growing on the mountainside. To one side, where the ledge narrowed, there was a ragged fissure in the rock face, three feet wide, which ran up to the ridge.

Minutes later he returned to Paula. He gave his birdcall, which warned her of his approach, before he came into sight. A joyful smile lit up her face when she saw him. His chest tightened as he spontaneously returned her smile.

PLEASED WITH HIS FIND, Paula was soon arranging a bower with the tall, feathery plumes of the wild celery that Tamubu had cut and lowered to her. She had rappelled down the natural chimney shaft on one foot, and had sent the harness back for Tamubu to use later when he returned from scouting. On her hands and knees, Paula made a small fireplace, and had a fire heating the water for tea when he returned.

Tamubu *roamed* the whole area, finding a mountain spring, edible mushrooms and ferns and sweet potatoes. He had also backtracked on the trail until he saw the band of apes, making their way along the distant narrow ridge. The bloody bull ape brought up the rear. He must have lost his place as leader, for he had bloody bite marks on his arms and shoulders. Tamubu watched these unusual creatures, and saw them uncover a nest of snakes under a rock. With frenzied excitement, the bull clubbed the snakes to death. As the new leader, he took the biggest snake, and biting it in half, gave a portion to a female with an infant at her breast. The rest of the troop vied for the remains, with the injured bull getting nothing at all.

This was a prime habitat for nesting snakes. They would find more before long. This then, had been the cause of the vicious attack. It was their food supply they were protecting. He wondered if the Ndezi knew of these apes, and if that was the reason for the fortress-like hut they had used last night.

He donned his clothes, and went back to gather the foodstuffs he had found, and to fill the goatskin at the spring. Nearby was a fig tree, where the fruit had not been harvested on the upper branches. At the edge of a boggy area, he found cabbage. His grass-gathering bag was full to overflowing when he arrived back at the chimney crevice. Whistling softly, he lowered the bag to Paula before he lowered himself.

Tamubu had watched Paula carefully when she rappelled down to the ledge earlier; but doing it, for the first time, was the experience of a lifetime. He had no fear of heights, but he also had no trust in the thin wire on which he must rely, as he swung out and down. At first he made small pushes and short drops, but with each success he became bolder, and was starting to enjoy himself when, all too soon, he touched the ledge.

Paula had hopped over to unhook the grass gathering bag, and had stayed to watch his descent down the defile. He reminded her of her first attempt at rappelling. It seemed that starting off with small pushes, produced better results. She was impressed by his perfect control of himself doing an entirely new exercise. She didn't want him to think she was concerned about his descent, so she scuttled back to her bower, tugging the gathering bag with her.

The chimney crevice would also make a perfect place for a pressure climb, but that required two good ankles. Her ankle was only a bit swollen and, oddly enough, did not hurt unless she put weight on it.

Tamubu anchored the harness under a large rock, so it could not be raised from above. He sat by the fire to sort the contents of the gathering bag and asked. "How is your ankle?"

"Fine, it only hurts when I jump rope."

Chuckling, he opened his medicine pouch. "I should poultice it again to keep the swelling down, and stop the aching. Then, if you get your diary out, I will do a drawing for you while the light is still good."

Paula offered him a cup of tea. He took it and asked for her cup too. He took a bit of powder from a small pouch and dissolved it in the tea.

"What is that?"

"It is a mix of several things: barley grass, yucca stalk, arnica and other plants for which I do not know the English names. It helps to purify the blood, and relieves pain and swelling."

"Does it make you sleepy?"

"Possibly, but you will awake easily, feeling refreshed."

Paula dozed until the light was gone and dinner was ready. She looked at the exquisite pencil drawing he had done and admired the lovely script description. "Tonight, will you tell me a story about the Zuri Watu?"

"I was going to tell you a story about a strange band of apes living in the mountains. Would you like that?"

"Yes, I would, especially after today."

"I have never before seen the manner of ape we met today. The bull ape had a different shape to his head and unusual facial features, with the eyes not so deep, the nose not so flat, the mouth not so full and a long neck for an ape. He immediately reminded me of the many stories told in my village about a band of apes, more human in shape, less like gorillas, not as heavy, not as hairy, but taller and terribly fierce.

"They were called Jagas. They seemed to appear out of nowhere several hundred years ago, coming from Central Africa. The Zulus came from Central Africa too, the part known as the Dark Continent. Possibly this is also where the Jagas began. They migrated through the West African nations before they disappeared more than a hundred years ago. For a hundred years before that, the Jagas were the scourge of

West Africa. Then they vanished just as mysteriously as they had arrived.

"The Jagas were not farmers nor were they herders. Their only agricultural interest was the making of palm wine—to which they were addicted. This addiction concentrated their raiding to areas where there were thickets of palm trees. Early in their migration, they organized themselves into a search and destroy culture that lived in mobile, fortified camps... attacking by surprise with fierce discipline to conquer tribes much larger than their own. The Jagas were a warrior army on the march.

"Legend says they killed the newborn babies, burying them alive with the afterbirth, so as not to be hindered on their relentless march. The barbarous Jagas adopted the adolescents of the conquered tribes. They also practiced cannibalism, as much for the terror it instilled in the enemy, as for the taste of it.

"It is said that the excesses of the men, their drunkenness, their cruelty, their rape of the women, their enjoyment of torture and mutilation, was their downfall. When the army reached the ocean, the women made a death pact. On a dark night, the women and female children, one and all, walked into the surf until they were drowned.

"After that, the Jagas were never again able to surprise a village. The war machine would arrive, but the village would be deserted. They worked their way back into the mountains, but never again were they able to take women as captives.

"In the mountains they came across a band of apes. The Jagas slaughtered all the bulls and took the females for their pleasure. According to legend, it is the offspring of these unions that we saw today. The female apes were able to escape the slaughter of their babes by fleeing into the trees. When they escaped, they did not return, for some had felt the sick cruelty of their new masters. The men of the war machine aged, sickened and died. There was no one to continue the horrible pillaging. It is told that the men had a terrible disease from mating with the apes, which killed them all.

"The female apes raised the offspring of the Jagas. These offspring had to breed among themselves, for there were no bull apes left alive to dilute the Jaga genes.

"The vicious mutant apes we saw today are thought to be the descendents of the Jagas. It would explain their ferocity and war-like aggression."

"The End."

PAULA WAS SHOCKED BY the story. It was brutal and gruesome. "I hope we never meet up with them again. I'm glad I didn't know that story this morning. I might have shot to kill and enjoyed it."

"Yes, they were an awful lot. But we are well away from them and safe here."

"Was that a word-for-word story? Do the Zuri Watu have many stories like that?"

"No, I left out the bloody details ... and yes, a good many. Some are about great chiefs or great medicine men. Some are about the slave traders when the Nation lived near the coast. Some are about the migration to the mountains to escape the slave traders. Some are about bad children or good children. There are many stories about the animals and birds. I think there is a story to illustrate any situation in life. It is their method of education."

"It sounds like a marvelous way to learn."

"Yes, I always liked school, but the teachings of the Zuri Watu were exciting and fun; more interesting and enjoyable than formal schooling."

"Do you have a favorite story?"

"Yes, it is the story of Shawna."

"Is it a long story?"

"No, very few of the stories, except the ones about the Nations, are long stories. Would you like to hear the story of Shawna?"

"Yes, I would very much like to hear it."

"Shawna was a ten year old boy. He was a disobedient boy. He was not respectful to his elders, and was mean to little girls. He was a bully, and was only liked by other bad boys. His father went to the Chief and said to him. 'My boy is a very smart boy, but he is not a good boy. Can you give me advice? He is our only son.' The Chief knew of Shawna. He had heard stories about his bad behavior. The Chief said, 'Go home; tell your wife to come and see me.' The father was startled by this command. His wife would be frightened.

What could the Chief possibly want with his wife? She was a good woman, a good wife, and a good mother. She was kind and forgiving. When the father told the mother to go and see the Chief, she wept. 'I have done nothing wrong. Why would he want to see me?'

"Her husband replied, 'You will have to go and find out.'

"She asked, 'Did he say when I was to go and see him?'

"'No,' he just said, 'Go home; tell your wife to come and see me.'

"Shawna's mother did not go immediately to see the Chief. She was very frightened. It was such an unheard of thing for a woman to do.

"When Shawna came home for supper, there was no supper. His mother was waiting for him and said. 'You are the cause of your father's grief. Now, you are the cause of my grief. You have been a bad son. You have been a bad person. You are no longer welcome at my pot or in my home.' Shawna was surprised, but he did not care. His mother was soft. He would spend more time with his friends. By bedtime, Shawna had been turned away from every home of every friend. He spent the cold, rainy night sheltering under the eaves outside his hut. In the morning, he approached his mother for the early meal.

"She said to him, 'Because of you, I have had no sleep. There is no meal this morning.' Shawna's father had left early on a hunt, and would be gone a few days. Again Shawna approached his friends, asking for a meal. Each friend refused him; their mothers would not allow them to share. The women knew that the Chief had summoned Shawna's mother.

"His anger at his mother and his friends drove him from the village to kill a rabbit or a quail for a meal. At the end of the day, he was no closer to a meal. There had been no game close to the palisade, and he had never ventured into the forest alone. He stole a few leafy vegetables from the gardens and ate them raw. Night found him very hungry and eventually, very cold and wet, for it rained heavily that night.

"In the morning Shawna went to his mother. 'I have been a bad son' he said. 'I will make a fire for you to cook the breakfast.' When the breakfast was ready, he sat down to eat, but his mother said. 'I did not make breakfast for you. Today I must go to see the Chief. I will tell him that if you do not change your ways, you will never be welcome at my pot again.'

"Shawna was desperate. He was very hungry. In his desperation he realized that he was not only hungry, he was lonely, he was afraid, and his future looked bleak. He loved his mother and father, but he had not shown it to them by giving them his respect and obedience.

"In his thoughts he saw the traders. He saw that the women and men exchanged their work and crafts for the goods they desired. He saw the men exchanging weapons. The bow maker exchanged with the arrow maker. The walinka maker exchanged with the spear maker. Everyone exchanged with one another to survive. He must exchange with his parents to survive, and the only things he had to give were his respect and obedience. He also realized he had been selfish. He had always taken, never given, and in so doing had shamed himself as well as his parents.

"Shawna said to his mother. 'Take me with you when you go to see the Chief. I will tell him that you are not to blame for my bad behavior. I will tell him that I will never again be disrespectful or disobedient. I will ask him to punish me, not you.'

"Shawna's mother went to see the Chief. He said to her, 'What do you wish me to do for your son?'

"Surprised she replied, 'I ask nothing for him.'

"The Chief said, 'Nothing? Are you sure?'

"She replied, 'He has been a bad boy, but he has promised to change his ways. He asks that you punish him, not me or his father, for his bad behavior.'

"'Tell me,' said the Chief, 'Why do you think Shawna was disrespectful and disobedient?'

"Shawna's mother was quiet for a long time after the question. She searched for an answer, and realized that she had allowed his bad behavior. She had done nothing to stop it, until the Chief had summoned her. Her love had been selfish, because she made it easy on herself. Her discipline had been selfish for she had done nothing to correct him, until she was frightened into thinking she would be punished. She had not earned Shawna's respect, because she had not taught him his place. He was disobedient, because she had not given him a reason to be obedient.

"'You are wise and understanding' she said. 'You are a great Chief and I am grateful that you have taken the time to show me the error of my ways.'

"The Chief said, 'Go and fetch Shawna to me.'

"Shawna did not know what had transpired.

"When he arrived, the Chief said. 'Your mother tells me you are going to be respectful and obedient. Why?'

"The question surprised the boy, but in his fear and hunger, he decided the truth, as he saw it, was the only answer.

"'Only this morning, have I seen that life is a trade. I must trade my respect and obedience for a home.'

"'Once your belly is full, will you go back to your old ways?' asked the Chief.

"'I have shamed my parents and myself. I have been a thief. I have taken and not given anything back. I must make amends to my parents and others, if they will let me.'

"The Chief told him, 'There is no life that is blameless. A mistake is a way to learn. But, all learning must not come from mistakes. Think well on this.'"

"The End"

"WHY IS THAT YOUR favorite story?"

"Because it is the essence of life; it is the essence of everything we do. If we always give to those who walk the path of life with us, we will always be the recipients of our efforts."

Taking her diary, Paula wrote down the final words of the Chief, and the explanation Tamubu had given to her. She would like to ponder on these bits of wisdom herself. Looking up, she said, "I loved your story; I am looking forward to hearing another one."

"It is now your turn to tell a story."

"We were not raised by stories as you were. Our stories were for entertainment. Some of the fables have a moral, but most were just for amusement."

"Well then, you must tell me a story that will amuse me." And so, she told him the story of: 'The little Engine That Could'.

"I thought you said your stories were just for entertainment. That story has a powerful message. One, I think, that you have made a part of yourself all of your life."

Paula was very sleepy. "Yes, now that you say it, I suppose that could be so... I just didn't realize I was doing it. It was always my favorite, childhood story ... night."

Tamubu wrapped himself in his cloak and lay beside the

fire. The sky was full of twinkling stars; he found the North Star and made a wish. It was the first time he had wished on a star since he was ten years old. He cherished his wish, but his thoughts turned to the sad fact that this journey with Paula was almost over. A few days were all that were left to him.

16

Jon Searches

JONATHAN CAULFIELD STARED INTO the fire, smoking his after-dinner pipe, while he considered the news brought by the runners a short while ago. There was not the slightest bit of information to be had from their contacts. The natives were usually over-eager to please the traders, for possible preferential treatment in their bartering exchanges.

But the native contacts were completely baffled. A white female traveling all alone—what nonsense was this? Upon further explanation that it was a white woman who had been captured, and who had escaped into the forest, the natives looked at the ground and shuffled their feet, a sure sign of bad news. The consensus of opinion was that she had been eaten, or maybe she had fallen into a sucking quagmire—it was highly unlikely that she was still alive.

Jon looked up as Max joined him. Max was haggard, for he blamed himself for Miss Thornton's impetuous flight into the wilderness. Max felt he should have tried to intimidate Bolbonga, when they were in the village and found Paula a captive, by telling him that the soldiers of Nigeria and the United Nations troops of Cameroon were looking for her. Bolbonga did not fear the traders, but he had a healthy respect for the soldiers whose reprisals were often harsh. The problem was that Max had no talent for prevaricating, so the threat didn't occur to him until they had already left the village, and it was too late.

Miss Thornton had escaped from the Ndezi Village five days ago. Max and Jon had hashed and rehashed her amazing and almost unbelievable escape into the trees. All people and animals leave marks of their passing. Only the birds and flying bugs go freely. To escape to the trees was one thing; never to come to ground, as she must for water, was quite another. The whole idea was really preposterous and a mysterious conundrum. Perhaps most amazing of all, is that the Ndezi found no *sign* of her passage.

"Jon, I want to get the news back to Enugu Station that there have been no native sightings of Miss Thornton. I am going to suggest that it would be best if the search party were to return to the Ndezi Village, and press the bearers, who were present at the kidnapping, into leading them back over the same trail to the yacht."

"I agree with you, Max. Our random travels for trading are unlikely to fetch any information about her. If she is alive, I think her only option would be to head back to the yacht—impossible as that may seem."

"Maybe we're not giving her enough credit. Dr. Miles thought her to be a Wonder Woman. If she is used to hiking in the woods in America, she might have the skills needed to find her way back."

It was this conversation, a kind of acceptance of her fate, which made Jon decisive about what he had to do. He went to the map kit and pulled out a map with the topography of the area, from the Ndezi Village to where they were camped near the Nguni, and eastward. He was still pouring over the maps when Max returned from the radio tent.

"I have disturbing news, Jon. It seems the Nigerians were not given permission by the **proper** authorities to send a military Search and Rescue Team into Cameroon. The emerging government of Cameroon now requires a request from the Expedition or from APCO, and a report from Captain Reverman and us. It is only our word that we saw Miss Thornton alive at the Ndezi village. With her escape, alone and unarmed, they now feel it is highly unlikely that she is still alive. I intend to call tomorrow and clear up the misunderstanding—but precious time will be lost. Jon, why the maps... have you an idea?"

"I am thinking about asking you to let me have three

bearers and Motozo, so I can set off to retrace the probable trail myself. I sense a *hot-potato* turf battle brewing here. By the time you get through the confusion, if you ever do, I could already be there.

"As you know, I like to read maps, and the first thing I did before we moved camp to base station four was to look at the possibilities. We know, from talking to Miss Thornton, that they traveled the ridge to the savanna, to the foothills, to the forest and the village.

"We are here, about twenty miles east is the gap into the Valley of the Devils. The gap, I am sure, is also a watercourse, and it continues through the first mountain range all the way up to the next ridge, which is the same ridge that drops down to the savanna and foothills at the edge of the Ndezi territory. With a Nguni guide to get us to the gap, we can then follow this stream all the way to the ridge where we can go either way, depending on what we find. A day to reach the gap... and two, maybe three days to reach the main ridge... what do you think?"

Max was excited. It was a bold, manly thing to do. Years ago, he would have done the same thing himself, but now, he had a large staff to consider and vendors expecting trade goods, all his responsibility. Also, it was most important that he deal with the officials who relied on him for accurate information. Now would be the worst time to ignore their requests. He looked at Jon and smiled. "This will be a much greater adventure than what was promised you when we were in the Congo. Let's go see who will volunteer to go with you."

When the venture was put to the bearers, both Max and Jon were surprised. Only one of the boys did not raise his hand to volunteer... only because he was getting married when he got home. So a bundle of twenty-nine straws was made with three short straws to draw lots. Once done, the rest of the evening was spent sorting through gear to send with Jon. A runner went to the Nguni village to hire a scout to lead the party to the gap tomorrow. By ten o'clock that evening the separated gear was all repacked and ready to go. Motozo came and requested that his regular helper, Obendi, be allowed to go with them, so they ended up with four boys, Motozo and Jon.

"Would you like me to contact your parents and tell them of your mission?"

"Not right away, give me a few days to get the lay-of-the-land first. Okay?"

"I understand, but do not put yourself at risk. You are your parents' only remaining son, and for all we know, Miss Thornton could already be dead."

"You can't tell me anything I haven't already told myself, but I find myself compelled to go. Each day the need to search for Miss Thornton has become more insistent—until I can think of nothing else. I can't explain why, I just know I have to try to find her."

"I understand, more than you think, and who knows, you may just be her salvation." Max took Jon's hand and pulled him in for a bear hug. He was going to miss this young man.

The runner returned early the next morning with the Nguni guide. After a hearty breakfast, and a last check of the gear, the party of seven was off as the sun rose above the trees. Jon had his revolver and both he and Kimbo had rifles. The other men had bows and arrows and their spears, the weapons with which they were proficient, plus knives and machetes and the ubiquitous walinka, used with unerring accuracy to kill small game.

Each man had a bedroll, spare clothes and a water bottle plus a bag of staples: beans, rice, dried meat, cocoa, oatmeal, sugar, salt and a cooking utensil. Motozo had packed the supplies into bundles, so if one bundle was lost, it would not be a disaster for the mission. Motozo carried his spices, herbs, the first-aid kit and a gathering net.

EACH BUNDLE WAS ABOUT a third of the load the men usually carried. Jon carried the maps, compass, binoculars, his revolver, ammunition, and his personal gear. Kimbo carried the radio, and two bandoliers of rifle ammunition. It was lucky for Jon that Kimbo had picked a short straw, for he was an expert shot with a rifle, from the years he had spent on Safari.

IT RAINED MOST OF the day and when they arrived at the gap in the early evening, it was almost dark. The guide knew of a good camping spot, where the fire and men would be out of the rain. It was an under-washed cave made by years of rampaging rainwater scouring the streambed. In the wettest part of the rainy season, the cave was probably flooded. But now, the stream was a good twenty feet away and just a bubbling brook.

In no time, Motozo and his helper, Obendi, had a fire started. The stew pot, which was a large turtle shell that was light to carry, was filled with dried meat, beans, rice, wild celery and bamboo shoots. Oatcakes, like pancakes, made with oatmeal, coconut milk, slivered coconut and mashed blackberries, cooked on flat rocks. They would have one each with dinner and eat the rest tomorrow at their mid-day meal with fruit and nuts. On the trail, breakfast was always porridge.

The cave was shallow, but long, so everyone was out of the rain, but lots had been cast for places next to the fire. Jon and Kimbo had insisted on taking the end places because they had the rifles. The Nguni guide chose to sleep on the ledge above the cave, under the bushes.

The Nguni tribe was quite different from other tribes. They did not build huts, but had open lean-tos that formed a large circle, which was surrounded on the backside by a thick thorn boma. Life was lived mostly in the open and the only privacy was behind a drape at the back of the lean-to. The Nguni were a gregarious sort, and enjoyed living closely together in the tribe, like one big family in a house that had many rooms.

The morning dawned clear, but there was a dense ground mist along the streambed, which delayed the start. The men used the time to forage on the hillsides for fruits and wild vegetables. Obendi found several plantain bushes with almost ripe fruits. This was considered a good omen by the searchers, as plantain were quite nourishing and had many uses, which would make the staples last longer. There would be nothing to gather, while walking in the streambed.

THE GROUP TRAVELED STEADILY uphill until early afternoon when they stopped for lunch. Jon climbed a tree to get above the dense surrounding foliage to see what progress they had made and to better judge the time it would take to reach the first ridge. He could see the summit, but did not expect to reach it before nightfall.

In the late African dusk, they found a large clearing above the watercourse. It was more open than they liked, but in a short time, they had used fallen trees and forest debris to fence in the area surrounding the fire pit. The area was not a habitat of lions, but there was still the leopard, and possibly the larger more aggressive black leopard, and maybe apes. But these animals did not usually prey on man; they preferred the African linsang, the mongoose, otter or genet; squirrels and monkeys, francolin and guinea fowl; the small antelope and duiker of the forest, and of course, the apes were omnivorous with a liking for snakes. But prey was prey and sleeping prey was even better, regardless of size. With this in mind, they cached the supplies in a pile and built a ring of fires around it and their bedding. In this way they passed a safe and comfortable night in spite of the horrific screams of the tree hyrax.

IN THE MORNING, WHILE porridge and cocoa were being prepared, Jon again climbed a tree to get his bearings. The watercourse gap continued, but curved almost ninety degrees south. They had no choice but to follow it, as the hillsides of the valley were covered with impenetrable undergrowth of thorn bushes.

All day they struggled along the rocky gully that was the streambed. At mid-day they had to hack a clearing for their brief meal and rest. Jon found a tree he could climb to get above the undergrowth, and saw that the gully of the crease took a switchback turn towards the high mountain ridge in just a few miles. Then, they would be on the lower reaches of the last slope, hopefully before dusk.

After the switchback turn, the gully watercourse became

narrow and difficult. Jon saw that the flooding rainwater had eroded the bank of the curve, to flow out of the rocky gully to go through the forest, rather than follow the torturous curve.

The watercourse up the last slope was wide, with good footing on both sides of the small stream. A well-used trail came in on the right. Kimbo said there were many recent tracks of apes, so many that the rain had not washed them all away.

Jon decided it would be best to be far away from this trail before dark; for through the minds of them all came the stories of the grotesque and vicious apes, more man-like than beast-like, that were supposed to inhabit the Valley of the Devils. With the stories as an impetus, the men traveled quickly and quietly for the rest of the day, coming at last to a forested plateau a mile or so below the towering mountain ridge.

THERE WAS NOT ENOUGH daylight left to climb the obvious, but steep trail, which snaked its way to the peak. So, Jon decided to use the remaining light to find a defensible shelter. He split the men into groups of two and all agreed to return to this same spot within the hour. Four men returned, without finding a suitable camping area. Only Kimbo and his son, Kybo had not returned. Jon was getting ready to leave a sentry and go looking for them when they heard the report of a rifle not far off.

Jon ordered the men to follow and stay together. "If we meet apes, form a circle but don't shoot to kill, only shoot at feet and legs." They had not traveled more than six hundred yards when they came to a small clearing, where Kimbo leaned over his fallen son.

Kimbo arose when he heard them arrive. "It's okay, he is only stunned. He had climbed this tree to get a better look at the ledge up there, when a huge female ape swung into the tree and knocked him to the ground. I fired a shot into the air to scare her away." Kimbo then knelt over Kybo and gently called to him as he poured a little water on his son's face.

Seeing the ledge that Kimbo had pointed out, Obu climbed rapidly to the limb that touched the jutting rock. "It is a cave.

Not large, but can only be reached from this tree. We should be safe here. I will go and look closer." In a few moments Obu was back. "There are some green branches in the back of the cave. It may be that the female ape is near her time, and had chosen this cave as a place to give birth."

Jon said, "We will have to rent it from her for the night. Obendi, you will need to contribute some of the plantain you gathered as payment." Everyone chuckled at Jon's humor. But it was a good idea. Obendi was not at all displeased. The plantain was a heavy load. He would be glad to part with some of it, for a safe night's rest.

The men were so well drilled in making camp, that it seemed only a matter of minutes before there was wood gathered, a fire going, water on to boil, and dinner preparations underway. Obu had snared a guinea fowl at the lunch break, which would be cooked tonight for tomorrow's lunch. Tonight it was stew and biscuits.

Kimbo had placed the banana rent payment in the crotch of the tree; and a fire had been built close to the edge of the ledge where they had entered it from the tree–just in case the landlady didn't think the rent offering wasn't adequate payment for the use of her lair.

Morning found the banana offering gone. After a quick breakfast, they were back on the trail. It was a daunting climb even in the shade and cool of the morning. Jon was glad that he had not attempted it last evening after a long and difficult day. It was almost noon when they arrived at the narrow, rocky ridge. Jon sent two men each way to scout the trail. Then he set up the radio while Motozo prepared the noon meal.

"Trader search calling Max camp. Come in. Over." Almost immediately there came a reply.

"Trader search, stand by. Over." A few minutes later:

"Trader search, Max here. Over."

"Max, we have reached the main ridge. The boys are out looking for *sign*. Except for a minor run-in with an unwilling landlady, all went well on the trek. Over."

"You made the right decision, Jon. The powers-that-be, as you had foretold, are dragging their feet. Nigeria won't go into

Cameroon territory again, and the government of Cameroon is in such a state of flux that the red tape is never ending, especially since the Expedition members are the guests of Nigeria. Report again when you have camp set up for the night. Over."

"That's a ten four, Max. Over and Out."

JON TOOK HIS BINOCULARS and went to a high rocky promontory further down the trail. It was a grand place, for the vista was limitless. Below, there was the dense rainforest giving way to tangled thorn bushes on the steep, rocky slopes with the occasional acacia tree covered in flowering creepers. Jon was secretly elated. He had always wanted to explore new areas, especially in the mountains where so few people went due to the difficulty of the terrain. Sitting down and enjoying a pipe, he was disturbed by a commotion from camp.

Kybo and Obendi, who had gone north, had returned and were quite animated. Jon returned to hear them talking about demon apes. Before long, he had the whole story.

While traveling down the trail looking for signs of passage, Kybo had found spoor from a large troop of anthropoids that had been feeding as they passed. Since the way was mostly open and the visibility was good, they continued on when, just past a crease that crossed the trail, they saw a number of huge, ape-like creatures feeding. The boys were convinced these were the vicious demons of the Valley of the Devils and had returned to camp as fast as their feet would carry them.

Jon wanted no encounters with a large band of apes. "We will eat and move on up the trail. Did you see anything else?"

"Yes, on the way back we found fresh marks and splintered rocks from gunfire and this." Kybo handed Jon a .22 Magnum cartridge shell. "At one place, beneath a tree off to the side of the trail, there were recent scuffled prints, possibly those of a native man and smaller prints, maybe those of a woman. In the tree some new-growth branches had been broken off and discarded."

Jon was elated, but puzzled: If the female print was made

by Miss Thornton, who had made the male prints? "Did you see any footprints before or after the tree?"

Kybo looked down and shuffled his feet. Uh-oh, Jon thought: but he said, "Whatever you think you saw, you must tell me; it might make sense to me even if it makes no sense to you."

Kybo looked up and said, "To the tree and after the tree, there were only the prints of a big man or a man with a heavy load. There were no other prints or even suggestions of prints of a woman. The prints of the male ended a few miles back near a copse of young trees and rocks."

Jon could see why Kybo had been reluctant to tell him what he had seen. "Then you saw no more prints at all? Did you check down the mountainsides?"

"Yes kigozi, we did and found nothing." As they had been talking, the other scouts who had gone south returned. Jon turned to them and asked for their report. "We have seen nothing new, some old tracks in sheltered places where the rain did not penetrate. They were not distinct enough to know which direction they were going, or exactly how long ago they were made, but one or two marks could have been those of a woman. About five miles up, there is a trail going down the side of the mountain. There are prints, male and female on this trail." Jon was pleased, but wondered why they had found nothing between here and there... odd, very odd. He turned to Kybo and questioned him again.

"Tell me, where did you start to see the spoor of the apes? Was it before the male prints ended or after?"

Kybo again lowered his head, but didn't shuffle his feet, and then looking up said, "We did not see the prints of the big man on our way down the trail. We saw only the spoor of many apes and did not look carefully among them for other prints. It was not until we were returning and saw the bright new marks on the rocks, and found the bullet shell that we started to look for other tracks. We found some prints of a big bull ape, but other apes had come along after him, and they obscured most of his prints. The ground became rocky scree and there were no tracks of any kind until we found the footprints under the tree beyond where the spoor of the apes had gone off into the brush. But we did see ape spoor, possibly a few bulls, further up the trail after the footprints of the big man ended."

Jon took his lunch back to the boulder vista, away from the constant chatter and laughter of the men. It was not only a wonderful view, but there were few distractions, which helped him think through the information that had been gathered.

Jon was going to assume the female print was that of Miss Thornton. It was highly unlikely that a native would travel alone with a woman. If a raiding party had captured a woman, there would have been many more male prints. If the woman was a tourist, traveling with a native guide, there would have been many more prints of male natives as bearers. Even if they had met disaster with the apes, there would have been dead bodies of apes, unless they were completely surprised... but... there had been no indications of a safari group.

Was it possible that Miss Thornton had picked up help from a lone traveler? That could make sense. Sometimes young men went on what they called *walk-about*. It was a time to be alone and think, a time to make decisions at the crossroads of life. Even so, this did not explain why the tracks stopped.

Taking his thoughts in another direction, Jon decided: if it was Miss Thornton, she was definitely headed back to the yacht. Maybe they had found a trail through the underbrush so they could be well away from the band of apes.

Well, we are definitely not heading back into the maws of the apes, so up we shall go and see what the trail over the mountainside has to offer.

17

The Zuri Watu

PAULA SLEPT LATE. TAMUBU had made a strong potion to ease her pain and to enable her to sleep deeply. Now, he needed to gather firewood. It might be a few days before she would be able to travel again. According to Paula, there was another day of travel on the ridge, a day on the slope, and a day in the forest before getting to the sea. He would go and see these trails.

Tamubu used the rappelling harness, for safety, when he pressure-climbed the stone chimney to the top of the ravine. There he left his possessions hidden while he *roamed* the trail to the beach. He found the cove, but there was no yacht. He scoured the beach for *sign*, and then saw a large white lump hanging suspended from the trees. Upon examining the anomaly, he found it was a cache of food and boxes in a net, with a white cover—possibly left for Paula by her friends before they took the yacht from the cove.

With the yacht gone, the situation between them had changed. With no one here for her, they could continue to travel together. Tamubu experienced a surge of joy. He had wished upon a star—was his wish being granted? Would they have more time together than the few remaining days it would take for her ankle to heal, and for them to reach the sea?

Tamubu found several sources of water and foodstuffs while *roaming*. He returned to his possessions and then went hunting/gathering. Once the supply nets were full, he returned to the edge of the cliff above the camping ledge, and signaled Paula with a bird whistle. She hobbled over to unfasten the faggot of wood that he had lowered on the rappelling line.

Tamubu then lowered the nets with their bounty. Paula then watched Tamubu rappel to the ledge; he seemed to be enjoying his newfound skill.

Once settled, Paula asked, "Where did you go?"

"I went to find food and wood for the fire." He didn't want to tell her that the yacht was gone. It would be best to let her see that for herself. "Does your ankle hurt?"

"Not until I start to dance," she said with a smile. "Your treatment is working well. I'm not at all uncomfortable. I made lunch while you were gone. I hope you don't mind my rooting about in your food bag."

"Not at all; what did you make?"

"I made sweet potato bread. I used one of the cooked sweet potatoes and mashed it in the turtle shell, added some of your ground oats, some chopped dates, some coconut slivers, some coconut milk, and a little grated vanilla bean, stirred it all together and topped it with sesame seeds. I baked it for an hour. It should be cooled soon."

The sweet potato bread had the texture of zucchini bread. Tamubu was delighted with her creation, for he loved breads, biscuits and muffins. They ate all of it with hot broth and fresh fruit. After lunch he sat to draw plants in her diary. Paula felt the need for a nap. Had he put something in the broth again? She didn't mind, she knew the body healed best while sleeping.

TAMUBU WAS IN HIS element. He had forgotten the joy of drawing. The afternoon sped away, until the sun dropped in the far west making deep shadows on the eastern ledge. The delicate shadings of a pencil drawing were difficult to do in this dim light, so Tamubu started the dinner preparations. There was plenty of the dried turtle meat, and near an old campsite at the edge of the ravine he had found squash and onions growing wild. Combined with the asparagus, mushrooms and peppercorns, they would have a delicious stew. As the stew cooked, he ground some more of the oats, and mixed it with the cassava, ground vanilla bean and the milk of a coconut to make biscuits to go with the stew.

Paula's amazement at the quality of the food never lessened; nor did her realization of her own inadequacy amidst such bounty.

Replete from the savory dinner, Paula wondered if she could coax a story about the Zuri Watu from Tamubu this evening. She had an endless curiosity to know all about them.

Gazing at the fire in the soft gray twilight, Paula thought of the spectacular sunsets on the western side of the mountain. Here on the east side, they were sheltered from the intense heat and glare of the western sun; but paid for the comfort with the loss of the magnificent display of the luminous sunset colors, which shimmered through the treetops in the shafts of fading light.

"I did some drawings today while you were napping."

"Wonderful, let me see... oh... these are marvelous. You are incredibly gifted with your art, but I think I have already told you that. It is amazing the depth of shading you are able to attain with an ordinary pencil."

"I liked pencil, charcoal and ink best; oils were too thick and watercolors were not precise enough for me."

"And you were just ten years old, amazing! My sister Sallee Anne didn't even start art lessons until she was twelve."

"I was going to start art lessons when I went to England for boarding school when I was twelve."

"You mean to say you have never had art lessons?"

"A teacher at day school, who had worked as a draftsman, gave me some lessons on perspective and a book on shading."

"I wonder if this was how it was with Leonardo da Vinci as a boy."

"Who is Leonardo da Vinci?"

"An Italian artist that lived a couple hundred years ago."

"He must have been famous to be remembered now."

"You could say that." She smiled at him coquettishly and said, "Since we may be here another day or two, what are my chances of hearing you tell the story of the Zuri Watu?"

Responding to her coquettish smile with his winsome,

impish grin, he said, "I could be persuaded, but why are you so curious about the Zuri Watu?"

Paula thought for a minute and then replied, "If you are a product of their culture, then it must be a very great culture—even without reading or writing, and I would like to know of it."

Tamubu was flattered by her words. "It is a great story—the history of the Nations and, in the manner of our people, it must be told, word for word, as I learned it."

"I was counting on that. It will be a wonderful experience for me, listening to you." Secretly Paula thought: ... and a great experience for you, thinking in English to tell the story.

"This is the story of the Nations of the Zuri Watu, as told from father to son, from mother to daughter; from the time of the great escape, to the time of the Great Chief, Sashono and his Medicine Chief, Manutu.

"Long ago, the Great Nations of the Zuri Watu lived in a settlement close to the sea, on the coast of the setting sun, in the land of Africa. They had lived and prospered in this place, for a very long time, before slave traders beset them. These evil men took their finest young men and women from the village, by extreme force, and carried them away in houses that lived on the sea.

"One day, when the slave traders came, the entire Nations, as the people called themselves, had vanished. The slavers used dogs to track the people through the dense jungle; but after four of the slavers met violent deaths, the evil ones returned to the empty village. It was a puzzle to them. All of the animals, possessions and people were gone. Only the palisade, the empty huts, the cold clay ovens, and the stripped vegetable fields remained.

"The Zuri Watu had, many moons and several rainy seasons ago, sent out scouts to find a new home for the Nations. The scouts had crossed mountains, and far away, had found an uninhabited valley with a beautiful lake and fertile soil. They scouted a week's march in all directions from the valley and found no other peoples.

"The scouts returned to the Nations to tell of the marvelous place they had found. The Chief, the Medicine Chief, and two of the Council elders made the long trek, guided by the scouts

in the heat of the summer, to see this new place for themselves. They found the valley good. Upon their return, the Council of Elders resolved to move to the new valley.

"It was decided that they would move out in groups, taking first the builders and laborers to clear the land and erect the palisade. Then, when the palisade was up, women and children, goats, chickens and dogs would form a part of each group. The trip was long and difficult, taking a moon to complete with children and animals. Once in the new valley the women erected huts for their families and pens for the animals. The workers had made piles of branches, cut from the palisade logs, of a size used in building huts and pens, along the inside of the palisade. The children mixed the dung, clay, water and dried grass into a plaster for the walls. Everyone helped.

"After the last woman, child and animal had left their ancestral village by the sea, a group of young men built animal traps on the trails. These were deep pits with sharp, pointed stakes driven in the ground at the bottom of the holes. The slavers knew the people hid in the forest when their ships were sighted. A sentry atop the bluff would sound his huge horn before the ship reached the inlet. Still, the bloodhounds found the young mothers with nursing babes and their strong protective husbands. They were the ones with strong scents and easiest for the dogs to track. Once captured, they would be taken away and never seen again.

"By now, the slavers knew the village would be empty when they arrived. They lost no time in setting the dogs on the scent. It had rained hard the night before, but the dogs followed the trails into the jungle. The scents were strongest on the trails. The traps were covered well enough to take the weight of the dogs, but not the weight of a man. Four men died in the traps before the slavers turned back to the empty village. The rain continued for days, and the spoor was washed away forever.

"Life was good in the new valley. The Nations grew and lived well. It was such a long time of peace, that there was no longer anyone living who had suffered the raids of the slave traders, or who had experienced the move to the valley. It was now just a frightening story of kidnappings, bloodshed and brutality.

"The Nations grew so large that another palisade was built on the other side of the lake beside the flat ground used for cultivation. A system of drawing lots was devised for those who went to the new place and those who stayed. The first son of the Chief and the first son of the Medicine Chief would be the leaders in the new village, subject to their fathers and the Council. It was not many years before the new village and its leaders became independent with their own Council. The Nations grew ever greater and stronger.

"With the growth in numbers came shortages of the old trade goods. Iron cooking pots were passed down to daughters, but there were more daughters than pots. There were only a few combs left and fewer mirrors. There was no woven fabric left at all. The women wore grass skirts or skirts made from animal skins. The awls used to punch the leather for sandals were just nubs and almost useless. There were no glass beads or wire, no silver or copper earrings or bracelets for the married women. The wonderful scrapers used to flense the skins were all worn out. Now they used pieces of shale, which often flaked and marred the hide. The men had resorted to hardening spear tips once again in the fire and to using shale rocks to sharpen into arrows. The hunting knives would no longer take an edge sharp enough to cut meat or hide.

"A Council meeting of both villages was held. It was decided to send out scouts to look for people with whom they could trade, but not towards the west. Travel towards the west had been taboo since the new village was established. Many moons passed before the first scouts returned. In the north, they found only poor villages, and even poorer people, some of whom they suspected might be cannibalistic. The people in the north were also subject to constant raids from the wandering tribes of the desert. It was bleak country and there was no trading available.

"The second group of scouts, who had traveled south, reported endless savannas of wild beasts and no villages. The area teemed with lions, leopards and cheetahs. Huge herds of elephants went anywhere they chose. Rhinoceros rampaged at the smell of man and charged in to stomp out cooking fires. Vast herds of wildebeest and antelopes stampeded across the plains when hunted by the big cats or packs of hyenas or wild dogs. Herds of Cape buffalo attacked men who passed too close to them.

"All now anxiously awaited the scouts who had gone east. When they did not return before the rainy season, a search party was sent to look for them.

"After weeks of searching the deep forest, the six scouts, who had been sent to the east, came to a wall of sheer cliffs. To save time, they split up. Three men went north and three men went south looking for a way across the cliffs. The plan was to travel two days out, then return to this place and share their findings.

"The three traveling north found a defile, which could be ascended on the second day. To make sure it was not a dead-end, they climbed up the ravine to the top of the cliffs where they saw a path leading into the valley below. Pleased, they retraced their steps until they reached a wide level area beside the ravine. It was a good place to make camp for the night. As usual, each would take a turn as sentry during the night.

"It was a very dark overcast night. The Usuku Wanaume smelled the campfire. It had been a long time since there had been trespassers. The men of the night *had uncanny skills: they were able to travel through the rocky ravine in the pitch dark, making no noise at all, as they advanced upon the sleeping scouts. Not one word was spoken. Not one nighttime critter was disturbed. They came up beside the sentry, downwind, raised their clubs and bashed in his head. Quick work was made of binding the hapless sleepers, as they never even heard a pebble roll. With an owl call, they summoned the others who would help carry the dead one back to the caves. Tonight there would be a feast!

"The party of three that had headed south had found a natural crease, which led to a gap, which led to a wide river. They could go no further, for they had to return to the meeting spot to share their findings with the others. It was getting dark when they reached the ridge, so they made camp on the summit. A sentry was posted, a fire made, a meal eaten and then they wrapped themselves in their deerskins to sleep.

"From a distance, the men of the night *saw the flickering campfire and again smelled smoke. More trespassers; they would be able to reach them before first light traveling on the ridge. Just before dawn when the night is the darkest, the men of the night *came upon the sleeping scouts. The sentry had allowed the fire to die to embers, so little light pierced the surrounding darkness. The sentry smelled the rotting smell of carrion and then smelled no more. The startled sleepers were overwhelmed, and their hands were tied behind their backs. *Their ankles were tied with a short length between them, so they could shuffle to a nearby cave. There they were tied to a huge log while* the men of the night *slept the day away. The captives were given no food or water until dusk, when the ugly Usuku Wanaume came back to take them to their lair. The Usuku Wanaume were in a hurry; they knew of the capture of the other trespassers, and expected preparations for a feast that night.*

"The Usuku Wanaume knew there were settlers many days march away, but they had no way of bringing back such large trophies. One foray to the palisade was enough to show them the great strength of the Zuri Watu, for the men of the night, feared reprisal; nor were they physically suited to travel in the dense forest. Plus the fierce beasts that lived there also hunted at night. It was always their hope that the settlers would explore to the east in small numbers. So it was that the Nations of the Zuri Watu had been unaware of their cannibalistic neighbors for their entire existence in the new valley.

"The Usuku Wanaume or the men of the night were gnomes in every way. They were hairy like chimps and only a little taller. They had large foreheads jutting out past black beetle eyes with pupils always dilated so the sun was painful to their eyes. Their long wide flat noses had huge flared nostrils, and their ability to smell was extraordinary. Under thin flat lips their faces slanted, chinless, to their short necks. Large movable ears provided hearing as good as any night animal. To move their kills, they had to dismember them and carry them in pieces. They are very strong for their size, but their arms and legs are short and stumpy. They do not run, except to waddle like ducks.

"These are a people forgotten by time. They are isolated beyond the sheer cliffs in a remote mountain valley. They live in dark caves, which are surrounded by deep thickets on all sides. In the twilight of morning and evening, they gather fruits and vegetables, and with deadly slingshots kill monkeys, chimps and baboons. Foraging, the elephant shrews they raise and hapless travelers are the staples of their diet. Their band is never large, for their life span is only that of an old chimpanzee.

"Everyone lives together in the deep caves. The men all share and use the women. Once a female finishes her courses, she is expected to accept all interested males until she no longer has her cycle. Such gross mating practices have given these gnomes grotesque and misshapen bodies; for it matters not, if it is the father, brother or son that mates with a fertile female. The lust of these squat evil men, with their fat tumescent organs is excessive. There are no amorous feelings attached to the act; it is just an itch that needs to be constantly scratched.

"The men of the night *have been in the mountains for a long time. Other tribes had come to settle in the fertile valley, but all eventually left, after they experienced the forays of the Usuku Wanaume. For once again tasting human flesh, the grizzly marauders would crave this delicacy and begin their stealthy raids on the settlers. With their animal-like senses, they could come and go unseen. Because of their physical limitations, they took only babies and small children. They did not raid the village often because they themselves were easy prey for the night hunting carnivores. In this way, it was often years before a tribe would become discouraged enough to move out of the valley.*

"The Zuri Watu had been safe for such a long time because they had brought the practice of building a palisade around their village with them from the coast. Most jungle tribes used the thorn boma for protection. It was effective against animals but not against* the men of the night, *the vile Usuku Wanaume.*

"The dazed Zuri Watu scouts had ropes placed around their necks, tying them to each other, and were marched to the main cave. Only the long twilight made it possible for them to walk without stumbling. As total darkness approached, they were prodded a ways off the trail to a wide, undercut shelf in the rocks. There they were again tied to a log. Cheered, but also dismayed, they found two of the three fellow scouts also tied to the log. Plaited green monkey vines were bound around their chests and upper arms. Their hands, feet and legs were free, but they could not lie down, only lean against the log. The Usuku Wanaume brought food and water and then they were gone.

"The scouts sat in silence for awhile, but hearing none of the usual sounds of a village, soon talked in low voices. It was told that Bonomo had been killed on sentry duty, and that they had been brought here early in the morning. The scouts had been led off before the butchering of their comrade and, as *yet, did not know these horrid, little ape men were cannibals. Soon they heard noises and smelled the smoke of a large fire. Later, when the fire had died to coals, they heard the excited revels and celebration of the cooking of their fallen friends. Had they known what was happening, their fear and terror would have been unbearable. They would have refused food and water so the pleasure of the cannibal's next feast would have been diminished.*

"A search party of twelve scouts was sent east to find the six scouts that had not returned by the time deadline. These were the scouts that had been sent north and south, for they had the most experience. Armed with bows and many poisoned arrows, their sharpened spears and walinkas, they set off following the trail of their comrades. They avoided the side trip explorations the first party had made, and followed their trail straight to the east. Late in the day, five days later, they came to the spot where the first party of scouts had split up at the base of the sheer rock cliffs. Since they did not know why the scouts had split up, they moved back into the jungle and spent the night in the trees, keeping a cold camp.

"In the morning, staying together, they tracked the trail to the north first. Late in the day they found the crease, then the ravine and the gap. They also found the campsite and, horrified, read the story it told. The search party retreated to the narrow trail in the deep ravine, where the enemy had to approach in single file. Again, the searchers kept a cold camp while they discussed strategy. The first scouts had been set upon by cannibals—the blood, the severed head, hands and feet all in a grisly heap, told the horrific tale. These were strong, brave men, but the gruesome campsite had reduced them to quivering masses of terrified nerves. No one was able to sleep much that night; and all were glad when the sun rose and the cannibals had not attacked.

"The plan was to press on slowly and carefully and follow the tracks. They prepared themselves with camouflage paint and placed ferns about their bodies and on their weapons. It was mid-morning when they started out and noon before they reached the path leading down to the *agiza mahili pango* (dark labyrinthine cave) with its deep recesses and twisting tunnels.

"The *Usuku Wanaume* did not post sentries at the cave opening. They had no close enemies. Their cave was a rabbit warren of tunnels and small dead-end rooms. The men of the night *lived far inside its vast reaches and guarded only this deep entrance. The cooking was done at the opening of the cave. This was a large and level area with many faults in the overhead rock, which made natural chimneys for the smoke to escape. Deep inside the mountain, where they feasted, they did not need fire, or even light, which hurt their eyes. They could see best in the dark. When they prepared for a feast, a fire was built in the twilight of the day. After it was glowing embers, they buried pieces of the flesh wrapped in wet moss and large green leaves to bake in the coals. So, the captives heard only the excitement of the gathering of materials for the great fire. The revels of the feast were held deep in the bowels of the cave.*

"The apprehensive search party approached the cave openings through the dense undergrowth at the edge of the trail, where the vegetation thinned, or the trail narrowed. They saw and, more importantly, heard nothing as they followed the small duck-shaped footprints that had led the captives to this area. The camouflaged scouts kept their focus low, for short men. Across the trail was a shallow cave surrounded by a thorn boma, but it looked deserted. Using extreme caution, they moved on to the larger cave opening. It was the same here, no guards, only the remnants of a great fire. The captives must be deep inside. Opting to go back to the shallow cave, so as not to be caught between two openings, the leader dashed across the trail to look behind the thorn boma.

"At a familiar signal, a second scout followed. It was this blur that caught the eye of a captive behind the boma. When the third scout dashed across the trail, the captive recognized him. The Zuri Watu use birdcalls as signals; the captive gave the call of the Yellow White Eye; a tiny, hummingbird-size bird with a beautiful shivering trill. It was the call of the hunter to announce his presence nearby. The leader, crouching next to the boma, returned the call of the Yellow White Eye and then heard soft voices. Peering into the darkness of the shallow cave, he heard his name and signaled his companions to keep their positions. They had found the missing scouts.

"There were only four of the scouts sitting tied to a large log. Quickly they untied the men who, although stiff from lack of movement, were well and unharmed. Shifting to the other end of the boma, they pushed it aside with their spears to make an exit. Once through, they pushed the boma back in place, as they had done at the other side.

"The leader had retied the knots in the vines, making it look as if the captives had disappeared—to give the cannibals something to think about. The freed men lost no time in retreating up the trail as fast as they could. While untying the men, the rescuers had told the captives about the Usuku Wanaume; and that they must flee as fast and as far as possible from the avenging horde of cannibals.

"On reaching the jungle, they stopped for a brief rest, a bit of food and water. The rescue party had buried the gruesome remains of the fallen sentry and had covered the bloody spots, so the freed scouts did not have to deal with that dreadful sight in their weakened emotional condition. Once refreshed, the party continued on through the night. Morning found them far from the mountains, but still determined to press on until noon when they would rest. The freed captives explained that the men of the night were so named, because they hated sunlight and were never abroad during the day.

"In forced marches, resting only in the heat of the day, they arrived back at the palisade in four days. The returned scouts were served a hearty meal, and given time to bathe and rest, while the Nations assembled to greet them and welcome them home. Everyone wanted to hear the stories they would tell the Elders and the Chiefs of their adventures. After the tale was told, the leaders realized they had gained nothing from their explorations, except two dead men, and the possibility of a relentless enemy."

TAMUBU LOOKED AT PAULA. "Are you asleep?"

"Oh, no; I have my eyes closed so I can picture in my mind what you are saying. It is a bizarre and incredible story. What ugly, horrible little men."

"Yes. Not really a good bedtime story. It is late. You need to rest. I will continue the story tomorrow. It is half told."

In the morning Paula wrote in her diary, bringing her narrative current to the story of the Zuri Watu. Tamubu had gone ostensibly for fresh vegetables and game, but she suspected him of also scouting the area for possible intruders to their privacy and safety. In the heat of the afternoon, after lunch, she napped while Tamubu drew and described more healing plants in her diary. He was tempted to read what she had written that morning, his curiosity all-consuming, but he could not betray her trust, so he reluctantly confined himself to the drawings.

Late that afternoon, it started to rain, but Tamubu had expected it, and had gathered large thick leaves, which stiffened from heat, to shield the fire pit on the side open to the valley. Sitting on their pallets within the shallow cave, after a leisurely meal, they were dry and warm with the little fire relieving the darkness and gloom of the rainy evening.

"Now, I will finish the story of the Zuri Watu, if you are ready for it."

"I am more than ready, I am anxious to hear the rest of it."

◈◈◈

"It was twilight; the time of the day when the women of the Usuku Wanaume went into the jungle to gather fruits, nuts, tubers and greens. This would be the first meal of the day, a cold meal as the cooking fire would not be lit that day. They'd had two feasts already and were saving the other captives for the future. So, this was the first food and water taken to the prisoners all day; the shock of finding the captives gone cast a superstitious pall over the tribe, for they were gone, but their bonds were still tied just as they had been early that morning. The thorn boma was still in place and the only sign was the footprints of the captives—too fresh to have been made upon arrival.

"A hunting party was assembled and, using their exceptional abilities to smell, followed the trail. It was when they saw the footprints of the rest of the scouts joining the fleeing party that the Usuku Wanaume knew their captives had been cleverly rescued. Traveling as quickly as their stunted legs would allow, they came upon the resting spot in the forest. The spoor was many hours old, but they decided to continue tracking—certain they would soon find their captives sleeping with the rescuers, and capture them all. The horrid little men followed the trail all night, but did not get any closer to their quarry. As night turned to the gray light of dawn, the men of the night had to build shelters from the sun, deep in the undergrowth. The men they chased traveled too quickly and had not stopped to rest at night. The Usuku Wanaume could not catch them now and were not prepared to travel further. They would go back when the soft twilight came and tell the others that the captives had escaped them.

"The Usuku Wanaume had a bigger problem, for the Zuri Watu now knew they were vulnerable during the day. This knowledge required them to build small caves from thorn bushes and leaves at guarded spots along the trail. There they could post sentries, for now they feared reprisal.

"The Elders of the Zuri Watu were still determined to find the trade goods they needed. After the rainy season, the same twelve scouts were sent into the taboo west. The scouts were instructed to take all possible precautions and they were to make no contact. Their mission was to observe only and to report back to the Elders.

"The coastal tribes of Africa had been so cruelly beset by the slave ships that those tribes that could, had escaped to the interior. In their peaceful valley, the Zuri Watu did not know that the slave ships had long since stopped raiding the west coast of Africa. So it was that the scouts could find no trails through the densely forested mountains and valleys to the west. They labored for weeks enlarging animal trails through the wilderness, using the sun to keep them on a westerly course. More than two moons passed before they reached the last summit where they could see the ocean shimmering in the distance.

"That night, from the top of a tall tree where they rested, the scouts could see tiny lights flickering in the clearing, where the blackness of the ocean began. The next day they came upon an old game trail, still used but mostly overgrown. They remembered the legends, which told of the pits and traps set to kill the slave traders. Staying cautiously to the edges of the old trail, they followed it all day. Climbing a lofty mahogany tree for the night, the scouts again saw the twinkling lights, like fallen stars, close to the ground. They knew not what to make of these tiny pinpoints of light.

"In the morning, as the first light tinged the night sky, they could see from an observation point high in the trees, the outline of a huge new palisade with large wooden boxes inside. These boxes had small areas on the walls that glowed with light.

"Keeping to their instructions, the two leaders crept closer under the cover of the night. Daylight found them perched high in a leafed-out old oak tree. Here they could see what was happening inside the fort. With great surprise they saw black men dressed in the same manner of clothing as the white men. The black men all seemed to like the white men and treated them like chiefs. These black men were not captives or treated badly. They moved about freely as did the women, who wore dresses made of beautiful, colored fabrics. All the children wore clothes too, and black and white children played together. Everyone looked relaxed and at ease, like they did back at the villages of the Nations. All looked well fed and the people laughed often. There was no sign of fear or hate. The two leaders spent all day in fascinated observation.

"It was a magical day. They saw sights that they had never even imagined. There were big animals like brown *punda* (zebra) pulling huge boxes supported by round discs that were filled with goods. They watched men cutting through logs by pulling handles attached to a long shiny board. Most amazing were the boys who went around on two round discs attached to thick sticks. They saw crates of fruits, vegetables and other interesting things outside of one of the big boxes with a long pointed roof. The women came and examined these things and took what they wanted.

"There were animals that looked like *gwase* (warthogs), but had no hair or tusks; and animals that looked like fat, curly haired *mbuzi* (goats) with black faces, but had no horns or beards; and in a pen were small *vasinyati* (Cape Buffalo) with brown and white hides. The wonders and sights were endless, and yet they saw no cooking pots.

"As night descended, so did the watchers who amazed their comrades with stories of the incredible things they had seen. Before dawn they were well on their way back to their village. It had taken them more than two moons to get to the ocean; but with the wondrous news and new trails, it took only one moon to get back to the Council.

"The Elders questioned each of the leaders alone, for it was difficult for them to believe the stories they heard. Once satisfied, the Elders allowed the villagers to gather about the central fire to listen to the tales of what the scouts had seen at the palisade where their ancestral village used to stand. The Elders wanted no misunderstandings about this important decision.

"In this way, it came to be decided that the second sons of the Chiefs would go west to the sea; taking with them the leaders of the scouts and a group of seasoned warriors The Elders gave them explicit instructions, which made them realize how very important the success of this mission was to the village. "An air of great adventure surrounded the group; for they took with them only the finest pelts and the most exquisite carvings. They had no ivory as elephants did not cross the mountains into their valley, but they had the teeth and claws belonging to the pelts and used them in clever ways to adorn the carvings, especially the ceremonial masks.

"In less than a moon, the trading group was within a day's journey of the new palisade. As directed, all the trade goods were hidden except for the items packed for the initial visit. The second sons bathed and put on new loincloths, the precious copper armbands and the feathered headdresses of Chief's sons. They had newly strung bows and many poisoned arrows in their quivers. Each carried a spear, a shield and a walinka. Armed, but not wearing paint or camouflage, they approached the wide, closed doors of this strange village. Two warriors, unadorned, went with them to carry the trade goods. The others climbed high in the trees to watch the historic event.

"Arriving at the town in mid-morning, they caused quite a stir as lookouts announced the arrival of armed natives. Since their approach was direct, calm and dignified, the gates were opened to them. A tall white man in white clothes wearing a headdress like a basket came to the gates to greet them. There were several men, black and white, gathered behind him, all quite curious.

"The tall white man raised his hand in greeting and asked them to identify themselves in Bantu, their language, but with a funny, different accent. After a moment, the Chief's second son understood his question and said, 'We are the Zuri Watu.' At this a low buzz of conversation erupted behind the tall white man. This was the ancestral home of the Zuri Watu, who had all been killed by the slave traders. The tall man turned and gestured for silence; then asked, 'Why have you come?'

"'We have come to trade.' At this, one of the young warriors stepped forward and placed a leopard skin on the ground. Upon the skin he placed three ebony and bone carvings of jungle animals; two bridal headdresses inlaid with polished stones that looked like diamonds and rubies; and two artfully carved ceremonial masks inlaid with tiny bits of a turquoise blue stone to look like tattooing. When the young man finished laying out the items, he stepped back to allow the white man to examine the displayed items.

"On his knee instantly, the tall white man could hardly contain his excitement. He was looking at museum quality African trade goods the like of which had not been seen in *over a hundred years. These were not just works of art; they were treasures, in perfect condition. He arose and said, 'I would be pleased if you would bring your trade goods to my sebula' (porch),' where we can talk out of the sun.'*

"The second son of the Chief said bluntly, 'Do you have any interest in these handcrafts? We seek iron cooking pots, combs, mirrors, fabrics, copper wire, glass beads, hunting knives, flensing knives, metal arrow and spear tips, needles and thread, scissors and machetes. Do you have these goods to trade?'

"The tall white man smiled at the earnest young man. 'We can supply you with anything you desire in return for these articles. You must tell me the number of pots and other things you want. Did you bring other items, besides these few things to trade?'

"'You must first tell us what these things will purchase in trade; then we will decide. We will wait here for your decision.' A stool was brought for the tall white man and a young boy held an umbrella over him to provide him some shade. The man took each item and examined it carefully. He wrote on a pad after looking at each item. The sun was getting high; the tall white man asked a woman to offer his visitors food and lemonade. The warrior escort stood silently aloof. When the tall white man finished, he said, 'You will have an account of a thousand dollars. It will enable you to buy whatever trade goods you require.'

"This was a new concept for the Chief's son. 'What is an account'?

"'It is the amount of money you have to use against the cost of the trade goods you desire. For instance, it will buy fifty cooking pots, fifty hunting knives, fifty machetes, and ten bolts of cloth; a hundred packets of needles, a hundred spools of thread, a hundred mirrors and a hundred combs. More goods than you can carry.'

"'What is this hundred, this fifty?'

"The tall white man held up his hands. 'This is ten. Each finger is a knife. Here is ten, and he laid his hands on the leopard skin, and signaled the watchers to help; here are ten more with another pair of hands, here are another ten and another ten and another ten.' When there were fifty fingers on the skin, the tall white man said, 'That is fifty; to make a hundred is to do it again.' Five more people added their hands to the circle. 'Now, you have a hundred fingers, and each finger represents a knife, or a pot, or a comb ... whatever items you choose. You can choose more of one item, like

knives, and less of another item, like bolts of cloth. Each item has a cost. The cost is different for knives than it is for combs. Do you understand?'

"It was amazing, but Ngarro did understand. He also understood they had been very successful traders. They could order whatever they wanted for they had many trade goods hidden in the forest. 'We will go now and decide how to use this account.'

"'You are welcome to stay here in the fort with us. There is a house for guests over there.' Ngarro turned and looked at the house. It looked like a jail to him. 'We are accustomed to sleeping in the forest; it is best for us. We will come back in the morning.'

"'Before you go, I would like to introduce myself. I am David Brookhurst. What we have here is called a dig. We are looking in the ground for artifacts, pieces of the old culture of the people who once lived here.'

"'I am Ngarro, second son of the Chief of the Nations of the Zuri Watu. This is Kimbata; he is the second son of the great Medicine Chief of the Zuri Watu. Our ancestors lived in this place. They left it long ago to escape the slave traders.'

"'Where did you go?'

"'I am not permitted to speak of any matters but the trading. We will return in the morning.' The goods had already been gathered and packed. So saying, Ngarro turned on his heel and left the fort. He signaled the warriors hidden in the trees to make sure they were not followed and continued on to the site of their cold camp.

"Here Ngarro and Kimbata decided it would be best to send the two warriors, who had gone with them into the fort, back to the Elders with the news of the trade. They were going to need many more bearers for the trade goods. By the time they traveled to the village, rested, were questioned and instructed by the Elders, and returned; more than two moons would have passed. Ngarro and Kimbata and the eight remaining warriors would stay to learn from these men.

"So began a favorable trade exchange. The ten natives arrived back the next morning. The tall white man, David Brookhurst, showed them all around the town; inside the buildings, explaining the grocery and dry goods store, the butcher, the horseshoer and ironmonger, and the grain and feed mercantile. The Zuri Watu were amazed. The houses were bright and busy, with tables and chairs and cooking places and washing places. The guesthouse had many beds and a place to bathe and a place called a privy. But most unusual of all was the house with all the bits and pieces of broken bowls, masks, jewelry and useless weapons. Even more senseless was the hole in the ground where men worked moving the dirt with tiny brushes.

"After the tour, they were invited to sit in the house without walls, called a gazebo, and offered a hot meal of roast pork, sweet potatoes with pineapple, squash, carrots and onions with biscuits and fresh fruit for dessert with coffee and chocolate. There was much excited jabbering over the meal and frequent laughter over a joke or an unusual answer to a question.

"When the meal was cleared away, Ngarro related the items he wanted to put on his account. He asked that a great many iron pots be ordered. He chose one of the women serving the table, whose dress he liked, to pick out the materials for him for five hundred women. David was astonished to hear the quantities. He quickly made sure Ngarro was aware of the vast quantity of cloth he was purchasing, for which he would have to send away. In fact his numbers were so large; it would greatly surpass his account.

Ngarro smiled, 'We have other trade goods; better things. Some things are over this hundred years old. You say you like old things.'

"David was speechless. Hundred-year-old African artifacts in good condition were unheard of ... 'Do you have these old items with you?'

"'One piece you might like. The woman who owns it wants to sell it for cooking pots for her granddaughters.' At a sign, one of the warriors dipped into his bag and brought forth a rabbit fur pouch and laid it on the table. Ngarro opened the bag and slowly drew out a child's death mask. It was carved from ebony. Every detail was perfect. The lashes of the closed eyes, the soft curve of the cheek, the sweet mouth, the tiny nose, the ears shaped like flowers with earrings of gold, and the hairline of kinky curls. Death masks were always buried with the dead. 'Why was this not buried with the child?'

"'The child drowned. Her body was never recovered. Her father always hoped Maridi would be found and have a proper burial. That was over a hundred years ago.'

"'This was priceless ... and to know the history that went with it... and the name of the child... David Brookhurst said, 'Your account is good for anything you want to buy. Anything! Just tell my secretary what you want.'

"So it was that the Zuri Watu started trading with the

American Archeologist in African Antiquities. So it was that there was no longer any shortage of trade goods. So it was that some of the men of the tribe went and stayed in the fort to learn the ways of metal, gems and glass.

"So it was that they learned of planes, automobiles, and engines. So it was that they learned of world war, armies and death. So it was that missionaries traveled to our village with quinine for malaria and taught us about the 'one true God'.

"But through it all the Zuri Watu prospered. The Nations stayed strong, and continued the way of life that had been so good to them with once-a-year trips to the fort for trade goods. The native crafts became sought after by many museums as they were done in the old manner, using the old ways and techniques.

"So it is they continue today, a great people, the Nations of the Zuri Watu, made stronger by adding a new God, the one and only God, the Supreme Being to rule the lesser gods who were often jealous and cruel. The story ends in the time of Sashono, the great leader and Chief of the Zuri Watu. The story ends in the time of Manutu, the greatest of the Medicine Chiefs of the Zuri Watu."

"The End."

Ambush Attack

"THE STORY WAS NOT what you expected, was it?"

"No, it wasn't. It was a marvelous saga, even though it was gruesome at times. But there was nothing about the Zuri Watu day-to-day life: no precepts or tenets explained."

"What are precepts and tenets?"

"The rules for moral conduct and the beliefs of a group."

"The Zuri Watu put only history in their history; sometimes adding unusual situations or tales of encounters with other tribes. I think what you want to hear are the stories that are told to the children, like the story about Shawna. It is through these stories that the children learn what is expected of them, why they should obey and the penalty for disobedience."

"Yes, I'd like to hear those stories, but, even more, I'd like to hear you tell a story about you, what you experienced growing up with the Zuri Watu."

Tamubu thought about her request and realized it was not the way of the Zuri Watu to talk about one's self, except to tell stories about encounters or situations. If this was the way the Americans and English talked, he would have to give it some thought.

"How is your ankle? I've seen you putting weight on it."

"It is better, but it gets sore when I use it. If I had crutches, I think we could move on soon."

"What are crutches?" Taking the diary, Paula drew a picture of a crutch and said, "These are made of sturdy, but light wood. With one on each side, they support the body while the good foot and leg swing forward." Then she explained the armpit and hand height measurements to him. "I know you must be anxious to move on. You have such a long way to go."

"It has been said, 'every journey begins with the first step; and that step is the only step of which we know the outcome.'"

"We have a saying too, 'Whatever will be, will be.' But that doesn't stop a person from planning what he or she wants to do next."

"In the morning, you can tell me your plans. I am like the grasses in the breeze... I bend in the direction of the wind." Paula turned to the wall so the flickering firelight wouldn't dance on the inside of her eyelids, wondering, what did he mean? He was like the grass in the wind; he bent with the breeze. Am I the breeze? It was an odd thing to say. Paula realized that she didn't want to move on just yet. She wanted more time with him than just the few days of travel that were left.

In the morning Tamubu was gone, but he left a coconut husk of oatmeal for her, which was still warm, and hot water for tea. Paula infused one of the two tea bags she had left. Days ago, she had taken to drying the bags and using them over again.

It was a glorious day. The rain had washed the forest clean. The air was fragrant with the smell of crushed flower petals, and the multi-denizen orchestra was playing a variation on a theme of crescendo, delightful!

Peeling a banana, Paula sat and watched the chiaroscuro, the patterns of light and dark, upon the backlit foliage change with the rising of the sun. The shafts of dazzling light peeked through here and there to illuminate the multi-hued petals of a dangling flower; making the drops of dew glitter like a decoration of diamonds. She would never forget the pageantry and the raw beauty of the rainforest; never forget hearing the primeval, yet harmonious sounds; nor would she ever forget the natural, earthy smell of Africa. It was like no other air she had ever breathed.

She heard a bird call nearby and turned to see Tamubu lowering a faggot of wood, then a bundle of feathery ferns.

She went and unfastened the sheaf. He said, "Wait! There is more." In a few moments, down came the woven grass gathering-bag. It was chock-full. There were coconuts, dates, sweet potatoes, the chard-like greens wrapped around asparagus and a plucked eviscerated bird, possibly a francolin: a larger quail-like bird.

Paula called out, "Are you planning on staying here until summer?" She heard him laugh and then he replied, "That's not a bad idea."

HER HEART RACED, SHE felt thrilled. It was a wonderful idea, but she had to get back and let everyone know she was all right; they must be worried sick about her. So she said, "We will run out of paper and pencil before then."

Touching down with a bounce, he turned and replied in his best British accent, "Well, that will never do!" The moment was brief, but still cherished. Tamubu didn't want this interlude to end either.

"Tomorrow we can be off. I have brought some branches that might make good crutches for you. Here, what do you think?"

He handed her two strong branches that had a soft curve at the top and horizontal branches sticking out an arm's length down from the top. Tucking one under her arm, she found it too long, but otherwise, a good fit from armpit to hand. "I brought some moss and threads from a sisal plant. I will wrap the hand supports for you." Tamubu adjusted the length of the crutches to suit Paula and then cleverly wrapped the hand and armpit areas. Paula watched him work, with a warm and happy feeling, until the crutches were finished.

TAMUBU PUT THE BIRD on the spit. He wrapped the sweet potatoes, which he had soaked in water, in tough stringy leaves before putting them in the hot ashes to bake. Finished with the meal preparations, he picked up her diary and began to work on the drawings again. Paula folded her now dry laundry and put it in her backpack. She then rearranged the pallets with the fresh new ferns.

As the light moved west, and the ledge cooled, Paula lay down and watched Tamubu draw. He was intent and totally focused. But she knew he was still aware of her, of the roasting bird and of all his surroundings. Impressed anew by his myriad abilities, and feeling a bit saddened by the short time left to them, she fell asleep.

Tamubu was pleased to hear the regular breathing of her sleep. She needed rest. Tomorrow would be a hard day. They would be walking up the rocky slope on the wide shoulder, with few trees to give relief from the sun. It was quite possible that they would not reach the mud hut before nightfall. It would be a long day, even with two good ankles.

After that, there was the arduous, winding trail down the mountain through the dense forest to the cove. Some places might be too narrow for the crutches; there he would have to carry her. It was going to be a difficult trip from here to the beach.

Tamubu struggled with his conscience. Should he tell her there was no reason to hurry to the cove... that the yacht was gone, and let her take additional time for her ankle to heal; or keep her hopes high, and her spirit willing for the strenuous trip to the beach... to reunite with friends that were no longer there. If the traveling proved to be too much for her, he could always tell her the yacht was gone; but once told, the devastating news could not be untold.

THE AFTERNOON LIGHT WAS fading into shadows, and the drawings began to lose their crisp definition. He closed the diary, and put it in the crevice next to Paula's pack. He turned the bird again, wrapped himself in his cloak and napped.

THE LOUD NOISE OF a splitting limb breaking off a tree awoke them both. Tamubu leaped up, grabbed the spit with the bird, his grass gathering-bag and the water skin, before he dove back into the cave-like crevice and his pallet. In only seconds, a huge branch came hurtling down to the ledge. Tamubu scampered to the edge of the platform next to the big boulder and looked up. He saw nothing, but heard again the splitting and crashing sound of another branch being severed from a tree.

"The apes," he said, "are building a ladder of branches to make their way down the cliff to reach us." Quickly he raced to the end of the branch and tried to push it off the ledge. It was too big and too heavy for him to shift. He heard the loud rustling of leaves above and leapt for the crevice as another huge limb came crashing down on the ledge.

Fighting his way through the branches, he reached the rappelling harness and detached it from the wire. Asking Paula for her rope, he made several knots in the end of it until he had a huge lump.

Paula asked, "What are you doing?"

"You are going to have to rappel off the ledge. Once you are safe, I am going to set these branches on fire. We don't have much time." He no sooner finished his explanation than another limb came hurtling down. "A couple more of these huge branches and the apes will be able to climb down to the ledge."

Paula quickly attached the line to the harness, stuffed her poncho, blanket and diary in her backpack, put on gloves, shouldered the pack and secured the straps. Tamubu took the line and wedged it under and behind the big boulder using the lump of knots as an anchor.

As soon as Paula was safely off the ledge, Tamubu set some of the leafy branches afire. The wood was green, but the attached leaves, needles, cones and pods were highly combustible tinder. While the fire grew, Tamubu hoisted the food sack, the turtle shell, the water skin and his weapons to his back. Once he was sure the fire would continue to grow and consume the apes' makeshift ladder, he tossed the grapnel and line to a podocarpus tree growing twenty feet away, and swung to safety.

PAULA HAD RAPPELLED DOWN to the sturdy branches of an ancient oak tree. She looked up and saw Tamubu jump off the ledge. He swung to the stout-limbed evergreen podocarpus tree. Ouch, she thought, for the long dropping swing brought him in fast and hard. But there was no other limb close enough or strong enough to support his weight. She watched as he made his way down the smooth bole of the many-branched tree and crossed to the oak tree to sit beside her. He looked sad. "What is wrong? Did you hurt yourself?" she asked.

"Your crutches, I forgot them." Paula laughed a little, then more and was finally consumed with mirth. Tamubu could not help smiling at her glee.

"What is so funny?"

"Here we are fleeing for our lives from murderous apes, who want to tear us into tiny pieces, and you are sad because you forgot my crutches! Well, do not be sad, they might be safe. While you were napping, I used them and then tucked them at the far back of my pallet. I wish I could see what is happening on the ledge with the fire. Do you think they know we escaped?"

"I don't think they saw you rappel down to the tree because the boulder obscured your escape; so they will not know about the rope. But, they probably saw me swing to the evergreen tree, which is an impossible feat for them without the grapple and line."

"Do you think they can get to us here?" Tamubu examined the steep slopes below them. "Probably not," he replied. "The trees here are mostly kola pines, with the occasional oak, aligna and young podocarpus; and those thickets are filled with poisonous, thorny vegetation." Although that won't stop them if they are determined to come after us, he thought. "That's the good news. The bad news is that we will have to go back the way we came once the fire has burned itself out; so I'm afraid we are here for the night."

"Believe me, there are worse things than having to sleep in a tree! Our first evening was spent in a tree and, even under the circumstances, I enjoyed it."

"You say the oddest things."

"Whatever do you mean?"

"Well, it would never have occurred to me that you had enjoyed being hunted and almost eaten by lions."

"I didn't say that! I said I enjoyed our time together in

the tree, once we were safe from the lions!" Tamubu smiled to himself. She was so easy to divert. One minute her face was white with fright, and the next, she was roused to indignation.

"I am going to climb up the podocarpus before it gets dark to see what has happened on the ledge with the apes. Are you comfortable where you are?"

"Yes, this is a lovely crotch, and here is a nice branch stub for my backpack. I can lean against this trunk and raise my ankle and foot to rest on that branch." Paula demonstrated her comfortable position. Tamubu smiled and left. She had to wriggle out on the limb a bit to watch his climb. She noticed that he had left the food and water close by, but took his weapons.

The light was fading quickly now, as it did on the east side of the mountain. The long, lingering twilight of the west was blotted out by mountain and vegetation. The visible sky was now a soft, copper cloud, with stratums of pink gold and salmon gold surrounded by a brilliant yellow-orange reflection of the distant, radiant sunset.

Paula reached for her water bottle. She was now glad that Tamubu had insisted on always being ready to depart quickly. Once something was used, it was put away. Washed clothes had to be folded and packed once they were dry. Food was taken out of the net bag only when needed; the unused portion was immediately wrapped and returned. Utensils were washed after use and put away. Extra food was carefully packed in leaves and small grass bags and put in the food bag. Her jacket or blanket, once removed, had to go into her pack. Only her poncho remained out on the pallet, because it was where she sat most of the time. Everything he did had a purpose and a reason. There was a precision to his trekking, akin to horse vaulting or to the quadrivial of the drill teams.

Once again, this quiet, unassuming man had known exactly what to do and did it without excitement or fuss. A bird warbled nearby. Paula turned and there he was just a branch away. How was he able to go about so quietly? She felt foolish. Her daydreaming had occupied her so completely that she had failed to hear his return. "What did you see?" she asked.

Tamubu wondered if he should tell her what he saw, and evaded her question with one of his own. "Are you hungry? I had planned the bird for our lunch tomorrow, but there's enough for two meals. Besides, there's little likelihood that I'll be able to whip-up a stew here."

Paula loved his British sense of humor, and replied. "Knowing you, dinner will be the usual gourmet meal; and I wouldn't be at all surprised if you did serve stew!" She enjoyed the badinage with Tamubu. He was a quick wit.

The bird was still warm. Tamubu had immediately wrapped it and put it in the food bag after he raced to escape the falling limb. There were dates, papayas and the sweet potatoes, which he always cooked ahead and used as a base for many of his recipes. No tea or broth, but plenty of water.

"You evaded my question earlier about what you saw back at the ledge."

"Yes, what I saw was unpleasant. Do you really want to know about it?"

"Yes, you cannot protect me from what is, only from what might have been."

Tamubu tilted his head to one side. Her receptive aura was emerging. She was floating to a higher plane of awareness... how far could she go? Linking her to his subliminal and mystical world, they floated up the tree until they came to a place where they saw the smoldering logs. Amidst the ashes, three ape bodies lay, charred, hairless, and grotesque. The other apes were gone. These impetuous males had perished when the brush pile collapsed in the flames, and they could no longer climb to the top of the cliff to save themselves.

While the apes could make a way to cross a deep, narrow ravine, or reach a ledge below a sheer cliff, they lacked the ability to foresee the eventualities. There was no *what if* in their actions. Tamubu's thoughts queried her. 'Do you see what has happened?'

'Yes, I see. But I do not feel sadness. They meant to harm

us, but instead harmed themselves. Do you think they will come back again?' Tamubu could honestly tell her.

'No, being able to produce a fire so great will remain in the memories of those who saw it; and it will make them wary of those who can do such a thing. They will not be back. It is late. We need to rest, for tomorrow will be a hard day.' Tamubu watched as Paula tied herself to the tree. He thought, 'Good Night'. Paula did not reply. The connection had been severed when she closed her eyes. Her psychic ability amazed him; it was so unexpected and strong.

THE NEXT MORNING, THEY decided to have breakfast later, when they reached the trail. Tamubu knew Paula would need a rest by then. It would be a hard climb one-footed. Buckling on the rappelling harness, Tamubu went up hand over hand on the knotted rope to the ledge. He hauled up their possessions, and sent the harness back down for Paula. Fitting a safety strap around each wrist, Paula reached up high with her left hand, then brought her right hand up to meet her left. She had assumed the 'L' position, using her strong thigh and buttock muscles to support her body weight, and anchor the harness, while she alternately slid her hands up the line towards the ledge.

Her muscles were trembling from the exertion when she reached the ledge. Tamubu grabbed the line as she rappelled out, and yanked her up on to the ledge, catching and holding her tight to take any weight off her injured ankle.

Paula took a few moments to catch her breath and oxygenate her tired muscles, making no effort to leave his comforting embrace. Never, in all her life, had she been so glad to be held, and leaned into him gently.

Tamubu responded by cradling her tenderly, savoring the fulfillment of his dearest wish. When her breathing quieted, he took her to sit next to the gear. Tamubu found the crutches, unharmed by the fire, and then guided her to the natural chimney. He would go up first, so she could send up the gear and the food. Paula had to rappel with one foot while Tamubu belayed a safety line from above. It was with great relief that Paula fell in an exhausted heap on top of the cliff.

Tamubu made a small fire while Paula rested. Breakfast was a sweet potato mixed with the last of the blackberries, vanilla bean and coconut slivers, and broth; the tea bags were gone. After three days of inactivity—and then more than an hour of intense physical exertion—she felt empty. But, by the time breakfast was over and the supplies repacked, she was feeling herself again. She took electrolytes and two aspirin for her throbbing ankle; now she was ready to go.

Paula had never used crutches before, and it took her some minutes to get the hang of them. She asked for the lead, saying he spoiled her cadence with his constant stopping to see if she was okay.

By the time noon and the hot sun arrived, Paula was more than ready for a meal and a needed rest. She took out her first aid kit, and trimmed the torn skin from the broken blisters on her palms, which she cleaned with hydrogen peroxide before applying ointment and then applied gauze around her palms and knuckles.

Tamubu watched the process, keenly interested. He knew water could contain germs that caused sores to fester, or worse, unless it was boiled. He was quite impressed with the bubbling fizz and said, "This would be great magic for a medicine man. I must learn how to make this 'an-ti-sep-tic'." he read from the boldly printed word on the plastic bottle.

Paula chuckled, "I wouldn't mind knowing how it was made myself."

Tamubu's lips thinned and widened; it was his expression of displeasure. "You don't know how to make this antiseptic?"

"I haven't the foggiest!" Tamubu looked at her askance and laughed with delight.

"My father used to say that! My mother would question him, saying: 'How did that dirt get on the carpet?' and he would reply, 'Haven't the foggiest' when his boots were covered with mud. So you must be avoiding something!"

Paula laughed at his reasoning. "Not everyone is trying to cover-up when they say they don't know something."

Tamubu sat quietly, thinking about this new memory of his father, which had popped-up out of nowhere, as so many memories did when he talked with Paula. He watched her put her first-aid supplies back in the kit; before she set about rewrapping the handholds on the crutches. She first wrapped the rolled cotton around the rough handles, then wide gauze to hold the cotton securely in place and lastly, wrapped the handholds evenly with cloth bandaging tape. She then peeled the bark off the armpit supports, leaving them smooth.

Over the lunch of francolin, dates and sweet potato mixed with papaya and coconut Tamubu spoke, "Each day I spend with you brings my past back to me in some way. Some are startling, like you saying, 'I haven't the foggiest'. Other times, in other ways, it is just a subtle remembrance of similar times, but different. Sometimes it is a vague feeling, or a thought not quite captured; but they change me and bring me closer to who I was so long ago." Tamubu looked into the fire for a few moments, and then raised his eyes to meet hers, and with deep feeling said, "I want you to know, before we reach the sea, that for as long as you need me, I will be there for you."

Paula wondered at this outpouring of loyalty. Did he know something she didn't? Or was it just a feeling of gratitude being expressed. Whatever the cause, she spoke her mind.

"You must be careful not to make commitments you will not want to fulfill."

"On the contrary, I just made a commitment I do want to fulfill." There! It was out in the open. He had told her he wanted to be with her, without obligating her in any way.

Paula was thrilled. Her spirits soared. She felt as if she would never be unhappy again—ever! But she dared not offer him encouragement, not yet. Too much was still unknown. First, she had to get back to the yacht. Second, she must not hurt his feelings, so she said, "It never occurred to me that you would not be there for me, if I needed you. Never has one person been so fortunate to find such a truly selfless friend, as I have found with you. I cherish your friendship more than I cherish my life."

◈◈◈

PAULA DID NOT KNOW it, but she had just sealed her fate to him. In the ways of the Zuri Watu, love was a feeling; sometimes you had it, sometimes not. It was like the passionate feeling that a mother has for her child, blind, selfless and all consuming. But if the person to be taken as a spouse could be looked upon as a friend, a friend who would put the other person's needs first, it could be a good marriage; for a deep, abiding love can grow in the fertile soil of friendship.

PAULA LAY DOWN IN the dappled shade of a teak tree. The lunch, combined with the unusual exertion, had her asleep in moments. Tamubu watched her as she slept. He was examining his emotions, which ran from delight in their togetherness on the journey to dismay at the disappointment Paula would feel when she arrived at the empty beach. She never complained, never showed fear, never faltered at the unknown. But, now she had a goal. What would her reaction be to abandonment? Would it be the blow that demolished her courage and determination? Realizing he was worrying like a little old woman (a first for him), he turned his attentions to repacking their supplies in case he had to carry her again.

The sun was past its zenith and mid-way on its descent to the horizon when Paula awoke from her nap. "Why did you let me sleep so long? Now, we'll never make it to the thorn boma hut before dark."

"If you were sleeping, you needed the rest; quite logical wouldn't you say?"

She had no defense before his reasoning, so she smiled and said, "Well Thomas, in that case, do carry on." He was surprised at the use of his given name; until he remembered that he had signed the plant drawings in her diary, *Thomas,* as he had done as a boy.

Moments later, they were trudging down the trail. In an hour, Tamubu was carrying her in his African version of a piggyback ride. He could move faster this way, as Paula used the crutches to move foliage out of his path. His pouches, the grass gathering-bag of food and the water skin were suspended from his neck, across his chest, and secured around his waist.

The weight in front acted nicely as a counterbalance. He carried his spear in his hand as a walking staff; the bow and quiver were attached to Paula's backpack.

He had carried a sick young man this way for days, but when the lad went unconscious, he had felt like lead. Carrying Paula felt like carrying feathers. Her weight moved away from his muscles at each stride, but she always stayed balanced. He wondered if this was how it felt for a horse carrying a skilled rider; there, but never interfering with the working muscles, the cadence or the motion.

Dusk found them far from the hut. "Look for a stopping place. I need to watch where I put my feet," he told her.

"I think we just passed a place that might do. It was a big cleft between two rocks. I couldn't tell how deep it was, for the opening was narrow. It is the only thing I have seen so far." Stopping, Tamubu released the tumpline from his forehead and Paula dropped her good foot to the ground. Supporting herself with the crutches, she went to sit on a low rock beside a sapele tree, while he unfastened the bag around his neck, asking, "How far back do you think it was? Describe the area to me."

"It was not far, look to the west. When you see boulders with the bright, evergreen foliage of the agauria at the base, look just beyond and you will see the cleft."

Paula barely had time to relieve herself before Tamubu was back. "You have a good eye for camping places. It will do nicely. With a fire at the entrance, it will also be safe. Come, I will carry our belongings. It is, like you said, not far."

The cleft was narrow, less than two feet wide, about four feet long, and led to an open space about ten feet square. Young trees grew on the periphery amongst the rocks and acted like a boma, preventing carnivores from leaping onto the rocks and attacking from above. The space was full of leaf and branch debris, providing fodder for a fire and materials for the pallets. They worked well together, so it was not long before the fire was going and the pallets were ready.

They had finished the cooked bird for lunch, but Tamubu still had the dried turtle meat, some of which he dropped in boiling water, with onions, mushrooms, barley, peppercorns and spices. Later he added the asparagus and half of a squash with a bit of rice.

The sweet potatoes he rolled in leaves and baked in the ashes for tomorrow's lunch. He would mix them with tapioca, which he soaked all night in water, from the cassava when they cooled and top them with slivered coconut and sesame seeds. He would roll the mixture in the chard-like leaves.

The dried manioc would make good flour for banana rollups, filled with fiddlehead ferns and slivered coconut, for breakfast. It was the last of the fresh foodstuffs. But, the forest to the sea was a garden of fruits and vegetables, with all the rain it received.

It was a deep dark in the forest, the black time before the moon rises and the stars are visible when they finished their meal. Paula again cleaned and tended her hand sores while Tamubu administered to her ankle. "I have thought of a story you might enjoy."

Pleased, Paula replied, "Oh good! What's the story about?"

"It's about a little girl who wouldn't cry."

"That's quite unusual. Is it one of the learning stories?"

"In a way, but it is a personal family story from the life of Sashono's father, Agurra."

"You mean this is a true story?"

"Yes."

Paula could hardly wait for the story to begin, but said nothing as Tamubu composed himself comfortably on his pallet before beginning his narrative.

19)

Emula

"EMULA WAS SEVEN YEARS old. She learned to walk when she was two years old. She never cried, although she fell down many times each day—for Emula had a clubfoot. Even when she lost a little finger in a snare, when she was four, she did not cry. Her mother died when she was five, still Emula did not cry. Neither did she speak. Emula had two brothers to care for: three-year-old Sammo, and the new baby, Huzunitoto.

The women in the village liked to gossip about this unusual little girl. She was likened to an old woman in a child's body. At such a young age, she took care of the family like a grown woman, and did so until her father remarried when she was six years old.

"Her father's new wife used Emula like a servant, letting her do most of the housework. But one day, before she was eight, Emula walked out of the hut, and did not return. Her father and stepmother were annoyed; there was work to be done. Where did she go? No one had seen her leave the village, yet she was nowhere to be found.

"This gentle, docile, obedient child was the example the village mothers used to their lazy daughters. A search party went out. It came back saying they had seen no sign of a child with a clubfoot.

"Months passed, and the village gossiped about the apparent death of little Emula by misadventure. One fine morning, five women, Emula's stepmother and her four neighbors, walked to the stream to fill their water containers. There, sitting on a rock, away from the edge of the stream was Emula, and she was crying. The women bombarded her with questions: 'Where have you been?' 'Why are you crying?' 'Why are you sitting on that rock?' Momentarily, they had forgotten she did not speak.

"At last, Emula held up her hand for silence. After a few

moments, she said to them, 'I came to visit you today... have you missed me?'

"Astonished that she was speaking, it took a few moments before the women replied, each said, 'Yes, yes.'

"Her stepmother became angry at hearing Emula speak for the first time, for now she felt she had been scorned by the child, and said, 'You have been a bad girl. How could you be so cruel to your father and me? He'll give you a good whipping when you get home. You have caused a great deal of trouble.'

"Taking no notice of her stepmother's mean words, Emula replied. 'I was born with a clubfoot. Because of my physical defect, I was neglected and ignored, even when I cried in pain and suffering. I had to crawl for two years before I managed to teach myself to walk. On that momentous day I promised myself that I would never speak, or ask for help from another person. You say, a two year old child cannot reason that way—cannot understand; but you are wrong. I was given great gifts to compensate for my crippled foot. But, no one paid any attention to me, not my mother, not my father, no one. Often I heard people say cruel things: Emula will never walk; she will never be of any help, only a burden; she will never marry, who would want her?'

"'The way a person looks goes no deeper than the skin. The way a person acts goes all the way to their hearts, and that is the only true judge of worth. On the day I left, I came to the river for water, and I saw a Shining Man on a camel. He said He would rid me of my club-foot if I went with Him.' At this Emula took her feet from the water, and the village women gaped in amazement when they saw two perfect feet.

"They were baffled. 'Then why are you crying?' a woman asked.

"'I am crying for you. Because of your callous treatment of me, you will never know the Shining Man on the camel. He sent me to you to make you understand that when a child is born with an affliction, that child is often given gifts no other child possesses. I could understand speech when I was a baby. I could speak a year before I could walk. I could reason and remember better than a full-grown man. But no one cared enough about me to find out that I had these gifts. I never had a happy day. I never had love from anyone. So, I went away. I came back to tell you that I am now happy every day, and loved every day, and I cry because none of you will ever know this happiness, for your lives will be filled with sorrow.' Emula slipped off the rock into the fast-flowing water and disappeared.

"The women were dumbfounded. What would they tell the others in the village? Who would believe them? The women made a pact. No one would ever speak of what happened this morning at the stream. There were supernatural forces at work here, which they did not understand and greatly feared.

"One by one, each of the women that had been at the stream, contracted leprosy, and became an outcast from the village. One by one, each realized that the spirit gods were punishing them for their senseless cruelty to a helpless child. One by one, they experienced the loss of love, and the degradation of neglect.

"Emula's stepmother was the last to be afflicted. A year earlier she had given birth to a little girl who was born blind. Every minute of every day was taken up with the care of this child whom she found repulsive. Her husband often beat her for giving him a blind child. In her terror one day, she blurted out the story of Emula at the water, saying that maybe the Shining Man on the camel would give their child sight. This story further enraged the father. He now believed his wife to be a liar. When she contracted leprosy, her husband insisted she take the child with her to live with the lepers, even though the child did not have the disease, nor would she ever contract it.

"Fifteen years later the village experienced an epidemic of typhoid fever. Because of her natural immunity, the blind child, named Myuma, was brought to the village to care for the sick. Those who were grateful for her ministrations and thanked her for her kindness and care eventually got well. Those who refused Myuma's help because she had lived with the lepers, and did not want her to touch them, or those who insulted her, eventually died.

"One of the many ill was a young man who became deaf from the disease. He fell in love with this dignified and tranquil young woman. A year later, Agurra wed Myuma. Two years later, twin sons were born to them; the blind Myuma thanked God for her healthy sons. On that day, her husband, Agurra, went to the stream for water, where he slipped and fell into the rain-swollen and turbulent stream. He panicked, and was about to drown when unseen hands helped him to the shore. There, he sat gasping for air, stunned to be able to hear the women calling for help.

"Agurra joyously returned to his wife's bedside, to tell her *his wondrous news. There, he found Myuma had died—and he then knew whose hands had pulled him from the raging stream. With his hearing restored, Agurra knew he had a destiny to fulfill and devoted himself to the sick, eventually becoming one of the wisest Medicine Chiefs in the history of the Zuri Watu. It was left to him to name the twin boys, and he chose to name the first born, Sashono; and the second born, Manutu." The End*

TAMUBU CONTINUED, "SASHONO BECAME Chief of the Nations of the Zuri Watu by popular acclaim, when the old chief and his family died in a fire, after lightning struck their abode, which had been built atop a little a hill. Sashono's wisdom is legendary. The Nations have known only peace and prosperity during his reign.

"Manutu became the greatest Medicine Chief in the history of the Nations, surpassing the abilities and knowledge of his father, Agurra. Since his birth, not one person has contracted leprosy or died of typhoid fever."

"What a wonderful story. Who do you think the Shining Man on a camel could have been?"

"I do not know what to think. I have seen whole villages caught up in a belief that had no basis for truth. It has happened in the Nations, but mostly from fear of an unknown, but natural happening. Her story was most unusual, as camels are not found in our area. We believe God controls life, but we have never known Him to carry away a living person. It remains one of those things that exists, but cannot be explained: like Agurra regaining his hearing after almost drowning; like being an Aliki Mzimu."(Wise ancestral spirit)

"Do things like this happen often in the Nations?"

"Every few years, it seems, something happens which is unusual and a legend is born."

"Sashono is your adopted father, is he not? Did he tell you this story?"

"No, Manutu told me the story —it was a lesson to teach me to look past the obvious."

Tamubu glanced at Paula. Was she going to a higher level of awareness?

Paula continued, "Who told Manutu the story?"

"Manutu had the story from Agurra before he died."

"Does Agurra still speak to Manutu?"

"Manutu is in touch with all the spirits of all the ages—he is: ule kubwa kasiroho," (the great living spirit).

Paula looked up at Tamubu and said, "It was a sad story; one that makes you feel melancholy for the stoic suffering of children. I feel children must always be cherished and loved."

"I agree. If you still want to hear stories, I will avoid the ones dealing with the suffering of children. But many of the stories are based on the sufferings of children; for it is children that the stories teach. Telling children about the sufferings of a grown man or woman, does not have the same effect on them, for there is no sympathy or mutual empathy."

"I never thought about it like that, but I'm sure you're right. I know bad things happen to children: I just hate to think about them."

"Then, we won't think about them. There are other stories—what I call boys stories, as they deal with boys learning to be men. But not tonight, you need to sleep."

"Yes, I must admit I feel weary. Goodnight."

A HEAVY RAIN AWAKENED them early. The overcast sky kept the air quite cool. Paula belted her poncho to keep it from tangling with the rough bark of the hand-made crutches, but the footing was greasy and the crutches slipped easily. The trek became arduous. By the time they reached the hut surrounded by the thorn boma, Paula was only footsteps away from total exhaustion.

They had an early lunch of the sweet potato mixture in the leaf roll-ups, nuts and fruit. Paula took electrolytes and aspirin with her hot broth. The heat of the small fire felt good and she lay down beside it. In moments, she was asleep.

Tamubu could see the lines of pain around her mouth and dark smudges under her eyes. She was near the limit of her endurance. Would she be able to make it to the sea? While she slept, he *roamed* the trail behind them to make sure the hideous apes had not followed them. The trail was clear and he felt he could safely *roam* for a few hours to look for a suitable camping spot for the night. He found nothing more than a wide space in the trail in a half-day march. Traveling on, he found a shallow cave, too open to attract animals as a lair, but good protection for them with a fire. But it was too far from the mud hut, at least a full day's travel at her reduced pace.

Later, when Paula awoke from her nap, Tamubu said to her. "It's a full day's travel to the next good camping place. I suggest we stay here for the night and start again in the morning, if that suits you."

"Yes, I'm afraid it does suit me. It seems a half-a-day on crutches in the rain is my limit. I hope I can do a full day tomorrow."

"It will not be as hard tomorrow. I will carry you on the steep, narrow part of the descent in the late morning. That should bring us to a wide spot in the trail for lunch. After that the trail widens as it curves its way around the slope of the mountain. There it will be easier for you with the crutches."

"I remember that part of the trail well. The Ndezi had just led me out of the thorny undergrowth in the woods, where there had been no trail, and I was thankful to see a wide, clear space and a worn trail. We are getting close. I can hardly wait to see my friends again."

Tamubu felt guilty for not saying anything. But the disappointment would be no greater for having waited to be seen. "If you are all right, I will go and find our dinner." So saying, he was gone.

Paula rested and wondered how he knew so much about the trail when he had not yet been there—or had he—but how could he travel so many trails in such a short time? Paula dozed off thinking about all the anomalies of their acquaintance and she wondered why she had not noticed them sooner?

Two hours later, Tamubu returned with bananas, loquats and blackberries. He had surprised a wild sow with piglets and had stunned a piglet with his walinka. They were in for a feast. He had found elephant's ear and figs, ferns and mushrooms. He moved the boma aside with his spear and glanced in the hut. Instantly, he was alerted. Paula was gone. Her crutches were gone; her backpack was still there. Reading the *sign*, he saw the tips of the crutches going off into the forest.

Following the marks, he came to a place where the plants were crushed and broken. It did not look like a skirmish, but as if someone had fallen. Tamubu called, "Paula, can you hear me?" Did he hear a groan? "Paula, answer me." Looking closely at the mashed vegetation, Tamubu saw that the masses of vines had made a natural trap; it looked like the ground, but actually, there was nothing under the vines, but air and the steep mountainside. Skirting the tangle of vines, Tamubu worked his way down the slope. His heart leapt into his throat when he saw her lying against the bole of a kola tree. She would fall no further, but he would need the help of a line to get her up the steep slope. Picking his way back carefully, lest he too slide down the slope, he went to Paula's pack for the knotted rope.

It seemed a long time to him until he was kneeling beside her—having stopped to tie the line around a stout tree above the steepest part of the ascent. She was unconscious, but nothing seemed to be broken in his brief examination. Hefting her onto his shoulder, Tamubu started up the tortuous climb of the rough slope. Several times he had to put her down and rest. It took an hour to reach the level footing of the shoulder. He was soaked in sweat and his leg muscles quivered from the exertion.

Carrying her to the hut, he laid her down on the pallet she had prepared earlier. Using some of the boiled water from her metal bottle, he washed her face, arms and legs. There were many abrasions and several cuts, which he cleaned with the peroxide from the first aid kit, but he could find nothing serious. Her ankle did not seem hot or swollen. In his efforts to make her more comfortable, he lifted her head, and found a huge lump on the back of her head. So, she had hit her head when she had fallen down the slope.

Going to his pouch, he took out a tiny pipe and filled it with a crumbled mixture. Lighting the pipe, he drew in the smoke and, covering Paula's mouth, blew the smoke up her nose. In a few minutes, the white bloodless look of her face faded and color returned. He took her backpack and placed it under her ankles and feet, then put her jacket under her head for a pillow, and covered her with the metallic blanket. He then emptied her plastic water bottle and filled it with the hot water from the metal bottle. Wrapping one of her shirts around the bottle, he tucked it in next to the soles of her feet, which were ice cold.

Tamubu built up the fire and refilled the metal bottle to heat water while he made dinner. She would not have an appetite when she awakened, but hot food was needed to help her body recover. Head injuries could be slight or serious. He would know soon. Every hour or so, he lit the tiny pipe and blew the smoke up her nose, washed her face and moistened her lips.

A stygian night had descended, for the sky was densely clouded and low; it would rain, and heavily, before morning. Tamubu gathered his cloak closer to go and check on Paula. She was warm under her cover but he would have to move her to the pallet he had prepared inside the mud hut before the rains came. The fire he had built inside was now burning hot and smokeless. He knew Paula hated the little airless huts, but dry was better than wet. The meal was cooked and keeping warm by the inside fire. He moved her gear into the hut and then, lastly, lifted her and carried her to the new pallet. As he again made her comfortable, he heard a murmur. Looking closely in the dim light, he saw her eyelids flutter open. "Where am I?"

"You are here with me, in the mud hut. It is raining."

"Good, I like the rain." Her lids closed and she slept. Tamubu was relieved. She was lucid. She would need rest, but she would soon be well again. He lay down beside her and used his body heat to help keep her warm. The night was raw and cold with the pervading dampness from the low cloud cover.

As he lay beside her, he remembered Manutu saying: 'Things that are worthwhile having... are often difficult to obtain. It seems the gods must test us for our worthiness before they allow us to attain our goals.' Were the gods testing him, or were they testing Paula? Or were they testing both of them?

Tamubu awoke when Paula moved. He whispered, "Are you all right?" She groaned a bit and said, "I have a terrible headache. Would you get me some aspirin from the first aid kit?"

"I do not think that is wise until you have been able to take in some food and keep it down. You have a nasty bump on your head."

"I am thirsty; did you make broth?"

"Yes, wait a moment." Tamubu slowly propped her up with his arm and handed her the plastic water bottle.

"You put the broth in here?"

"Yes, when the water was hot, I made the broth and put it in the plastic bottle to warm your feet, that way I could use the metal bottle to heat more water."

"I'm sorry to be so much trouble to you. I went out for the necessary and when I leaned on the crutch, it just kept sinking. I lost my balance and fell; I rolled on landing, but I don't remember anything else."

"You will be fine. You are recovering quickly. Are you hungry?"

"No, the broth was enough."

"Are you warm enough?"

"Yes, I am, even my feet feel warm." Paula lay back and was instantly asleep.

Tamubu thanked God for His mercy. He replenished the fire and again lay down beside Paula. This time his thoughts were on the near future thinking about their traveling to Kenya together; but would she be able to do that now with her injured ankle... or would she even want to trek so far? Could he have been wrong in his feelings that she enjoyed the traveling? Or was she just making the best of the difficult situation that had been forced upon her? Maybe she would want to go to the nearest town to contact her friends. He sighed, whatever she wanted, he would be there for her... if she needed him.

◈◈◈

IN THE MORNING, PAULA sat up and had a few bites of the roasted pork and vegetable medley. Her headache was gone, but she was stiff and sore. Tamubu suggested she drink some broth with his herbs, rather than take the aspirin, and she acquiesced. The rain had stopped, and she asked to go outside when it dried up a bit. The hut had the pervading smell of decay that she disliked so intensely.

She slept again and then badgered Tamubu into helping her go outside. She breathed deeply of the fresh, sweet air and felt much better. Sheltering under the deep eaves of a mud hut was one thing, being inside another. She was glad it was the last time; she never wanted to sleep in a dark and smelly mud hut again.

WARM AND COMFORTABLE UNDER the long eaves, she dozed; and in her dreams she heard Tamubu say, "Knock, knock, hello there! I say, am I ever so glad to see you again! You have given us all a dreadful fright!" Then she heard Tamubu reply, "Hello, what do you mean, we have given you a dreadful fright?" This dream was just too silly, with Tamubu having a conversation with himself; so she opened her eyes, but she was still dreaming. The young man that had come to the Ndezi village with the kind and grizzled trader, Max, stood before her. Jon was looking away from her, so she turned her head and saw that Tamubu had emerged from the hut where he had been smoking portions of the piglet.

The young trader seemed to be astonished. He said, "I'm so sorry. I was talking to Miss Thornton. We've been searching for her."

"Why have you been searching for her?" Tamubu asked.

"I know this man, Tamubu. He is a trader. He came to the Ndezi village the day I escaped. He and his partner tried to get Bolbonga to release me—but Bolbonga refused to let me go—so they made their prices so high that no one wanted to trade with them. They left to get help—but Bolbonga sent warriors with them, so they couldn't go for help."

"On the contrary my dear lady," Jon said, "as soon as the warriors left us at our camp, we radioed to Enugu Station in Nigeria for help. The next morning soldiers arrived in helicopters and captured the village. When Bolbonga and his warriors returned from searching for you, they too were captured. But you were gone without a trace.

"Captain Reverman, who led the soldiers, did not believe Bolbonga's story of your disappearing into thin air, so he contacted us at our camp; and we patched him through to Enugu Station; who patched him through to the *Norsk Star*; who patched him through to the *Just Cause*. Dr. Miles told him, 'If she can reach the trees, she will be gone. She is a monkey when it comes to climbing and is fearless about heights.'"

Tamubu was pleased to hear some of the details of her story. Paula had talked little about her ordeal, except for a few references to events that happened on the trek to the Ndezi village.

Jon continued, "It has greatly bothered both Max and myself that we were unable to free you before we left the village; and that we were unable to tell you of our plan to radio for help once we reached our camp. Bolbonga would not let us see you again before we left the village. Later, after your escape, we were extremely troubled and worried about your ability to survive alone in the wilds of Africa; but here you are—safe, with someone to look out for you—who obviously knows the ways of Africa."

Jon turned to Tamubu, "I am so sorry. In my excitement at finding Miss Thornton, I totally forgot to introduce myself. My name is Jonathan Caulfield. I was tagging along with Max Mason, a trader, for a bit of travel and adventure before settling down to tea farming in Kenya. When we arrived at the Ndezi village to trade, we became embroiled in the fringes of Miss Thornton's abduction and the subsequent rescue effort.

"A few days ago, when there had been no news of Miss Thornton at all, we decided to mount our own search effort. What a jaunt that has been—and even better, what a marvelous conclusion—I'm absolutely delighted!"

A huge lump had come up into Tamubu's throat. His chest felt constricted and he thought he would suffocate. Pictures were dancing in his mind, the little voice, "Thomas, where are you?" rang in his ears. He could not speak, could not even breathe, so he raised his hand, index finger pointed up, the universal sign of: wait a moment, please; and ducked back into the hut. He could hear Jon chattering on and then finally, Jon said, "Listen to me nattering on–I should return to my group, and get a message off that you've been found. We'll pop back later."

Paula was very excited and wanted to talk after Jon had gone. "Tamubu, where are you? What do you think of his news? I seem to have a habit of disappearing just before the troops arrive. Tamubu, answer me. Are you all right?"

Paula started to struggle to her feet when Tamubu came out and sat down beside her. He looked straight into her eyes and Paula saw tremendous anxiety. He took her hands in his and said, "I don't know what to do; I need your help and advice". He looked away and Paula thought she saw his eyes brim with tears. Whatever could be so wrong? She thought. Tamubu turned back to her and said softly, "I think that man was my little brother, Jon."

Paula was incredulous. "Oh, my gosh! That's wonderful!"

"No! No it's not! I'm not ready for this! It is exactly what I feared! He did not treat me as an equal. He didn't even ask me to introduce myself. He didn't extend his hand when he introduced himself. Who I am was unimportant to him. He did not see me as a person worthy of respect and common courtesy."

"Oh Thomas, Jon was so excited at finding me alive that he was beside himself, and manners were the last thing on his mind." Paula thought for a moment, as she eyed his troubled countenance, before she continued, "Why don't we just continue on as we were? You don't need to say anything until you find out about his plans. After all, you did lose most of your memory. Later, you can always say that something triggered your memory, for that has been happening, hasn't it?"

"Yes, it has and you're right. We'll just wait and see what happens. There is no need to rush into explanations. When the time is right for declarations, I will know the right thing to do—for everyone involved."

Paula was elated for Tamubu. He's such a wonderful person; anyone would be proud to know him, and even prouder to be related to him. He just needs to regain his usual self-confidence. His memories of the class distinctions of his childhood are probably unfounded today—so much has changed. But even so, he is not a native, he is a member of their family, no matter how he now looks or acts.

Paula could still see his tenseness and worry. She laid her hand gently on his arm saying softly, "You must be you, for you can be no one else. You must walk tall, for regardless of race, you are a paragon among men—there is no man living who is better than you. You have been chosen, and this is your destiny."

Tamubu closed his eyes. He felt as one with Paula. He then knew she was speaking for the spirits who watched over him. When he opened his eyes, the tension and apprehension were gone. He was himself again, and her relief was palpable.

With his coy, dimpled smile he said, "I will trust to my destiny."

Speculation

JON HURRIED BACK TO the place where he had left Kimbo and Kybo, before going on to the hut alone. The bearers were close enough to see the hut, but they were too far away to hear the exchanges. They could, however, see the joy on Jon's face, and knew he was bringing good news.

"Hallelujah! Miss Thornton is found, Kimbo, and she is fine. Let's get cracking. I can't wait to tell Max the jolly good news."

"Jon calling Max at base camp four. Over." The radio crackled with a flurry of static, and Jon thought, Oh no, not battery failure, not now! Just then, the radio crackled again and Jon was overjoyed to hear:

"Max here, Jon. How are things going with you? Over."

"Things here are just smashing! We found Miss Thornton about an hour ago and she is just fine, except for a sore ankle. There's always the unexpected, you know. Seems Miss Thornton has an African escort, who is guiding her back to the cove. I was so excited to see her that I didn't ask how they happened to meet. Over."

"You don't know how good that makes me feel. I'm glad you followed your instincts, my boy. I will radio the tanker and the yacht with the good news. What are your plans now? Over."

"I have decided to go with them to the beach. As I mentioned, Miss Thornton has a sore ankle, and we can help with the portage, as the slopes may be quite steep in places. Over."

"That's a good decision on your part. Now, I have a surprise for you: Miss Thornton's parents are in Africa, at Yaoundé. They are planning to sail to the cove to await Miss Thornton's return. Over."

"Do you know their ETA? Over."

"No, I just heard this morning that they were to arrive in Yaoundé today. I expect it will take two, maybe three days for them to arrive at the cove. When I heard of their arrival, I thought it was a foolish thing for them to do, but it has turned out to be exactly the right thing to do. I think it would be wise to keep this information close to yourself, just in case their plans hit a snag. Over."

"Max, this may be the last time I'll have radio transmission, as the mountain may block radio signals from here to the beach. But, I will get word to you about what is going on, and our future plans as soon as I can. Over."

"Leave word for me at Enugu Station. I am going back to Enugu now to get another cook and a few more boys to help with the goods. My next stops will be to villages that I only visit once every few years, as they are quite deep in the mountains. I'm sorry you will be missing them. They are the ones that seemed to interest you most. Over."

"I'm sorry to miss them too, but I've had a terrific adventure this past week. Thanks, old chap, for all your help. Over."

"Good Luck to you, Jon. Over and Out."

Motozo served the stew he had prepared while waiting for Jon to return. He was glad that the white woman had been found, unharmed. Over the years, he had gained a great deal of respect for Max Mason, the kigozi, (leader) and his selfless missions to free white captives. He hated to see the depression of futility that had settled over him. The young and inquisitive kisha (associate), who had brought a good deal of fun to the trading safari, was also distraught. Motozo was looking forward to meeting this Safi Mitiriki (white tree goddess). It would be an exciting end to a grand adventure; one that would thrill his grandchildren when he returned home.

THE PIPE JON SMOKED after a meal was the one he enjoyed the most. With a replete and contented feeling from his meal,

Jon often contemplated the course of his life, his past and the possibilities for the future. Today, he had experienced a joy like none he had ever known before, when he approached the hut and saw Miss Thornton resting in the lee of the roof, alive, safe and still stunningly beautiful, just as he remembered her.

Jon could not explain his joy to himself. It was out of proportion to their previous association of an hour or so. Maybe he was transferring his desperate desire to find his brother to the finding of Miss Thornton. Half a loaf is better than none... but oh, how he yearned for the whole loaf.

Casting his mind over Miss Thornton's situation, questions began to arise about how she had managed to meet someone who was clearly caring for her. It defied all rational probabilities—and the person was unusual too. In thinking more about him, Jon realized he had not asked his name when he had introduced himself. But he remembered that Miss Thornton had called him Tamubu, definitely a native name. Yet he knew from looking at the man that he was not a native; topaz blue eyes, honey color hair, narrow nose and lips, he was only dressed like a native. He did not suspect mixed blood either, even though his hair was curly. The man and his presence with Miss Thornton was a complete enigma to him.

Well, one step at a time. First, sort through the gear and get the men set up to stay the night here. Jon would again take Kimbo with him, when he went back to the hut to let them know that he had reached Max; and that Max would relay the news of Miss Thornton's good health and whereabouts to the tanker.

TAMUBU SERVED PAULA a lunch of slivered pork mixed with squash, mushrooms, onions and a bit of garlic with a pinch of kimmea. She would sleep for a few hours, giving him time to *roam*. His curiosity about his brother was overwhelming. He shadowed Jon on his return to his camp and listened to the radio conversation between Jon and Max. He had mixed feelings about the imminent arrival of Paula's parents. He was glad for Paula because he knew the empty cove was going to be a devastating blow for her. But he was disappointed at the loss of his innermost desire: the long months alone with Paula while traveling to Kenya. His destiny had become like a desert mirage: always changing, always promising, and then when closer—disappearing.

Tamubu would have been heartened if he had known Jon's postprandial thoughts; for he had decided to intercept Jon at the wide spot on the trail where Jon had left the two bearers earlier. There they could sit and talk and not disturb Paula's rest.

As Jon and Kimbo approached the little clearing, Tamubu stepped out onto the trail and raised his spear in greeting. Surprised, Jon returned the greeting by raising his rifle. Kimbo was instantly alert. Tamubu sensed Kimbo's wariness and to allay his fears said, "Miss Thornton is asleep. I thought we could talk here without disturbing her."

Jon noticed for the first time that Tamubu spoke English with a British accent—this was becoming curiouser and curiouser as Alice would have said. "Of course, by all means; by the way, I hope you will forgive my bad manners. I neglected to ask your name earlier."

"I am called Tamubu by the tribe of the Zuri Watu."

"I see, are they near here?"

"No, the Zuri Watu are many days travel from here, a moon or more away."

Jon thought: this isn't getting easier; his every answer makes things more complicated.

"You must forgive my bluntness and curiosity. How did you ever meet Miss Thornton?" Tamubu smiled, and Jon was stunned to see his dimples, which made his heart jump a bit—for a fleeting moment, this man reminded him of his lost brother.

"I was watching the panic flights of the roosting birds, and was curious as to the cause, when I happened to see Miss Thornton coming through the trees, to descend and hide under a devil plant. It was such an unusual sight that I climbed a nearby oak tree to see what else might happen. Soon, many warriors came searching everywhere, but they did not find her under the devil plant. Later, the warriors went back to their village. When Miss Thornton came out from under the devil plant, I followed her.

"I would have soon gone on my way, but the trail she took led straight into lion territory and the dens of the simba-jike. Later, when the simba-jike were stalking her, it was necessary for me to show myself to allow her time to escape into the trees. When she asked for my help to return to the cove and the yacht, I agreed—for she was ill-prepared to travel alone in the wilderness."

Jon was speechless at Tamubu's short narrative. His search would have been in vain if it were not for the curiosity of this man. How the fabric of life hangs by a thread—and how intricately we are all woven together by these slim threads amazed him.

"Well, we are here to help in any way you feel we would be useful. Miss Thornton said she had hurt her ankle. We could make a litter and carry her if you like."

"I had planned to carry her myself. The trail is steep in places and a litter would not be safe. But you could carry our foodstuffs, her backpack and my weapons. That would be a big help."

"Done! Anything else?"

Tamubu did not want Jon to know how much he knew, but he did want to caution him against telling Paula the yacht had left the cove. "You might not want to question Paula about her plans. Her goal right now is to return to the cove, and her friends. It is what keeps her going."

Jon cocked his head and Tamubu's heart jumped into his throat. How often had Jon done that when they were boys, when he suspected that Thomas wasn't telling all he knew? To gather his wits about him, Tamubu abruptly turned and headed back to the mud hut. Jon and Kimbo followed.

Paula had awakened to find Tamubu gone and was mulling over the twists of fate that had conspired to bring them all to this end... or was it a beginning. She was feeling better now, and was anxious to start on the last leg, the return to the beach. Hearing voices, she arose to see Tamubu leading

Jon and a native to the hut. She waved to them and seated herself in such a way that she would be facing them across the little fire, with her back to the hut.

When they were inside the boma, Jon said, "This is Kimbo. Kimbo, this is Miss Thornton." Kimbo laughed, nodded his head and went to sit at the far side of the hut, leaving the space around the little fire for Jon and Tamubu. Jon said, "Kimbo is shy, but he is very brave."

Tamubu said, "Pull up a chair, Jon, while I make us some tea. Paula looked worried; tea, what tea? I hope he hasn't saved those used up tea bags! Jon made small talk about his trek through the rainforest to reach the ridge and asked if she had used her sidearm on the trail.

"Why, yes I did. How did you know?"

"Kimbo saw the ricochet marks on rocks and found an empty cartridge. Were you shooting at snakes?"

"No, apes—actually just one, a bull ape who resented our sudden appearance on his turf. He charged and I fired into the rocks to scare him off."

Tamubu listened quietly to the conversation until he served the tea, made from spices and mint. He said, "Jon, you and Kimbo must join us for dinner. We are having roast pork, sweet potatoes and asparagus."

"We would like that, thank you." Jon was feeling a bit detached from reality. Here in the midst of the African wilderness, inside a thorn boma beside a mud hut, life was going on much like it did at home, on the tea plantation, when guests arrived near the dinner hour.

"You are in for a treat, Jon. Tamubu is a marvelous cook. He has made some of the best meals I have ever eaten—anywhere!"

Kimbo offered to help and was asked to fetch some more firewood. Tamubu had used most of the wood that had been stored in the hut and he wanted to replace the cache.

Jon's offer to help with dinner was also refused; "There's no room in here for two of us, but thanks anyway—dinner will be ready soon."

Jon smiled at Paula saying, "After dinner, you must regale

us with the story of your escape from the Ndezi village. You have no idea how many hours Max and I mulled over the possibilities, and I'm sure we never even came close to the truth."

Paula laughed, "I'm sure you didn't. I, myself, am often surprised at how it happened."

Tamubu called out, "I can hear just fine in here if you want to start your story now. I too, would like to hear about your escape."

Jon was astonished that Tamubu didn't know about her magical escape. What had they talked about?

Paula talked into the long dusk of the coppery evening. Kimbo helped with the serving of the meal and then insisted on doing the clean up chores.

Jon was intrigued and amazed during the telling of her story, and found it hard not to interrupt with questions.

Paula ended her story with her escape from the lions and getting acquainted with Tamubu in the tree. For some reason, she wanted to keep the details of her unique association with Tamubu to herself; she didn't want to share their instant camaraderie with anyone. It was like a fragile, beautiful butterfly, the close examination of which could only mar its beauty.

"You were right, Miss Thornton..."

"Call me Paula, please..."

"If you like, Paula; Max and I never came close to actuality in our speculations. What a story! You were right about the cook's ability too, it was a marvelous meal. Thank you, Tamubu, for asking us to join you for dinner."

Kimbo also added his thanks and drifted off to the other side of the hut.

Jon and Tamubu arranged themselves on either side of Paula under the deep overhanging eaves for the night. Paula was soon asleep. Jon thought over the conversation of the evening, and wondered even more about Tamubu's origins.

Tamubu, who had seen Jon's astonishment when he smiled at him, wondered if Jon had begun to sense the truth: that he was his long-lost brother.

Actually, Jon had been looking for the smallest of clues about Thomas in such obscure places, that coming face to face with him was much like hiding an object in the open for all to see... so, no one saw.

MORNING DAWNED BRIGHT AND clear, with only wisps of the usual low-lying mist. The men went into the forest, which gave Paula some privacy, so she was washed, dressed and had her things packed by the time they returned. Tamubu laid out his plans for the day over a breakfast of bacon, biscuits, oatmeal, fruit and coffee, saying he was going to carry Paula as he had before, if Jon and the men would carry their gear.

Paula was conflicted; she hated the ignominy of being carried, but looked forward to being so close to Tamubu again. Time did not allow her the luxury of examining her feelings, for Motozo and the rest of the men arrived at the hut.

Introductions were made and Jon gave Obu the honor of carrying Miss Thornton's backpack, which meant that he would have to remain close behind her should she need something from her kit. The rest shared a portion of the gear, each wanting to carry something that belonged to the Safi Mitiriki. Motozo was elated when he was given the mongojo (walking sticks) to carry. It was a happy group that set off down the trail.

Kimbo and his son, Kybo, cleared foliage overhanging the trail and stray branches underfoot. They worked with a rhythmic chant, which made the time pass pleasantly. Paula was so relaxed and at such ease, that had it not been for her need to grip Tamubu's hips with her thighs with just the right amount of pressure, she could have fallen asleep. The nearness of Tamubu was a great comfort to her. She reveled in his clean manly smell and the feeling of his muscles working with the beating of his heart as he breathed deeply to oxygenate his muscles. The sensations she felt while riding his hips were distracting.

WHEN THEY CAME TO the badly eroded hairpin turns, Paula had an idea. Locking the grapnel in the open position, she tossed it over a stout low branch. When everyone was below her on the trail, she too swung down and was caught by strong arms to keep her from having to use her sore ankle on landing. Obu, on Kybo's shoulders, then retrieved the grapnel. Her idea worked so well, and was such fun, that they used it for all the eroded gullies that fissured the trail.

After one particularly wide chasm, Jon laughed and said, "I could get used to this, Kimbo. It is great fun, better than slogging through the muddy bottoms."

Kimbo surprised everyone by replying, "You can make a man out of a boy, but you can never take the boy out of the man."

With all the help and ingenuity, the group arrived early at the clearing beside the trail. Motozo had a fire going in no time and Tamubu infused his concoction of herbs for tea. Lunch was usually a prepared, cold affair, but today there was time to fry some of the ham Tamubu had smoked, before wrapping the thin slivers in the prepared pancakes with a bit of cassava. Tea, fresh fruit and small talk finished the meal. Paula retired to the pallet Tamubu had arranged for her and was soon asleep.

Tamubu and Jon discussed the rest of the day. It was decided that Jon, Motozo, Obendi and Obu would go on ahead. The rock formation above the shallow cave was quite visible from the trail, and they could get the evening fire and meal started. This would allow for longer rest stops after the arduous portions of the trail. Kimbo and Kybo would stay with Tamubu and Paula, supplying support in front and behind on the steep descents. Kybo, like his father was a big, strong man–and also shy.

After Jon and his men had gone, Tamubu realized that his deep fears of being treated as an inferior had been unfounded. Paula had been right... again. Jon's oversight at that first meeting had been due to his excitement at finding Paula alive and well. Since their first conversation at the little clearing, Jon had treated him with the respect of a contemporary and equal. Tamubu found that he liked Jon as the man he had become. He was a gregarious eager and indomitable young man, much the same way as he had been as a boy.

Paula slept for two hours before Tamubu awakened her. She was grateful to see the men move off into the woods to give her some privacy. Now that she thought about it, they gave themselves some privacy too.

During the afternoon, Kimbo and Kybo taught them a marching chant. Kybo said, 'Mabari-yoko' (what's up with you)? Kimbo sang in a singsong voice, some unintelligible things in his dialect, and then Tamubu and Paula were to say, 'Mawajambo-leo' (we're all right today). It was distracting and fun, which made the afternoon pass quickly. Sometimes, Tamubu and Kybo would laugh at the things Kimbo said, but they would not tell her what it was that had made them laugh. Paula suspected some of Kimbo's comments were risqué.

The longer rests were a boon. Paula's muscles were strong, but unused, and she was a bit stiff and sore from the constant tension. Once they were down the steep hillsides, Kimbo rigged a litter for Paula, using his kitamba for a seat. She missed the nearness of Tamubu, but her aching muscles told her that Tamubu was probably sore too—from carrying so much unaccustomed weight on his hips.

The jolly group arrived at the shallow cave in the early evening. Jon and the boys had heard them coming, for they were still singing the ditty and laughing. Motozo had a stew and biscuits ready. He had also made his specialty, a coconut pudding, which he served warm with coffee laced with vanilla. The entire dinner conversation and most of the laughter revolved around Paula's use of her *5in1* to eat the stew. Jon did not use his fingers either, he had a wooden utensil that was a spoon at one end and a two-pronged fork at the other end; the whole of which was about six inches long. He said he had whittled it and a few others while in the Congo with Max, when they had come upon some discarded branches from a timbered teak tree. When he saw the cooking spoon Tamubu used, Jon immediately plunged into his pack and produced another of his spoon-fork creations, which he offered to Tamubu, saying, "I made these for Motozo and Kimbo, but they would have none of it. I would be very pleased for you to have one."

Tamubu saw that the size of the utensil was much better than his cooking spoon and said, "Thank you. This will be better than my cooking spoon. It is a clever idea, small and light enough not to be a burden."

For some reason, this small praise thrilled Jon beyond its meaning. A small, nagging wisp of deja vu whispered to him and was gone.

Paula said, "We have an after-dinner custom. Someone must tell a story. Jon, you are next on the list. The only rule is that the story is history, or a family saga, or has a moral to it; or it can be a personal story, like your story about your trek to find me."

"Well, I don't see why I am next on the list since I told my story last night. I think it is Tamubu's turn, since you told of your escape from the Ndezi on our first evening."

Paula smiled and looked at Tamubu. "He's right, you know. It really is your turn."

Tamubu glanced around the camp. Motozo and the boys were ranged around the outside of the fire while he, Jon and Paula were seated under the rocky roof. He knew fireside stories were a great delight to Africans. It was their way to share history and family accomplishments. Tamubu smiled; he knew the story he would tell.

"There was a young boy who was quite ill. He suffered from chills, fever, ague and delusions. At times he was a normal boy, but he was weak and frail. Much of his time was spent in bed listening to stories, which were told to him by a wonderfully kind woman, while she worked at her loom weaving beautiful fabrics.

"One day a missionary doctor visited his home, examined the boy, and left medicine for him. The medicine eventually made him well. The boy was so happy to be leading a normal life again; so happy to be able to go out and about; and he was even happier still, when he was given a special teacher, who taught him about the wild animals, the birds, the trees and plants, the stars and the moon. For years his teacher

taught him the lessons of life and the lad's life was full and happy.

"Years later a great sadness befell the now young man. The woman, who had always cared for him from the time he was so ill, and who had told him so many stories, was near death. On her deathbed, she told him another story, a strange story; strange because as she told the story, the young man remembered some of the things she told him, for he had lived through the times she described.

"The young man thought long and hard about the facts she told him during her deathbed story. This story had brought him to a great crossroads in his life. He knew he would have to leave a way of life that he loved; a way of life that had nurtured him; a way of life that had fulfilled his every need. He knew he would have to go and find the truth of the deathbed story. He had to find his destiny.

"When the kind woman was laid to rest, the young man set out on a quest to unravel the mystery the deathbed story had woven for him. The story was her last gift to him and she had said, "To live your life and fulfill your destiny, you must know who you are—not who you think you are—and once you know, you will be free to choose the path that is yours, and yours alone."

"The young man left his home for a long trek, and no one has yet heard of him.   The End."

PAULA COULD SEE THE consternation on the faces of the listeners, so she spoke up and said, "Did you know this young man, Tamubu?"

"Yes, I know him well." Tamubu said.

"Do you know where he has gone?" asked Jon.

"Yes, he has gone on walk-about to the east coast of Africa."

Jon was astonished, "Do you mean to say your friend is walking to the east coast of Africa from the west coast. Why, that's more than two thousand miles from where we are now. Can anyone walk so far, alone, in safety?"

"What is safety? At any moment disaster can strike. Only a person who wants to live in misery would dwell on the possible adversities of life. It is best to learn the basic precepts of living in the wilderness: watch and prepare, listen and prepare, smell and prepare."

Motozo knew Tamubu was speaking of himself, of his childhood and upbringing; but he wondered why Tamubu was speaking in riddles, naming no names, placing no places, so he asked, "Was this young man also a member of the Zuri Watu? Do you know what was told to him in the deathbed story that made him go on walk-about?"

Tamubu looked at Motozo. He was a wise, old man. He knew the truth of his story, knew that the story was about him, so he replied.

"Yes, the young man was the adopted son of the chief of the Zuri Watu, Sashono, and his wife, Nanoka. In her deathbed story, Nanoka told him he had another family, and that her death would free him to go and find this other family, so he could know himself completely."

"It seems odd that the boy never questioned Nanoka about his life before he was adopted by them." Jon spoke softly.

"It is odd, but the boy did not remember his other family. He never spoke of them in the long time of his illness. By the time he was well; Nanoka and Sashono had adopted him and considered him their son. As such, the boy was treated with deference and respect. It was a wonderful life and the boy especially loved his teacher, Manutu, who was the Medicine Chief of the Zuri Watu."

"You are saying the boy grew to manhood and was happy," Jon persisted.

"Yes, the boy and man had a happy life and wanted no other until Nanoka's story, when he realized that his recurring dreams were not really dreams, but fragments of memory of another life, a life before the Zuri Watu."

Paula said, "You can go on talking, but I hope you don't mind if I turn in."

"Not at all," Jon replied. "The hour has grown late and I could use a good night's rest myself. I think I'll turn in too." The bearers moved to the other side of the rock formation. Paula's pallet was under the over-hanging rock with Tamubu's pallet on one side and Jon's pallet on the other. She felt quite safe with this arrangement and the fire at her feet.

Tamubu had left the campfire after Paula had called it a day. She and Jon were both asleep when Tamubu returned. Motozo and the boys were ranged around a fire beyond the jutting rock wall. Kimbo had taken the first watch.

It would be a good night, if it did not rain again.

21

To The Cove

JON AWOKE WHILE IT was still dark. He'd no sooner put his head down last night than he was gone... he usually outlined his next day before nodding off. The adrenalin rush of finding Miss Thornton, and the short nights and long days before that, must have caught up with him. He had a nagging feeling, like he was supposed to do something, but had forgotten what it was... when Tamubu's campfire story leaped to mind.

How could I have gone to sleep, when I had so much to think about? His story didn't strike a nerve until the end... when he said he had two families. I began to wonder if similar events could have happened to Thomas. He turned on his back, put his arms behind his head, drew up his knees, and thought about the possibilities. It was a logical progression of incidents: the plane crashed; Thomas was the only one alive; he escaped the plane, and was found by natives; but then became sick... probably with malaria; he was sick a long time like Tamubu; and during the illness, he forgot about his past life like Tamubu. Could this man be his long lost brother? Jon's mind scrambled over the details; Tamubu's hair was a darker shade of his honey blond color, his eyes were the same clear blue, and his age seemed right. The dimples! He had dimples just like Thomas, and his smile with that slight tilt of his head; that had stunned me.

It was too exciting, too good to be true. Jon was elated and thrilled, but first he had to get control of his emotions. If it was just a series of coincidences, he could be in for a big disappointment. After all, Tamubu knew Jon's name was

Caulfield and that he came from a tea plantation in Kenya, yet he had said nothing.

Maybe it was not familiar to him because he was another lost boy and not his brother at all. It would be best to go slowly here. Time would tell the tale and solve the puzzle.

The birds started to chirp and Jon sensed that Paula and Tamubu were awakening. Even with his doubts, Jon still felt a boundless elation.

BUSYNESS WAS THE USUAL morning state in camp. Everyone had a job to do and did it while managing to find some privacy for personal functions. Motozo made oatmeal, which he cooked with slivered coconut and served with fresh mixed fruit, while he grilled the oat-based pancakes for the cold pork lunch. Paula sipped the fragrant coffee, which had a hint of vanilla and cinnamon, and thought it was the best coffee she had ever tasted. She praised his coffee and his cooking, which greatly pleased Motozo.

The boys packed the kitchen gear and cleaned the campsite. Jon and Tamubu talked about the trail over coffee, and decided the best way for Paula to travel would be by litter. Obu and Obendi could spell Kimbo and Kybo, taking turns to carry the litter. They hoped to reach the beach by late afternoon.

Paula's pleasurable thoughts at seeing the yacht and her friends again made her amenable to whatever they decided. Motozo came and offered her the remainder of the coffee for her hot-bottle canteen.

The sun had just begun to pierce the dense greenery with diffused shafts of light, making the forest seem otherworldly, when they started down the trail. Kimbo began his drill-like chant, which set the pace with a rhythmic beat. Jon was leading the group, followed by Obu and Obendi, who cleared trail where necessary, and then came the litter with Kimbo in front and Kybo behind, followed by Motozo, who carried Paula's backpack. Tamubu brought up the rear, somewhere behind, for he was not always in sight.

The morning progression was slow. Every hour they changed litter bearers and took a short rest. Where the hillside trail was steep and narrow, Tamubu carried Paula piggyback, until they could use the litter again.

Before noon, the trail became a pleasant downhill series of lazy switchbacks with long winding paths in between. Paula had not seen this stretch of trail before as her captors had led her through the deep trackless forest.

Around a bend, the group came upon a small run-off pool, which had eroded the entire trail. It was a good place to have lunch and rest. Paula hobbled to the water's edge, sat down, took off her shoes and socks and soaked her feet and lower legs. The hours of sitting on the litter with her legs dangling from the knees down had made her ankle ache. The cool water was a marvelous relief.

Tamubu saw the relief on Paula's face as she soaked her foot, and took Kimbo aside to discuss some revisions to the design of the litter. While Paula napped, Kimbo found longer poles for the sides and a short one to use as a footrest, which was ingeniously attached between the side poles with long thongs. Now the full length of her legs would be supported and she could use her good foot to brace herself from sliding forward, since she rode mostly tilted, on the downhill trail.

After lunch and a short rest, Jon and Motozo left the group to go ahead and prepare a campsite for the evening. Tamubu had told them about the place where a cache was suspended in the trees, and that they would need to make a clearing in the underbrush to avoid getting wet at high tide.

It wasn't until Jon and Motozo were well away on the trail that Jon wondered how Tamubu had known about the cache suspended in the trees. No scenario he could devise gave him a suitable answer to the riddle, except that somehow, Tamubu had been to the beach after the cache had been left in the trees and the yacht had left the cove.

TAMUBU HAD EATEN LUNCH with the others before drifting off into the forest. When he was far enough away, he hid his things and *roamed* to the beach. The trail was clear. No one had come this way since he had last *roamed* here, ten days ago. On his return, he saw Jon and Motozo. Jon had seemed preoccupied this morning when he was not sneaking sly glances at him. Tamubu was pleased. His fireside story was having the desired effect. Jon was already wondering if he could be his lost brother. When the truth finally came out, Jon would be ready for it.

Tamubu though, was having trouble containing his joy that here was his brother, Jon, the little voice he had never forgotten. But Tamubu wanted Jon to reach out to him in some way, before he revealed himself. With the return of much of his memory, including the class distinctions, he needed some reassurance that he would be accepted for himself; at this moment, he was much more a native than an Englishman.

Tamubu watched Jon and Motozo for a while. Jon's trekking skills were good. He seemed aware of his surroundings and saw the mamba slither across the trail; and waited prudently until the fast-moving snake had time to hide itself in the brush; when threatened, the black mamba was deadly. Wanting to stay and watch, but needing to be back with Paula, Tamubu left to bring up the rear of the little cavalcade.

PAULA WAS THE FIRST to smell the ocean and she cried out, "Oh, do you smell that? I can smell the sea. We are nearing the beach." Tamubu was surprised, because all he could smell was Obu, who was up wind of him. In a matter of minutes, the trail widened and Tamubu came up to walk beside Paula. He wanted to be near her when she saw that the cove was empty, and the yacht was gone.

THE WESTERLY SUN MADE the beach hot and the little procession walked in the bits of shade at the edge of the rain forest. When they topped the rocky remnant of the volcanic wall, Paula saw the empty cove. Tears brimmed in her eyes and she took Tamubu's hand as she said, "Oh, my! They're gone!"

Jon, who had been waiting at the high point of the rocky rim, came forward in time to hear the utter dismay in her voice. He saw Paula reach out to Tamubu for comfort. This was an unexpected display. Was there a deeper connection between them than a guide to a lost woman?

TAMUBU TOOK HER HAND and said, "It looks like there is a cache hanging from those trees down the beach. Maybe it was left by your friends; there could be an explanation there as well."

Paula said, "Oh, yes, I see it. Let's hurry and see what's there." Now past the barnacled rocks and onto the beach, the boys Obendi and Obu picked up the pace towards Motozo, who came out onto the beach from the forest edge, where he had been making a clearing for their camp. In moments, Obendi was up the tree and released the rope holding the cache. Kimbo and Kybo laid the canvas and net-wrapped ball on the sand and Paula hobbled over to sit on the tarp and examine the contents.

Most of the contents were wrapped, except for the tins of food, and a plastic envelope that was pinned to one of the canvas packages. She unpinned the envelope and drew out the letter. Tears brimmed in her eyes as she read:

My dear Paula,   Saturday, January 30, 1960
It is with regret that we are leaving the area. The yacht was removed from the cove on flotation devices into the open sea, and it is a choppy anchorage.

The United Nations Search party lost your trail after the heavy rains; so staying here would not help you in any way. If you are reading this letter, you have made it back to the cove where we have left supplies and a two-way radio for you.

The Norsk Star will be docked in Port Harcourt, about a hundred miles away, until the 10th of February. They might be able to pick up an SOS signal, if you are unable to establish radio contact. Irrespective, the distress signal will be picked up by passing ships and relayed to the authorities.

We are taking the Just Cause south to the Ogooué River in Gabon, about 325 miles from the cove, where there was no tsunami damage to the flora.

The previous plan to dock the Just Cause at Port Harcourt for the April through June hiatus in the States has been changed to docking her at Port-Gentil in Gabon.

I remain, as ever, your friend and mentor.
George Miles

Paula passed the letter to Tamubu, who read it and in turn passed it to Jon. Jon took the boys aside and told them the gist of the letter while Paula inspected the contents of the cache. There were tins of beef, chicken and tuna; packets of mayonnaise and mustard; tins of soup, grapefruit, pears, stews, chili and several gallon jugs of fresh water. There was instant coffee, tea and cocoa; powdered milk and sealed packages of cereal, sugar and salt; a sealed can of oatmeal and one of flour and of all things, a small can of baking powder; a plastic bag of rice, a bag of split peas and several bags of elbow macaroni; an aluminum drip coffee pot, a fry pan, and two pots, one small, one medium; a can opener, a rubber scraper and a wooden spoon with a box of aluminum foil; a package of paper plates, napkins and wood matches.

In a separate package were personal items, clothing and a large, extensive first aid kit. Included too, was another blank book to be used as a log, pencils, pens and extra batteries for the two-way radio.

PAULA SAT DEVASTATED. How could they abandon me like that? Dr. Miles' letter made it seem as if I'd called in sick, and missed a field trip. Without warning, she became angry and indignant. If I had been kidnapped at home–all the stops would have been pulled out to find me. Life would have revolved around getting me back! But, get abducted in Africa and it was: ho-hum! "Staying here won't help you..." Was his ego so anal that he had no idea of the atrocities I would have been subjected to if I had not escaped? Was the success of the Expedition to be purchased at any cost? Any suffering? Any life? When you came right down to it, what had he done, personally, to help me, or to find me? Nada! Nil! Zip!

But, a man I had known for less than an hour had put his life and financial interests on hold to go looking for me. Another man I had known for even less time had given supplies, his best men, equipment, and moral support to aid in the search for me. The person, in whose care I had been placed, did nothing... wrote a letter... left some supplies... '... being here won't help you'!

And none of it would have mattered... were it not for a total stranger's curiosity and concern.

Paula glanced around at the group... at the people who had put their lives on hold to help her. She gave thanks to God for each one of these caring souls, for she had never known better people in her whole life.

MOTOZO NOW HAD A fire going, so Paula filled the coffee pot with water and, using one of her crutches, took it to the fire. She was going to make tea, enough for everyone. The last package she opened had held two tins, one of individually wrapped cookies and one of crackers, wrapped in packages of four–probably from Dr. Miles' personal locker–here's a cookie, I hope you don't give a lion indigestion!

Tamubu approached her warily. He could see the shock, confusion and anger on her face. "I think it would be best to take what you need now from the cache and hoist the rest of it back into the trees."

Paula looked at him, saw his concern and smiled. "Yes, that's a good idea. As soon as we've had tea, I'll sort through it again."

Jon came over and said to Tamubu and Paula, "I'm going to scout down the beach to the cliffs with Kimbo and Kybo. We need more firewood and some elephant leaves for the lean-to roofs. Obu and Obendi are busy hacking out another clearing, about fifty feet away, for the men. Motozo is getting the lean-to organized for dinner. Seems he found some onions, garlic, spinach-like greens and wild squash growing near an old campsite beside the trail. With all the rain, it seems seeds sprout easily into new plants."

"Motozo, would you like to have one of these packages of macaroni for your stew tonight?" Paula asked. "It should be added near the end, like green beans, before the stew is finished; it will also absorb some of the broth."

"Yes, Missy, thank you. We have no potatoes for tonight; I plan to make biscuits. You have many good things in your cache. Your friends were good to you."

"Motozo, if there is anything else in the cache that you can use, please help yourself."

"Pots, pans, paper plates, Missy?"

"Take anything you like, now or later."

Paula hopped back to the cache; Motozo followed. She gave him the things he wanted and kept out the new log and pencils for Tamubu; the new first aid kit, the tea, cookies and cocoa for herself. She covered the rest for Tamubu and Jon to hoist back into the trees. Paula wondered where Tamubu had gone. He frequently disappeared, only to come back with delicious foodstuffs; but gathering wasn't necessary right now.

PAULA HAD NEVER BEEN able to sustain her anger; she vented her spleen and, once done, it was over; but this time, her rage simmered, fueled by her reflection on Professor Miles' outrageous indifference and his total lack of responsibility or concern for her.

She gazed out at the cove and pictured the *Just Cause* riding on anchor at high tide. She was not only incredibly angry with Dr. Miles, she was extremely hurt that the yacht and crew were gone too; but something else bothered her. Underneath all else was a deep, wrenching feeling of sadness, like the loss of a puppy. It came to her... soon she would lose Tamubu and Jon, Motozo and the boys. These kind people had saved her life. They were there for her, when others had abandoned her, when she desperately needed help. When they were gone, a most important chapter in the book of her life would close.

There would be no one with whom she could stand, shoulder-to-shoulder, to face the future. Well, that's not going to happen; not now, not ever! Paula knew one thing for certain: she did not want her association with Tamubu to end. She was almost positive he felt the same way, from the things he had said to her ... 'for as long as you need me, I'll be there for you ...' and she would take the steps necessary for them to remain together.

These past three days Paula had not written in her diary, nor had Tamubu made any plant drawings. She decided to divert her mental focus—for she knew fretting changed nothing—and bring her diary up to date; for now Tamubu could draw while she wrote.

JON RETURNED TO CAMP with a bag full of coconuts; Kimbo had a huge bunch of the large, waxy leaves called elephant ears; and Kybo carried a large faggot of firewood. They left part of their gleanings with Motozo and continued on to leave the rest with Obendi and Obu. Later, when they came back for tea, bringing Obendi and Obu with them, Tamubu had still not yet returned.

Over tea, Jon said, "I do wish Tamubu had not gone off again. He said something to me this morning that has been in my head all day."

"What was that?" Paula asked

"He said I would find a cache in the trees on the beach. How did he know that?"

Paula smiled to herself at the question. Days ago, she had sensed that Tamubu's transcendental powers allowed him to do things and go places that were beyond the normal abilities of most Medicine Men. "I do not know," she replied. "You will have to ask him when he returns."

"You can be certain of it. I can think of nothing else!"

After tea, the men went to finish the lean-tos while Jon fiddled with the radio. Paula continued writing in her diary. Leaning back in the shade of the tree, Paula closed her eyes for a bit and nodded off; the diary fell open in her lap.

Jon's noiseless approach in the sand, stirred Paula not at all. The softly fluttering pages drew Jon's attention. He caught glimpses of exquisite pencil drawings of plants, and beautiful script as the pages turned lazily in the breeze. He thought Miss Thornton was indeed a talented woman, and wished he had been able to get to know her better before she had met Tamubu. He strode away to sit at the surf's edge, smoke a pipe and ponder the irony of life.

THE LONG, SOFT DUSK began as the sun fell into the sea, behind the towering remnants of the west rim of the sunken volcano. Tamubu had returned while Paula napped, and he had wandered over to Jon, who was still sitting, Indian style, at the edge of the receding surf.

"The weather has been good to us," Tamubu remarked.

Jon turned and looked at this extremely handsome and congenial man and said, "Yes, with the streaky salmon sky, it could be that tomorrow will be a nice day too. By the way, you have given me a conundrum that has puzzled me all day."

"I have given you a what?"

"A riddle; this morning you said in your instructions that I would find a cache in the trees on the beach. How did you know it was there?"

Tamubu thought, the time is not yet, but said, "I had already scouted the trail to the beach, while Paula was recovering from a fall; I wanted to know the hazards of the trail. That was before you came to our camp."

Jon asked casually, "How long did it take you to do that?"

"I'm not sure; I did some hunting, caught the piglet, as well as the usual gathering on the way. I was gone most of the day."

"Were you not concerned for Miss Thornton's safety while you were gone?"

"Goodness me, no! I would not have left her if there had been any danger."

Jon was transfixed. He felt as if a bolt of lightning had struck him. Thomas used to say that, 'goodness me, no', when Jon made bizarre statements or wild presumptions when they were young. It sounded just like Thomas too, same inflection, same tone of voice. Unbidden, tears brimmed in his eyes, and a lump that threatened to suffocate him arose in his chest to cut off the wind in his throat.

Tamubu didn't notice Jon's distress, because he was standing just behind him. "I came over to ask you if you would mind if I gave Motozo the foodstuffs I have in my gathering net. It would be best to use them while they are still fresh."

Staring out to sea, Jon managed to gulp out, "Not at all."

Tamubu left. To hide his discomposure, Jon dropped his head to his knees, which he had brought up close to his chest. Tamubu was Thomas. Jon was sure of it... how could he be wrong? There were too many things that fit, like pieces in a jigsaw puzzle. His hopes were so high. What if Tamubu said he was mistaken? Could there be so many coincidences, and still have a mistaken identity?

Dinner was a fine affair. Everyone enjoyed the stew with the macaroni in it, which was a first-time treat for the natives. Motozo was pleased by the many compliments. He delighted one and all with the vanilla and coconut pudding he had made earlier, and had cooled in seawater; desserts on the trail were almost unknown, except for fruit. Paula and Jon had tea while everyone else had chocolate Ovaltine from Paula's cache, another unusual treat.

Conversation during dinner was limited. The roosting bird-life made such a cacophony of strident cries and with such volume that only monosyllabic comments were understandable. Later, when the avian hordes were settled and finally quiet, Jon returned to the fire from his after-dinner pipe and walk along the shore. Motozo and the boys had retired to their own little clearing and fire, where they were playing a game of skill with black and white pebbles on a checkered cloth.

Paula asked, "What is the game they play with such obvious glee?"

Jon replied, "As far as I can say, it reminds me of an ancient Greek game called Pente."

"The object of which, is?"

"To get five of your color pebbles in a row in any direction."

"I think I would like to learn that game. Do you know how to play it?"

"Yes, but I won't play with the boys. They are very sneaky and cunning and I always lose. Max and I have been known to indulge on occasion, but he is sneaky too."

Paula laughed. "The more you say about the game, the more I think I would like it."

Jon chuckled too. "Yes, I guess you would like it. It appeals to people that are multi-talented, both physically and mentally adept, and people who like puzzles. Do you like puzzles too?"

"Yes, very much, I especially like word puzzles, such as cryptograms."

Jon looked quizzical. "I think I am out of my league here; I can't even do a crossword puzzle."

"What do you like to do, Jon?"

"I like languages, especially the African dialects. I like horticulture too... which reminds me... I happened to see some of the drawings in your diary today; I had stopped by to chat with you, and the pages were turning in the breeze while you were napping. They looked like pencil drawings of African plants. Are they the plants you need for your research?"

Paula was intrigued. "Yes, do you know these plants?"

Jon said, "I have seen some of them, but I haven't studied their properties. Most of my experience is limited to cultivated plants. The drawings were marvelously done; even at a brief glance I could see you have tremendous talent. My lost brother, Thomas, liked to draw, and he too, was very good at it."

Paula didn't know what to say. She didn't feel it was her place to explain that Tamubu had done the drawings, so she let the moment go and said, "Have you never had any news of your brother since he was lost?"

"No, none; it was one of the reasons why I joined up with Max Mason. He trades with the tribes that are closest to the place where they found the plane wreckage. I felt that I would know Thomas if I ever saw him among the natives of those tribes."

"You don't think he's dead?"

"No, I don't. Thomas always seemed to land on his feet, no matter what the situation. He is one of those people who are completely gifted."

"What do you mean by gifted?"

"Thomas had a sixth sense, one that kept him from making mistakes–like not stepping on a rotten step–he just seemed to know these things."

Paula was curious. "How old were you when Thomas was lost?"

"I was going on eight, Thomas had just turned ten."

"How long ago was that?"

"I will be twenty-two this summer. Thomas is twenty-four."

Paula thought Tamubu to be older, (she would turn twenty-five in March) but said, "So it has been fourteen years since you last saw Thomas. People sometimes change a great deal when they mature."

Jon replied, "Some things, little things mostly, never change. They are a part of you that you don't even know exists; but other people see them and know these things about you. Like your voice, or the things you say inadvertently, or the tilt of your head when you are amused, or your laugh. Your laugh never changes."

Paula thought: he knows Tamubu is his brother, Thomas. Why doesn't he say anything?

"I didn't know that about a person's laugh. That's quite interesting. How did you find that out?"

"I sat in on a Criminology lecture on Missing Persons at school."

"So you have been thinking about Thomas for a long time."

"Yes, I have never stopped thinking about him. His disappearance left a big hole in my life. One I have been unable to fill... even friends were a disappointment, compared to my camaraderie with Thomas."

Oh my, Paula thought. He knows, but like Tamubu, he is afraid of letting himself believe; in Jon's case, he fears disappointment, while Tamubu fears rejection.

The dusk had turned to night but the moon and stars were not yet visible, making the night very dark. A shadow passed beyond the fire, dark against dark, and Paula said softly to Jon. "Something has just passed by along the beach." Jon quietly reached for his lantern when he heard a muffled noise.

"I hope you are not reaching for your pistol, Jon."

"Oh, Tamubu! I saw a shadow and it made me remember the chuima."

Tamubu came and sat by the fire, and Jon said. "You had an encounter with a leopard?"

"Yes, but according to Tamubu, I was safe even if only ten feet away."

"Are you still annoyed with me about that evening?" Tamubu asked.

"No, I guess not, but you did just give me a fright. Where have you been anyway? It has gotten late and you haven't been here since dinner."

Tamubu looked deep into Paula's eyes and said, "Forgive me, if I frightened you. It will not happen again." He turned to Jon and said, "Tomorrow, I want to go up the beach to the north. Will you go with me?"

Jon answered, "Of course, what are we looking for?"

Not wanting to alarm Paula, Tamubu replied. "I need your help to catch some fish. Is anyone tired besides me? The boys are asleep, Kybo is on guard and I'm ready for my bed."

Paula realized her fatigue was from tension; and her short temper was provoked by Tamubu being gone all evening. She had not been that startled. She had been worried instead. The uncertainties of the next few days were going to be hard on her nerves. Covering up, with her ankle supported on her backpack; Jon on one side and Tamubu on the other, she was soon asleep.

Jon, on the other hand, was thinking about being alone with Tamubu tomorrow. He could ask him some ambiguous questions about his past, or his age, or how he came to be in the rainforest. The simple answer to these questions would tell him, once and for all, if Tamubu could really be his brother, Thomas.

TAMUBU NOW KNEW BEYOND a doubt that Jon longed for him—no matter what had happened to him these past fourteen years. Tamubu had spent the evening listening to Paula and Jon's conversation, hoping to hear the very sentiments he had heard. Relief flooded his being. He was going home!

22

On The Beach

THE RAIN HAD COME in the night. It was still drizzling when the birds began their morning chatter. Motozo built a new fire under the large lean-to for breakfast. Everyone crowded around the fire for the meal. Paula remarked, to no one in particular, "It will be a good day to catch up on my writing. What will you do, Jon?"

"I'm going to try to contact Max via Enugu Station; but it may be further than I can transmit without a high auxiliary antenna. Even so, I may pick up a passing ship that could patch me through. He'll want to know that we've arrived here in good order. He can contact the authorities and the *Just Cause* for us."

Tamubu said. "Could I help you?'

Jon tried to keep the pleasure he felt from showing in his voice. "I could use another pair of hands, thanks."

Paula thought: I wish I could be a flea in Jon's pocket today, as she hobbled back to her lean-to alone. Until the rain stopped, the bearers would be at their game of stones, and the resultant bonhomie would be too distracting for composition.

Jon and Tamubu gathered the radio gear and a small tent and headed off to the ragged stone jetty–the best place for reception. Paula watched them make their way to a high point, far out on the rim, towards the open sea. Jon led the way until he found a suitable place to erect the small, one-piece, one-man tent, which would keep them and the radio out of the wind and rain, cozy and dry inside.

"Jon Caulfield calling Enugu Station. Come in. Over." The

radio crackled and the static noise was annoying. Jon checked the equipment, looked at Tamubu and shrugged.

"Jon Caulfield calling Enugu Station or anyone receiving. Come in. Over."

"This is the *Merry Mermaid*, a fishing trawler, off the coast of Malabo. Over."

"Hello *Merry Mermaid*, are you able to contact Enugu Station in Nigeria for us? Over."

"Yes, I can do that. Over."

"Please tell them that Jon Caulfield and Miss Thornton have arrived at the cove off the Bight of Biafra, and all is well. Over."

"That's a ten-four. Will you wait for a reply? Over."

"Yes, thank you. Over and Out."

TAMUBU WAS FASCINATED BY the two-way radio. The first time, when Jon had talked to Max up on the mountain, he had been too preoccupied with the content of the conversation to wonder about how it was happening. Now, sitting here, he was thrilled by the experience. Jon had talked to someone, somewhere out on the sea in a fishing boat, and he would soon talk back; amazing!

"How does that box do that?" Tamubu asked Jon, "Make people talk to you from far out on the sea?"

Jon smiled. "The energy, which is like a tiny bit of lightning, is stored in the batteries inside the radio. This energy is used to create radio waves... similar to dropping a pebble in a pond, which then causes ripples to move across the surface of the pond. Well, radio waves are just like those ripples; they travel a long way in the air, but they are neither seen nor felt. When the radio waves ripple past places where other radios are turned on to receive, they make contact and the messages are heard."

Tamubu understood the concept immediately. It was like those who had the power to communicate with the spirits. This radio had the power to communicate with other radios.

He said, "I understand. This box has special powers."

Jon was amused by his correlation. "Yes, this box has special powers."

The radio crackled as Tamubu sat mulling over the information.

"Enugu Station calling Jon Caulfield. Come in. Over."

"Jon here, Enugu. Over"

"Jon, we have relayed your message from the *Merry Mermaid* to Max Mason. We will notify the authorities and the *Just Cause* of your safe arrival at the cove off the Bight of Biafra. Is there anything else we can do for you? Over."

"No, nothing just now. I will check-in every morning with an update. Over and Out."

As Jon put the microphone down, the radio again sputtered and crackled and a voice was dimly heard through the static.

"... Thorn ... call ... cove ... read ... ver."

Jon quickly snatched the mike and responded. "Jon Caulfield to Thorn. Come in. Over."

The crackling and static worsened. Jon was getting ready to call again, when loud and clear, he heard. "Charles Thornton calling Jon Caulfield. Over."

"Receiving you five by five, Charles. Over."

"We are Paula Thornton's parents. We are en route to the cove where the yacht was stranded. Our ETA is mid-afternoon tomorrow. We are anchored at Limbe, as visibility is too poor to continue on today. Over."

"That's a ten-four, Mr. Thornton. We will have a smoke signal for you south of your anchorage tomorrow. Over."

"Is Paula okay? Over."

"Paula is better than okay, sir. See you tomorrow. Over and Out."

Charles turned and hugged his wife, Lisa. He didn't want her to see the tears that had welled-up at hearing Jon's last transmission. What a nightmare these past weeks had been for them. First, they had the news of the yacht and Paula being swept away, out to sea, by the tsunami. Then they heard that the yacht had been found, but Paula had apparently gone ashore and was missing; and, later, the inconceivable news that the yacht was leaving the cove and going several hundred miles south. After hearing that piece of perfidious news, Charles and Lisa resolved to go to Africa. They would be there for their daughter when she returned.

On reaching Yaoundé, they had received a message that Paula had been found, and was traveling back to the cove. But that had been all. It was wonderful news ... but parents always want more. 'Paula was better than okay.' What grand words! The awful uncertainty was over. Tomorrow, they would be with their precious daughter again.

Jon turned to Tamubu and said, "I suppose you heard that Miss Thornton's parents are on their way here to the cove; I guess-timate that they are about a hundred miles away."

"Her parents are a long way away. How can they be here tomorrow?"

"They have rented a boat. If it is a sailboat, they can do maybe eight to ten knots, which is about nine and a half to twelve miles per hour with the prevailing winds along the coast. (Jon knew about the doldrums, but this was the time of year that the effect of the tides lessened.) That means that in ten hours or less of sailing, they could be here by late afternoon tomorrow, if they leave at first light. On the other hand, if they have rented a cabin cruiser, they may be able to do twenty knots per hour, but with the tides and swells, they might average fifteen knots per hour and be here in five or six hours. At any rate, I have promised a nice, smoky fire going tomorrow at noon, right here, where we are sitting."

"Have you done this sailing?"

"Yes, when I was at school in England. I often went sailing or yachting with friends."

"Is there a difference between sailing and yachting?"

"Yes, sailboats move through the water by the wind pushing at large sails of canvas or nylon, attached to tall masts. They have small engines for docking or when becalmed. Cabin cruisers, on the other hand, have no sails but big engines, which turn propellers, called screws, beneath the boat so fast, that they push the boat through the sea."

"What is becalmed?"

"Becalmed is no wind, not a breath. Only boats propelled by sails can be becalmed."

"Which do you like best?"

"I suppose I like sailing the best. With a sailboat, there is always something to be done to keep the boat moving with the wind, across the sea. The difference between yachting and sailing is mainly skill. It takes a great deal of skill and knowledge to sail a boat. A poor skipper can get into trouble quickly with a sudden change of wind, weather or seas. Cabin cruisers are less affected by winds, tides, or weather; but in a storm all boats are at risk."

"What is a skipper?"

"A skipper is the person in charge of running the boat, also called the Captain. He is the Chief on his vessel and his decisions are final."

Jon and Tamubu had reached the beach, where they stashed the equipment, to be picked up on their return–after their fishing jaunt north on the beach.

"Where did you see the fish you want me to help you catch– and what are we going to use to catch them?" Jon asked.

"I said that because I didn't want Paula to worry, but I think we have been followed to the beach."

"What makes you say that? Did you see something?"

"Yes, I saw the tracks of four men. They did not use the trail. They went through the forest. I did not backtrack very far, as the light was almost gone. They came out of the forest not far ahead; we will follow them and see."

"See what?"

Tamubu tilted his head, looked at Jon and gave him a small smile before he said, "We will see where they are going."

Apprehensive and without thinking, Jon stopped and said, "Thomas, we have no weapons. What if these men are hostile?"

Tamubu stopped and turned back to look directly at Jon. "Why did you call me Thomas?"

It is now or never. Jon thought. A slip of the tongue has forced my hand. He stood straight and tall, squared his shoulders and said, "I wonder if you would answer a question, by way of a reply. The story you told at the campfire of a lost boy—was that about you?"

"Yes."

"How old were you when you were lost in the rainforest?"

"I was ten."

His voice shaking slightly, Jon asked, "How were you lost?"

Tamubu knew the moment had arrived. He had to control his emotions, which were dangerously near the surface. He too stood tall and erect as he answered. "The engine of our plane caught fire. The pilot tried to land in the river and hit a submerged log. He and my teacher were killed. I escaped through the smashed windscreen to the tree trunk and then to land."

Jon, using every ounce of his self control, then asked, "Do you remember your birth name?"

"Yes, I remember my name; it is Peter Thomas Caulfield, the second, called Thomas because my father is called Peter."

With tears brimming in his eyes and a severe tightening in his throat, Jon said, "Then you knew who I was when I introduced myself. Why did you say nothing?"

"For the same reason that you, who had also guessed, said nothing."

Jon flung his arms around Tamubu and Tamubu held on tightly. Jon said softly, "I am so glad I have found you. My life has been so lonely without you. I am so pleased that you have been happy and well treated all these years. My heart overflows with joy, dear brother. Forgive me for not saying anything sooner, but I was so afraid that you didn't remember me, and I couldn't bear that reality."

Tamubu gently released Jon and looked straight into his brimming, blue eyes when he said, "Your voice was one of the few things I did remember: one of the memories that I never forgot. For a long time I thought your voice was just a recurring dream: a dream of a soft, warm hand and a happy voice saying, 'Come on, Thomas, let's go' ... or the same happy voice crying, 'Thomas, where are you? I'm ready now'!"

Now the tears did fall. Jon felt so euphoric—he could say

nothing. Tamubu, who had been taught to be stoic in all things, was speechless from the lump of joy stuck in his throat. Tamubu put his arm around Jon's shoulders, and coaxed him towards the forest where they could sit. They were together again. Tamubu's misgivings and doubts had fled. He knew now that the love of the brother would be doubled by the love of his parents when he returned home.

IT HAD ONLY BEEN moments, but already Tamubu felt the tribal mien slipping away, displaced by the memories and feelings of long ago. As he gazed at the surface fog floating above the sea, he saw Manutu arise before him. Manutu was smiling, but black tears ran down his cheeks. Tamubu heard Manutu say, "Great joy often brings great pain. Everything has a price and sometimes the price is too great to pay." As he watched the vision of Manutu fade, Tamubu understood the meaning of his words; but he was determined to take each day as it came to him; for already the sorrow of his loss was upon him. The time was not yet when he had to choose, but it was not far off.

A GREAT BREEZE BLEW in from the sea, and the haze cleared away and the clouds scudded towards the mountain while the sun shone through wispy clouds in glorious shafts of brilliant light. Tamubu heard the spirits chant. He heard the women lament. He was inspired as he had never been before. He was not lost to them—not yet. Someday, he knew he would go back to Manutu.

JON HAD COMPOSED HIMSELF. He looked at Thomas and said, "Even the Gods are shining down on our happiness. I thought I heard the angels sing."

"It is possible that you did, dear brother, for I thought I heard them too."

Tamubu removed his arm from Jon's shoulders and said, "Let's see where those footprints lead."

Together they headed up the beach. Each questioned the other about their lives during the past fourteen years. They came to the place where the footprints came out of the forest and marched down into the water. They passed them and walked along the surf, but they saw no other *sign* or footprints. Engrossed in deep conversation, the time passed swiftly.

Tamubu was about to suggest they return when he sensed they were being watched. He took Jon by the arm and turned him to look out at the sea before saying, "I think we are being watched from the forest. Do not do anything to indicate that you know someone might be there. Act just as you did while we walked down the beach. Now urinate." Jon was surprised at the unusual command, but actually, he felt the need for relief. "Good, now let's turn around and go back the way we came. Tell me about the first year you went to England for school. Did you like it?

"Yes and no. I liked school very much, but I hated being away from home for such a long time. Weekends and holidays were spent with Aunt Margaret and Uncle James and the rambunctious cousins, but it wasn't the same as home.

Aunt Margaret was a socialite, and always talked about what people would think. Her children paid no attention to her whatsoever, and ran absolutely amuck. We had great fun together. One Friday evening when Aunt Margaret and Uncle James were at a posh fete, the cousins and I took the mattresses off the bunks and used them for sleds to race each other down the curving twin staircases to the foyer. Most of the servants had the evening off, as they would be needed for Saturday brunch after the Ride to Hounds or foxhunt the next day. It was glorious fun and Brompton, the dithering old fool, was too busy polishing silver to even notice."

"Keep talking, you are doing fine. They are gone, whoever they were. I am anxious to get back to those footprints. I think I was misled."

"I would like to know more about your years with the Zuri Watu. What did you do each day, once you were well?"

"Jon, I am going to have to tell the whole story when I get home. I would rather tell it only once, can you bear with me in this?"

"Yes, I suppose I can, but I might expire of curiosity before we get back home."

"It is more important that I hear you talk of your life. The things you say sometimes bring back memories that have been long forgotten. I need to bring back as many of these buried memories as I can. There are so many holes. Things I don't remember at all. Like I didn't remember Aunt Margaret or Uncle James or the cousins until you started to talk about your mattress races. With each picture you painted, a wisp of memory floated back. I need your help in this, Jon."

"It will be as you wish. I will fill you full of boyish doings and family lore."

Jon talked on, and before long they were back at the footprints. Tamubu knelt down and examined the prints closely.

"It is as I suspected." He said to Jon. "The men walked out of the forest into the sea, probably to bathe, and walked back to the forest in the same footprints. They have probably been watching us all morning. In itself, this is not bad. If they had been hostile, and saw we were unarmed and out-manned, they would have attacked us when we stopped to urinate."

"Great! What would we have done then?"

"Gone swimming, I suppose—you do swim?"

"Yes, of course I swim!" Jon couldn't get over how calm and seemingly indifferent Tom had been about such an eventuality.

Tamubu was anxious to return and warn Motozo; and to *roam* the forest alone.

Motozo was preparing a hot lunch, after the damp and cool morning, when Jon and Tamubu plunked down the radio and gear.

Jon announced, "We were able to reach a ship that patched us through to Enugu Station. Max and the authorities know that we have arrived in good order. Don't say anything to Miss Thornton, but her parents should be here tomorrow afternoon. They are fogged-in at Limbe, or they might have been here today. Thomas, you wanted to warn Motozo about

the natives that shadowed us this morning... where did he go?"
Jon looked around but did not see Thomas at all.

"Did you see him leave?" He asked Motozo.

"Maybe he went to talk to Missy Paula," Motozo replied.

"At any rate, we should keep a sentry posted."

Jon ambled down the beach to the lean-to where Paula was still immersed in her compositions. Thomas was nowhere to be seen. "Was Thomas here?"

"No, not recently." So now Jon knew for sure, Paula thought, and was extremely pleased. "I assume when you say Thomas, you are asking about Tamubu?"

Jon went all smiles and barely contained his joy. "Yes, he is my long, lost brother, can you believe that? I made the mistake of calling him Thomas this morning and then the truth came out. I was so worried that he didn't remember me, but he said my voice was one of the few things he did remember."

"I am so happy for the both of you. I know you will have many wonderful hours of catching-up to do."

"We've already started, but he has asked me to wait until we get home for the full story. He says hearing me talk helps him to remember."

"Yes, I know. While we were on the trail, some things I said triggered recollections. Now I can tell you, for I felt a bit dishonest at the time, Thomas did the drawings in my diary, not me. He is enormously gifted with his art."

"When I saw the drawings flapping in the breeze, I thought of Thomas and all the pencil pictures he had made for me when I was young. There were so many little things that made me hope and then there were things that made me feel I was hoping in vain. But that is all over now. If you did not see him, I wonder where he has gone."

Paula said, "You must get used to his going off alone. He did it so often on our trek here, that I soon gave it no thought at all. It will take a while for him to change his habits."

Jon thought about Paula's advice. She's right. I must not smother him. He's not used to having a doting brother, and might resent too much restriction by affection. We can go along as we were, getting to know each other slowly. I must use some restraint on my emotions and be patient. I am too impetuous anyway.

"How's your ankle? I don't see any crutch marks in the sand."

"I'm not using them anymore. I can walk a few steps without discomfort. I just have to be careful not to twist it; so I put an Ace bandage on it this morning."

This woman had so much pluck and courage that Jon found it hard to resist telling her of the imminent arrival of her parents, which would give her so much joy. Instead he said, "Motozo has lunch ready. Would you like me to bring it here to you?"

"Actually, I would like that. It is kind of you to offer."

Jon got up to fetch her meal when he saw Obu and Obendi carrying gourds and paper plates of food coming up the beach. Obu's face lit up with a smile as he said. "It is lunch for Missy Paula and kisha. You eat here—big space."

Paula offered Jon a packaged towlette, but he said. "Save them for your own use, I'll wash up in the sea."

Motozo had made a fish chowder using pork broth, fish, rice, tapioca, green onions and guava. It was an unusual combination, but delicious, as were the fluffy biscuits and the fresh, sweet pineapple for dessert.

Paula was going to miss these trail meals. She had never eaten better food in her life—and said as much to Jon while they ate their lunch. Jon told Paula that Motozo was the best trail cook Max had ever had, and that he had let him go reluctantly. When lunch was finished, Paula wanted to be alone to think. She made her excuses to Jon, and lay down for a nap.

I MUST DECIDE WHAT I am going to do. The authorities will be here in a day or two, and logically, I have to go back to the Expedition, if only to have my day in court, so to speak. Jon and Tamubu will go home to Kenya; and Motozo and the boys will go back to Max Mason. What then? I wish Tamubu would ask me to go with him to Kenya. I wish I knew what he wanted... 'I'll be there for you as long as you need me.' Once the authorities are here, will he feel as if I don't need him anymore? I wish I knew what he was thinking.

Her thoughts, as they often did, drifted back to meeting Tamubu in the tree, with the enraged lions roaring below. She had been terrified by their noise and great size. When he spoke, she was astonished by his British accent—and their unusual relationship had begun.

It was two weeks ago today, but so much has happened, that it seems like months. Here I am stranded in the wilds of Africa, and I don't want the experience to end—silly me!'

TAMUBU HID HIS CLOAK and pouches in the dense underbrush. He *roamed* to the footprints that went down to the sea, where he found other tracks along the foliage going north. No care had been taken to obscure the tracks at all. This seemed odd to him. Near the place where he and Jon had turned around, there had been a small camp in a clearing not far from the water's edge. The camp was now abandoned, but Tamubu wanted to know more about these men and continued to follow their tracks.

He heard excited voices, just before he came upon a sight that made him want to laugh. These were boys. In some tribes, when the boys reach the age of twelve, they go out into the forest by themselves, for several weeks. It is a ritual of manhood. They cannot return home until they have killed a wild piglet. This is a dangerous and difficult assignment for the tusks of the sow are lethal, her temper short and nasty, and the piglets themselves are faster than lightning. These boys looked to be Fulani, and were jabbering away about the dangerous foreigners they had seen on the beach.

One boy was limping badly and Tamubu could see that he had an infected wound on his foot, below the ankle. The foot was festering and the boy needed care immediately. While watching, Tamubu heard the tallest boy give out orders, saying, "Kabanza, make a clearing for a fire; Nashutu, you help him."

Kabanza seemed to resent the order and said, "What are you going to do, Mguru?"

"I am going to look for spring water for Kasuku's wound. I

think the pond water was bad. We should go home, but Kasuku is not able to walk that far."

Tamubu made a decision and *roamed* to the top of the trees. There, he spoke to the boys. "Mguru, Kabanza, Nashutu, Kasuku–listen to me–you must go to the camp of the foreigners–they have medicine for Kasuku–a medicine chief from the Great Nations of the Zuri Watu is with them, he will help Kasuku–go now–do not make camp–walk openly on the beach."

Needless to say, the boys sat cowering in abject terror. Tamubu gave them a few moments to control their fear and moved closer to them.

"Mguru, you are the leader–you must be strong."

"Kabanza, you must help–not hinder–or the spirits will be angry with you."

"Nashutu, you know the pain of Kasuku (Tamubu had seen the long scar on his leg) –remember your own injury–help him."

It was too much. The terrified boys quickly packed their things and helped Kasuku to the beach. Here Mguru said, "I will run ahead and tell the Medicine Chief of the Zuri Watu that we need his help. That way Kasuku will not have to walk so far."

Tamubu was pleased with his results and *roamed* back to his cached possessions. When he entered the camp, Paula immediately asked, "Where have you been? You missed lunch."

Tamubu looked at her with soft eyes and a slight smirk. "You missed me! I'm glad to hear it."

Paula started to retort, then laughed. "You're right! I missed you, but you are so smug, I won't do it again!"

"Good, because I have to leave again."

"Where in the world are you going?"

"Someone needs my help. Kybo is going with me. Don't fret; I'll be back for dinner."

Tamubu gathered his pouches and fresh water while Kybo gathered some food as directed. Jon was going to ask if he could help, but a slight shake of Thomas' head let him know his help was not needed. Just past the other lean-to, Tamubu turned back and returned to Paula asking, "May I use your first aid kit?" Paula turned to her backpack and pulled the kit from its pocket and handed it to him. Their eyes met and Tamubu saw Paula's desire to help, and the frustration of her present physical limitation. He said, "Asante," and he was gone.

Once across the stony rim, Tamubu and Kybo picked up a ground-eating jog along the water where the sand was wet and firm. It wasn't long until they saw Mguru running towards them. Tamubu motioned to Mguru to follow, and kept on, until they saw the other boys struggling down the beach on the wet sand. Kybo glanced at Tamubu and thought: 'this man is much more than he seems. I am honored that he chose me to help him today.'

When the boys saw Tamubu and Kybo coming fast with Mguru bringing up the rear, they diverted from the water's edge to the shade of the rainforest. Kasuku could hardly walk. His friends had supported him between them and half dragged and half carried him with his injured foot raised and supported under his shin by his kitamba.

"Kybo, we can only do first aid here. Give the boys the food and water and then support this boy's foot across your legs. You," Tamubu pointed to Mguru, "make a small, hot fire." To a cup of cold tea, Tamubu added a bit of powder, which he gave to the boy, Kasuku, to drink. Then, slowly and carefully, Tamubu cleaned the wound with sterile gauze pads and hydrogen peroxide from the first aid kit. He then took a small steel cup from the first aid kit, added a bit of water and placed it by the fire where it came to a boil; to this he added some herbs and set the cup aside. He then wrapped the heel and ankle with a winding gauze bandage, putting gauze pads over the injury, between the layers of the bandage. When he was finished, he poured the warm mixture in the steel cup over the bandage, wetting it thoroughly.

The boy clearly had a fever. Tamubu cleaned the cup; added a bit of water and put the cup beside the fire to boil before adding several different herbs from his pouch. Glancing at the food, he took a bit of the coconut and added it to the cup before taking some of the leftover sweet potato, which he mashed into the mixture in the cup. With Jon's gift spoon, Tamubu fed the mixture to the sick boy.

The herbs were bitter but the cooked coconut released its strong sweetness and the sweet potato gave substance to the potion and nourishment to protect the stomach. In a few moments, the boy was asleep.

Tamubu turned to the remaining boys and said, "The spirits called to me to come and help you–is this so?" The boys all nodded agreement.

"Who among you called the spirits for help?" Each boy looked at the others and finally, Nashutu raised his hand.

"You did the right thing, son. How are you called?"

"My name is Nashutu, this is Mguru, and this is Kabanza. The sick boy is Kasuku. Thank you for coming so quickly. Are you really a Medicine Man from the Great Nations of the Zuri Watu?"

"Yes. I am on walk-about, lucky for you. We will let your friend sleep for a while and then Kybo will carry him back to our camp. Finish the food we don't want to have to carry that back too." The boys gladly did as they were told; hunting had been scarce, mostly birds.

KYBO SAT IN UTTER amazement thinking: there was much, much more to this man than anyone suspected–if the spirits had told him there was an injured boy not far away that needed the help of a medicine man. Tamubu had also found and saved Miss Thornton. Motozo had told them that he was dogo mungu soon after they had met. But none of them had ever known a *little god*, as the living emissaries of the spirit gods were called, and they all doubted if Motozo had ever known one either. But Tamubu had just said that the spirits had sent him to help the injured boy. Motozo was right after all; Tamubu was dogo mungu.'

IT WAS A SAD little group that arrived at the camp later that afternoon. Kasuku had not awakened after Tamubu's ministrations, so Kybo found poles to make a litter, using the boy's kitamba for support. He and Tamubu carried the litter while the other boys held another kitamba above the litter, to keep Kasuku out of the sun.

When Paula saw the sick boy, she immediately wanted a recap. When Tamubu was finished, she said, "He needs antibiotics. I have some sulfonamide tablets. He will need one tablet every six hours, which is four times a day, with plenty of water. We will start him with two tablets now, if you can wake him." Tamubu roused Kasuku, and told him to swallow the medicine and drink all the water.

With the help of Obu and Obendi, the boys built another lean-to nearby. Jon gave up his space with Paula and Thomas to Kasuku and went to stay with Motozo, while Kybo bunked in with the young boys. Motozo sent a shell full of stew down to the boy's lean-to for dinner. They were going to refuse the food until Tamubu said, "One sick boy is all I need. You will work for your keep over the next few days and do Kasuku's work too." Once they knew it was not charity, the boys ate with gusto.

Kasuku slept until late evening when Tamubu awoke him for a bite to eat and his medicine. Kasuku was frightened to see Paula, but Tamubu quickly calmed him, saying, "This woman is also a healer. She has agreed to help me with your care. Her name is Paula. You must accept her ministrations as you did mine."

In the morning, Tamubu went to the new lean-to and told the boys to go and see their friend. He was awake and asking for them. When Kasuku's friends arrived, Tamubu helped Paula to leave. They would go and have breakfast with Motozo and the others and let the boys comfort Kasuku alone.

After breakfast and the examination and repoulticing of Kasuku's wound, which was looking better, Paula decided to bathe in the sea. Tamubu and Jon looked at each other, laughed and decided to accompany her—to keep the sharks away. Paula didn't like the idea of sharks and kept to the surf, which was receding from high tide. Paula took her laundry with her to the sea; and with a bit of playful keep-away splashing and dunking, the clothes were finally washed. It had been the first bit of carefree play since she came to Africa—and it felt good!

IN THE MORNING, MOTOZO sent his men out hunting, or on food-gathering forays, while the three young lads had been sent out to gather wood for the fires. There were now twelve mouths to feed, and there was much work to be done.

23

Surprise Visit

JON TOOK THE RADIO, tent and binoculars and headed for the western end of the stone jetty, where it met the open sea. Tamubu followed, gathering the materials for a smoky fire. While erecting the tent, Jon handed Thomas the field glasses, saying, "Do you remember how to use binoculars?"

"I'm not sure, show me." Jon demonstrated how to focus the lenses, and how to zero-in on a particular object. Thomas practiced with the binoculars, while Jon was on the radio.

"Jon Caulfield calling Enugu Station. Come in. Over." Jon repeated his call and was getting ready to change the frequency when he heard a spotty message.

"Jon Caulfield calling Enugu Station, or anyone. Come in. Over."

He fiddled with the squelch and heard: "Charles Thornton here, Jon. Is everything okay? Over"

"Oh yes, quite! I was just checking in with the base station for an update. Where are you now? Do you have an E.T.A.? Over."

"We are about thirty miles away. We should be there is less than two hours. Over."

"So you have chartered a cabin cruiser. We wondered about that. Over."

"Yes, in a way. There were no boats available for hire. Captain Jones offered us the use of his private motor yacht to go to the cove. Over."

"The signal fire is being prepared for you as we speak. The camp is south of the signal fire, but the only anchorage is north of it. The cove is basically a tidal basin. Over."

"That's a ten-four, Jon. Over and Out." Jon changed the frequency on the radio to the one they had used at Enugu Station when calling the *Norsk Star*.

"Jon Caulfield calling Enugu Station. Come in. Over." The reply was immediate.

"Enugu Station here. Come back, Jon. Over."

"Mr. and Mrs. Thornton are about two hours away from our position. It will be a wonderful surprise for Miss Thornton. She was quite distracted when she found the Expedition yacht was gone. Were you able to contact the *Just Cause*? Over."

"We contacted the harbormaster at Port-Gentil. He relayed the news to the *Just Cause*. They were overjoyed to hear that Miss Thornton had been found in good order; and it seems the resultant celebration might have been the reason for the *Just Cause* running aground. Now they are having an airboat flown in for the collection of samples. Over."

"See if you can get an update on the *Just Cause* and the airboat. Miss Thornton will want to hear what's going on with the Expedition. Will you send Max a message for me? I want to tell him that I have found my brother, Thomas. It was Thomas, called Tamubu by the Zuri Watu, who was responsible for helping Miss Thornton through the wilderness after she escaped the Ndezi. Over."

"Will do, right away. Enugu Station over and out." Jon went to stand-by just in case Max was near the radio.

"Have you seen anything with the binoculars, Thomas?"

"Yes! I saw many whales. I remember father reading the story of the white whale, but these were gray and seemed peaceful. They just plunged along blowing plumes of water into the air." Jon took the binoculars and scanned the sea. The whales were gone. Too bad, he would have enjoyed seeing them.

Thomas had found a depression in which to build the signal fire, for the wind over the jetty was strong even with the receding tide, and quickly blew the thick smoke away.

"It is not much of a signal, Jon."

"It is enough. Smoke is visible for a long way at sea." Still looking through the binoculars, Jon panned back to the camp.

He saw Kybo walking towards them with a bag slung over his shoulder.

"I think lunch is on its way," he said as he handed the glasses to Thomas. After a quick look, Thomas said, "Kybo was overly impressed yesterday. He thinks the spirits sent me to rescue Kasuku."

"Well, it is curious how you knew about him."

"It was the footprints in the sand. They were enlarged to make them look like the prints of a man, and the right foot of a set of prints was very shallow compared to the other sets, indicating a lack of pressure on the right foot. The footprint to the left of the shallow print showed a heavier side on the right edge of the print, which could mean that person was providing support. After that, it was merely a matter of returning with the first aid kit and Kybo."

Jon thought... and all I saw was a bunch of depressions in the sand... amazing!

"Kybo told me the boy called Nashutu thinks you were sent to them by the spirits?"

"It is only natural that, faced with a serious problem, at least one of the boys would pray for help. It was a way to get them to accept my ministrations."

Tamubu thought to himself, I managed to avoid revealing myself this time, but I will have to be very careful from now on—that I don't expose my abilities and, in so doing, set myself apart.

Kybo arrived with lunch and asked why we had set a signal fire. Once explained, Kybo grinned from ear to ear. Apparently, Kybo had never seen a boat before, nor had he ever seen the sea until two days ago. The cold oatmeal, nut and berry roll-ups went well with the gourd of coffee. Motozo was a clever cook with combinations; they were always a flavor treat.

Jon said to Kybo, "We are waiting for a radio reply. Would you go back and tell the others we may be here a while longer."

"Yes kisha, I will go now."

When Kybo had gone, Jon said to Thomas. "I think you

were right. Kybo was impressed yesterday. He has now decided that you are the leader."

"I noticed that. Kybo is a good man, an honest and reliable man. I like him."

"Yes, he is a good man, but too much honesty can be a fault. A little dissimulation is a virtue."

"A little what?"

"False pretense or hypocrisy—saying one thing and meaning another; he could think kisha, but it would have been nicer if he had said kigozi."

Tamubu smiled; Jon had always been concerned with small differences: did you get three jellybeans? I only got two! And he had not changed. He had been kisha to Max Mason; kigozi on the search; and was now kisha again—to me.

A small indignant silence fell as Jon smoked his pipe. Thomas scanned the ocean for more whales, or other marine life, until the radio broke the spell.

"Max Mason calling Jon Caulfield. Come in. Over."

"Max, this is Jon. It's just great to hear from you. Over."

"Jon, I'm over the moon with the news that you have found your brother. What a jolly good show! That he was with Miss Thornton is an incredible coincidence. You said you felt compelled to go and search for her, and look what you found! We will be with the Zuri Watu next week. Can I take a message for your brother? Over."

Jon handed the mike to Thomas; "Push the button to speak, release it to listen."

"This is Jon's brother. My tribal name is Tamubu. Please tell Sashono and Manutu that I am well; and that my blood brother found me in his search for Miss Thornton. Tell them that I will have great stories for the talking fire when I return. Thank Manutu for his words of wisdom. Over"

"That's a ten-four, Tamubu. Jon, what are your plans? Over"

"We have no plans. We are taking it one day at a time. Miss Thornton's parents will be here soon. Tomorrow, when I call Enugu Station there may be plans. Over."

"Whatever you want to do will be fine with me, Jon; tell

Motozo I miss his cooking and tell the boys I miss hearing them play their game of stones. Over and Out."

Tamubu said, "This Max... is he your chief?"

"Not really. We were partners on a trading journey. I had asked him to go much further north to the plateau nearest the Benue River—where the plane wreckage was found—to look for you among tribes he rarely visited, or had never traded with before. It was possible that we could get there and find they would not trade, or had nothing that we wanted in trade. The trading journey could be a financial loss, so I paid half of the expenses against earning a profit from trade goods. It must have worked out well, or Max would have changed his route once I was gone."

"Did you like the trading?"

"Oddly enough, I did. It was an adventure going deep into the wilderness to trade with tribes that rarely saw a white man. I studied African languages in school, and it was always a source of pleasure when the natives opened up and talked to me. Basically, that is one of the reasons why traders don't go so deep; few know the subtleties of the languages or the dialects.

Max had to hire more help after I took Motozo and his boys. He told me he was going to choose men that spoke the dialects of the deep forest. Max is an amazing man. He is a bundle of energy and is always ready for something new. I very much enjoyed being with him."

"How did you meet Max?"

"I met him on a tour of the Congo River. Max and I went on a side-trip to the Pygmy villages. We got on well together from the start. Max told me about his trading and I told him about you. Soon we had worked out a plan, on a map, of villages where you might be living.

"After the Ndezi, we went north, away from the base camp supply line. My leaving to search for Miss Thornton changed his plans; for Max needed to go to Enugu to get replacements for Motozo and the men.

"When the Nigerian rescue attempt failed, both Max and I were plagued with worry and regret. Max had started out in the guise of a trader, many years ago, to rescue a boy taken from a safari camp. It pleased him to help people, so he kept on trading, and kept on rescuing lost or abducted people. Miss Thornton's rescue was his first failure, and it upset him terribly.

"Me, I kept thinking about you, and how I was right there, and doing nothing to help Miss Thornton. It obsessed me. I had to go and search for her even though I had only known her for an hour. Much of my feeling was subconscious; it was as if by finding her, I would somehow be relieving the need to find you. Never, not once, did it cross my mind that I would find you with Miss Thornton."

Tamubu wondered if Jon might be a subliminal receptor too. On his journey from the valley of the Zuri Watu, he had constantly tried to remember more about Jon, his sisters and parents. Several times, he saw fleeting images of a smiling Jon in his mind. Had he actually summoned Jon without knowing that he was doing so? It was as Manutu said, 'Great love can produce great results.'

"Jon, what is that I see?" Tamubu asked as he passed the binoculars to Jon. Jon focused the lenses and saw a multi-level luxury cruiser with a canopied rear deck.

"I think we are about to meet the Thorntons... who are arriving in grand style! Let's go to the beach." They gathered the gear and left it at the end of the stone jetty before going to greet the Thorntons. Sitting on the dry sand, they watched the cruiser arrive and anchor out with her bow into the now incoming tide. A large dinghy was inflated, lowered overboard and a crewman descended to the dinghy, where he manned the ladder for Mr. and Mrs. Thornton's descent. Once embarked, the crewman rowed to the beach.

When the dinghy touched the sand, Jon and Tamubu helped them out of the dinghy while the crewman stowed the oars. Tamubu and the crewman dragged the dinghy above the water mark on the beach before Tamubu returned for the introductions.

As he walked back to the group, Tamubu observed the newcomers. Lisa Thornton was an older, more rounded version of her daughter with the same smile lines around her mouth. Charles Thornton was the epitome of the dedicated outdoorsman: lean, wiry and exuding good health. Up close, Lisa Thornton also had the same captivating blue eyes and lily-like skin as her daughter.

Tamubu heard her ask Jon, "Where is Paula? We thought she would be here to greet us."

"Paula has a twisted ankle. She is resting at her lean-to ... we did not tell her of your imminent arrival. She was devastated when we reached the cove and the *Just Cause* was gone. We didn't want to chance another disappointment, in case you were delayed. Paula is probably taking a nap now, just the other side of the jetty. Let's go along, shall we?" Jon said.

"Wild horses couldn't hold us back." Charles Thornton replied in a well-modulated voice that held a timbre of authority.

The preppie-looking crewman, whose name was Phil, said, "I'll stay here with the dinghy. He handed Charles a two-way radio. If you need me, just call on channel three."

The four of them walked off with Lisa Thornton asking, "How did Paula hurt her ankle?"

Tamubu replied, "She stepped back and her foot became wedged between two rocks." It was the first time Tamubu had spoken besides saying hello.

Mrs. Thornton said, "Why you speak English with a British accent. I suppose all the locals do."

Jon was annoyed that Mrs. Thornton had brushed Thomas off as a 'local' and hastily interposed: "Mrs. Thornton, Thomas is my older brother. He was lost in a plane crash in the wilderness when he was ten years old. Thomas is the person who brought Paula more than a hundred and fifty miles through the wilds of Africa safely back to this beach. Were it not for him, more than likely, you would never have seen Paula again! Thomas and I have just been reunited, for when I found Paula she was safe in his care."

Charles Thornton, immensely chagrined spoke, "We can't thank you both enough... now or ever! We owe you a debt we can never repay. Lisa and I are so out-of-our-element here, that we beg you to forgive us if we say or do the wrong thing."

Tamubu looked at Jon and with a tiny shake of his head told him that he had been too hard on Mrs. Thornton. Jon replied, "It is I who must ask forgiveness. I was being overly protective of a brother who has been lost to me for fourteen years. How were you to know?"

AT THAT MOMENT, KYBO stepped out onto the open beach and saw Jon, Tamubu and the visitors coming towards him. He immediately told Motozo and the other bearers before turning to go and be with Kasuku and the lads.

"Why there are many people here. I don't know why, but I thought it was just the three of you." Lisa said.

"I brought five men with me", Jon replied. The wilderness is a dangerous place. Alone, death is just around the next bend in the trail, unless you are extremely skilled in wilderness travel. Yesterday, Thomas came across four lads, one of whom has an infected foot. In all there are twelve of us here."

Jon waved a hand to let the men know to follow them to the reunion. Paula was indeed asleep. Mr. and Mrs. Thornton stood gazing at their precious daughter, who sat on her poncho, leaning against the tree trunk, a book in her lap, with the pages gently fluttering in the breeze.

Tamubu gave his bird whistle, the call he had used to alert Paula to his arrival back at camp. She immediately stirred and opened her eyes. She saw Tamubu and Jon standing there, smiling at her. Beside them were Motozo, Obendi, Obu and Kimbo. When it looked like she would speak, Tamubu and Jon moved aside and made a gesture of presentation toward her parents who had stood just behind them.

Paula cried, "Mom! Dad! Oh, my gosh! How did you get here?" Tamubu had gone to Paula's side to help her to her feet and then her parents rushed to embrace her. Her father said through his tears, "We have a cruiser on the other side of the jetty." Her mother said, "We wanted to be here for you, when you returned and found the Expedition yacht gone, dear."

Paula was so thrilled she couldn't speak. Leaning back,

she looked at these two wonderful parents who had come so far to be here for her. Everyone left them to their reunion, and went to the lad's lean-to where Kybo had already told the boys what was happening. Big smiles greeted them and were returned, for reunions were special events.

They all sat with the lads while Tamubu told them the story of meeting Jon at the thorn boma hut and their travels to the beach. Motozo had taken Obu and had gone to serve refreshments to Paula and her parents. He had made coffee and scones, biscuit like muffins made with mashed bananas, coconut, dates and nuts. After serving Paula and her parents, Motozo and Obu returned to hear the story. No matter how many times a story is told, there was always magic in the telling.

WHEN THE FIRST RUSH of emotions had subsided, and Motozo and Obu had gone, Charles Thornton said, "We thought we would find you half-starved, but we should have known better. You have always had a penchant for five-star dining. These scones are marvelous and the coffee ... I've never had better."

"Some of the best food I have ever eaten in my life has been served in the wilds of Africa by Tamubu and Motozo."

To keep up the light banter, her mother added, "Maybe they will give me lessons." Both Paula and her father laughed. Her mother was not a cook; she did salads and Charles barbequed. Sallee Ann, her older sister had learned to cook, in self defense, before she was in her teens.

"You must tell us everything, darling." Her mother said.

"Yes, we will do that later, after dinner; Motozo has been cooking all day..." an odd feeling passed over her before she continued; then we will all sit around the fire, and Tamubu, Jon and I will tell our stories. That is the way it is done here; everyone will listen.

"That's fine with us dear," Lisa said, "but who is Tamubu? We have not yet met him."

"Of course you have! He is Jon's brother who stood right next to him! Tamubu is his tribal name, and I'm used to calling him that. Look, here they come now."

Motozo and Jon decided that the enlarged clearing before Motozo's cooking lean-to, where they ate their meals, would be the best place for them to gather for the story telling.

Jon came up to Paula and said, "When you are ready, come to the fire."

Charles said to Jon, "We must inform Captain Jones and his crew of our plans. What do you suggest we tell Phil?"

"Do you want to spend the night on the beach with us? If you do, radio Phil and ask him to bring whatever clothing and gear you'll need when they join us for dinner. Everyone is invited." Jon replied.

"Lisa and Charles exchanged glances and Lisa said, "Yes, we would like to sleep here on the beach, if it's not too much trouble."

Paula added, "Mom, Dad, you can sleep here with me. Jon and Tamubu can sleep with Motozo. They enlarged their lean-to this afternoon..." the odd feeling became a knowing look, and her mouth dropped open. She looked at Jon and said, "You knew my parents were coming! Oh Jon, you really are a sly one!"

Jon smiled at Paula and said to Mrs. Thornton, "Tell Captain Jones and his crew to join us for dinner, in about an hour."

Paula said, "I'll help with the list. Did you bring sweats? They would be good to sleep in. Plan to wear shorts and a tee shirt or long-sleeved cotton shirt tomorrow. I have bug spray. You'll need your ditty bags and wide-brimmed hats. Knee socks and canvas sport shoes. You will need rain ponchos for a ground cloth and sleeping bags; it gets cold at night. I think that's it; any suggestions?"

"None, you are your usual efficient self." Lisa finished the notations and Charles contacted Phil at the dinghy.

"Mom, Dad, let's chat here for a few minutes, I want to know what is going on at home." For an hour, her parents talked about the events at home. They had a way of talking together, never interrupting one-another, but somehow all talking at the same time when they talked about family and friends. There wasn't much news since they had last been together on New Year's Day, seven weeks ago. The biggest event had been their decision to come to Africa, to be here for Paula when she returned—after they heard that the yacht had gone south to the Ogooué River.

Her father asked, "What are your plans now, Paula? Are you going to go south to join up with the Expedition on the Ogooué River?"

"Dad, it is a very complicated decision. Except for the lads, these people put their lives on hold... as well as put them at risk to find me or care for me. Without their selflessness, I wouldn't be sitting here talking to you—now or ever again... and I do not exaggerate! They traveled long distances, endured great danger and put their financial interests in jeopardy. I have to consider them before I consider myself. I don't know yet, what Jon and Tamubu want to do; I only know that whatever it is, they will do it together. Jon will see to the welfare of the men when a decision is made. My ankle is still unstable, so there is time to see how things will work themselves out. What are your arrangements, Dad?"

"Well, I'm on sabbatical, so there are no restrictions on my time. Your mother has Julie coming to the office full time to cover for her. It is tax season you know. But we are here for you and what you want... is what we want."

JON CAME TO FETCH them to the fire. "You have us all on pins and needles. Come along now."

"Jon," Paula said, "What are your plans now that my parents are here?"

Jon looked at Paula earnestly and said, "I haven't thought about it. I suppose, if there is room in the boat, Thomas and I could go back to Douala with you. From there, we could fly home to Kenya. I haven't asked the men if they want to fly home or trek. I imagine it is close to two hundred miles from here to Enugu.

"The biggest consideration is our patient, Kasuku. It will be a few more days before the infection is gone, and he can travel. I don't think Thomas will consider leaving Kasuku before then, nor would I ask him to do so. We can stay behind, if you are ready to leave with your parents."

"Oh, it's nothing like that. I just wondered if you had talked about what you might do after my parents arrived, since you knew they were on their way yesterday."

Jon tilted his head much like Thomas: "Actually I knew when they landed at Yaoundé, three days ago." He said with a crooked smile. "The radio, you know."

"Oh Jon, I'll never trust you again! How could you be so cruel as to keep something like that from me?"

Jon grimaced at Paula, and looked sheepishly at her parents. "We thought it would be crueler to tell you: the yacht is gone, but your parents are in Africa and might meet us at the beach."

Paula gaped like a fish, and then lowered her head. "Everyone has been so good to me, so thoughtful and considerate. I hardly rate such good friends. You were right— of course, you were right!"

Charles said, "I can't wait another minute to hear your story. We'll sort out our plans tomorrow, let's go to the fire!"

24

Fireside Story

PAULA, LISA AND CHARLES arrived at the talking fire to find Motozo, the men and the lads waiting to greet them, using their best English to do so. Obendi had drawn the short straw, so it was he who had to ask if it would be possible for them to visit the boat. It was at this moment that Captain Jones and his crew arrived at the camp.

Hearing the question, Captain Jones replied, "I would be pleased to have everyone visit the motor yacht in the morning." There was an immediate round of cheers with big smiles.

Charles Thornton drew the newcomers towards the fire. "Everyone, this is Captain Jones, and his crewmen, Phil and Steve."

Jon arose and said, "We are delighted that you came ashore to be with us Captain. Come, you must join us around the fire. Paula is going to tell us the story of her adventures after she was washed out to sea by the tsunami."

Captain Jones smiled, "Aahh, we wouldn't want to miss a tale like that now, would we?"

When everyone was settled around the fire, Jon, who had remained standing said, "My name is Jon Caulfield, this is my brother, Thomas Caulfield, and sitting beside him on his right is Paula Thornton, and next to her are her parents, Lisa and Charles Thornton. Over here is Motozo our cook, his helpers Obu and Obendi, and our scouts Kimbo, and his son Kybo. These young men are Fulani lads who are visiting us, Mguru, Kabanza, Nashutu and Kasuku. Kasuku has an infected foot, but he is recovering nicely. If we stay here much longer, we will have to find women to build huts for us." The Africans laughed uproariously, and while the others didn't understand the joke, they joined the laughter. For their benefit, Jon explained. "In tribal Africa, the women do all the hut building, and new villages are often started with as few as twenty people. There are seventeen of us sitting around this fire." Again, there was laughter.

After Jon sat, the natives started a rhythmic "huh-huh-huh-aaah, huh-huh-huh-aaah." Paula knew that when they stopped, she would be expected to begin her story.

"Night had come early from the threatening storm when I went aboard the yacht to stow my gear. Had it not started to rain, I would not have closed the hatch, and you would not be hearing this story. I had finished my chores, and was walking through the galley to the companionway, when I was suddenly forced to my knees as the deck rose beneath me, and tossed me about the cabin, knocking me unconscious. A tsunami wave had struck the tanker. The yacht was ripped from her moorings and flung into the sea, behind the crest of the huge wave. She was taken out to sea on the massive ebb tide, where she rode the violent stormy seas. At some time, I managed to get into a bunk and lower the storm net; a device that I'm certain saved my life." Paula smiled at her father, who nodded his head in reply.

"The tidal seas eventually tossed the yacht and me into this cove. When I was recovered, I found I could not sail away because of the volcanic rim surrounding the bay; so I began to explore ashore. My first day on the beach, I saw six native warriors. Their savage looks frightened me. I hoped they had not seen my trail, where I had walked in the edge of the surf. Desperate to return to the yacht, but not wanting to leave a trail, or be seen walking in the open water, I returned here through the trees.

"After two days, I thought the natives were gone; so I ventured ashore again to collect more samples. It was just as I returned here to the cove, that I heard a helicopter. I dropped from the trees and rushed to the water's edge to fire a flare, when the natives threw a net over me and took me away – captured.

"We traveled to the Ndezi village for seven days. The day after I arrived at the village, the traders came: Jon here, and his partner, Max Mason. They tried to obtain my freedom, *but Bolbonga, the Ndezi chief, wanted me for his wife." Her audience gasped. "The chief's first wife, as was her right, challenged me for status. I was given no choice; I had to fight her in an unusual and ritualistic fashion.*

"We were slicked up with grease. Our left arms were bound to our sides and her right ankle and my right ankle were tied together, with about a foot of cord between us. The object was to make your opponent fall without falling yourself. I had seen such a fight in the past hour and knew I could win only by surprise. When the drums signaled the start, I instantly threw my upper body forward into an aerial, which I knew could not be completed, but I hoped it would fell us both. Kira, my opponent, was so surprised by my action, that she stepped back; a movement that allowed me to raise my tied ankle higher, the force of which, forced her to fall backwards and allowed me to land on my hands, flex my elbows, and push off for a backspring onto my free left foot. In four or five seconds, it was all over. As the winner, Bolbonga gave me the knife to kill Kira." Again her audience sucked air in surprise. "I pretended not to understand his intentions, and just nicked her ear as had been done to the loser of the contest I had seen earlier. I then returned to my prison aerie."

THE FULANI LADS SPOKE almost no English, so Kybo was translating in hushed tones on the other side of the cooking lean-to. All of Max's bearers spoke good English as well as Swahili and other native tongues.

"That night I escaped through the smoke hole in the roof to a stout branch above it. I used the survival belt that my father had designed for us when we were mountaineering, to reach the limb. Not wanting to leave a visible trail, I stayed high in the trees. With the full moon, I could see well enough, but my progress was slow—but more importantly, I was not leaving a trail to be followed.

"Shortly after first light I left the forest trail I had been shadowing to find a devil plant." Another gasp, tinged with horror, came from her audience. Paula smiled, and continued. "I found a huge specimen and, covering myself completely, I used a branch to raise the leaves, so I could crawl under and

hide inside from the searchers that would soon be coming to look for me.

"While I did not know it at the time, Tamubu had seen me seek refuge under the devil plant. After the searchers had returned to the village, his curiosity made him follow me— and that curiosity saved my life."

Paula took Tamubu's hand and gave it a squeeze, a gesture that did not go unnoticed.

"I again fled through the trees, for I did not know that the Ndezi had gone back to the village. Two days later, I came out of the forest into the bush. I had followed the wrong trail in the forest and came out in a different place.

"Thorn bushes and boulders covered the hillsides. There was no path. I walked along the base of the hills until I saw a path, which I followed. Rounding a bend, I saw a huge lioness before me. I stood frozen. My only defenses were my whistle and Bolbonga's knife.

"Tamubu, who had been following me, fired my gun and frightened the big cat away. He had seen Bolbonga toss the pistol into a thicket, just before calling off the search, and had retrieved it for me, having noticed my empty holster.

"Tamubu had already helped me make good my escape when the lioness came back and confronted him. She was too close to outrun, so Tamubu rushed at her as if to attack. Startled by such unexpected behavior, the lioness arose from her crouch. Tamubu used his spear to pole-vault onto a large rock, where he then leapt for the lowest branch of an oak tree. The lioness made a lightning fast leap for the boulder and narrowly missed snagging him."

Again Paula squeezed Tamubu's hand, which she still held.

"It was in a lofty oak tree, in the wilderness of Africa, that we first introduced ourselves to one another. After sharing his rations with me, Tamubu left to find a better camping place, while I took a nap to recover from the enervating confrontation with the lion. Later that night, after the simba-jike had gone off to hunt, Tamubu took me to a ledge, high above the trail, where we made camp.

"The next day it rained and Tamubu suggested we stay put for the day while he roasted a bird and cooked other delicious food. It was during this lull that I realized I would never make it back to the yacht alone, which was probably a distance of a hundred and fifty miles or so. Later, I asked Tamubu to help me to get back to the yacht; he agreed.

"The next day we traveled through the rocky and thorny foothills to a sheer cliff below the savanna plateau. On the fourth day, we crossed the savanna to the base of the mountain shoulder. We camped on the ground beneath a massive rock near a pond, fed by a mountain spring. That night a black leopard came to drink and found her territory invaded. I was in a state of shock by the time she left, for the leopard had come within ten feet of where I was sleeping on the ground. Tamubu had taken the food and climbed to the top of a tall podocarpus tree, knowing I was safe, as he later told me: 'With the smoky fire to cure the turtle meat and the firelight reflection from your blanket, you were all but invisible'. I am here, so he must have been right.

"On the fifth day, we reached a traveling hut the Ndezi had used on our trek to their village. There, I took a nap that lasted all afternoon. We stayed the night at the hut, telling one another campfire stories.

"On the sixth day, we crossed a series of narrow creases bisecting the uphill trail. Upon climbing out of a crease, I came face to face with a gruesome ape. He was about fifty feet away and became mad with rage when he saw me. He charged and I fired my pistol at the rocks around his feet. Between the noise and the pain of the rock-slivers, he turned and fled, but not for long. A few miles later, the bloodied ape again challenged us for the trail: this time by leaping out from behind a large boulder with a big club in his hand. I again fired, hitting the club in his hand, which sent wood splinters, like tiny arrows, into his arm and chest. Again, the bloodthirsty ape retreated; but I had stepped back, in my surprise at his leap onto the trail, and twisted my ankle.

"Tamubu carried me piggy-back until late afternoon, when he found a wide ledge part way down the mountainside. It was thirty-five feet down and had a cave recess for shelter. The drop from the ledge was sheer for another fifty-five feet below. Here we spent two days while I rested my ankle. Late on the second day, the apes started to drop huge branches onto the ledge, so they could climb down and kill us. Using the survival belt harness, Tamubu sent me over the edge to rappel into the trees below, before he set fire to the mounting pile of greenery.

"He then escaped by using the grapnel and line to swing to a tree about twenty feet away. I had taken my pack with me, and Tamubu managed to bring the other gear along with the food and water. We spent the night safe in the trees. "Now, it was the ninth day. We returned to the ledge and found three dead bull apes. From there we reached the mountain trail, using the survival belt device. Tamubu had made crutches for me and I was able to move along under my own steam, but after lunch and a nap, Tamubu insisted on carrying me piggyback again. We camped for the night in a small space surrounded by large boulders.

"On the tenth day, I managed to go under my own steam until we reached a mud hut surrounded by a thorn boma. The Ndezi had used this as a stopping place too. While Tamubu was out gathering, I went into the woods for a bit of privacy. There my crutches went through the bottomless greenery, and I was pitched forward down an embankment. I ended up hitting my head on a tree and it knocked me cold. Somehow, Tamubu found me, and carried me up the steep ravine to the hut. He treated me for shock and concussion.

"In the late afternoon of the eleventh day, I was dozing outside of the traveling hut, when I heard an English voice say, 'Knock, Knock, hello there!' I wondered why Tamubu was being silly, and then I heard him reply to himself. I opened my eyes to see Jon standing on the other side of the thorn boma. Later, Jon radioed that I had been found and the next day he and his men arrived at our camp and we all set off for the beach.

"It took two days to get here, without mishap, but with plenty of help. We have been here two nights; tonight will be the third night. In all, it has been the adventure of a lifetime!"

The End

❖❖❖

NO ONE SAID ANYTHING, so engrossed were they in feeling her experiences, until Jon started to clap. Then everyone clapped and praised her courage.

Motozo said, "Dinner is ready. There is food for everyone." Indeed there was. Motozo had prepared a feast. He had spit-roasted three large guinea fowl. He had baked sweet potatoes in the ashes, which he had cut in strips and drizzled with coconut syrup; there was cut asparagus with squash, biscuits and coffee, with fresh pineapple for dessert.

Captain Jones arose shortly thereafter and said, "That was the finest meal I have ever eaten–anywhere! Motozo, if you ever need a job, just look me up in Douala. We must get back to the yacht. What time should we come ashore for you in the morning?"

Jon replied, "High tide will turn about eight tomorrow morning." Jon looked around but no one made any comment.

"That's the time then," Captain Jones agreed, "eight in the morning. Good night to all and again, thank you for your grand hospitality. This has been a memorable evening, one we will never forget."

Phil and Steve approached Paula and shook her hand. Steve, who looked more like a flower child than a sailor said, "You are a brave woman and I am proud to have met you." Phil added, "Me too." They thanked Motozo for the dinner, said their good nights to the others, and followed Captain Jones down the beach.

Tamubu and Paula prepared a clean dressing for Kasuku's infected foot. The red puffiness had diminished, for the hot Epsom Salt soaks had drawn off a great deal of the pus. He no longer had a fever and Paula had stopped giving him the sulfa drugs. Tamubu had found a good substitute, a natural antibiotic, which he had dried and powdered and sprinkled on the wound before it was bandaged for the night. Kasuku had been a good patient. He had been stoic through his pain. He would soon be well.

As they worked, Paula asked, "Tamubu, what are your plans now that my parents have arrived?"

"I have not given plans much thought. It is up to you and your parents, and possibly Captain Jones, what will happen next. I must stay here until Kasuku is well enough to travel home. I imagine Jon and I will then go to Kenya together, but we have not discussed the future."

When they had finished with the bandages, Kybo took Kasuku to be with the other boys in their lean-to, where Kybo now spent his nights. Motozo, Obendi and Obu were cleaning up from dinner and preparing the pallets for the night. Kimbo had escorted Captain Jones and his crew back to the tender and had not yet returned. Jon had escorted Lisa and Charles back to Paula's lean-to so they could get ready for the night in privacy.

When Jon returned, Paula said, "Let's take a walk on the beach." Tamubu looked at Jon and smiled mischievously. They scooped her up on their linked arms, and strode off towards the water's edge.

"You two are a pair! I can imagine you gave your parents many a gliff when you were young. Take me to the dry sand, we need to sit and talk."

Tamubu asked, "What is a gliff?

"It is a scare or surprising moment."

It was very dark, the sliver moon was still low in the sky, but millions of stars glittered in a black velvet sky. Paula leaned back with her forearms behind her head, drew up her knees, and looked at the beauty of the star-filled sky without light pollution, and thought: civilization has given up the joy of so many natural wonders in exchange for conveniences; I wonder how many living Americans have ever seen this many stars?

Jon and Tamubu assumed similar positions and, deep in thought, they too gazed at the infinite luminescents above them.

Tamubu had put off thinking about this moment, for he didn't want to face the possibility of separation from Paula. But here it was, and it had come in such a way that he didn't have a choice. He must stay with Kasuku until he was well. Tamubu loved looking at the stars, and thought of Manutu's words–this trip had been a great joy, but now, it might also bring great sorrow.'

The silence grew long before Paula spoke. "I know that Tamubu plans to stay with the lads until Kasuku is well enough to travel home. What are your plans, Jon?"

"I'll stay with Tamubu. I'll do whatever it is that he chooses to do."

Tamubu smiled in his mind. Each day he remembered more of why had loved this brother so intensely. He was loyal; he was thoughtful; he was kind; he was humorous; he was spontaneous; he was basically a happy person and his happiness was contagious. He loved unconditionally. He had no faults, except for his smelly pipe. He was the perfect companion. Tamubu's heart ached for all the lost years; for all the boyhood fun they had missed; but he clenched his jaw, determined that not another day would ever be lost again.

Tamubu added, "After Kasuku is well and the lads have gone home: Jon and I will travel to Kenya together."

Jon's heart sang with joy, the joy of his youth. Here was the old Thomas, the Thomas that was so strong, so reliable, so dependable and so knowledgeable. In a day and a half, all the years between them had been washed away by the remembered camaraderie of their youth.

"What are your plans, Paula?" Tamubu asked.

"I will go to Douala with my parents. From there, I must go to the Expedition yacht at Port Gentil. I have important matters to settle there. My future plans are uncertain, and hinge on other things: like my ankle and the decisions of Dr. Miles."

"When do you plan to leave?" Tamubu asked, dreading the reply.

Paula smiled to herself and said, "When Kasuku is well enough to travel home." Tamubu's spirits soared with joy.

Paula asked, "Has your crew said how they plan to travel back, Jon?"

"Not yet. We will see how they like being on the cruiser tomorrow. Maybe Captain Jones will take us for a short trip out to sea? If they like it, and if there is room enough, they can go to Douala with us and then fly home to Enugu."

Paula said, "I'm sure there is plenty of room. The cruiser berths twelve plus the crew. Did you know that Captain Jones offered his boat to my parents when he heard they could not find a boat for hire? His explanation for his unusual generosity was, '...I just want to help!' He volunteered his cruiser '... for however long it takes to find your daughter.'

"No, I had no idea! What a marvelous chap he is to do that!" Jon said.

Paula said, "We are going to be here for a few more days. Let's go to bed. I'm tired." They picked her up and carried her to the lean-to where her parents sat chatting and said, "Good Night."

Pleased to see her return, Charles stood and helped her to her pallet, saying, "What a perfectly marvelous evening we have had … and your story, we're so proud of you! Never, in all our days of teaching you to be self-reliant, did we ever expect you to have to face the hardships you have encountered here in Africa. Did you talk to your friends about their plans?"

"Yes, I did. We have decided to stay here together until Kasuku's ankle is healed enough for him to travel home. Do you think Captain Jones will mind waiting a few days before we all leave?"

"I can't say for sure." Charles replied, "We'll have to ask him tomorrow. He offered to sail off into an unknown situation, and did it gladly, without strings. I think this is the most adventure he has had in a while, and I am of the opinion, that he likes adventure."

Lisa said, "So do I; do you think we could do some exploring tomorrow? Do you think either Jon or Tamubu would lead a little hike—maybe show us the trail back to the thorn boma hut?"

Paula laughed. "I'm sure they would. It's only a day's hike if you're not carrying the wounded! The view up there, at dusk, is the most spectacular you will ever see in your life!"

"We'd better get some sleep if we are going hiking tomorrow," Charles said as he slid into his sleeping bag.

PAULA PUT ON HER jacket and covered her legs with the thin metallic blanket. She had a feeling of contentment. The conversation at the edge of the surf had taken away the feeling of impending gloom. She was obligated to return to the Expedition, but she was glad to put it off for a few more days.

Only Kimbo, who was the sentry and Kybo were awake. Kybo was deep in thought. He was considering plans that would change his life completely. It was possible that he would never again see his family—or Laalu, his special friend since he was twelve. Kybo had put off settling down because he did not want to be tied to living in the village; he liked the travels of the traders. Laalu had not seemed to mind his absences—maybe it would not be too hard on her if he never returned. But he did not yet know if these things would come to pass. He had not yet asked the question.

Shortly before eight in the morning, after a light breakfast of porridge, nine excited souls trooped up the beach to the other side of the jetty, with Kybo carrying Kasuku. Paula and her parents chose to stay behind with Jon and Kimbo, who had agreed to guide them to the thorn boma hut.

Over breakfast, when Paula mentioned her parents' desire for a hike to the thorn boma hut, Jon offered to guide them and suggested they plan to camp overnight there. Kimbo said he would go with them as bearer, and made the preparations needed for their comfort on the hike. The four of them left a little after nine.

Phil brought the tender to shore on the last of the high tide. He was early, but glad to be alone for a bit, for he was addicted to mystery stories and had a new copy of Ellery Queen's Mystery Magazine in his pocket. The tender held fourteen comfortably so there was plenty of room for the visitors, who were clearly awed and thrilled. Captain Jones took the visitors on a tour of the cruiser while the tender was being winched aboard its davits.

The anchor was raised and Captain Jones moved the *Wind Drift* into the open sea. There were ten anxious faces standing at the rail in the bow as the cruiser picked up speed. It was a grand day for a cruise; the sea was calm on the receding tide. The anxious faces and stiff movements of the nascent sailors soon gave way to relaxation and laughter. Tamubu had a natural ease on the ship and soon had the boys enjoying themselves. It was his first time aboard a ship too, yet he found a great pleasure in the sea and the vastness of the ocean, which he could not readily explain.

Captain Jones had filled the spare gas drums for the journey with the Thorntons, not knowing when he would again be near a port with fuel; even so, he kept the pleasure excursion to an hour, to allow plenty of fuel for exigencies on the return trip to Douala.

It was a thrilled and exuberant group that came ashore two hours later. The lads jabbered amongst themselves about the stir their experience would cause when they arrived home with the small replicas of the cruiser on a key chain, which Captain Jones had given everyone for a souvenir.

Tamubu lagged behind the group as they talked excitedly on the walk back to the lean-tos. He deftly moved into the underbrush to *roam* and to scout the trail where Jon was leading the hike to the thorn boma hut. Later, on his return, he would gather some of the herbs and plants he carried in his pouches; for his supply was dwindling.

The hikers had made good time and were not far from the wide space by the trail where they would stop for lunch. Tamubu passed them and went on to the thorn boma hut. All was well. There was no *sign* of the apes, but he wanted to be sure; for after their encounters, the apes would be vengeful. In retracing the wide trail on the shoulder of the mountain, he found the place where the apes had gone into the valley, a long distance before the thorn boma hut. The rains had washed out their spoor but not the damage to the flora, for the apes had broken off many plants and moved downed logs, limbs and stones while searching for food.

It took Tamubu the better part of the afternoon to go back and gather all the plants he had found while *roaming*. When he returned to Paula's lean-to with his gathering-net full, she was elated. "You must tell me about each one of these plants. Where you found them, what they do, how to prepare them and how to administer them. You must also add them to the diary. You have not drawn in days."

"No, there has been much to do." He looked up in his whimsical way, with the smirk of a smile that she had come to know, was his way of inferring humor.

Only too glad to banter, Paula replied, "I don't know how you can say you've had 'much to do', when Motozo has been doing all the cooking and the men and boys have been doing all the hunting and gathering."

Tamubu chuckled—amused; "I have been doing what I like

to do best." Paula loved the repartee and his quick wit, but she was stymied by his answer. "And what is that?"

"I have been looking after you and Kasuku; it is my responsibility to keep us all safe." Tamubu looked into Paula's eyes as he spoke, for he was quite serious. Danger lurked all about them in one form or another. His senses told him that there had been watchers in the forest. He had seen no one, but he saw the *sign* of the recent passage in the forest of a group of men who had crossed their trail to the beach. Tamubu hoped it was just the Fulani looking for the lads.

26

Decisions

TAMUBU SPENT THE REST of the afternoon preparing the herbs he had gathered, and drawing the specimens in his splendid new book, called a logbook. He told Paula of their uses when she returned from tending to Kasuku, who was beginning to chafe from his confinement.

Kasuku felt much better. Even the sea trip this morning had not tired him, although Kybo had to carry him in the soft sand. He wanted to get out and about with his friends. He sat thinking of this morning's exciting trip out on the big water... he pictured himself telling his family of his adventure when he heard, "Pssst, pssst." Glancing about but seeing no one, he returned to his reverie, and again he heard, "Pssst, pssst." Then he saw the forest foliage part and his father's face appeared. Kasuku arose and hobbled around to the back of the lean-to, where he went for privacy.

"Father, what are you doing here?"

"I came to find you, my son; you have been gone a long time. Are you a prisoner? I heard the voices of the British."

"Oh, no, father. I am a patient. I injured my foot and these kind people have been taking care of me. I was very sick when they found me. Mguru, Kabanza and Nashutu are out gathering firewood for the fires. Are you alone?"

"No, the other fathers are with me and two uncles."

"Father, would it be alright for you to come to the dinner fire this evening? If you just walk down the sand to the dinner fire, no one will bother you. The Medicine Man of the Great Nations of the Ziri Watu and an American woman have made me well, and you could thank them."

Sombu knew his son spoke the truth. He had been watching all day, but had been frightened by the lads going off on the boat. Interference with the manhood ritual by a family member could bring shame on the boy and the family. He said, "I will think about it. If we do not come, it is not because we are ungrateful, but because we do not want to shame you."

"I understand, Father. I will be able to travel in a few days. Tell mother I am safe. I must go back before I am missed." Kasuku's father smiled. Sombu was very proud of this son, who had a thoughtful regard for his father's dignity. Many sons would only think of sparing themselves embarrassment, and be annoyed by a father's concern.

With great stealth, Sombu made his way through the undergrowth to the other men awaiting his return. "We must go now using much speed! All is well with the boys." Sombu, when he heard Kasuku refer to Tamubu as a medicine man of the Zuri Watu, knew they had to leave the area immediately. He had heard of these medicine men who were reputed to be able to travel as spirits, and who could also commune with spirits. Kasuku had said he was safe, but were skulking intruders safe? Not a moment was to be lost in putting distance between them and the medicine man of the Great Nations of the Zuri Watu.

The British had conquered the Fulani rulers at the turn of the century, and had taken over the rule of the villages; but there were still some remote villages of the tribe living in the old ways, and Sombu did not want to bring attention to their presence.

THE EVENING TWILIGHT APPROACHED as Jon, Lisa and Charles continued on to the top of the trail at the mountain's wide shoulder. Kimbo stayed at the thorn boma hut to prepare dinner. It had rained off and on most of the day, and there had been a low haze. As they approached the almost level shoulder, the updraft breezes blew the haze away.

The group crossed the wide clearing, towards the deep the ravine on the far side of the grassy shoulder, just as the low westerly sun broke through the scudding clouds. For a long moment–every droplet on every leaf, and every flower petal became a glistening crystal illumination of light, with the multi-hued prisms of their reflection dancing in the breeze; like a million fairies touching their wands in unison. The sight was magical, and so was the effect on Lisa, Charles and Jon– who stood awed to their bones.

The clouds would swirl and thicken and the wondrous illusion would fade away–to reappear again–when the breeze scattered the puffs into wispy clouds, which parted to let the enchanting show began anew–on other droplets, on other flowers, on other leaves–singled out by the filtered shafts of light reflecting through the tiny prisms of moisture, and bursting into myriad and spectacular colors dancing about in fascinating and brilliant icy-like sparkles. Mesmerized, they stood absolutely still, enthralled, until the last rays of the evening sun dropped over the horizon.

"For the first time in my life, I'm speechless!" Lisa murmured. Charles smiled to himself as he appreciated the irony of her assertion; it was an understatement.

Jon said, "I've seen a good bit of smashing beauty in Africa, but that display was a show-stopper!" Charles agreed and said, "It's a shame Kimbo missed it."

"I not miss it." The three turned to see Kimbo standing just a few feet away. Deep in the ecstasy of nature's panoramic display, no one had heard him arrive. "You gone long time; I am worried." Jon glanced at his watch; they had been entranced for two hours. Kimbo continued, "We go back now; soon very dark."

The little group trekked down the trail, reaching the campsite by flashlight. The long twilights of Africa are over in a moment. In the rainforest, the canopy of flowering vines in the treetops and the tall leafy vegetation close out all the light from the stars and most of the light from the moon phases, except the full moon, which manages to dimly filter through the thick vegetation... if the sky is clear.

Kimbo's little dinner fire was a beacon in the clammy, clinging darkness. Silence fell while they ate the stew and biscuits. Lisa and Charles both had the same disturbing thoughts: Paula had been alone, escaping the Ndezi, on nights just like this one...

Jon sat remembering: when Thomas had emerged from this hut that fateful afternoon. He sensed now that he had been summoned, by powers stronger than his will, to go and look for Miss Thornton. Wisps of dreams he had forgotten floated just out of reach—but he knew these wispy dreams. They had instilled in him the obsessive need to search for Paula. He had seen this hut before—before he had arrived here—before he spoke to Paula. Why had he not remembered that until now? Jon softened his gaze until he saw only the periphery and there, encased in the shadows, he saw emanations that looked like Thomas and an old man with kinky white hair. He tried to focus on the images, but the shadowy figures faded and were gone.

"Jon, are you falling asleep, sitting up?" Charles asked. Brought sharply from his reverie, Jon felt surprised to see his companions. The wispy thoughts were lost. He could not remember what he had been thinking.

He replied, "No, not asleep yet... but soon."

It rained hard most of the night, and the hikers were grateful for the long overhang of the thatched roof. Kimbo had moved his embering fire inside the hut, but he, like the others, slept outside. Morning came in a dense mist, which was very cold, for it was actually a low cloudbank. In a mile or two, they had walked down out of it. The heavy rain had turned portions of the trail into mud slicks and Kimbo and Jon found themselves breaking trail in the forest to avoid the treacherous footing. On one such diversion they came upon a game trail which, when checked with the compass, was found to be going in the same general direction as the main trail. Kimbo had to hack away the vines, branches, and the ever-present, thorny wait-a-bit, but the footing was good.

They stopped for a cold lunch, where it was decided to head back to the main trail, for Kimbo felt that they were below the badly eroded and dangerous sections they wanted to avoid. During their brief rest, Kimbo closed his eyes to think about what Kybo had told him yesterday morning. He did not want to see his son go off on a lifetime mission, but he could offer him no reason to stay. Kimbo felt a sharp prick on his arm; he swatted at it and his hand hit a spear. His eyes flew open to see a group of six men, all pointing spears, surrounding him.

"Who be you? What you want? Why you here?"

Kimbo moved not a muscle, but answered their questions. "I am Kimbo, a Nigerian. I do not want anything, but to travel to the beach with the friends of my kigozi. I serve the Medicine Man of the Great Zuri Watu."

Sombu said, "Close your eyes. Finish your rest." Kimbo did as he was told. He heard nothing. Were they still there? Curiosity got the better of him and he peeked through lidded eyes. The men were gone. He arose and went to the others. They were still asleep. He decided this was one incident he was going to keep to himself. If it were not for the blood on his arm, he would have thought he was dreaming.

The day cleared in the afternoon, making the forest steamy and humid. It was a great relief when they felt puffs of the ocean breezes and later heard the surf, and greater relief still, when they were able to go for a swim in the incoming tide. Somehow, the trek down the mountain had been more wearying than the climb up it.

AT DINNER, PAULA SAID, "We have news. Kasuku was able to walk alone in the firm sand at the edge of the water today. His wound is healing nicely. In a few more days, he will be able to leave with his friends."

Kybo added, "The lads killed a piglet today. So, when Kasuku is ready to leave, they will be able to go home."

Lisa asked, "Are we eating the piglet for our dinner?"

Kybo replied, "No, The lads will smoke their piglet for food on their trip home. The piglet you are eating, I killed. Motozo is a wizard when it comes to cooking piglet." Everyone agreed with Kybo; the roast pork, the taro baked with cabbage and Motozo's special spices, the freshly baked farina and banana scones; all of it was a meal fit for kings. Even kings didn't have tapioca pudding and coffee with a hint of vanilla for dessert in the wilderness.

Paula smiled and said, "No offense, Mom, but I've never eaten better or tastier food than I've eaten on the trail with Tamubu and Motozo. Both know Mother Nature and her bounty, better than you or I have ever known the grocery store!"

Tamubu looked at the happy group and asked, "Whose turn is it to tell a story tonight?" He turned to Motozo who said. "Me have not English for story." His gaze went to Kimbo, who repeated Motozo's excuse. The rest of the boys scattered and Tamubu turned to Charles Thornton. "It is a tradition of the traveler's campfire. Maybe you would tell us about your trip to Africa to find Paula?"

"Oh, Dad, please do. These people are as close to me as my brothers. They, too, are family. Share your story with us."

With this kind of a plea, Charles knew he had no choice. He looked at Lisa and asked, "Do you mind if I tell a story?"

"Not at all, dear. You're a good story-teller." Lisa smiled at the double-entendre.

Charles took a moment to mentally formulate the progression of his tale.

The natives started the chant, "huh-huh-huh-aaah" until Charles raised a hand and began.

"It seemed she was an ordinary child, but she talked early, walked early and at the tender age of two, could often be found sitting in my armchair reading a children's book. By the time she was three, she was horseback riding and at four, she was riding her pony alone. She started gymnastics with her twin brother when she was five, and they both started horse vaulting when they were eight. By second grade, she was reading books at a sixth grade level and this was to be the norm for her development. When the twins were eight, we bought the sailboat. The family took to the water and the easy camaraderie of sailing, but Paula excelled. She soon knew as much about sailing as I did and then surpassed me with her skill.

In the winters, our family liked to hike and camp in the woods, and friends were often invited to join the fun. When the twins, Paula and Eric, our youngest children, were twelve, we added cliff face climbing and rappelling to our weekend hikes. Everyone looked forward to the outings, but Paula was gung-ho for them. Even after Scott and Sallee Anne went off to college and Eric was involved helping the local Veterinarian, she continued to sail, hike and climb and ride; often taking friends along to fill the gaps left by her missing siblings.

"We were all surprised by her turn to biology and plants. This girl, who was never still, would now sit for hours drying flowers and herbs for a compendium she was making, and to supply Sallee Anne with materials for her realistic still-life paintings. It was no surprise, though, that she excelled at her craft.

"We were even more surprised when Paula decided to continue with biology as her major in college. But it was logical, really. Both Paula and Eric had always wanted to know how and why things worked, or what caused things to work as they did.

"When Paula was included in the biological Expedition to Africa, as an assistant to Dr. Miles, she was thrilled and her career seemed well under way. When the news came that Paula was lost with the yacht after the tsunami, we had hope. If the yacht is seaworthy, Paula will be able to manage her.

Then came the news that the yacht had been found, marooned in this cove; but Paula was gone and might have been abducted. But the worst news was that the yacht had been removed from the cove and was sailing south to the Ogooué River. We still had hope, for if anyone could cope with such appalling problems, it was Paula.

"Then the news came that Paula had escaped her abductors just before the rescue troops arrived at the Ndezi village. The yacht was gone and there would be no one here for Paula when she returned... and we felt deeply that she would return. There was nothing else for us to do, but to come here to Africa to await her arrival.

"Getting to the cove proved a problem. The boats for hire were all engaged in taking supplies and relief personnel to the site of the tsunami. We looked for a boat for two days, until Captain Jones heard of our plight and offered to take us on his private motor yacht to the cove to find our daughter. His exact words were, 'For as long as it takes to find her.' We will never, ever forget those words, spoken by a man who knew us not at all, but who was and is deeply generous and incredibly gallant.

"But Paula had met Tamubu, and later Jon, and these paradigms of noble manhood and knights in shining armor *had, with the help of their companions, brought her safely back to the cove. We will be eternally grateful to each and every one of them, for their honorable and selfless concern, for our treasured daughter." The End.*

THERE WAS A ROUND of applause when Charles finished. Paula's face was pink. Her father had never been sentimental, nor had he ever bragged about his children; so the story was completely unexpected. She glanced at Tamubu and Jon, who showed their enjoyment of his fatherly ruminations. His gratitude and compliments embarrassed them not at all.

Charles continued, "I talked with Captain Jones on Jon's radio just before dinner, and he has agreed to take us all back to Douala. From there, he can take Paula south to Port Gentil, for he has been asked to take four missionaries to Lambaréné, who want to go up river to study with Dr. Schweitzer at the leper colony. We did not know if the men would wish to go to Douala and then fly to Enugu or not; but Captain Jones has assured me they will be welcome to go with us, if they choose to do so."

Jon spoke with deep feeling; "It is men of good heart, like Captain Jones, who make this a better world for all of us. His generosity, it seems, is boundless. Why did he not join us for dinner?"

Charles replied, "He said he had quite a few things to do to get the yacht ready for the trip to Douala tomorrow."

Paula spoke in surprise, "Tomorrow! I thought we were going to stay until Kasuku was able to go home."

Jon caught her glance and told her, "Thomas and I will stay here with the lads. They must be able to travel home by themselves, as they are out on their manhood trials. It is more than fifty miles to their village. Kasuku will need to be healed, or he will run the risk of incurring another infection by the reopening of the wound. We can't expect everyone to sit around and wait; nor do we want to abuse of the good will of Captain Jones and his crew. My men have agreed to go on the cruiser to Douala tomorrow, and fly home from there."

Much to the amazement of everyone, Kybo spoke. "I will stay with the kigozi and his brother, if they will have me."

Kimbo knew this was coming, but he had hoped Kybo might change his mind. He would have liked to stay with the kigozi too, for he had no ties to the village anymore; but he felt obligated to the trader, Max, who had hired him in a permanent position; not just for the trading junkets.

Tamubu looked at Kybo with a smile of satisfaction and, with a nod, accepted his loyalty.

"What is everyone doing?" Paula cried. "I'm not ready to leave yet!"

Surprised, her father said. "We could not presume upon the generosity of Captain Jones to remain here for another three or four days. Now that we know you are safe, we must return home to our jobs and you to your Expedition. These men," he said, sweeping his hand in the direction of the bearers, "are in the employ of the trader Max Mason, and are under contract to him. We cannot, in all fairness, delay our departure on whimsy."

Paula was dumbfounded. Rising, she stomped as best she could—with only one stomping foot—to her lean-to. Her father, unaware of the undercurrents, was chagrined by Paula's outburst. Lisa, who had suspected some sort of attachment, was apprehensive.

No one followed her. Alone, the tears came and she raged inwardly. I'm not ready to leave! I need more time! We haven't discussed the future; no decisions have been made... what am I going to do?

This was the moment she had dreaded, and now, without warning, it was here. Ever the pragmatic soul, Paula soon dealt with the surprise of a decision in which she'd had no say, and began reasoning: We have this evening—if I don't waste it sulking. Paula washed her face and combed her hair and returned to the campfire.

Tamubu arose when she arrived and said, "Do you feel up to taking a walk with me?"

"Yes, I would like that." They strolled to the wet sand and walked along the dark edge of the water in silence. Walking in the sand, even the wet sand made Paula's ankle ache, so she said, "Let's sit here for a bit." When seated, they both lay back and looked at the starlit sky. At length she asked. "Have you and Jon made plans too?"

"Only to care for Kasuku until he is well. We have not talked beyond that. I told him I wanted to cross the continent on foot. He thought me mad, but agreed, reluctantly, to go with me. It is unspoken but understood—we just haven't discussed the traveling. I would like to follow the Congo River to the Ruwenzori Mountains and cross into Kampala at Lake Edward, then cross Lake Victoria to Kisumu and home."

"How long do you think that will take you?"

"When I mentioned the idea to Jon he said, '...that's more than two thousand miles. If a person could travel twenty miles a day, it would take a hundred days—or more if you had problems'. I thought it would take longer when I started out, at least a rainy season and a dry season."

"That's six months! How do you know the route... if you've never been there?"

"Manutu told me. He knows most of Africa from his talks with visitors. Manutu was also a traveler; he traveled to Lake Chad, the great Sahara Desert and the Congo River."

"Will you go to Douala at all?"

"It is possible. From there we could follow the Nyong River east to the Ngoko River to the Sangha River, which empties into the Congo River. The Nyong River empties into the sea below Douala. I will have to discuss the route with Jon. Why do you ask?"

"I thought we might meet in Douala in ten or eleven days, before you set off on your great journey. I have affairs to settle with Dr. Miles." (And, she thought, that's putting it mildly.) "It's also possible that the Expedition will shut down early." (Once mister-too-important-to-care-about anybody else hears what I have to say!) "So, I won't know until I talk to him what my obligations are going to be."

"What will you do then? Go to America with them?"

"That's not what I want to do at all. Right now, I'm obligated to return to the Expedition, and until I do, I can make no other plans, but I intend to resign. That's why it's so important that I see you again, before you leave on your journey."

Tamubu felt encouraged. Her commitment to these Expedition people had to be resolved—it was like Motozo being responsible to Max for a trading season. His anxiety evaporated. If they met in Douala, it was possible that they could travel together again.

"I will talk to Jon about Douala. You go to bed, get some rest, and we'll talk again in the morning." Back at the lean-to, her parents were ready for bed, but sat quietly chatting, waiting for Paula to return. Tamubu made a late check on Kasuku. Kybo had changed his bandage and had done an expert job. He then went to find Jon, who was not at the lean-to. The odor of pipe tobacco wafted towards him and he followed the scent until he found Jon sitting on a fallen palm tree, enjoying his smelly pipe.

"How did you find me?"

"I have a nose."

"Oh, my pipe; is Paula still upset?"

"Yes, I think it was the suddenness of the decision to leave that took her by surprise."

"My fault; I took Charles' suggestion and asked Paula if we could use the high tensile wire from her survival belt for a high antenna in the trees. It worked, and I contacted Max from the cooking lean to. I think it was my subsequent natter with him that put the bee in their bonnets. Max asked me how much longer I expected to be gone with his best men. I know Max said that for the men to hear, by way of a compliment, not as an admonition, but apparently, the Thorntons felt the imposition. By dinner time, leaving tomorrow was a fait-accompli."

"It was a what?"

"Sorry, old chap—it means a thing already done, beyond change."

"So, Captain Jones expects to leave with the tide tomorrow?"

"Yes, and the tide turns about ten—or midmorning."

"Have you had any thoughts about us, after the lads leave?"

"Yes, I have decided to do whatever you want to do... the way you want to do it."

"Do you mean you will trek with me across the continent? Do you really want to do that?"

"Actually, in the beginning, I thought it a dreadful idea. I just wanted to get you home. But, the more I thought about a long journey, the more I thought I'd have a go at it—we have so much catching-up to do—and I dearly love to travel and explore. Now, I think I'm actually looking forward to it. I would only add one stop on the itinerary."

"Add one stop on the what?"

"Sorry, an itinerary is a list of places where you will stop on your travels."

"What stop would you add?"

"I feel we should go to Douala or possibly to Yaoundé. There we can have English clothes made for you, and then shipped to Kenya, ready for your arrival. Also, while there, we can send a telegram to our parents to let them know you have been found, and that we are traveling overland to Kenya."

"I can see that being with you will be an education as well. You will send what to our parents?"

"A telegram; it is a message sent over telephone lines to an office near the destination, where it is written and then delivered to the recipients... recipients: people receiving something."

Tamubu laughed uproariously while Jon sat and looked at him as if he had two heads.

"You sounded just like Paula. She explained words to me in the same way."

"I wondered about that. Your English is very good for someone who hasn't used it since he was ten years old."

"For the first few days with Paula, she had to explain words in her every sentence. I was thinking in Bantu, and speaking in English, the result was awful. Then I started to remember things, especially when Paula started giving me lessons in the evening. When I took a pencil and started to write, it was as if the clouds parted and the sun was shining. I started to remember all sorts of things for I had forgotten most of my childhood, but I remembered I could draw.

It was these memories and the drawing of plants for her that made my boyhood education come back to me. Were it not for the time Paula spent tutoring me, I would never have revealed myself to you."

"You what! Why ever not?"

"I am not ashamed of my tribal associations, in fact, I am very proud of them. But I remember that our parents thought of the natives as inferiors, socially and intellectually. I would not want to shame them with my tribal ways."

Jon was quiet, thinking: Thomas was right, but that was then. Things are different now, so he proceeded to explain. "The natives, who worked on the tea farm when we were children, were uneducated, were slothful and slovenly and had no interest in learning or bettering themselves... at that time. But there have been great changes. The children now go to school. The adults have been taught sanitation and cleanliness. There is a night school for those adults who wish to learn to read and write and do sums."

"Are they ever invited to sit in the parlor?"

"No, nor are they asked to dine in the dining room. But, there are now two festivals a year: one after harvest, and one after planting. Mother supervises a great feast, served outside, and everyone eats together. Neighbors are invited and they accept our invitations. Some of the other planters have followed our lead and the lot of the native is greatly improved.

We pay wages now, not just keep. They are hired, they can be fired, and they are free to leave at anytime. The education is free, the children five and over have chores, which is mostly raking, or sweeping up, or watching the babies and feeding and changing them. Medical care is free. They make their own cloth, sew their own clothes, and tend their personal gardens. We have cattle for meat and a slaughterhouse. A meat ration is part of their pay. Every child, to six years old, is allotted a quart of milk a day from the dairy. Adult workers are allotted a pound of cheese each week, which is also a part of their pay.

Those that don't gamble their salaries away are able to save, and some of the farm children have actually ended up going to boarding school in Nairobi. Every day, people show up at the office asking for jobs. Our tea production has increased and Father has planted a vineyard. We now have managers, Negroes, who manage the workers and their schedules. It is a very big business—one you and I will inherit some day."

Tamubu was amazed... and he was proud. His parents were good, caring people and they had improved their world. Secretly, Tamubu agreed with the observation that the natives were lazy and slothful. It was because the women did all the work in the tribe and this attitude probably remained with the men, even after being hired to do a job. Work was for women! Men were hunters or warriors.

Curiosity made him ask, "Are the men good workers?"

Jon laughed. "I see you are familiar with the native male mentality. But, those who come looking for jobs know that the men must work as hard as the women or they will not be hired. Men used to come, wanting us to hire their women, but not themselves. We said everyone must work to obtain a home and benefits with us. Anyone found not giving a full day's work would see his family out on the road. But Father made up a list of jobs that he felt were more suitable for men, as they required strength, and this difference seems to keep the men happy in their work. The men do not harvest the tea, prune the bushes or cultivate to weed the ground; but they do dig trenches to plant new bushes and vines or dig out the old ones: set new posts, run equipment and care for the stock."

"I can see I have much to learn and that there is much for us to talk about while we are traveling to Kenya. How long do you think we will stay in Douala or Yaoundé?"

"I don't know if there is a good tailor in Douala; one that is capable of making the wardrobe you will require. If not, we will go to Yaoundé. In Douala, there will be garments available off the rack, work clothes, safari clothes, underwear, socks and boots, if you choose, but the rest will have to be made to order. Why do you ask?"

"Paula wants to meet us in Douala."

"When?"

"In ten or eleven days."

"How does she plan to do that?"

"I don't know—she didn't say."

"Well, if we are here another four days, and it takes five days to get to Douala, we will be there in nine days. If there is a tailor in Douala, it will take another two days for measurements and fittings. So, we should be there in ten or eleven days. We can ask the Thorntons the name of the hotel they used and plan to meet Paula there; how's that?"

"Perfect. Let's get some sleep."

26

Farewell

BREAKFAST WAS A LIVELY affair, considering the sun was barely over the horizon. The lads came down to the cooking lean-to to watch the preparations for the momentous departure on the cabin cruiser, and questioned Charles, with Kybo translating: "How far was America from Africa? Could the cruiser take them to America? How many days would it take to go to America? Could you go there on the water from Africa?"

Kybo explained to Charles, that the answers to these questions would be told to the whole tribe when the lads returned home. So Charles added details for the lads: he described the people and places where the planes stopped; the number and type of planes it took to get to Yaoundé; and the time it took for them to reach Yaoundé from Philadelphia. He also drew a map in the sand, which delighted the young boys, who said to Kybo, "This was amazing knowledge and will make a very good story."

When translated, Charles said to Kybo, "I would like to be a flea in the lad's ear, so I could hear the changes this story will undergo when it is retold."

Kybo replied, "Every word will be repeated as I translated it. Nothing will be changed."

"I don't see how that's possible. There were so many details, and the ideas were so different from their life experience." Charles replied.

"The lads have been trained, since they could speak, to repeat messages, or stories, exactly as they were told to them. It is not necessary that they understand the message—only that they repeat it exactly as it was told to them. To change one word, would shame them."

Charles thought of the impact this little story was going to have on his students. Every word will be told just as you said it. Nothing will be changed. Amazing!

Lisa was helping Paula with her packing, while Kybo and the lads helped tote the gear up the beach to the place where the tender would come ashore. Kybo helped Motozo sort through the foodstuffs: some to take with them, most to leave behind, which included what was left of the supplies that Dr. Miles had left in the tree net for Paula.

THE THORNTONS WERE SOON ready and sought out Jon and Kimbo to thank them again for the marvelous hike up the mountain to the thorn boma hut. "It gave us an understanding about the wilderness of Africa, and a feeling for the tropical rainforest that few tourists ever experience. We are at a loss for words to adequately thank you and your men for your selfless assistance in helping Paula in her hour of extreme need." Kimbo, who stood a few paces away, nodded his acceptance of the gratitude and left. Charles Thornton clasped Jon's hand firmly and pulled him into a manly hug.

Lisa continued, "Should you ever be in the States, make sure to look us up. Then we will take you on an American wilderness hike. Here is our address and phone number Jon, please keep in touch." She reached up and kissed him on the cheek.

Jon was a little flustered at such a show of gratitude and emotion and said, "I'll only come if you can promise me a smelly thorn boma hut!"

Lisa smiled, saying: "Would an Indian teepee do?"

Jon replied, "That would be smashing!"

WITHOUT BEING NOTICED, PAULA and Tamubu had slipped away. "I think you'll be happy to hear that Jon had already planned for us to stop in Douala. I am to be measured for clothes to be sent on to Kenya. We should be in Douala in nine or ten days, and be there for at least two days, if a good tailor is available. How is it that you expect to be there in ten or eleven days?"

"I don't know what to expect when I arrive back at the Expedition yacht. I know the Expedition crew is supposed to return to the States at the end of March. With the delayed start and the problems they have had on the Ogooué River, it may be that they will shut down this phase of the exploration early. I must formally resign before I can come back to Douala with Captain Jones after he finishes his business. He told my father that he had to be back in Douala by the 5th of March, which is eleven days; that's why our stay here was cut short."

"What if something happens and you cannot be there in eleven days?"

"I will telephone the hotel in Douala and leave a message for you."

Tamubu thought: your leaving me today is like a knife in my chest, but your words and your desire to meet again give me hope. Softly he said, "What can come of our meeting in Douala?"

Paula thought: if I am there, I will be able to go with you on your trek to Kenya. But she said, "Deep inside, I have the feeling that it is most important that we see each other again... that our association does not end here."

Tamubu had the same feeling: it was vital that this was not good-bye. "Yes, I agree with you." he said and tried for a higher level of communication with Paula, but she was too intent, too distracted and therefore, not receptive.

"Then it is agreed? Douala in eleven days."

"Yes," he said, "Douala in eleven days at the hotel."

Paula took his hands in hers and reached up to kiss him on the cheek. "You know I'm more grateful to you than mere words can express. Instead, I want to tell you, that the past nineteen days have been the happiest of my whole life."

Tamubu looked deeply into her eyes and replied, "Yes, we will meet again, for our time together is not yet finished."

RETURNING TO THE COOKING site, Tamubu found the lads had moved in with Kybo in Motozo's lean-to, and Tamubu's and Jon's things were in Paula's lean-to. All the other gear had been moved to the loading place, waiting for transport. Tamubu gave Paula his arm for support as they walked up the beach to the just-arrived tender.

The last few moments flew by in the hustle and bustle of loading gear, and the exuberant last good-byes—with Paula giving big hugs to those who stayed behind. Tamubu, Jon, Kybo and the lads, sat on the beach and watched until the cruiser disappeared around the volcanic rim south of the anchorage.

IT WAS A QUIET group that returned to a cold lunch of leftovers. Tamubu went to the little lean-to he had built for drying his herbs, and was soon absorbed in the various preparations of them. Once finished with the herbs, Tamubu turned to the logbook to do a few drawings, where he found a note from Paula:

> *Dear Tamubu,*
> *I have taken my diary with your drawings in it with me. I see that you have already started to use the new unlined writing book, left in the tree-net by Dr. Miles. I have left the new pencils, one hard lead, one soft lead and a nice gum eraser... not that I ever saw you need an eraser. We will meet again, for your drawings will be the catalyst (ask Jon) of our continued association.*
> *Love, Paula*

As if summoned by telepathy, Jon strolled up. "Where have you been?" Tamubu asked.

"I have been on the jetty using the radio. Since Paula took her rappelling wire with her, it is the only place where we have reception. I wanted to bring Max up-to-speed on the current arrangements. I told him that I kept the radio, and we would be here a few more days with the lads before we travel to Douala. He said he was glad I kept the old radio; he plans to buy a new one from my share of the profits."

"This Max sounds like a hearty person."

"Yes, that is the perfect word to describe him, hearty!"

"I have a letter from Paula... here, read it." Jon read the note and said, "That which makes other things work–or you could say... your drawings are the reason we will have a continued association, not very encouraging is it? But she does sign it, Love, Paula, which, I suppose, is better than Sincerely, Paula."

"Are you trying to be a pain-in-the-ass?"

"Dear me, when did you learn that expression?"

"Paula called me that one day when I insisted she keep the camp ready for departure at any moment."

"I suppose I feel a bit jealous. You must know Paula has strong feelings for you."

"Yes, I sensed that, but she has not committed herself to me in any way."

"Because, at the moment, she is committed to others; she said she would meet us again in Douala."

"Well, Douala is at least nine days away. We must deal with the here and now first."

"Right! What, in heaven's name, are we going to do on this beach for another four or five days?"

"Well, you'll be busy hunting and cooking."

"Me... hunting and cooking? What are you going to do?"

"I am going to draw plants and write descriptions in this book. I am going to tend to Kasuku's wound, teach the boys a little first-aid, and dry and powder the herbs we will need on our trek to Kenya. Once we are away from the rain forest, I may not find the plants I need."

"What about Kybo? Can't he cook?"

"I am sure he can, but the important question is: do you want to eat what Kybo can cook?"

"Why do I get the feeling that I made a mistake in not leaving on the cruiser this morning?"

Tamubu laughed aloud and said, "I knew Motozo and Kimbo had spoiled you."

Jon went to Motozo's lean-to and sorted through the foodstuffs to see what he would be able to put together for dinner tonight. Actually, there were a good many things already cooked. There was pork, a breast of fowl, sweet potatoes, a shell of taro and cabbage and scones. Well, that will be dinner tonight, Jon thought, tomorrow can take care of itself.

WHEN THE LADS RETURNED with their daily collection of firewood, coconuts, fruits and berries, Jon stayed with them and questioned them about their tribe. His fluency in their language soon had the boys talking freely, and the rest of the day passed quickly while he listened to them speak of home, family, and of their experiences during the manhood ritual.

At dinner, Tamubu said to Jon, "Tomorrow you and Kybo should go and hunt in the early morning, while the boys gather firewood and fruits. I will stay here with Kasuku, do my drawings and prepare the herbs. But the next day, I will go and hunt while you stay here and do the laundry. Each day, whoever stays in camp will help Kasuku to walk in the firm sand at the edge of the water to get his strength back. We did two walks this afternoon, and he is getting much stronger."

Jon knew Thomas wasn't giving orders, he was planning the best use of time and personnel, but it felt like orders... something Jon was unused to receiving. Then he smiled; but he wasn't used to having a big brother either and big brothers, he remembered, liked to arrange things. In retrospect, the four days actually flew by. Jon was not much of a hunter and Kybo's knowledge and skill fascinated him. He would have spent all his waking hours hunting with Kybo if they had not had other duties.

ON THE FIFTH DAY, the lads made an early start. Kasuku carried his own gear using a walking stick to help support his healing foot. Once the lads were gone, Tamubu and Jon dismantled the campsites, hefted their gear, and journeyed south along the beach, going over the jagged cliffs to find a narrow rocky beach on the other side. While on the beaches, they walked side-by-side, and the conversation was almost constant; with Jon doing most of the talking about home, school and family. Tamubu told Jon of his recurring dream-like memories.

Discussing them with Jon, gave substance and meaning to his wispy recollections, fleshing them out into meaningful events. From there, the floodgates opened, enabling Tamubu to recall many other forgotten incidents from his boyhood.

On the third day, the sheer rock outcroppings into the surf forced them to go inland. Here the conversation ceased, for vigilance in the forest was the first precept of safety. They had found a much-used trail from the beach, which eliminated the hazard of hacking through the vegetation, so Kybo followed them. The trail led inland several miles to a small village of the Fulani, but not the village of the lads. Jon made a big hit with the chief with his knowledge of their language and customs, while everyone treated Tamubu like royalty. The following day they took their leave, with many gifts of food and a detailed route to Douala.

In the late afternoon of the second day, after leaving the Fulani village, the wide trail opened out into a dirt road, and again walking side-by-side, Jon remarked. "This has been a pleasant trip; Motozo and the men would have enjoyed this long walk, don't you think, Kybo?"

"Yes, kisha, it has been an easy walk."

Tamubu added. "Manutu says there are many trails in the forests used by the natives. With your skill at languages, Jon, we may be able to obtain information about existing routes all the way to Kenya."

"Speaking of skills, I was impressed by the respect accorded you by the Fulani. It was as if they knew of you."

"They know of Manutu. I stand in his shadow."

"How do they know of Manutu?"

"Manutu once traveled to the Congo River, helping and healing as he traveled; his reputation became legendary. Now, the drums talk, traveling natives talk, and we are the news at the campfires.

"Even when I traveled alone, the villagers often knew my path and left gifts for me, hoping I would go to their village and visit with them. Once, a man waited in my path with his sick son. The boy was swollen with fluids, which is sometimes a reaction to a particular food. I gave the man all my powders from a plant that makes you urinate and told him to add one new food each day to the boy's diet to find the food that had caused the problem. A half moon later, two men approached me and gave me this amulet, which is over two hundred years old. It was a gift from the man whose son was now well. It seems the man was the tribal witch doctor who was frustrated by his inability to help his son, so he sought me out in the guise of an ordinary man."

"So, you have been trained as a Medicine Man by the legendary Manutu, and your reputation precedes us. I say! That's a jolly good show! I had visions of slogging our way through thorn-infested forests for thousands of miles, eating berries and sleeping in trees. What a relief!"

"Well," Tamubu smiled, "it's possible you won't be disappointed. There may be times when your visions will come true."

Jon became quiet, thinking. There is more here than meets the eye. The Fulani treated him like a God, not like a visiting Medicine Man. There was something nagging at him, something unusual, but he just couldn't put his finger on what it was.

In the late afternoon, they came to a native village nestled in a copse of huge old oak trees. Kybo went over and chatted with an old man sitting in the shade of the roof eaves, while Jon and Tamubu waited on the road. Kybo returned and said. "I will stay here for tonight. Tomorrow I will travel to the Wahutu village near Edea, on the banks of the Sanaga River. I will visit my cousin, Nashani, and her family. It is about two days travel from here. I will wait for you there."

JON AND TAMUBU ARRIVED at the Douala Hotel just before dark. Jon went to the desk and booked a suite: two bedrooms with baths on either side of a sitting room. He felt Thomas might be more comfortable alone, away from observation, in the almost strange environment. He knew that he was certainly going to enjoy the first privacy he had had in months. Tamubu, who was engrossed by the ornate lobby, wandered around until Jon found him peering into the coffee shop. "Are you hungry?" he asked.

"No, I just followed my nose to the delicious smells."

"Then let's go to the suite. I'm anxious for a bath. We can have coffee and pastries sent up to the sitting room."

Tamubu had never been in a hotel before, and was fascinated by the spacious room arrangements and all the services available. He did, however, remember taking a bath, and was soon immersed in hot water.

Douala boasted a fine tailor and haberdasher, a branch of the main store in Yaoundé. Thomas was somewhat embarrassed by the attention, but Jon assured him, it was perfectly normal for gentlemen to have their dress clothes made to order. The tailor was efficient and, in less time than Jon expected, they were again at liberty. He suggested to Thomas that they use the time to tour the town and wharf. Tomorrow, they would return for a fitting of the cloth patterns.

Jon hired an open landaulet with a liveried driver and footman, pulled by a richly caparisoned horse with ivory inlaid in his patent leather harness. The footman, was about seven years old, and wore a red jacket with a sky blue collar and pants and a matching pillbox hat. Jon negotiated, in French, with the driver, and it was apparent that the man was pleased with the outcome, for he told his diminutive footman to open the small door.

The driver eyed Tamubu from head to toe. He then smiled and tipped his hat to him. Tamubu recognized the deference and nodded in return. He was no longer dressed in his native clothes. He had on a safari shirt and walking shorts with knee socks and his sandals. His kitu-kina, which he had received from Manutu and the spirits, he wore in the fashion of a cape over both shoulders fastened by the two hundred year old amulet, which was ornately carved out of a solid piece of ivory with a heavy, twisted gold chain.

The tailor had been stunned when Tamubu had used his kitu-kina as a footcloth during the fittings, after which he picked it up and shook it out, before tossing it once again over his shoulders. Once ensconced in the carriage, Tamubu said, "This is a good idea; soon, there will be enough walking."

"Actually, I had a purpose. We will not only see the sights better, but we are going to the barbers; we both need a shave and a haircut. The driver says the best barber is uptown. It will be a sightseeing ride." Tamubu knew that Jon was doing things in a specific way, because it was the way his family lived and traveled, when he was a boy. The Land Rover had only been used to go to Nairobi, or for emergencies.

Tamubu said, "I am delighted to ride. The view is better. I would not have thought of it." After the barbers, they stopped at an outdoor café for tea and sandwiches. Tamubu remarked on the quality of the bread and the lack of crusts. Jon chuckled and said, "They cut the crusts off."

"What do they do with the crusts?"

"Make a bread pudding I suppose."

"We must try this pudding made of bread." For dessert they had bread pudding and Tamubu found a new food that he quite enjoyed and asked the chef to come out and explain how the pudding was made. Pleased that his pudding was a hit, the chef listed the ingredients while Tamubu questioned him on the assemblage.

"I can see why I have not had this pudding before, too many perishable ingredients. You could only make it in a village, never on the trail." And so the day went, from one new experience to another, until they arrived back at the hotel at the dinner hour. Tamubu said, "Can we do this again tomorrow? There is still much to see." So Jon engaged the driver for the next day at ten in the morning, after the fitting of the cloth patterns.

Jon checked the desk to see if there was a message from Paula; nothing. He then ordered dinner to be served in his suite, for the hotel required formal dress in the dining room, for dinner.

27

Port-Gentil

CAPTAIN JONES WAS DELIGHTED to have Paula's company for the trip south to Port-Gentil, saying: "It was a propitious encounter, the day I met your Father and Mother; they were quite frustrated by their inability to hire transportation to take them to the cove. It seems providence had a hand in putting us together; I'm glad I was there for them—and for you; it was a memorable trip. Someday, I would like to meet your brothers and sister. If they are anything like you, I'm sure I'll be impressed."

"Actually, they are more talented than me, especially Sallee Anne."

Conversation with Captain Jones was relaxed and easy. He was a gifted conversationalist who asked many discerning questions about her abduction, her escape, and her travels with Tamubu. He always knew the right thing to say and the two days of ocean travel passed quite pleasantly.

The missionaries came away from their prayers and studies in their cabins, only for meals; and then had little to say to these worldly people.

ON REACHING PORT-GENTIL, IT was a surprise to see the *Just Cause* tied up at the pier. Coming alongside the pier, Captain Jones hailed the *Just Cause* from his speakers. Heads popped out of the hatch, and shouts of surprise and delight followed. The five men scrambled off the yacht onto the pier, towards the cruiser.

Captain Jones invited the Expedition members aboard the *Wind Drift* for a Champagne lunch. The missionaries retreated before such immoderation, and ate lunch in their cabins. Captain Jones was a marvelous facilitator. He sensed the Expedition members might be chagrined and a bit embarrassed at having left the cove, and that Paula was harboring resentment–possibly strong outrage–at being abandoned.

With the reunion awkwardness smoothed over by the savoir-faire of Captain Jones, they had an enjoyable lunch together before leaving the *Wind Drift* for the *Just Cause* and business.

Dr. Miles and Paula went down to the lab where he asked her to complete the acquisition data on the specimens she had collected. He had made little progress; a few plants had seemed promising, but none had produced as good a result as had the pods and seeds she had gathered before her abduction.

Later, they moved to the dining booth and the maps to talk about the location of the specimens that Paula had gathered before her abduction.

Dr. Miles said. "We are in the right place here, at the right time, but we are not finding the right plants. I sometimes wonder if the samples were hoaxes. But why would the APCO research lab fund a project based on inadequate evidence?"

Paula replied. "I don't think the samples were hoaxes... but I have reason to believe the interpretation of the sources named was incorrect."

Dr. Miles looked down his nose, over his little half-glasses, with his eyebrows raised. "What makes you say that?"

"Language: the Swahili word for vine is: mzabibu. A word for plant is: mbegu, and one of the words for flower is: uamaua, and a word for pod is: mfuko. Words are combined: so to say flowering vine, it could be said, uabibu and to say flowering pod could be mauabibu, which is so close to mzabibu–flower on a vine, that it could easily be misunderstood; especially if Swahili is being used as a second language by the informant– or by the interpreter. So, instead of looking for a flowering vine–maybe you should be looking for a flower growing on a vine."

Dr. Miles was not pleased by the succinct explanation. Who

does this little nobody think she is—lecturing me? With the patronizing tone of an intellectual snob, he said. "You seem to have become remarkably well informed during your absence. I assume you have some sort of a basis for your explanation and reasoning."

"Yes, I do. First, but not least, you have been unsuccessful in isolating plants with the new alkaloids, the ones APCO believed came from this region. Second, the pods I found were growing on a vine, but that is not to say that the plants that produced the seedpods were a product of the vine. There are many plants whose seeds are dropped by birds in their excrement and this excrement clings to the vines, which grow up the trees below the nests of the birds. These seeds find a fertile growing medium in the rich manure and downward movement of moisture. These plants could be called uamfuko or maumbibi, depending on whether you were saying flowering vine or flower on a vine. So, my samples could have been from flowers on a vine, and the parent genus may grow mostly in other places."

"I was under the impression that you had been abducted by hostile natives —not Rhodes Scholars." Dr Miles replied in a sarcastic tone.

PAULA LOOKED AT HIS tight lips and hard eyes and realized that the helpful and interested professor she had known at the University was gone; an obsessed egoist now occupied the remains. The nice guy façade had been just that: a façade that had masked a morally shallow narcissist.

She didn't hate Dr. Miles, she just didn't have any respect for him as a human being, and his supercilious attitude was quite offensive. She could no longer see the man she had once esteemed.

She thought: I'm the victim here; you were the indifferent leader who put his vanity before my life. Of course, you're embarrassed—especially since your unimportant and nascent assistant is offering logical explanations for the failure of the viability of your samples. But, your arrogant attitude is unforgivable.

Still, Paula was accustomed to speaking with respect, and politely explained: "I came by my knowledge on the arduous return to the cove; after narrowly escaping physical and sexual mutilation by the Ndezi. I would not have made it, were it not for the help of strangers; men who did not know me; men who had no responsibility for me or for my safety; men had no vested interest in my future; but they were truly valiant men who felt compelled to help another human being in trouble... one of whom was an African languages specialist. It was he who explained some of the subtle nuances of African languages to me."

PIQUED, AND POSSIBLY OVERWHELMED, Dr. Miles replied, "This project has been beset from the beginning... from the tsunami until now. To have to listen to your inane conjectures and martyrized explanations is annoying. I have better things to do." Dr. Miles arose to leave.

If he kept us this outrageous attitude, malice was going to be easy, she thought. All her subdued anger and pent-up frustration at his callous abuse and neglect burst its bounds. Charity and forgiveness went out the door and slammed it shut. Putting this insufferable egomaniac in his place was going to be a pleasure. If he finds these simple linguistic variations hard to swallow, he's going to choke to death when he sees my diary.

"JUST A MOMENT, DR. Miles; I would like to show you something you might find of interest." Paula pushed her diary across the table toward him as he sat down with a look of contempt. Paula said, "Start at the back... the front is just personal."

Dr. Miles opened the diary to the last page. He was immediately riveted, and drew in a startled breath. His mouth fell open as he looked at the drawings and read the words, turning page after page.

Paula reached over and gently removed the book from his hands... pausing mid-table to fan the pages slowly... as she said, "This is the tip of the iceberg... and I control the iceberg."

Dr. Miles was flabbergasted. Long moments passed before

he overcame his awe and consternation, and managed to speak to her. "How did you obtain all this information? I didn't know you were such an accomplished artist!"

"I obtained the information during my travails in the wilderness. Some of these plants have the properties to do exactly those things, which you are seeking with your Expedition.

"There are plants here that make you fall asleep and rest deeply, yet allow you to awaken refreshed and alert without grogginess or languor. Plants that take away anxiety completely, but they do not make you listless or dull or short-tempered. Plants that take away local pain by topical application, and plants that relieve deep pain with a feeling of relaxation and tranquility, yet they are not addictive.

"There are plants here that are natural diuretics. There are antibiotics too. They work synergistically with the body to improve and aid the immune system to fight infections... and there is more... so much more."

"I am stunned. I cannot think! How did you come by this knowledge?"

"I met a man... a special man... who has the knowledge of the ages. He saved my life several times after I escaped from the Ndezi. We traded: he drew plants–I taught him English."

"Do you have any idea what even one of these plants is worth?"

"Oh, yes, I know. But do **you** know that your abandonment of me after I was abducted... even after I managed to escape... and your immediate replacement of me with another assistant eliminated any claim to my findings... by you... or the University... or APCO?

"My contract states: '... *Paula Thornton will assist Dr. Miles in obtaining specimens and will help in the preparation of said specimens, as required, in exchange for* all *expenses: travel, room, board and* care... *this contract will be considered null and void once a replacement for her services is obtained...'*

"I was not receiving room or board... and most certainly not care... not even concern! I was ignored. I suspect that you thought that if you replaced me, you were rid of any obligation to me. Turns out, that's a two-way street!

"You're not obligated to me... and I'm not obligated to you or to any of your associates. I understand my replacement was waiting here in Port-Gentil when you arrived, after freeing the yacht from the tidal basin... before you went up the Ogooué River.

"Discarded associates are not employees... replaced associates are not employees... so at the time of my discoveries, I was no longer under the auspices of the Expedition.

"If you had used the APCO resources to field a search and rescue effort... or if you had sent help when you learned I had escaped from the Ndezi... or if you had returned to the anchorage north of the cove... or if you had sent someone else to be there for me... if you had cared at all... but you did nothing! Your depraved indifference was inhuman."

Dr. Miles had never been at a loss for words, but they failed him now. He was culpable and he knew it. He had known it when he took the yacht from the cove; but he wanted to salvage the Expedition... and his dreams of glory... far more than he wanted to spend precious time dealing with a missing assistant.

There had been bitter arguments and nasty recriminations from the crew about his decisions. To a man, they had been angry and had avoided him. In his mind, they had sabotaged the mission with lackadaisical attitudes... spending time playing cards, almost refusing to attend to duties.

He had abandoned his scruples when he abandoned Paula, and possibly, he had abandoned his career.

Paula watched as the realization of the enormity of his situation came over him, and she said, "My one reason for coming here to Port-Gentil was to talk to you in person. Your Expedition is a dead-end. It is based on erroneous information. It can never succeed."

"You must hate me very much..."

"No, I can't be bothered with hate, it is useless. You brought the demise of the Expedition on yourself... all by yourself. I have already written and sent my formal resignation to APCO, listing cause. I have notified the University that I will be taking the rest of the year off... and I have requested a new advisor, also listing cause. My parents, who came to Africa to do your job for you, have been kind enough to see that my letters were photocopied and mailed with the proper 'copy' documentation for me.

"Goodbye, Professor. I wish you decency and loyalty." Paula left without waiting for a reply, but she would have waited in vain.

Dr. Miles had begun to realize the heinous position in which he had placed himself... she has written letters... with copies! I remember now, she is pretty well connected in academic circles... why had I forgotten that? Because I wanted to see my name in a Medical Journal... gone! I wanted to be considered for the Nobel Prize... now, never! Her corroborated accusations will always be a huge blot on my record... I might even lose my job! How could I have been so stupid? With the Expedition in ruins, he was seeing his perfidy clearly now. How could I have been so vacuous? What is left for me now? Nothing but stigma and ridicule!

DR. MILES LEFT THE afterdeck and headed to his cabin, hollering, "Arthur; is there any coffee left?"

"Yes, sir; I made a second pot."

"I'll get the whiskey, you heat the coffee!"

When Dr. Miles came into the galley, Arthur handed him a mug of fresh, hot coffee and watched as he dumped half of it down the drain, before he topped the mug with whiskey.

He sat, saying, "I always knew she was a strong, self-reliant woman. I liked that! I hate clinging vines..." Dr. Miles laughed at the irony saying, "Actually, I just hate **vines...** clinging or otherwise! Arthur, have a drink! I don't want to get drunk alone."

CAPTAIN JONES WATCHED AS Paula made her way to the *Wind Drift*. From the sagging shoulders and stiff body movements, he knew she was upset. He had not been told about the plant drawings, so he attributed her distress solely to her resignation from the Expedition.

Looking up, Paula saw Captain Jones, and requested

permission to come aboard, which was not really necessary, for she was still considered a passenger.

"Permission granted, lassie. Ha' ya made oop yer mind aboot goin' wi' us to Lambaréné?" He asked with his best brogue, for it usually made her laugh... right now, he'd be pleased with a smile.

Indeed, she did smile. "How long will you be gone?"

"Ah, jus' a day oop, and jus' a day bak... cannet ye spare it?"

Now there was a laugh. "I su'poos I can spare it, if ye promise to talk prop'r!"

They both laughed. "Done!" he said.

"When do we leave?"

"Tomorrow morning, first thing."

"Would you please send someone over to get my bags from the *Just Cause?* Arthur said he'd put them up on deck by the gangway."

It's over then; Hannibal Jones, fumed. He sensed that George Miles had been brutal to Paula. The man was everything he disliked: an elitist snob, an egoist and a bore, who was also morally shallow. "I'll send Phil right away. You'll need your best bib and tucker... I'm taking you out for dinner! I want you to meet a friend of mine. You'll like her; she's a lovely lady. She owns a Guest House here in Port-Gentil. Her name is Anna Chumley. She expects us at six!"

Paula was relieved to be alone in her cabin after Phil brought her bags. She was also glad to be going out for dinner. It would keep her from mentally replaying the disagreeable afternoon with Dr. Miles, which she did as she opened her bags for something to wear. She needed to reorganize her stuff: a pile of things to be sent home, a pile of things for Kenya and a pile of things for a long trek. She kept aside a sleeveless blue and white printed cotton jersey jumper with a full flared skirt, a white cotton sweater and her white sandals.

Paula showered, washed her hair and dressed. The knock on the door came just as she put on her earrings. "Yes?" She called.

"Captain wants to know if you are ready, ma'am?"

"Tell him I'll be along in a minute."

"Yes, ma'am; the carriage is here."

A jitney was waiting by the pier. Hannibal Jones handed Paula into the horse-drawn shay and began his tour-guide patter. It was something he enjoyed doing and he was good at it: "In 1956, exportation of crude petroleum began from Pointe Clairette, which is just north of Port-Gentil. It brought an influx of experts from Europe and America, who overflowed Pointe Clairette down to Port-Gentil, causing it to flourish as well. We are going to a new and elegant little French bistro, which has marvelous Crêpes Suzette."

Anna Chumley was already seated and waiting for them. Paula liked her at first sight. She was petite, with auburn hair piled high and merry green eyes with hazel flecks. She smiled often and had even white teeth and one dimple in her right cheek. She greeted Hannibal warmly, with a hug and intimate kiss. Aha! Paula thought. This is a special friend!

Little did she know that at one time, Hannibal Jones had serious romantic leanings toward Anna... but she had been quick to tell him she hated the sea, and while he waited for her to change her mind, he continued to admire her, but their deep friendship never progressed to romance.

The conversation was brisk and interesting. At one point, Captain Jones asked Anna if she had any maps for the Ogooué River.

"Why? Are you going to Lambaréné?"

"Yes, and so is Paula. Would you like to come with us?"

"When are you leaving?"

"Tomorrow morning, first thing... but we could delay until nine or so, if that would be better for you."

"When will you return to Port-Gentil?"

"The following day; it is just a day up and a day back. I am delivering some missionaries to study with Dr. Schweitzer."

A big smile lit Anna's face, as she thought: River travel is not at all like sea travel: no tides, no swells... just smooth sailing. "Yes, I think I would enjoy that. Mammaleo will be able to do without me for a day or two. She already believes she runs everything. This will give her a chance to see just how much I do, too!"

Paula smiled, "Who is Mammaleo?   She sounds interesting."

"She is Anna's housekeeper at the Guest House. She is very impressed with her own importance, but she is *one-in-a-million*, with a heart as big as Africa." Hannibal replied. "I found her begging in the streets of Douala. Her family had all died of a mysterious disease, like dysentery. The village witch doctor said she was evil, and made her an outcast. When I finally pried the story from her, I began to suspect her family had been poisoned, for the witch doctor claimed her hut when she was gone... saying evil spirits lived there... and only he was immune to them."

"Why didn't she die too?"

Hannibal grimaced saying, "Mammaleo doesn't eat dessert. She has a sugar problem. So, she did not eat the pineapple dessert that day. Only her family ate it. Her husband had brought it home as a surprise for them. It was part payment for a job he did for the witch doctor... need I say more?"

Anna added, "She is a wonderful person, who has suffered much. You will find her an irreverent wit when you come to stay with me."

Lambaréné

I<small>T WAS A FOGGY</small> and rainy morning. Captain Jones was glad he had delayed their departure until nine o'clock so Anna could join them. The thick mist didn't break up until the sun was up over the trees. Even then, there was still a low-lying mist on the river; a mist that could obscure log snags, pirogues or the occasional hippo that surfaced for air in the deep water.

Paula rode up on the flying bridge with Captain Jones, which afforded a good view, even with the mist. Anna chose the afterdeck with her book and camera. Steve manned the fathom chain while Phil used a pole to push logs and river debris away from the yacht. Captain Jones liked having Paula on the bridge; her skill as a yachtsman was apparent; she was adept at spotting obstacles in the river: mud bars, water logged limbs, lone hippos and branchy snags that could damage propellers, and the pirogues, which could be swamped by a strong wake. He explained the controls to her, and when the way was clear, let her take the helm.

Watching her, he thought: She has an innate feel for ships and the water, which seems to be second nature to her. She has such effervescence; it makes doing things with her more enjoyable.

E<small>XCEPT FOR THE WIDE</small> deeply curved channels on the riverbanks, made by the hippos going ashore to graze at night, the shoreline was mostly thick vegetation and uninhabited. They passed an occasional fishing landing, where the pirogues were pulled high into the clearings, with high platforms for storing supplies, which also provided a bit of people safety, on occasion The hippos are ornery and will ransack a village at night, if it is built to near the shore. The crocodiles too, with their camouflaged and stealthy ways, made living close to the water a constant danger, especially for children.

Mostly the river was pastoral, allowing time to enjoy the variety of birds: herons, kingfishers, pelicans and the regal great white egrets. The flight of the distinctive hammerkop with his backward-pointed crest balanced by a long pointed bill drew their attention with his high-pitched and raucous cackling.

OVER THE LOW HUM of the diesel engines, the ever-present jungle-like noises were heard in stereo surround-sound, muted at times by patches of low-lying mist, which gave their progress, an end of the world feeling, as it thickened and thinned, parted and dispelled.

Every now and then a bull hippo materialized with gaping maw. Seeing the frightful chasm of long sharp teeth, Captain Jones remarked, "You do know that hippos don't swim."

Paula looked at him with raised eyebrow, unsure.

He smiled at her doubt and continued, "They push off strongly with their back legs to skim over the river bottom... or to surface in deep water. They can hold their breath for up to five minutes, when they must surface for air, before sinking again, for their specific gravity is greater than water. That is the reason they prefer water depths that allow them to stand where they can keep their eyes and ears above water, and can occasionally lift their snouts to breathe. Aggressive bull hippos, like the one we just passed, can be a death knell for a pirogue and its occupants. A hippo weighs about thirty-five hundred pounds and surfaces in deep water to breathe, without warning"

THE OGOOUÉ RIVER FORKED to the right for Lambaréné, where they anchored for a bite of lunch on the afterdeck. Jonas had set up a buffet with navy bean soup and sandwich makings. The air was festive as they gathered together for the meal.

Anna said, "I haven't had a day off in so long, that I don't know what to do with myself."

"Maybe, you'd come up on the bridge with me after lunch?" Captain Jones smiled at her in an alluring way.

Anna laughed and said, "I'd love it! Now that the mist is gone, I want to take some pictures. All I saw this morning through the view finder was mist. I might have gotten a picture of the hammerkop though."

Paula said, I hate to miss anything, but I need a short nap."

"We're all going to take a short nap after lunch, Captain Jones said. The missionaries can pay for the trip by keeping watch for an hour or so. Speaking of which, why didn't they come up for lunch?"

Jonas, the cook, replied, "They came down to the galley earlier and took hard-boiled eggs, scones and coffee to their cabins for lunch. I'm glad they are keeping to themselves. They're an unusual lot! All hand signals, no talking... very weird!"

THE *WIND DRIFT* DOCKED at Lambaréné before four o'clock. A town official was on hand to greet them and took them, in pirogues, to the hospital. The hospital was not on the island of Lambaréné, but on the mainland, across a sluggish pea-soup tributary to the Ogooué River, about a mile away.

The path to the hospital was just a worn dirt rut through the dense bushes. The visitors trooped single file: town official, Paula, Anna, Captain Jones, Phil, Steve and the missionaries; until they came to a large clearing and the native village. Captain Jones had asked Jonas to stay with the yacht, at the town official's suggestion, as theft was rampant. The paddlers had also stayed behind with the pirogues, for the same reason.

THE VILLAGE THEY CAME upon was also the hospital compound. There, a man directed them to an area where Dr. Schweitzer was directing workers, many of whom had bandages on their hands and feet stained with gentian violet.

Paula was surprised to see the workers (and later the house servants) wearing these bandages, which meant they were lepers.

Dr. Albert Schweitzer is a man with a large frame, who, at one time, had more flesh on his bones. Even so, he is an imposing personage. You see his shrewd and assessing eyes first, amidst a distinguished face, surrounded by gray hair. He greeted his guests warmly, in French, before excusing himself to return his attention to the workers, instructing them, also in French, how to continue in his absence. We later learned that he spoke no African language or dialect, although he knew Latin, Greek, Hebrew, English, French and German.

DR. SCHWEITZER TOOK US on a tour of the facility, where he asked to see the hands of some of the worst cases. He remarked in English. "Do not touch the bare hands... ever." And continued, "Nowadays, my rounds are more for moral support, and to maintain a presence, for we now have a staff of medical doctors tending to the actual work."

While he showed us around, he told us that leprosy was one of the least communicable of diseases. It was thought that contagion of the mycobacterium leprae is through unsanitary and overcrowded living conditions, especially those found in damp and humid climates. He, himself, had lived among and ministered to the lepers for more than fifty years without ever contracting the disease.

Paula was surprised to find the hospital so primitive. It had no running water and no hot water, except what was heated in a kettle over a wood fire. It had no electricity, except for what was generated for the operating room lights, and no radio or telephone communications. There was no autoclave to sterilize instruments, no cold storage for perishable medicines or blood samples, and no monitoring equipment for surgical patients. Yet, great work had been done here, even with such primitive facilities... Dr. Schweitzer had saved thousands.

THE HOSPITAL BUILDING IS unique. Dr. Schweitzer designed it himself; he built a long and narrow structure, which was divided into small cubicles, fronted by a long open porch. The patients have low platforms for beds, covered with vegetation. (When changed, the used vegetation is burned.)

Outside each cubicle, the family of the patient has a fire to cook the meals for the patient. The smoke from these many cooking fires and the burning of used bedding, helps to keep the mosquitoes away, greatly reducing the incidence of malaria among the patients. The hospital village is open from six in the morning until six in the evening. It is considered too dangerous to navigate the waters in the other hours, when the hippos move to and from land to graze. The last place visited on the tour was the insane asylum, which was nothing more than small huts, built like cages, similar to, but much smaller than, her prison aerie in the Ndezi village. The poor souls that are violent and dangerous have to be caged. If they were not, their relatives would murder them. After seeing the fetid cells, Paula thought murder might be a mercy.

The guests were ferried back to the establishment on Lambaréné. Dr Schweitzer is famous for his hospitality. No one is ever turned away; neither guest nor patient, no matter the length of the stay. He has built accommodations for many guests, and while Spartan, they are clean and comfortable, with screens on the window openings and locks on the doors.

Theft is so rampant that everything is kept under lock and key. This problem is a severe trial for this moralistic man, who came here to devote his life to their welfare... for they will steal anything, even those things for which they have no use.

DR. SCHWEITZER HAS, WITH a great effort of will, built all the buildings using the lepers for workers. "But it is difficult to keep the men motivated, as they are apathetic laborers. They are accustomed to the women doing all the work. So, while they are working, I call out a drill sergeants' ditty. They like that, and it keeps them happy and productive. The men are more like children than adults, and make little progress without constant supervision." He lamented.

PAULA WONDERED ABOUT THIS ambiguous comment. Indeed, the

native man does not do manual labor, he only hunts or fights or tends livestock... work is for women. But, they will labor to help themselves: they build bomas and shelters when they are out hunting. They gather their own food, flense their own skins and cook their own food. They do it to survive; here they must work to get better. Pretty much the same tenet: I must do this to survive. So, there must be another reason for their poor work ethic, even an illogical one.

Paula watched as Dr. Schweitzer showed a man how to place a post. The man stood there shaking his head, yes, as Dr. Schweitzer explained it to him. With the next post, he looked puzzled, like he didn't have a clue. Dr. Schweitzer had to repeat his instructions all over again.

Paula wondered: Is it possible that they want to be reassured all the time... to make sure the job is done to his satisfaction? Done only the way he wants it done? The reasons for doing a job in a certain way might make no sense to the native, making him fearful of doing it wrong... or fearful of reprimand. The native mind is a product of thousands of years of superstitions and quirks; how could any white man know what their reasoning might be? She would ask Tamubu about this when they were together again.

WITH MORE THAN FIVE hundred souls in the hospital village, the industry is ongoing. Except for those bedridden, everyone has a job to do. Some transport fruit and vegetables, from Dr. Schweitzer's personal garden, in old packing boxes, affixed with poles protruding fore and aft for handles. Some wash laundry; some iron it with flatirons; some use foot treadle sewing machines; some weave cloth; some weave palm fronds or make wicker ware items; some tote wood or water; some gather fresh bedding; some distribute the fresh bedding to the sickbeds.

The jobs are myriad, for the little village is totally self-sufficient for the sick and their families; except for medical supplies, stationery supplies, books and the manufactured personal items that come with the regular medical shipments.

ALL THE WORKERS RECEIVE seven bananas a day: these are plantain, a course fibered but nutritious fruit, which can be cooked with other vegetables in a stew. These are meticulously meted out. When the doctor was questioned about such scant provisions, he was quick to remark: "There is a river filled with fish and a forest filled with fruits and coconuts, if they are still hungry." It is a never-ending incredulity to him that the natives make almost no effort to help themselves.

THE GUEST QUARTERS ARE constructed similarly to the hospital, but the rooms are larger and open out onto a wide covered walkway. The dining room is a long room with a table that seats at least twenty people, and usually does. There is a piano against the wall behind Dr. Schweitzer's chair.

When the tour was concluded, Dr. Schweitzer insisted they join him for dinner, seating Anna to his right, with Paula to Anna's right. To his left, he seated Captain Jones, then Phil and Steve, with the missionaries finding places at the foot of the table. The food was plain, but quite good. A nurse, sitting beside Paula, told her that dinner was her favorite meal of the day. Breakfast, she said, is served Continental style, with coffee or tea, toast and jam with porridge and fresh fruit. Lunch is a vegetable stew, with biscuits and fresh fruit. Dinner is begun with a broth soup or salad, depending on the state of the garden. It progresses to a fish entrée, served with either rice, macaroni or sweet potatoes and a medley of vegetables comprised of squash, onions, peppers, peas or beans, depending on what was ready to pick in the garden. There is always a big wooden bowl of fresh black bread, like pumpernickel, passed with the soup. A fruit cup medley is served for dessert with tea and coffee served later.

Paula saw why guests tended to linger... even if they were obliged to work for their daily fare. Transient guests, like themselves, who provided a service or, like the American author, who had added Lambaréné to his definitive tome on Africa are not asked to work, but they might be called on to lend a hand for a bit.

Meals are just that, meals, and they are usually finished in thirty minutes or so. After dinner, while the table was cleared, everyone gathered around the piano to sing hymns with the good doctor skillfully playing the piano. Upon returning to our seats at the table, Dr. Schweitzer gave a reading from the scriptures, and a short related sermon. After the services, coffee and tea were served and general conversation (to be differentiated from the small talk during meals) commenced.

Dr. Schweitzer asked both Paula and Anna if they played a musical instrument. Both said, no, but Paula added, "My older sister has all the talent in the family; she is a concert pianist. Dr. Schweitzer became animated at this news, for he is of the opinion that while most people like music, there are few that understand it. Encouraged by a discerning ear, he returned to the piano and played a Beethoven Sonata, ending with a casual remark, "You need an organ to properly play Bach."

He persisted in his conversation with Paula, and was impressed with the idea of using African plants for medicines. She briefly described the kimmea to him and Dr. Schweitzer asked her to please write him, when she could, of her findings about the plants.

He then told of his visit from an American author several years ago. He had found him quite interesting and knowledgeable, as well as a good conversationalist. He had learned much about the rest of Africa from him. He then talked about his one visit to the United States. He had gone to Aspen, Colorado for the Goethe Festival. He still remembered all the fuss and attention he had received... like a royal personage. "Americans are an enthusiastic people, I like them."

He then turned his attention to Anna. "Are you, by any chance, related to Alexander Chumley, the cartographer?"

"He was my husband, sir," Anna replied.

Dr. Schweitzer was immediately delighted and began a verbal treatise on maps and the making of maps, which fascinated him.

Listening to Albert Schweitzer speak, Paula recalled how Captain Jones had praised him during the casual luncheon on the afterdeck, saying, "He is truly a *man of the ages*, like

Goethe or da Vinci; a man whose talent and intellect far exceeds his contemporaries. His interests are incredible and varied: He is an ordained minister with a doctorate in theology. He is a licensed medical doctor, whose thesis was a psychiatric study of the mind of Jesus Christ. He also has doctorates in music and philosophy and has written comprehensive books on those subjects, as well as a history of civilization. He won the Nobel Peace Prize in 1952. Sitting here now, listening to Dr. Schweitzer speak, made her hardships in Africa worthwhile, for this experience was an unprecedented pleasure; a time never to be forgotten!

The missionaries had retired after the sermon, as had the doctors, nurses and staff. The good doctor turned to Captain Jones and thanked him for his generosity in bringing the missionaries to Lambaréné. "Won't you stay a few days?"

"I would like nothing better, but I must get Mrs. Chumley and Ms. Thornton back to Port-Gentil, but I thank you for your offer." It was then decided that Phil and Jonas would be Dr. Schweitzer's guests for breakfast in the morning. Dr. Schweitzer had noticed the Ellery Queen Mystery magazine in the leg pocket of Phil's cargo pants. He thought he would enjoy knowing about his acquaintance with Agatha Christie, whom he had met at a writer's symposium in Vienna.

Dr. Schweitzer did not shake hands, but nodded at each one, before he turned and left the dining room. As they walked back to the yacht, savoring the events of the evening, the lantern escort told them, that Dr. Schweitzer wrote in the evenings into the small hours of the morning.

IN HER BUNK ABOARD the yacht, Paula thought about all she had seen that day, and all she had seen in the last two months, and all that had happened to her, and sleep fled. She arose and lit the gimbaled lantern, took out her diary and scribbled away into the wee hours of the morning, while her impressions and memories were fresh and undimmed by time.

THE TRIP BACK TO Port-Gentil was anticlimactic. The conversation was only of Dr. Schweitzer and their observations and impressions. They had all felt the magnitude of his presence. Phil regaled Steve, while keeping watch at the bow, about Agatha Christie following Dr. Schweitzer around at the symposium in Vienna, jotting notes in her little book. When Dr. Schweitzer asked her if he could be of help to her, she had just replied that she only wanted to observe him, if he didn't object. With a twinkle in his eye, he had asked Phil, "Do I remind you of a certain Belgian detective at all?" Phil was ecstatic at the possibility of a secret that only he, Dr. Schweitzer and Agatha Christie shared.

Jonas made his special recipe Danish pastries filled with lemon curd, for the breakfast meal. Dr. Schweitzer was delighted, for he missed the delicious pastries of his youth. Jonas relived the kudos, and dreamed of becoming a famous chef.

29

Exposé

JON AND TAMUBU AROSE with first light, had an early breakfast of porridge, melon, fresh bread and coffee. After tasting his coffee, Jon remarked, "I'm sure this is good coffee, but after Motozo's coffee, it seems flat."

"I agree. The food does not taste as good as it did in the forest. I wonder if it is because I didn't have to find it and cook it myself."

"You're right, that's it, of course. The self-satisfaction is missing." Jon glanced out the window and said, "Looks like a lovely day. I'm ready for a sniff of fresh air." Smiling a crooked smile, Jon continued, "I never thought I'd see the day when I would miss walking!"

Tamubu replied with amusement, "You may not miss it for long."

THE TAILOR HAD THE muslin patterns ready. There were only a few minor adjustments needed, before Jon and Tamubu chose fabrics. Tamubu did not care for the fine wools, but preferred the angora and silk blends. "My, you have jolly good taste. You'll be the envy of the town. In fact, I think I'll order a dinner jacket of this white angora and silk blend myself." The tailor measured Jon saying he was a perfect size and would not need another fitting.

FIFTEEN MINUTES LATER THEY were back at the hotel where the landaulet was waiting for them. In French, Jon directed Ben, the coachman, to drive them to the wharf

"Where are we going today?"

"First, to the wharf."

"Why are we going to the wharf?"

"Did you not tell me that Captain Jones would bring Paula to Douala in eleven days? Well, today is the eleventh day. Unless you don't count the day they left on the cruiser. Then it is only the tenth day. We can ask when Captain Jones is expected."

"I am not accustomed to keeping track of the days, just the moons. I'm glad you remembered." Secretly, Tamubu had been counting the days, which in truth, he did not usually do; for his thoughts had not long wandered from seeing Paula again.

Arriving at the busy wharf, they left the landaulet and walked down to the piers for private boats. The dockhand on duty told them, "Captain Jones said he would be back today or tomorrow; but he often gets side-tracked and goes off somewhere else. He has a permanent berth over there, on the pier with that tall light pole. That light comes on at dark and goes off at sunrise all by itself," the dockhand said, clearly impressed. "Captain Jones had it brought here all the way from California, U.S.A."

THEY LEFT THE WHARF and drove along the coast into the countryside where wealthy Europeans had impressive chateaus high on the bluff. It was a scenic drive enhanced by a gentle cooling breeze from the sea. The cart way was a gradually rising shelf, which wandered inland and back again to the sea in a series of gentle climbs and straight-a-ways, before coming to a wide clearing shaded by a grove of sepele trees, where there was a panoramic view of the harbor and the bay.

Ben, the coachman, led Goldie, the big Belgian horse, to a clearing among the trees, where a small pool of water had formed from a mountain spring. He scooped water into a small bucket for the horse to drink and used the leftover water to sponge the horse's neck and chest. He half filled the pail again for all to wash their hands before lunch.

Ben's wife had sent a picnic lunch of cold roast chicken, a cabbage salad mixed with bits of pickled asparagus and slivered nuts, sliced fresh fruit, sun tea and bread pudding for dessert. Ben arranged the trays, which Gomojo served to the gentlemen seated in the carriage.

Tamubu was surprised, but Jon explained that Ben had offered to bring lunch today, saying his wife, Tirini, was a wonderful cook.

Indeed, her picnic lunch was even better than his trail food. Tamubu spoke to the driver in Bantu. "Ben, please thank your wife for us. It was the best lunch we have ever eaten. The bread pudding had a delicious flavor. We are very pleased."

Jon watched in amazement. The aloof driver was all smiles with a gracious inclination of his top-hatted head. Again, Thomas was being treated like he was royalty. It gave Jon that nagging feeling again, like there was something he should remember—something unusual and important. But whatever it was, it still eluded him.

Jon wanted to stretch his legs, and suggested a little stroll along a narrow path on the grassy mountainside. It brought them to a small cottage tucked away in a crease, sheltered on three sides, but open to the sea. An old woman sat in a rocker, knitting. They were upon the cottage before they realized it was there, when the old woman looked up and smiled. "I was hoping for company today," she said in French.

Jon replied, "We were just taking a postprandial stroll. We didn't realize the cottage was here. We beg your pardon."

"Not at all, most of my visitors come upon my house unexpectedly. I sit here on sunny days and hope someone will take a walk and end up at my door. Come, sit for a minute, and tell me who you are, where you come from and where you are going. It is my only connection to the outside world except for my son, who brings my groceries."

Jon translated for Thomas and immediately he was sitting on the porch steps, at the feet of the little old woman.

"My brother speaks no French, so I will have to translate. Do you mind?"

"Of course not, but if you speak French, why doesn't your brother speak French?"

"We didn't go to the same schools. I went to school in

England. My brother, Thomas, went to school in Africa. We are here for a short visit before traveling to Kenya. We have a driver waiting and cannot tarry too long."

The old woman looked deeply into Tamubu's eyes and said to Jon, "Your brother is a healer, yes?"

Jon was amazed. "Yes, you could say that. How did you know?"

"I felt the power of his aura. Will you ask him to lay his hands on my knees, they are bad today."

Jon was so startled by the concept of the request that he forgot to translate it to Thomas; but watched in amazement, as Thomas raised his hands and placed them gently on the old woman's knees. He then closed his eyes, and swaying slightly, chanted in a singsong manner that Jon had never heard or seen before. Jon stood in shock, as if turned to stone—how could this be? What was going on here?

The old woman had closed her eyes when Tamubu placed his hands on her knees and when she opened them, she said, "Merci beaucoup mon ami, c'est tres bien votre effleurer sur moi." Tamubu arose and said to Jon, "We can leave now. She will sleep for a while." Jon looked down at the old woman, who had thanked Thomas for putting his hands on her knees... and indeed, she was asleep with a small smile on her lips.

TAMUBU WALKED AWAY; JON followed, but his thoughts were whirling about in his head. What had happened back there? Had Thomas made the old woman's pain go away? If so, how had he done that? In a flash, he knew the reason for his persistent nagging feeling. How had Thomas known there was an injured boy needing help, that day on the beach? Somehow he had known, for he had taken Paula's first-aid kit with him, when he took Kybo and went out again. This was the something unusual that had been bothering him. That falderal about the tracks in the sand had been pure nonsense, and Thomas had known about the net hanging in the tree on the beach. Jon now knew it was an all day trek, one way, from the thorn boma hut to the beach.

Was this the reason the Fulani had treated him like

royalty? And a witch doctor had sought him out, in disguise, to heal his son? And the reserved driver, Ben, fawned on him, and had his wife make a wonderful lunch? Was his brother really a gifted healer?'

When they arrived back at the sepele trees, Ben asked, "Did you see the old woman?"

Tamubu answered. "Yes, she will feel better for awhile. When we return to the hotel, I will give you some powders to take to her another day. She should stay out of the damp wind, and only sit out on dry sunny days."

Now Jon was even more perplexed. Had Ben brought us here so Thomas could meet the old woman? Was this the reason for his deference to Thomas? But the walk had been spontaneous. Actually, it had been my idea. I led the way.

Tamubu said to Jon, "You must accept that which you cannot understand. One day soon, you will know the answers to your questions."

Jon was stunned. Now, this is quite something else! Does he know what I'm thinking? Or was it just a coincidence? Was Thomas referring to his ministrations to the old woman? Or did he read my thoughts? These impossible ideas occupied Jon's attention completely, as he searched his memory for other anomalies on their return to the wharf. Captain Jones had still not arrived.

AT THE HOTEL, JON inquired if there were any messages for him? There was still no word from Paula. It was teatime, and the hotel lobby was busy. Thomas had gone to his room to fetch the powders for Ben to give to the old woman.

Jon just wanted to bathe... and to think. His clothes should be back from the laundry by now, hopefully, with all the sand out of them. Back in the sitting room, Jon had drawn out paper and pen to leave Thomas a note when Thomas returned saying, "Ben is going to meet us again tomorrow morning at ten, unless you have other plans."

Frustrated by the unique surprises of his extroverted brother, Jon replied, "No, not at all! Are you going to make the blind see and the lame walk—what?"

"I don't know, Ben didn't say."

Jon realized his mouth was wide open; he clamped his lips shut, then said, "I'm going to take a bath. I have ordered dinner for seven here in the sitting room—and there has been no word from Paula." Jon walked to his room and closed the door.

Tamubu understood what a surprise the afternoon had been for Jon, for he had been transmitting his thoughts subliminally to Tamubu on the return to the wharf. Jon was not yet consciously aware of his abilities, but he too, was a spirit savant. He had used his fine-tuned senses all his life. It was the reason why Jon was so happy-go-lucky. He instinctively took the path of least resistance. He had always been able to avoid unpleasant situations; he always knew the safest way to turn, and wasn't even aware that he was doing it.

But Tamubu knew only Jon's thoughts, not his feelings. He did not realize Jon was feeling shut out and alone again.

FOR JON WAS THINKING to himself: everything has been so great between us; we picked up where we left off as children. We understood one another as we did of old—now this... this notoriety. It makes me uncomfortable. I feel like I have a sign on my back, saying: kick me.

In the bath, Jon's anxieties faded and his thoughts became contemplative. The shock of finding out about his brother's bizarre abilities was lessening. He began to talk to himself, man-to-man. What has changed? If I'd just found out that Thomas was an international concert pianist, sought after by one and all; recognized by one and all; would I feel this way? No, of course not, so why does this sort of distinction upset me so?

Answer yourself Jon, why? Because it is not the accepted thing to do, and it is bad form to be singled out for being different—right? Right! He's not a classic bay horse—he's a blue-eyed piebald—black patches on white—with a streaked mane and tail. He will always stand out. How are you going to cope with that reality? It is here—it is now—it is the way things are going to be. Don't compare Thomas to society, he is head and shoulders above them; and don't compare yourself to Thomas—complement him. Remember, your blood and his are identical.

Yes! That's what I'll do! I'll be the Dr. Watson to his Sherlock Holmes. I'll help him be who he is, and I will be who I am—what a great team we'll make!

Jon's bath was cold by the time he finished talking to himself and his skin was all wrinkled, like the old woman today. Feeling much better, almost back to his old self, Jon dressed in clean, sand-free clothes and went to the bar for a cocktail before dinner.

He saw a crowd gathered off to one side, and wondered: something must be going on. Jon squeezed his way to the bar and ordered his cocktail. While he sat on his high stool, the crowd parted and he saw Thomas surrounded by a bevy of women. Now what? Jon hitched himself higher on the bar stool and just watched. Eventually, a lady from the inner circle of the crowd passed by, and Jon asked, "I say, what's going on?"

The woman, all flushed from excitement, replied, "My friend laughed suddenly and an olive got stuck in her throat and she couldn't breathe. That tall man picked her up around the middle and almost threw her up in the air. When she came down, out came the olive, but she fainted. I'm going to find her husband. He went out to get a newspaper or something."

I GUESS I'LL JUST have to get used to this, Jon thought. Seems like that's the way things are going to be from now on. I wish Paula would get here so we could leave for Kenya.

Jon heard his inner voice saying... one minute you can't find enough to do to put off the trek... and the next minute, you can't wait to leave. Seems to me, old boy, you're trying to hide.

Jon waited until Thomas was leaving; then slipped through the crowd to fall in behind him, saying. "I'm glad we're having dinner in our rooms. You'll be safe from the hungry hordes there."

"Manutu told me I should stay away from crowds,

but I didn't understand why at the time; I'm feeling a bit overwhelmed myself. It will be good to get back to the serenity of the forest."

AFTER BREAKFAST THE NEXT day, the eleventh or possibly the twelfth day, the 4th of March, when there was still no message at the hotel from Paula, Jon said, "Let's go down to the harbormaster's office and radio the *Just Cause* to find out if Paula is still there.

"That's a good idea; it will be a nice walk too."

"DOUALA HARBORMASTER TO THE *Just Cause*. Come in. Over."

The call was answered, "This is the *Just Cause*, Arthur speaking. Over."

"Arthur, this is Jon Caulfield. Is Dr. Miles there? Over."

"No. Everyone has gone home to the States. I'm the only one here. Over"

"Did Miss Thornton go to the States too? Over."

"Miss Thornton left first. Then Dr. Miles and the others left three days later. Over"

"I am at the Douala Hotel. If you get news of Miss Thornton, please contact the Douala Harbormaster and leave a message. Over."

"That's a ten-four. Over and Out."

JON WAS PERPLEXED AND dismayed. Looking at Thomas, he knew he was extremely upset by the news, as his lips were flattened in a grimace—like he used to do as a boy when he was thwarted.

Tamubu was flummoxed. The news was so unexpected. Whatever could have happened to make her change her mind? Why had she not even called or left a message for them?

Tamubu seemed to take the news stoically, but inside he was bereft. In the short time they had been together, he had come to know Paula as a person of her word. He could not imagine a reason for her to change her mind so completely. For the first time in his life, his spirits drooped, he felt empty and deflated.

On the walk back to the hotel, Tamubu said to Jon, "Why don't we leave today? Ben can drive us until the road narrows." Tamubu yearned for the deep forest and the solitude that went with it.

"Yes, that's a good idea. I'm anxious to get going myself. It won't take me long to pack and settle things with the hotel." When Jon paid the account, he posted a letter he had written to his parents last night. He told them only that he was traveling overland to Kenya. He had not mentioned finding Thomas. The long wait would be too much for them. He would telegraph the happy news when they were closer to home.

They had their gear waiting when the landaulet arrived. Ben was dismayed that they were leaving, but he and Gomojo would be glad to take them to the trailhead to the Wahutu village. Both Jon and Tamubu were quiet during the long ride. Both were occupied with thoughts of the trip to come and Paula's inexplicable lack of communication with them.

Later, when the dirt road started to climb steeply, Ben pulled onto a wide level spot beside the road, in the shade of tall old trees. Here a little rivulet of water gushed from the mountainside providing a cool drink for Sunny, Goldie's full brother, who was on duty today. "Tirini has made a nice lunch for you," Ben said. "She has made her special sausages and fresh bread, with hard boiled eggs and a fruit compote for dessert."

Tamubu replied, "Tirini is very kind to strangers. She is a good woman, as well as a good cook."

Gomojo had gone to pull grass for the big golden horse; when he returned, they sat down to lunch. During the delicious meal, they discussed the trail; Ben gave them directions to the Wahutu village, which was near the Sanaga River.

Ben said, "Gomojo and I have been pleased to share your company these past few days. We wish you a successful journey, and hope to see you again one day."

"I plan to return some day. I wish you well until then." Tamubu replied.

Jon added his farewell, "Adieu."

JON AND THOMAS HEFTED their gear and took the first steps of two thousand miles of steps. As the long dusk waned, they came to the Wahutu village where Kybo was awaiting them. Nishani had been surprised and happy to see Kybo; the only family she had seen since she married and left home. Kybo had caught her up on the news; and now, her family was honored to have Tamubu and Jon visiting too. After the formal dinner for visiting dignitaries, the talking fire was lit and Jon regaled the villagers with stories of his travels and the Pygmies; while Tamubu talked far into the night with the tribal medicine man.

30

Gone

THERE CAME A GENTLE tapping on her door. Paula arose and opened the door to find Anna Chumley standing there with a note. "This was just delivered from the harbormaster's office. I do hope it's not bad news. I know it's quite late in the day for an invitation, but if you have no other plans for this evening, I'd be pleased if you would join me for dinner."

"Thank you, Anna, I'd like that." Closing the door, Paula went and sat at the desk to read the note:

"March 1st - Miss Thornton, I will arrive at Port Gentil on the 3rd. Have your bags packed and on the pier, ready to shove off at noon. H. Jones."

Paula had sent Captain Jones a message yesterday, on the 29th, telling him she had forgotten about leap year, and that she was to meet Tamubu and Jon in Douala in eleven days, which would be March 4th–not March 5th. Now that she knew Captain Jones' schedule, she could leave a message for Thomas.

When Paula joined Anna Chumley for dinner, she used her phone to call the Douala Hotel.

"Hello, I would like to leave a message for Mr. Thomas Caulfield. Please say I am delayed and will not arrive until late in the afternoon of the 4th; signed, Paula."

The message was properly placed in Mr. Thomas Caulfield's box under his room key. He had checked in, but must have gone out for the evening.

TAMUBU DID NOT LIKE his bedroom at the Douala Hotel. It was airless and smelled of cigars. Outside the French door windows was a balcony. It was here that Tamubu slept and here that he kept his gear, behind a large potted hibiscus. He had instructed the maid to leave the room unlocked, for he did not want to be bothered fetching the key. The maid understood at once, sensing his wishes were to be obeyed without question.

Tamubu never went to the Main Desk. Jon took care of all the details, arranged for the suppers, and paid the bill. The message from Paula was left, gathering dust with the unused key, until Paula arrived in the late afternoon on the 4th, when Jon and Tamubu were already gone.

PAULA SPOKE SHARPLY TO the desk clerk, "What do you mean? Mr. Caulfield has checked out!" How could they be gone? Why would they go without leaving me a message? She thought. She again rang the bell and said, "I would like to speak to your Manager."

Mr. Pandi came out of his office and with quiet authority said, "Yes? What can I do for you, Miss?"

"The problem is that I left two messages for your guests and neither one was delivered to them. I want to know why?"

"That's not possible. When did you leave the first message?"

"The first message was on the 26th of February to Mr. Caulfield. He had not yet arrived but was due in a few days." Mr. Pandi remembered a desk clerk asking him about the proper disposition of a message to a guest not yet arrived. He went and spoke with him. They both returned and the clerk went into the file and found the message–To Mr. Paul Field, filed under "F".

"I am sorry for the mistake. The telephone lines are often noisy."

"Well, what about my other phone message to Mr. Thomas Caulfield?" Mr. Pandi looked at the register, then turned and went to the key box and plucked out the message. "The message was never picked up. Just a moment, please." Mr. Pandi talked with the other main desk staff and found that none of them had ever seen Mr. Thomas Caulfield. They had only dealt with Mr. Jonathan Caulfield. He had paid for the suite and all related charges. Mr. Pandi returned and explained to Paula, "Mr. Thomas Caulfield never came to the desk—not even for his key—only Mr. Jonathan Caulfield had come to the desk. I am quite sorry for the problem. Is there anything else I can do for you Miss?"

"Can you tell me where they went?"

"No, Miss, I cannot. It seems they were going on walk-about."

WITH OVERWHELMING FEELINGS OF frustration, Paula went into the tearoom and ordered a pot of Earl Grey tea. She felt devastated by the chaotic chain of events. Sipping the soothing tea, her agitation diminished; and it occurred to her that the only way they would have been able of get in touch with her, when they had not heard from her as arranged, was to radio the *Just Cause*. They knew she was going back to the Expedition yacht in Port Gentil. She returned to the desk and booked a room. "How long will you be staying, Miss?"

"I don't know. I need to find someone who can tell me where Mr. Jonathan Caulfield and Mr. Thomas Caulfield have gone—maybe someone with whom they had dealings."

"Mr. Caulfield hired the carriage each day. Maybe the driver knows where they have gone. Ben will return to the hotel, in the morning, around eight. He drives a landaulet pulled by a big, Belgian horse, but he does not come out in the rain."

PAULA BOOKED A ROOM and freshened up before returning to the pier, where she surprised Captain Jones when she asked, "permission to come aboard."

Stepping back on the flying bridge, he said, "Permission granted, but what brings you here?" He had, just an hour ago, taken her to the Douala Hotel.

After her brief explanation, Captain Jones soon had the *Just Cause* and Arthur on the horn. Matters were muddled even further when Arthur said, "I put all of her things on the dock; I thought Missy Paula was going home. The next day, the Expedition was cancelled, and everyone else went home."

Paula took the mike and asked Arthur, "Did they give you any message?"

"Only to call the Douala Hotel if I heard any news."

Arthur was contrite, "I thought you had gone home, Missy. No one told me differently. If Mr. Caulfield calls again, what should I tell him? Over."

"Tell him I will leave a message, detailing my plans, with the manager of the Douala Hotel, a Mr. Pandi. Thank you, Arthur. Over and Out."

BUT, SHE HAD NOT gone home; she had gone aboard the *Wind Drift*. The next morning, she and Anna Chumley had gone with Captain Jones to ferry the missionaries to Lambaréné.

No wonder they had gone. Arthur had told them I had gone home to the States. What must they think of me? They no longer had any reason to tarry in Douala—but how was she going to find them? Her only clue was the carriage driver who, the desk clerk thought, might have driven them away—but the carriage driver wouldn't be back until tomorrow morning.

CAPTAIN JONES INVITED PAULA to stay for an early light supper. "I need to go to bed early, but I can't sleep on a full stomach. Jonas has made a nice shrimp chowder and, after I dropped you off, I bought some just baked French bread." Paula was pleased to stay. Captain Jones' repartee would take her mind off her dilemma for a few hours. He was funny, witty and interesting to talk to, and the thought struck her, as she sat listening, that if she had her way and found Tamubu and Jon... sadly, she would never see him again.

IT WAS PAST MIDNIGHT when Paula finished a letter to her parents, and put her head on the pillow; but she remained awake—remembering...

She never let her mind dwell on the gut-wrenching fear of her abduction by the frightful Ndezi. Nor did she give much thought to the rigors of her escape—or the horrible fate that the Ndezi Chief had planned for her. Instead her thoughts always turned to the heart-stopping confrontation with the lion—when Tamubu had saved her life by putting his own in jeopardy; and he had saved her life, not just once, but several times during the next twelve days.

Her thoughts always turned to getting acquainted in the lofty branches of the old oak tree, and the instant rapport that passed between them; and Jon—dear sweet Jon—who had given up his trading adventure to go and search for her—when he learned of my escape from the Ndezi. A man who had only known me for an hour or so in the Ndezi village—the man who knew me least... was the man who had cared the most.

I must find them again. Nothing else matters.

Afterword

Dear Reader,

It is my sincere hope that you found the story worthy of your time and that it lived up to the quotation:

"That is a good book, which is opened with expectation and closed with delight and profit." A. B. Alcott

I put myself in your shoes at the ending—I would want to know, as a reader, if Paula finds Tamubu and Jon again—and I wouldn't want to have to wait until the sequel came out for an answer.

Yes, Paula does find Tamubu and Jon and Kybo. But suffice it to say, villains arise, and plans go awry.

The adventures continue in the sequel: Surviving in Africa.

Marie Pierce Weber

Glossary

Agiza mahili pango	Dark labyrinthine cave
Akili Mzimu	Ancestral spirit
APCO	Asher Pharmaceutical Company
Asante	Thank you (Swahili)
Baharike	Sea Goddess
Boma	Fence of thorn bushes
Burnoose	Arabian/African hooded cloak
Camaraderie	Fellowship
Chiaroscuro	Artist's treatment of light & shadow
Chosen	A specific destiny to fulfill
Chui	Leopard–male
Chuima	Leopard–female
Cicitrix	Scar tissue designs on body and face
Clitorectomy	Surgical removal of the Clitoris
Daktari	Medical Man
Devil Plant	Laprodis or Kamikiza
Dock	Wild celery: grows to eight foot high
Dogo Mungu	Little god
Dulband	Turban–Persian headdress
Esoteric Mystique	Internal mind altering abilities
Gusa	Taboo (Swahili)
Gwase	Warthog
Habari	Hello (Swahili)
Haliiki	Goddess of Nature
Kamikiza	Devil plant – laprodis
Kigozi	Leader

Kimmea	Plant that relieves anxiety and aids sleep
Kisha	Associate – assistant leader
Kitamba	Cloth capes – men
Kitu-kina	Cloak from the spirits
Kuzimu Akili	Spirit walker – spirit talker
Landaulet	Open carriage with facing seats and rear hood
Laprodis	Devil plant – kamikiza
Mabari-yoko	What's up with you?
Mafuu	Crazy
Mawa-jambo-leo	I'm just fine today!
Mbuzi	Goat
Metaphysical	Beyond the laws of nature
Mitirike	Tree Goddess
Mongojo	Walking sticks (crutches)
Mzimu Akili	Wise ancestral spirit
Mzuzu	Tenderfoot - novice
Nahuku	Is here
Nyani	Ape
Nyoka	Snake
Pambisha	Sari-like dresses – women
Pirogue	Dugout log canoe
Possessions	Tamubu's gear
Psychotropic	Capable of modifying mental functions
Punda	Zebra
Quadrivial	Simultaneously radiating four ways
Roam	Spirit travel
Safi-Mitiriki	White Tree Goddess
Sebula	Open porch or gazebo
Sign	Marks left by man or beast
Simba	Any lion – or male lion

Simba-jike	Lion – female
Siyo gusa	Don't touch
Subliminal	Below the threshold of conscious awareness
Survival belt	Rappelling harness – grapnel and line
Tamubu	Sweet Gift
Touched	Gifted – Special – Unique
Transcendental	Beyond common experience
Tumpline	A wide band on the forehead to support a rear load
Ule Kubwa Kasiroho	Ule (the), Kubwa (great), Kasi (living), Roho (spirit)
Usiku chungu	Night pot
Vasinyati	Cape Buffalo
Walinka	Throwing club – used to kill small prey

Miscellaneous Names

The *Just Cause*	62' yacht- designed by Adam Wesley for the Expedition White w/purple
The *Merry Mermaid*	Fishing trawler–Bight of Biafra
The *Norsk Star*	Tanker that ferried the *Wind Drift* to Africa
The *Wind Drift*	95' Motor yacht–Hannibal Jones, Skipper

Main Characters & Families

Peter Thomas Caulfield, II

a.k.a. Tamubu ~ 1st son of Lady Mary & Sir Peter ~ lost in a plane crash at age 10 ~ adopted by the Chief of the Zuri Watu ~ protégé of Manutu, the Medicine Chief of the Zuri Watu ~ 24 yrs old ~ 6"2' tall ~ 290# ~ long curly honey blonde hair ~ topaz blue eyes ~ engaging smile w/dimples.

Jonathan Edward Caulfield

2nd son of Lady Mary & Sir Peter ~ educated in England in Horticulture and African Languages ~ fluent in French & German ~ 22 yrs old ~ 6"1' tall ~ 175# ~ short wavy dark blonde hair & bushy eyebrows ~ dark topaz blue eyes ~ dimples.

Paula Mahree Thornton

M.S. Biology ~ Ph.D. Fellowship University of Pennsylvania ~ world class gymnast ~ rockface climber ~ pilot ~ horseman & distance rider ~ yachtsman ~ 24 yrs old ~ 5"9' tall ~ 135# ~ chin length ash blonde hair ~ sapphire blue eyes ~ captivating smile.

Charles Scott Thornton

Paula's Father ~ 56 yrs old ~ College Professor ~ Inventor ~ yachtsman ~ horseman ~ tennis Pro.

Lisa Wagner Thornton	Paula's Mother ~ 54 yrs old ~ Tax Accountant ~ horseman ~ breeder & trainer ~ top tennis player.
Charles Scott Thornton, Jr.	Brother ~ 30 yrs old ~ Captain U.S. Air Force ~ Pilot ~ outdoorsman.
Eric Arlen Thornton	Paula's twin brother ~ Vet student ~ horseman.
Sallee Anne Thornton	Paula's sister ~ 28 yrs old ~ concert pianist ~ artist ~ clothing designer ~ tennis player.
David Thornton, Esq.	Paula's Uncle - her father's brother ~ Patent Attorney ~ U of P Alumni.

Expedition Characters

Brown, Arthur	Ship's cook, fluent Bantu, Swahili, French, English
Connors, Sandy	Radioman, electrical systems expert, U.S.N. Ret.
Miles, Professor George, Ph.D.	Leader of the Expedition – recruited by APCO to head the Holistic Psychopharmacology Program. Professor–U of P, Paula's Advisor.
Nils, Captain Ole Johann	Master of the tanker, *Norsk Star*
Thornton, Paula Mahree	Protagonist of story
Ulman, Greg	Mechanical Mr. Fix-it; fluent French & Spanish
Wesley, Adam	Shipwright, sail maker; fluent French & German

Other Characters

Ace	APCO helicopter pilot
APCO	Asher Pharmaceutical Company
Brookhurst, David	Archeologist – Legend of the Zuri Watu
Chumley, Mrs. Anna	Proprietress of the Port-Gentil Guest House
Jamison, Mr.Thomas	Caulfield's teacher – killed in plane crash
Jonas	Antisocial cook of the *Wind Drift*
Jones, Captain Hannibal	Skipper of the luxury motor yacht, *Wind Drift*
Julie	Office help for Lisa Thornton
Mason, Max	Maximillian Mason (55) South Afrikaner, wife deceased, Mercenary turned Trader; fluent in Dutch, French, English, Bantu and Swahili
Pandi, Mr.	Manager – Douala Hotel
Peters, Dr.	Veterinarian – Eric Thornton's mentor
Phil & Steve	Deckhands for the *Wind Drift*
Reverman, Captain	Leader: Nigerian Peace Keeping Force – Search & Rescue mission
Schweitzer, Dr. Albert	Universal Man: Architect, Author, Medical Doctor, Ordained Minister; Organist, Linguist, Head of the Leper Colony at Lambaréné in Gabon.

Native Characters

Agurra	Father of Manutu & Sashono, husband of Myuma – past Medicine Chief of the Zuri Watu
Ben	Landaulet driver in Douala – son, Gomojo (Little One), wife, Tirini
Belgian Horses	Goldie & Sunny
Benima	1st son of Manutu & Kibi (2nd son Kenga)
Bolbonga	Chief of the Ndezi (38 yrs old)
Emula	Story Character, brothers: 3yr. Sammo – new baby: Huzunitoto (sad child)
Fulani Lads	Kabanza, Kasuku (infected foot) Mguru and Nashutu
Gomojo	Son of the landaulet driver, Ben & wife, Tirini
Jomba	Husband of Mruna, Ndezi military advisor, Mistress, Sutto
Jon's Bearers	Kimbo & his son, Kybo, Obendi, Obu & Motozo (the cook)
Kaizii	Native wildlife teacher for Thomas & Jon Caulfield
Kenga	2nd son of Manutu (1st son, Benima)
Kimbi	Ndezi prison sentry/guard (night)
Kimbata	2nd son of the Zuri Watu medicine man in legend story
Kimbo	Traders' head guide – father of Kybo
Kira	Wife of Bolbonga (32yrs) Sons: Ngunna (16) – Basuku (13)
Kybo	Bearer for Traders – son of Kimbo
Laalu	Kybo's friend (since age 12)
Loboda	Son of Kaizii, (wildlife teacher) (8yrs)

Mammaleo	Housekeeper at Port Gentil Guest House
Manutu	Medicine Chief of the Zuri Watu – son of Agurra & Myuma, twin Brother of Sashono, Zuri Watu Chief Myuma blind daughter of Emula's father and stepmother, mother of Sashono and Manutu
Maridi	Child of death mask – Legend of the Zuri Watu
Masula	Son of the Ndezi Medicine Man, Suruna (19yrs) captured Paula with Mbundo
Mbundo	Son of Bolbonga, Chief of the Ndezi (18yrs) captured Paula with Masula
Misha	Bolbonga's mother, Ndezi Headwoman, hostess to Paula
Motozo	Traders' head cook – helpers Obendi and Obu
Mruna	Jomba's wife with infant son – contest with Sutto
Myuma	Step sister to Emula, born blind – married Agurra
Nanoka	Wife of Sashono, Chief of the Zuri Watu – adopted mother of Tamubu (Thomas Caulfield)
Ngunna	Eldest son of Bolbonga and Kira, age 16
Ngarro	2nd son of the chief in Zuri Watu Legend
Nishani	Kybo's cousin – lives in Wahutu village near Douala
Obendi	#1 helper for Motozo, trader's cook
Obu	#2 helper for Motozo, trader's cook
Sampson	Trader's base camp radio operator
Samo	Trader's bush camp radio operator
Sashono	Chief of the Nations of the Zuri Watu – adopted father of Tamubu, son of Agurra and Myuma – twin brother of Manutu, Medicine Chief of the Zuri Watu
Scouts	Zuri Watu legend: Dubo & Kiku

Shawna	Bad boy in story
Sombu	Kasuku's father (Fulani lad)
Suruna	Medicine Man of the Ndezi, eye tattoos like Zorro's mask
Sutto	Jomba's mistress – contest with Mruna, his wife
Tamubu	Means: Sweet gift, adopted son of Sashono & Nanoka
Tirini	Wife of Landaulet driver, Ben, mother of Gomojo

Tribes in the Rainforest

Fulani	Mguru, Kabanza, Kasuku and Nashutu (Lads on beach)
Jagas	Warring tribe of story: Conquerors and sadists
Ndezi	Warriors, hunters, gatherers – tribe that abducted Paula
Nguni	Guide: Jon to valley of the devils
Tutus	Cannibal tribe, archenemies of the Ndezi
Usuku Wanaume	Hairy dwarf cannibalistic cave dwellers – night people
Wahutu	Tribe near the Sanaga River and Kybo's cousin, Nishani
Zuri Watu	Craftsmen, herdsmen, gatherers, tribe of Tamubu

Pg. 29 —
green knee-length
tights ?

9 781438 973036